PARADIGMS LOST

D0887424

Baen Books by Ryk E. Spoor

Digital Knight

Phoenix Rising

Phoenix In Shadow (forthcoming)

Paradigms Lost

GRAND CENTRAL ARENA SERIES

Grand Central Arena

Spheres of Influence

Baen Books by Ryk E. Spoor and Eric Flint

Boundary

Threshold

Portal

Castaway Planet (forthcoming)

For a complete list of Ryk E. Spoor books and to purchase all of these titles in e-book format, please go to www.baen.com.

PARADIGMS LOST

RYK E. SPOOR

BAEN

PARADIGMS LOST

This is a work of fiction. All the characters and events portrayed in this book are fictional, and any resemblance to real people or incidents is purely coincidental.

Copyright ©2014 by Ryk E. Spoor

All rights reserved, including the right to reproduce this book or portions thereof in any form.

Portions of this novel appeared in substantially different form as *Digital Knight* (copyright © October 2003 Ryk E. Spoor).

A Baen Books Original

Baen Publishing Enterprises
P.O. Box 1403
Riverdale, NY 10471
www.baen.com

ISBN: 978-1-4767-3693-8

Cover art by Stephen Hickman

First printing, December 2014

Distributed by Simon & Schuster
1230 Avenue of the Americas
New York, NY 10020

Library of Congress Cataloging-in-Publication Data

Spoor, Ryk E.
  Paradigms lost / Ryk E Spoor.
     pages ; cm
  "A Baen Books Original."
   ISBN 978-1-4767-3693-8 (softcover)
  I. Title.
  PS3619.P665P37 2014
  813'.6—dc23

                                          2014034545

10 9 8 7 6 5 4 3 2 1

Pages by Joy Freeman (www.pagesbyjoy.com)
Printed in the United States of America

I want to thank my beta-readers for all their support, commentary, and criticism that made Paradigms Lost *a better book.*

This book is dedicated to:

Jim Baen, for giving me a chance;

*Toni Weisskopf, for giving Jason Wood a **second** chance;*

my wife, Kathleen, for her constant support;

the "Butcher of Baen" for his invaluable help.

Foreword

Paradigms Lost is a greatly expanded edition of *Digital Knight*, my first published work. It is not just a polishing and slight reworking of *Digital Knight*—indeed, in many areas I have tried *not* to touch the writing overmuch, as I don't want to damage the "flavor" that made it work in the first place.

What I *have* done is add incidents and actions that would have happened—foreshadowing and "crossover" events that are part of Jason's universe—but which I didn't fully know when I first wrote *Digital Knight*, some portions of which were written as far back as 1987 and 1988. I have also reconciled a few contradictions and confusing incidents to make more sense and clarified the *dating* of the stories, as some readers might have found it unclear; Jason's adventures begin in April 1999.

In addition to these changes—some of which are quite substantial—I have included two more of Jason's adventures, "Shadow of Fear" and "Trial Run," to make this a truly worthwhile read for those of you who may have read the original. Overall, this means that more than a short novel's worth of material has been added to *Paradigms Lost*; the original *Digital Knight* was about 103,000 words, while *Paradigms Lost* runs well over 160,000.

Jason's world is very like ours... but not precisely, and it *changes* for him as time goes on. His adventures also connect—sometimes in surprising ways—with other stories and events in his universe. Those who have read *Phoenix Rising* will perhaps not be surprised to see his encounters with a certain young man, and possibly make other connections with things that have happened... or will happen.

Join Jason, then... on the day that everything changed.

PARADIGMS LOST

PART I

Gone in a Flash

April 1999

CHAPTER 1

Dead Man Knocking

I clicked on the JAPES icon. A second picture appeared on the Lumiere RAN-7X workstation screen next to the digitized original, said original being a pretty blurry picture of two men exchanging something. At first the two pictures looked identical, as always, but then rippling changes started: colors brightening and darkening, objects becoming so sharp as to look almost animated, a dozen things at once. I controlled the process with a mouse, pointing and clicking to denote key items that would help JAPES interpret the meaning in the image and bring out details.

Fortunately, I had a lot of pictures of the same area—and the same individuals—from the same batch of photos Lieutenant Klein had given me, which provided me with a considerable amount of material for enhancing and interpreting what was in this photo. JAPES, which stood for Jason's Automatic Photo Enhancing System, was the whimsical name I'd given to my own specialized image analysis and processing suite which combined multiple standard (and not so standard) photographic enhancement techniques into a single complex operation controlled partly by me and partly by a learning expert system.

I stiffened; suddenly I was overwhelmed by the sense that I was being watched. Some people say they get that feeling often when they're alone; since I live alone, and work in the same building I live in, I've never been prone to that sensation. But the feeling was so strong that I turned quickly to the plate-glass window that was the front of Wood's Information Service.

For *just* an instant—that split-second between turning and focusing—I thought I saw something: a very tall figure in the mist of evening, dressed in what seemed—in that vague glimpse—to be robes or a longcoat of some sort, with a peculiar wide-swept hat like nothing I'd ever seen. Long white hair trailed off below the hat, and the figure was leaning on, or holding, some kind of staff.

But when I focused, I could see there was nothing there at all; just mist and the cotton-fog glow of a streetlamp beyond. I stared out for several minutes, then shrugged. *What the hell, brain?* I thought to myself. *Not even seeing things that make* sense.

The delay had, at least, allowed JAPES to complete its work. The computer-enhanced version was crisp as a posed photo—except that I don't think either the assemblyman or the coke dealer had intended a pose. *Yeah, that ought to give Elias Klein another nail to put in the crooks' coffins.* I glanced at my watch: eight-twenty. Time enough to digitize and enhance one more photo before Sylvie came over. I decided to do the last of Lieutenant Klein's; drug cases make me nervous, you never know what might happen. *Come to think of it,* I realized, *that's probably why I had that weird feeling; I'm twitchy over this one.*

So let's get back to it. I inserted the negative into the enlarger/digitizer, popped into the kitchen for a cream soda, sat down and picked up my book. After seventeen minutes the computer pinged; for this kind of work, I have to scan at the best possible resolution, and that takes time. I checked to make sure the scan went okay, then coded in the parameters, set JAPES going, and went back to *Phantoms*. Great yarn.

After the automatic functions were done, I started in on what I really get paid for here at Wood's Information Service ("Need info? Knock on Wood!"): the ability to find the best "finishing touches" that make enhancement still an art rather than a science.

A distant scraping sound came from the back door, and then a faint clank. I checked the time again: nine twenty-five. Still too early; Sylvie's occult shop, the Silver Stake, always closed precisely at nine-thirty, and besides, Syl would just ring the bell or walk in from the front. "Lewis?" I called out.

Lewis was what social workers might call a displaced person, others called a bum, and I called a contact. Lewis sometimes did scutwork for me—as long as he was sober, he was a good worker. Unfortunately, when he was drunk, he was a belligerent nuisance, and at six-foot-seven, a belligerent Lewis was an ugly sight. Since it was the first Friday of the month, he was probably drunk.

But I didn't hear an answer, neither his voice nor the funny ringing knock that the chains on his jacket cuffs made. Instead, I heard another clank and then a muffled thud. At that point, the computer pinged again, having just finished my last instructions. I checked the final version—it looked pretty good, another pose of the assemblyman alone with his hand partly extended—then downloaded all the data onto two disks for the lieutenant. I sealed them in an envelope with the original negatives, dropped the envelope into the safe, swung it shut, pulled the wall panel down and locked it. Then I stepped out and turned toward the back door, grabbing my book as I left. Just then the front door-bell rang.

It was Sylvie, of course. "Hi, Jason!" she said, bouncing through the door. "Look at these, we just got the shipment in today! Aren't they great?" She dangled some crystal and silver earrings in front of me, continuing, "They're genuine Brazil crystal and the settings were handmade; the lady who makes them says she gets her directions from an Aztec she channels—"

There was a tremendous *bang* from the rear and the windows shivered. "What the hell was that?" Sylvie demanded. "Sounded like a cannon!"

"I don't know," I answered, "but it wasn't a gun. Something hit the building." I thought of the photos I was enhancing. It wouldn't be the first time someone had decided to erase the evidence before I finished improving it. I yanked open the righthand drawer of the front desk, pulled out my .45, snicked the safety off.

"You're that worried, Jason?"

"Could be bad, Syl; working for cops has its drawbacks."

She nodded, her face serious now. To other people, she comes across as a New Age bimbo, or a gypsy with long black hair and colored handkerchief clothes. I know better. She reached into her purse, yanked out a small .32 automatic, pulled the slide once. I heard a round chamber itself. "Ready."

One of the things I have always liked about Syl: she isn't afraid of much and is ready to deal with anything.

She started towards the back. "Let's go."

I cut in front of her. "You cover me."

I approached the door carefully, swinging to the hinge side. It opened inward, which could be trouble if someone slammed it open. I took a piece of pipe that I keep around and put it on the floor in the path of the door so it would act as an impromptu doorstop. Then I yanked the bolt and turned the handle.

I felt a slight pressure, but not anything like something trying to force the door. Sylvie had lined up opposite me. She glanced at me and I nodded. I let the door start to open, then let go and stood aside.

The metal fire door swung open and Lewis flopped down in front of us. Sylvie gasped and I grunted. Drunk like I thought. I reached out for him. That's when he finished rolling onto his back.

His eyes stared up, glassy and unseeing. There was no doubt in my mind that he was very dead.

I stepped over the body, to stand just inside the doorway, and peered up and down the alley. To the right I saw nothing but rolling fog—God must be playing director with mood machines tonight—but to the left there was a tall, angular figure, silhouetted by a streetlamp. Pressing myself up against the doorframe in case bullets answered me, I called out, "Hey! You up there! We could use some help here!"

The figure neither answered nor came closer; he just seemed to melt silently into the surrounding fog. *It's a night for seeing men who aren't there, I guess.* I watched for a few seconds, but saw nothing else and turned back to Lewis.

Fortunately, there wasn't any blood. I hate blood. "Aw, Christ..." I muttered. I knelt and gingerly touched the body. The weather was cool for a spring evening, but the body was still warm. *Dammit.* Lewis was probably dying all the time I was reading *Phantoms*.

"Jason, I have a bad feeling about this," Sylvie said quietly.

"No kidding!" I snapped. Then I grinned faintly. "Sorry, Syl. No call for sarcasm. But you're right, this is one heck of a mess."

She shook her head. "I don't mean it that way, Jason. The vibes are all wrong. There's something...unnatural about this."

That stopped me cold. Over the years, I've come to rely on Sylvie's "feelings"; I don't really believe in ESP and all that crap, but...she has a hell of an intuition that's saved my job and my life on more than one occasion. "Oh. Well, we'll see about it. Now I'd better call the cops; we're going to be answering questions for a while."

Normally, I might have asked her more about what she meant; but something about the way she'd said "unnatural" bothered me. I zipped back to the office and grabbed up my phone; I had the local police station on speed-dial. I worked with them a lot. The sergeant on duty assured me that someone would be along shortly. I was just hanging up when I heard a muffled scream.

I had the gun out again and was around the corner instantly. Sylvie was kneeling over the body, one hand on Lewis' coat, the other over her mouth. "What's wrong? Jesus, Syl, you scared the daylights out of me! And what the hell are you doing even *near* the body? You know what—"

She pointed a finger. "Explain that, mister information man."

I looked.

On the side of Lewis' neck, where the coat collar had covered, were two red marks. Small red dots, right over the carotid artery.

Two puncture marks.

"So he got bit by a couple mosquitoes. Big deal. There are two very happy bugs flying high tonight."

Sylvie gave me a look she usually reserves for those who tell her that crystals are only good for radios and jewelry. "That is *not* what I meant, and you know that perfectly well. This man was obviously assaulted by a nosferatu."

"Say what? Sounds like a Mexican pastry."

"Jason, you are being deliberately obtuse. With all the darn horror novels you read, you know what nosferatu means."

I nodded and sighed. "Okay, yeah. Nosferatu. The Undead. A vampire. Gimme a break, Syl. I may read the novels but I don't live them. I think you've been reading too much of your woo-woo book stock lately."

"And *I* think that you are doing what you always laugh at the characters in your books for doing: refusing to see the obvious."

I opened my mouth to answer, but at that moment the wail of sirens interrupted, which was something of a relief. *That's the craziest discussion I've ever been in and maybe we can just forget she started it.* Red and blue lights flashed at the alleyway—jeez, it must be a quiet night out there. Besides the locals, I saw two New York State Troopers; they must've been cruising the I-90 spur from Albany and heard about Lewis over the radio. I felt more comfortable as I spotted a familiar figure in the unmistakable uniform of the Morgantown PD coming forward.

Lieutenant Renee Reisman knelt and did a cursory once-over, her brown hair brushing her shoulders. "Either of you touch anything?" she asked.

I was glad it was Renee. We'd gone to school together and that made things a little easier. "I touched his face, just to check if he was still warm, which he was. Sylvie moved his collar a bit to see if he'd had his throat cut or something. Other than that, the only thing I did was open the door; he was leaning up against the door and fell in."

"Okay." She was one of the more modern types; instead of scribbling it all down in a notebook, a little voice-activated recorder was noting every word. "You're both going to have to come down and make some statements."

"I know the routine, Renee. Oh, and I know you'll need to keep the door open during the picture taking and all; here's the key. Lock up when you're done."

I told the sergeant we'd be taking my car; he pulled the PD cruiser out and waited while I started up Mjölnir. It was true enough that I could afford a better car than a Dodge Dart, even a silver-and-black one, but I kinda like a car that doesn't crumple from a light breeze ... and it wasn't as though Mjölnir was exactly a factory-standard car, either.

Sylvie's statement didn't take long; apparently she chose not to expound on her theory to the cops, which proved she had more common sense than most people. Mine took a couple of hours since I had to explain about Lewis and why he might choose to die somewhere in my vicinity. A few years back, I'd been in the area when two drug kingpins happened to get wiped. Then Elias got me involved in another case and a potential lead fell out of a closed window. I was nearby. Cops don't like it when one person keeps turning up around bodies.

It was one-thirty when we finally got out. I took a left at Chisolm Street and pulled into Denny's. Sylvie was oddly quiet the whole time. Except for ordering, she didn't say anything until we were already eating. "Jason. We have to talk."

"Okay. Shoot."

"I know that you don't believe in ... a lot of the Powers. But you have to admit that my predictions and senses have proven useful before."

"I can't argue with that, Syl. But those were ... ordinary occasions." Admittedly, ordinary occasions where she gave me a warning in time to save my life, when I saw no way she could have known what was going to happen ... "But now you're talking about late-night horror movies suddenly doing a walk-on in real life."

She nodded. "Maybe you can't feel it, Jase, but I am a true sensitive. I felt the Powers in the air about that poor man's body. And that *noise*, Jason. Big as Lewis was, even he wouldn't make that kind of noise just falling against the door. Something *threw* him, Jason, threw him hard enough to shake the windows."

I nodded unwillingly. I'd already thought of that; honestly, I didn't think Lewis could have made that kind of impact even if he'd been trying to batter the door down.

"Jase, it's about time you faced the fact that there are some things that you are not going to find classified on a database somewhere, comfortably cross-indexed and referenced. But I'm not going to argue about it, not now. Just do me a favor and check into it, okay?"

I sighed. "Okay, I'll nose around and see what I can find out. No offense, but I hope this time your feelings are haywire."

Her blue eyes looked levelly into mine. "Believe me, Jason, I hope so too."

CHAPTER 2

Picture Imperfect

I got back to Wood's Information Service at two forty-five. The cops were gone but one of those wide yellow tapes was around the entire area. *Damn.*

I went to the pay phone on the corner (*luckily there still* are *some . . . pretty soon, I'll have to get a cell phone myself*), dialed the station, and asked for Lieutenant Reisman. I was in luck. She was still in. "Reisman here. What is it, Jason?"

"You know, I happen to live in my place of business. Do you have to block off the *entire* building?"

"Sorry," she said. "Hold on a minute."

It was actually five minutes. "Okay, here's the deal. You can go in, but only use the front entrance and stay out of that back hallway."

"But I store a lot of stuff there."

"Sorry, that's the breaks. Tell your informants to die elsewhere from now on. Anything else?"

"Yeah. This thing has Sylvie spooked. She's really nervous about this, and being in the business she is, it gives her weird ideas."

"So what can I do?"

"Just give me a call when the ME report comes through. If there's nothing odd on it, it'll make things much easier."

She was quiet for a moment. "Look, Jason, medical examiner reports aren't supposed to be public knowledge, first off. But second, what do you mean by 'odd'?"

I grinned, though she couldn't tell. "Believe me, Lieutenant, you'll know it if you see it."

"Huh." She knew I was being deliberately evasive, but she also knew I probably had a reason. She'd push later if events

12

warranted. "All right, Jason, here's what I'll do. If the ME's report is what I consider normal, which includes normal assaults, heart attacks, and so on, I'll call you and tell you just that, 'normal.' If I see something I consider odd, I'll let you know."

"Thanks, Renee. I owe you one."

"You got that straight. Good night."

I went back to my building and up to my bedroom. I was drifting off to sleep when I sat bolt upright, suddenly wide awake.

The figure I had seen in the alley, backlit by a streetlamp. I thought it had moved away too fast to follow in the fog. But the "Tamara's Tanning" neon sign had been on its left, and the lit sign for WKIL radio on its right. One or the other should have flickered as it passed across them.

Both had stayed shining steadily. But that was impossible.

It was a long time before I finally got to sleep.

✧　　✧　　✧

I got up at twelve-thirty; that yellow tape would keep away the customers who might drop by, and as a consultant I keep irregular hours anyway. I was just sitting down with my ham sandwich breakfast when the phone rang. "Wood's Information Service, Jason Wood speaking."

"This is Lieutenant Reisman, Wood. I've just read the ME report."

"And?"

"And I would like to know what your girlfriend thinks is going on here, Mr. Wood."

"Syl's not my girlfriend." *Not exactly, anyway*, I thought. "What did the ME find?"

"It's what he *didn't* find that's the problem." Renee's voice was tinged with uncertainty. "Your friend Lewis wasn't in great shape—cirrhosis, bronchitis, and various minor malnutrition things—but none of those killed him. He'd also suffered several bruises; someone grabbed him with great force, and after death the body was thrown into your door. But death was not due to violence of the standard sort."

"Well, what *did* kill him, then?"

"The ME can't yet say *how* it happened," the lieutenant said quietly, "but the cause of death was blood loss." She took a breath and finished. "There wasn't a drop of blood left in his body."

I made a mental note that I owed Syl a big apology. "Not a drop, huh?"

"Well, technically speaking, that's not true. The ME told me that it's physically impossible to get *all* the blood out of a corpse. But it was as bloodless as if someone had slit his throat with a razor and then hung him up to drain. The thing that's *really* bothering the ME is that the man had no wounds that account for the blood loss. He'll have the detailed autopsy done in a few days, but from what he said I doubt he's going to find anything."

"You're probably right. Well, thanks, Renee."

"Hold on just one minute, mister! You at least owe me an explanation."

"Do you really want one?"

She was silent for a minute. Then, "Yeah. Yeah, I do. Because there's one other thing that I haven't told you yet."

I waited.

After a few moments, she said, "All right, here it is. This body is not the first we've found in this condition. The others all had wounds that could explain the loss...but the ME told me privately that there were certain indications that made him think that they were inflicted after death."

"Okay, Lieutenant, but you are not going to like it."

"I don't like it *now*, Wood. Let me have it."

"Sylvie thinks we are dealing with a vampire."

There was a long silence. "Would you repeat that?"

"A vampire. As in Dracula."

Another silence. "Yeah. And damned if I don't half-believe it, either. I must be getting gullible. But no way can I take this to my supervisor. He's the most closed-minded son-of-a-bitch who ever wore blue."

I laughed. "I don't expect you to do anything about it. Just keep an eye out. I'm going to start some research of my own. If we *are* dealing with something..." I trailed off, paused, then force myself to say it, "...paranormal, I doubt that normal approaches will work."

"God, listen to us. Vampires? I'll call you later, Jason. This is too weird for me to handle right now."

I cradled the receiver. I couldn't blame her for needing time to sort it all out. Hell, I was stunned that she accepted it as much as she did. Somewhere in the back of her mind, she must already have decided that something was very wrong about those other deaths.

All right. Let's get to work, Jason.

I went upstairs into my library, started pulling down books—folklore references I'd collected over the years, mostly, including *Vampires: A World Survey*, which was the closest thing to a scholarly compendium on the subject I'd ever found. Most of these things came from my information addiction overlapping with my fiction reading; I couldn't resist trying to fact check even my horror novels. Bad facts didn't stop me from *reading* them, of course, but I liked to know what was real and was wasn't.

I sat down at my workstation, started keying in information from each book. The *World Survey* emphasized what I'd already known: the vampire myth existed in some form in almost every corner of the world—from South America to Japan, China to Europe. The abilities and weaknesses of the creatures varied wildly, from the original shambling zombielike corpses of Eastern Europe to China and Japan's strange "hopping vampires" to...

I glanced back at the shelves and wondered if I should include anything from the fictional side. Yes, at first glance that sounded stupid, but if I was going to assume there *were* such things as... vampires, there was the possibility that one or more books had been written by people who knew that they existed and something of what they were like.

And... again if I was right... they'd already apparently shown two of the characteristics often attributed to fictional vampires: superhuman strength and the ability to disappear or turn into mist.

I sighed, got up, and picked out a selection of vampire novels—the original *Dracula*, Yarbro's Saint Germain books, Rice's *Lestat*, a few others that covered a range of tastes. *I'll extract the key points as possibilities and put them in with a low but significant weight.*

After three hours, my neck and arms started getting really cramped. I broke for a late lunch or maybe dinner, headed back towards the computer just as the phone rang.

"Wood's Information Ser—"

"Hello, Wood."

I knew that gravel-scraping voice, even though it usually didn't call before the night shift. Then I looked at the clock and realized it *was* the night shift. *That's what you get for sleeping until after noon.* "Hi, Elias. I've got your photos done."

"Anything good?"

"Let's just say I'll be real surprised if we aren't electing a new assemblyman soon."

He laughed, a quick explosive chortle. "With an attitude like that, I don't see you getting on jury duty, that's for sure. Listen, I'll be over to pick 'em up soon. 'Bout an hour and a half good?"

"Sure thing, Elias."

I needed a break from blood-sucking freaks anyway. I pulled the envelope from the safe, rechecking the pictures on the disk against the negatives. By the time my recheck was done, Elias was there. "Hey there, Jase," he said, ducking slightly as he entered. He really didn't have to—the doorway's seven feet high and he's six foot six—but it was a habit he had. Add a gangly frame, a sharp-edged nose, black hair, black eyes, and a slight stoop; Elias Klein always reminded me of a youthful buzzard. He came into my office to get a quick look. He liked them all, until we got to the last one.

"Nice joke, Jason."

"What do you mean, joke? It looks pretty good to me."

"Oh, sure, Assemblyman Connors looks just lovely. But without Verne Domingo to complete the picture it's nothing but a publicity shot."

I pointed to the next to last. "What about that one? They're swapping right there, what more could you ask for?"

"That's just a second-string doper, Jason! Domingo's the big man, the guy we've been after the whole time I've been on this case, and *that* is the photo that should show him."

I shrugged. "Too bad. Next time make sure he's in the picture."

"Don't give me that, Wood! I *know* he was in that shot, I was the one looking through the viewfinder."

I handed him the negative. "Look for yourself."

He stared at it. "What the hell?" Then he swung towards me. "Wood, you'd better not be dicking around with the evidence! I've been on this for eight damn months, and if you're—"

"Oh, cut the tough cop act, Elias. You know damn well that I only play jokes; I don't mess with my clients' stuff. If I did, would the city PD be paying me ten grand a year? That negative is the one you gave me and it's in the same shape as it was when it got here."

"But that's impossible." Elias glared at the negative as though a hard stare would make the missing figure materialize. "If you look through the viewfinder of an SLR, what you see is what you get. Besides, dammit, look at your own enhancement. He's got his mouth half-open, saying something, and he's about to shake hands. Then look at that angle. Do you put your hand out twenty feet from the guy you're going to shake with?"

"Nope." I was mystified now. Then the memory of a quote spun across my mind:

This time there could be no error, for the man was close to me, and I could see him over my shoulder. But there was no reflection of him in my mirror!

I took the negative and stared at it again. "You're right, Elias. Mr. Domingo *should* have been in this picture. That leaves only one explanation."

He looked at me. "And that is...?"

"That you are dealing with someone whose image doesn't appear on film."

Elias didn't like that at all, but he had to admit that I had no motive to screw around with the negatives. "So what're you saying? He's got some kind of *Star Trek* cloaking device that wipes his image off film? I won't swallow it."

"Trust me, Elias, you don't want to know what I think. Since this negative is worthless as is, mind if I keep it? Maybe there's some kind of latent image I could bring up."

"Dammit, Jason! Tell me what is—" He broke off, having caught sight of the pile of books and papers on the desk.

He looked at them. He picked them up, examined them. Looked at me. "And Reisman said..." he began, then stopped. He glanced at the negative again. Back at me. A long pause. "You're right," he said finally. "I don't want to know. Keep the negative." He grabbed his hat and sunglasses, left quickly.

I went back to typing.

The phone rang again.

"Hello, Jason," said Sylvie. "What have you heard?"

"Enough. I apologize for doubting you, Sylvie. We've either got ourselves a real honest-to-God vampire here, or someone who is doing his level best to fake it. And with the technical problems of faking some of this, I'd rather believe in a vampire than in a faker." I glanced down. "And I think I've found our bloodsucker, too." I gave her a quick rundown on Klein's negative.

"But, Jason, isn't that an incredible coincidence?"

"I thought so myself, at first. But I've been thinking, and it isn't as far out as it first seems. In most legit businesses you have to do business in daylight hours at some point. Maybe a vampire *can* live in a musty coffin underground all the time, but I'll bet they sure don't want to. They want all the creature comforts they can enjoy and that means money. So they'll just naturally gravitate to the 'shady' side of commerce, pardon the pun. And with their natural advantages, it isn't surprising that one might be high up on the ladder."

"I hadn't thought of it that way. But drug deals happen in the daytime, too."

"If you've got muscle to back you up, you can get away with a lot of odd quirks. Avoiding sunlight might be possible." I nodded to myself. "And Lewis acted as an informant to me; might have done so to the police, or—more likely—he'd tell me and expect I'd get it to them. So if Lewis had seen something and come to tell me..."

"Oh, the poor man," Syl said softly. "But you're right, it does make sense. And, by the way, apology accepted. I've been calling around and getting my better occult acquaintances on the alert. They'll see what they can find."

"Good." Privately, I didn't expect much from Sylvie's pals. Sylvie herself might have something, but most of the people who visited the Silver Stake were your typical muddled New Age escapists who confused Tolkien and *Star Wars* with real life. "I'm working on something here that might help. Stop by after you're done, okay?"

"Sure thing, Jason. Just promise me no more bodies, huh?"

"I make no guarantees. Bodies never consult me before arriving. See you."

"Bye."

It was ten o'clock by the time I finished. Then I put WISDOM to work. Wood's Information Service Database Online Manager can analyze information using many different statistical methods and a lot of other heuristics. WISDOM was instructed to examine the information on all different kinds of vampires to construct the most likely abilities that an actual vampire might be expected to possess. It took WISDOM only a few minutes to do its calculations. I sat down and read. It was grim reading.

CHAPTER 3

Contingency Planning

"What in the world are you doing?" Sylvie asked.

I put down the loading kit. "Preparing. I figure that if I'm going to deal with a vampire, I'd better have something other than conventional ammo."

She picked up a cartridge. "Silver? I thought I read somewhere that you actually couldn't make silver bullets; something about balance?"

"I heard that too, but it's a silly statement on the face of it. Lead's softer and just as heavy, and they've been making bullets from lead as long as they've been making guns. Yes, you have to make a few adjustments, but nothing prevents a silver bullet from working as a bullet." I checked the fit of another bullet. "Not that I expect those to be of much use. WISDOM only gave a twenty-five-percent chance of vulnerability to silver. That seems more of a werewolf thing."

She examined the other kinds of ammo. "Well, I'll say this for you, you have one heck of an assortment." She reached into her purse, pulled out a small wooden box. "Here, Jason."

"What's this?" I opened the box. On a slender silver chain was a crystal-headed hammer, handle wrapped in miniature leather thongs, the head an angle-faced box. "It's gorgeous, Syl! Thank you!"

"I remembered how much you like the Norse pantheon—you even named your car after Thor's hammer—and if you look real closely on the hammer head, you'll see *Mjölnir* engraved there in Nordic runes."

I squinted closely at it, and I could just make out the spiderweb-thin runic lines. "It's really beautiful, Sylvie. But why now?"

"I was actually saving it for your birthday next month, but with this vampire thing going on, I decided it was best I give it to you now." She saw my puzzlement. "It's not just a piece of jewelry, Jason. I made it especially to be a focus, a protection against evil, for you."

"But you know I don't really believe in that stuff."

She gave a lopsided smile. "Jason Wood, how in the world can you believe in vampires and sneer at crystals and spirits?"

"Touché." I slipped the chain over my neck. It felt cool against my skin. The three-inch-long hammer made a slight bulge below my collar. "This could look a little strange. I don't wear jewelry often. I think I'll put it on the wall. Or on Mjölnir's rearview mirror."

"No, Jason." Sylvie had her "feeling" face on again. "Wear it. Even if you don't believe, it will make me feel better if you keep it on you."

I wasn't about to test her accuracy now. I was about eighty-five percent convinced we were dealing with some kind of creature that might as well be called a vampire, and one-hundred percent convinced that Syl had some way of knowing things she shouldn't. "Okay."

"Now what else has your machine come up with?"

"Nothing good. The problem is that there are so many versions of the vampire legend in myth and fiction that the best I can do is estimate probabilities. Problem with that is that even a low-probability thing could turn out to be real." I picked up a printout. "But I can't prepare for everything. So I've constructed a 'theoretical vampire' using all the probabilities that showed a greater than eighty-percent likelihood." I started reading. "Strength, somewhere between five and twenty times normal human, with a heavy bias towards the high end of that range; he—or she, let's be equal-opportunity with our monsters—can probably tip over a minivan like I can a loaded shopping cart and leap small garages in a single bound. Invulnerable to ordinary weapons. What *can* hurt it is a nice question; only one thing cleared the probability threshold—fire—with a bunch more clustered at between twenty-five and thirty percent: the movie standbys of sunlight and a wooden stake, running water, holy symbols or weapons as a general class, some sort of symbolic material like rice or salt, and so on. Does not show up on mirrors; after that photo I think we can take that as proven."

"Maybe he just doesn't show on film?"

"The legend started long before there was film. Stands to reason the mirror business had something behind it. Okay, where was I? Shapeshifting. This might have started as a blending of the werewolf and vampire legends, but most are pretty emphatic that vampires can either change shape or make you think they look different than they are. Plus what I saw the other night pretty much convinces me our target can either go invisible or turn into mist. Changes those bitten into others of its kind; that's how they reproduce."

Sylvie shook her head. "No, Jason, that's silly. If a vampire bite made more vampires, we'd be up to our earlobes in bloodsuckers in nothing flat."

"So I simplified it. Some kind of additional condition has to be met—maybe exchanging blood, maybe some kind of a ritual. As an aside, if that happens, there is a fair chance that the new vampire is controlled by the old one. And speaking of age, the legends also tend to emphasize that the older the suckers get the tougher they are."

"Anything else?"

"Yep. They tend to be inactive in the daytime, and may have psychokinetic abilities. One other interesting note: many legends state that a vampire, or similar spirits, cannot enter a personal dwelling—house, apartment, whatever—without the permission of a legitimate resident therein. However, once given, the permission is damned hard to revoke. Some of the legends have the idea that there is a particular location the vampire must return to, or carry with them, that old 'home earth' requirement." I put the printout down. "That's about it. Lower down on the list you get some really odd stuff."

Sylvie sat in frowning thought for a few minutes. "So fire is the best bet?"

I waved a hand from side to side. "It's chancy. How you're going to set him on fire without getting killed isn't very clear to me. The problem is that while it's pretty likely that the vampire is somewhat vulnerable to sunlight—most of them do not walk during the day, and I have to assume there's a reason for that—the degree of vulnerability is highly variable. If they're vulnerable at all, any vampire would die if you could stick it out on a Miami beach thirty minutes from shade, but if it's not just an instant kill, in the first twenty minutes it could do a lot of damage to anyone in the area. Several of the legends emphasize that an old and powerful vampire becomes more and more able to resist their normal vulnerabilities. Besides, I doubt he'd answer an invitation to a beach party."

"So what are you going to do?"

"See if I can get a handle on him somehow, so he has to come to me. And I think this negative is the key."

CHAPTER 4

Flirting and Clues

Two hours later, I wasn't so sure. "Funny, Jason...that picture looks the same."

"Oh, very funny, Syl." I stared at the screen, willing a faint outline to appear.

"Sorry, Jason. But this is not exactly the most exciting date I've ever been on."

"I'd have thought last night would have been all the excitement you could handle. Besides, we are not dating."

"Oh? So you kiss your male friends goodnight too?"

"Okay, then I won't do that anymore." I pounded another set of instructions into the machine, a little harder than was really wise. Syl always rattles me when she gets on that subject.

"Oh, honestly, Jason! Don't sulk like that. I didn't mean to pressure you. It just strikes me funny."

"What strikes you funny?"

"You, Jason. You can face down an angry policeman, send crooks to jail, run a business, and you're calmly trying to track down a vampire...and you fall apart whenever a woman smiles at you."

"I do not fall apart!" With dismay I watched the entire background turn a pale lavender. Hurriedly I undid my mistake. "I just...don't want to get involved. I don't have time. Besides, we are off the subject here." I ignored her tolerant smile.

"So what are you doing now?"

I turned back to the screen, then shrugged. "Nothing, actually. I've tried everything and it's no use. Either he simply does not show on any wavelengths or else, more likely, this film just

23

has no sensitivity at all in any non-visible spectra. I can't bring up something that the film doesn't have on it." I slumped back, depressed. I really hate losing.

"Well, then, why not work with what has to be there?"

I looked at her. She looked serious, but there were little smile wrinkles around her eyes. "What exactly do you mean?"

"Well, this vampire's solid, isn't he? I mean, you don't shake hands with a ghost."

"Right. So?"

She pointed to the area in front of Connors. "He's standing right there somewhere. So his feet must—"

"—be on the ground there...and he'll be leaving *footprints*! Syl, you are a genius! And I am an idiot!" I selected the area in front of Connors where his invisible opposite should be and started to enlarge it.

A few seconds went by as I searched. Then I smiled and sat back.

On screen, in the gravel of the pathway, were the unmistakable outlines of two shoes. A sprig of grass was caught underneath one shoe, showing an impossible half-flat, half-arched outline. "Syl, I could kiss you!"

"I'll bet you say that to all the guys." She looked pleased, though.

I saved the data and hid the disk away. "For that, I'll buy you dinner."

CHAPTER 5

An Invitation You Can't Refuse

I knew there was no point in calling Elias in the morning; he was still on the night shift. The police removed the yellow tape that day, and I found myself busy with regular customers until six-thirty: two major literature searches for a couple of professors at RPI, a prior-art and patent survey for a local engineering firm, and a few simple source searches for a few well-heeled students who'd rather pay me than spend hours in the library. Sometimes I wonder if I'm doing people like that a service, but what the heck, they'll pay for it one way or another. At seven I locked up and called Elias.

He protested at first, but eventually gave me what I asked for: Verne Domingo's phone number, which was of course unlisted. As I hung up, it occurred to me that Elias had actually not fought very hard. According to regulations, it was illegal for him to hand out that information, so he had to have wanted me to get it. I remembered him looking at the books yesterday. Maybe he just didn't want to get directly caught in the weird.

I punched in the number. After a few rings, it was answered. Yes, Mr. Domingo was in. No, he could not come to the phone. No, there would be no exceptions. Would I care to leave a message?

"Yes. Tell Mr. Domingo that I have a photograph that he is not in."

The dignified voice on the other end was puzzled. "Excuse me? Don't you mean one that he is in?"

"I mean exactly what I say. Tell him that I have a picture that he is not in. I will call back in one half-hour." I hung up.

I booted up a secure VOIP (Voice Over Internet Protocol)

package I'd found and heavily customized, tied my phone into that. Someone trying a traceback on the call would find it going to various service providers, since I'd hacked together an effective anonymizer for VOIP work. The package also included some signal analysis packages for the incoming signal; if they were using conventional phone lines, I'd be able to tell how many lines were in use.

Precisely thirty minutes later, I called back. A different voice, with a faint accent I couldn't place, answered. "Verne Domingo speaking."

"Ah. You got my message."

"I did indeed. A most peculiar message. I must confess that my curiosity is piqued. What, exactly, does it mean?"

I felt a faint tinge of uncertainty. Could I be wrong? I dismissed it, though. The photo was unmistakable evidence. He was playing it cool. I looked at an indicator; there were more than two people on this line. "Are you sure you want me to talk about it with all those others listening?"

There was a fractional pause, then a chuckle. It was a warm, rich sound. "Very good, young man. I suppose there is no harm in talking to you privately. The rest of you, off the line."

The indicator showed four connections dropping off. *Quite a staff he has; unless he called in the cops, but I really doubt that.* "All right, young man ... what should I call you?"

"Call me ... um, John Van Helsing."

That got a pause. "Most ... intriguing. Go on. Tell me about this picture."

"I have a photograph that could place you in a very difficult position. A photo of you involved in a felony."

"You said that I was not in the photo."

"Indeed. Your accomplice is, but even though you should undoubtedly be in the photograph, there is no trace of your image."

He chuckled again. "Obviously the photographer made a mistake."

"Not in this case, Mr. Domingo. You see, even though you do not appear, your physical presence left definite traces, which modern technology could define and discover. I think that you would find life even more difficult if this photo were publicized than if you simply went to jail."

I heard no humor in his voice now. "I despise clichés, Mr. ...

Van Helsing. But to put it bluntly, you are playing a very danger-ous game. Vastly more dangerous, in fact, than you may think, and I will credit you with the intelligence to have already realized considerable danger lay in making this call. You sound like a young and, it would seem, impulsive person. Take my advice and stop now. I am impressed by your initiative and resources . . . not the least of which is your ability to nullify my tracer. But if you do not stop this now, I will have no choice but to . . . convince you to stop. And no matter the result of that attempt, you will remain in more danger than you can imagine."

That response confirmed everything. If he hadn't been a vam-pire, he would have dismissed me as a nut. "Sorry, Mr. Domingo. It can't be dropped. This is a matter of life and death. Several deaths. I'll be in touch."

I hung up the phone immediately.

Now I had to figure out what to do. I'd verified my guess. Domingo was the vampire, no doubt about it. Now what? I couldn't just march up to him some night and hammer a stake through his heart. Never mind the technical difficulties like bodyguards and the fact that he'd probably be less than cooperative; I'd probably be arrested for Murder One and put away. But aside from just killing him, what other choices were there? Lieutenant Reisman would believe me, and maybe Elias Klein if I pushed him. But try getting a warrant for a murderer with no witnesses except a photo that doesn't show him and some wild-eyed guesses.

I decided to sleep on it. Sometimes the subconscious works out solutions once you stop consciously worrying at it. I had din-ner, watched *Predator* on cable, and finished reading *Phantoms* before I turned in.

I woke up suddenly. I glanced at the clock; it was three-thirty. What had awakened me?

Then I heard it again. A creak of floorboards. Right outside my bedroom door.

I started to ease over towards the nightstand; I keep my gun in that drawer at night.

The bedsprings creaked.

The door slammed open, and three black figures charged in. I lunged for the nightstand, got the drawer halfway open, but one of them smacked my wrist with the butt of a small submachine gun. "Hold it there, asshole. Move and you are history."

I used to think Uzis looked silly on television, like a gun that lost its butt and stock. There was nothing funny about the ugly black snout with the nine-millimeter hole ready to make a matching hole in my head. My voice was hoarse and my heart hammered against my ribs. "Okay! Okay, I am *not* moving! What do you want?"

"It's not what *we* want," one said, his voice neither angry nor gloating, but simply factual. "Mr. Domingo wants to talk to you. Now."

After a nasty but impersonal frisking, I was dragged out to a large car. My captors made it clear I was to sit down and shut up. The ride was fast and silent. We pulled up in front of a very large house, fenced and guarded; I recognized the location as we approached. I'd actually driven by here a few times, but never realized there was anything like this on the other end of the gated drive.

The three hustled me out and into the hallway. "Ah, very good, Camillus," said a gentleman with a perfect English accent, dressed in the impeccable formalwear of a Hollywood butler. "I'll take the young man from here."

The one addressed as Camillus looked narrowly at me. "Don't give Morgan here—or anyone else—any trouble, Mr. Wood. If you do, I'll be back with a pair of tinsnips and you won't ever need to worry about having kids. Got it?" I didn't doubt he meant it.

"Please, Camillus, this gentleman is not one of our . . . more obstreperous visitors. I am sure he does not need such crude threats." Morgan bowed to me. "If you would come this way, Mr. Wood?"

Morgan led me into a library that looked like Alistair Cooke should be sitting in it for the next episode of *Masterpiece Theatre*. I sat down in one of the chairs to wait. I'm glad it was a cool night; if it had been hot I might have been sleeping in little or nothing, and my captors had shown no inclination to let me change clothes. As it was, a red-and-blue running suit looked pretty silly.

Of course, I supposed that what I looked like was the least of my problems. But if I didn't think about inane topics like this, I'd probably be screaming.

I hadn't heard the door open again, but a voice suddenly spoke to me. "Good evening, Mr. Wood. Welcome to my home."

I guess I was jumpier than I thought. I leapt out of the chair and whirled. "Jesus!" He smiled slightly as I did a double-take. "Son of a . . . you even look like a vampire!"

He did, too. Not the walking-corpse kind; he looked like a taller Frank Langella. "Fortunate casting on their part, I assure you." He smiled again, and this time I noticed pointed teeth. Two fangs. It suddenly felt very cold. "Sit down, please." He rang a bell; the door opened almost instantly, framing the silver-haired butler who'd guided me upstairs. "Morgan, bring a suit of clothes for my guest here." He rattled off my measurements in a lightning-fast stream. "And send up some hors d'oeuvres; I have yet to meet a young bachelor who isn't hungry at all hours."

What in hell is going on? I expect to be taken out back and shot. Now he's treating me like a visiting dignitary? This is very weird. "How in the world did you find me?" I asked once the butler left.

He shook his head, looking amused. "Mr. Wood, you are indeed a very clever man. But you are, I am afraid, not an expert in espionage or covert operations. Certainly you left no direct clues, but consider! From my conversation with you, I knew the following: you were a young man—your voice, manner on the phone, and approach left me with little doubt on that score; you were in possession of a photo which, from your description, could only have been obtained from a covert surveillance camera; you were certainly not the police; you had considered possibilities that most people would dismiss offhand; you had either access to someone with the ability to, or you yourself actually possessed the ability to, process the images on that film and from them discover the evidence you and I discussed recently.

"In short, then, I had to look for a young man who was on close terms with the police, who worked with computer-enhancements or had access to them, who had an open mind, and, from the tone of your voice, who had had at least one death recently that he was personally concerned with. I think you will admit that the field of choices becomes very narrow."

I flushed. *Nice work, moron!* I had set myself up perfectly.

The clothes and food arrived; he directed me to a small alcove to change. I came out feeling almost human again and I was actually hungry. "So, what are you going to do with me? I presume that if you intended to kill me, you'd already have done so."

"I do not kill unless in self-defense, Mr. Wood. You are entirely mistaken in your impression of me. I have killed no one since I arrived here three years ago."

The last thing I expected here was denial. "Entirely mistaken? Are you saying you are not a drug dealer?"

He winced. "I dislike that term. I am a supplier of substances which your government terms illegal, yes."

"Then you've killed hundreds by proxy. That's even worse."

He glanced at me; his expression was mild, but his eyes appeared to flame momentarily. "Do not seek to judge me, young man. What your culture calls illegal is its business, but I do not acknowledge its sovereignty over me or others. I walked this world long before the United States was even a possibility, and I will exist long after it has gone and been forgotten in time. If members of your population choose my wares, that is their affair. I do not sell to children, nor do I sell to those who do. Adults make their own choices of salvation and damnation. I supply the means to make that particular choice. I live in comfort on the free choices of these people."

"Once they're addicted, it isn't much of a free choice! And some of them—many of them—turn to drugs because of their dead-end lives."

He flicked a hand in a negation, red light flashing from a ruby ring on his finger. "Mr. Wood, this lecture of yours is at an end. I did not bring you here to discuss my business affairs. But I will say that I target my wares to those who can afford them. They have both the choice and the resources to make or unmake the choice. I take no responsibility for the idiocy of others." He held up the hand as I started to answer. "No, that is enough, Mr. Wood. You are a well-meaning young man, and I would enjoy talking with you on other subjects. But this discussion is closed.

"To the point, Mr. Wood. I presume that you believe that I killed your . . . friend, Lewis. Would you tell me why I might do such a thing?"

Could he be that dense? "Obviously you were hungry."

He nodded. "I see. And can you think of any other reasons?"

"Lewis was one of my contacts. Maybe he knew something about you or your operation."

He began to smile, then he laughed. It was as warm and rich as the chuckle, ringing like a deep bell. "Come with me, Jason."

He led me out of the library, down a hall, and into his own chambers. He pointed at a cabinet. "Open that."

I pulled on the handles. The rosewood opened to reveal a large refrigerator. Inside were dozens of bottles filled with red liquid.

"I can obtain blood legitimately from several sources, Jason. It can be expensive, but I have many millions. I can even warm it to the proper temperature. I can eat normal food, though I derive no nourishment from it, and it gives me what a mortal would call cramps; but thus I can maintain a masquerade."

I was stunned. I had missed all this totally. How could I be so stupid? "But what if Lewis knew something? You—"

"Really, Mr. Wood, you can't think that I would personally kill him? I have people—such as Camillus—for that, who can use bullets or their bare hands, or strangle with generic wire, or cause automobiles to go out of control at convenient locations. What earthly reason would I have to kill someone in a fashion so bizarre as to draw just this sort of attention?" He led the way back to the library. "You are a reasonable man, Jason. Unless you believe me so insane that I have lost any semblance of rationality, then you cannot believe I am responsible for these terrible killings."

I nodded. How could I argue? I should have realized all this without having to have it rammed down my throat. "Then what you are saying is that there is another vampire in the city?"

"I see no alternative."

I cursed, earning me a scandalized raise of an eyebrow. "Sorry. But this puts me back to square one. Now I'll have to sort him out from a hundred and fifty thousand people in the area."

"I may be able to help you."

He sure had my attention. "How?"

He leaned back in his chair. "Normally, I do not get involved in ..." he paused oddly, then continued, "... squabbles between my other brethren and you mortals. If they are stupid enough to be discovered, they deserve the fate that you weaker but numerous mortals will inevitably dispense. But in this case," his voice grew hard, "this one's actions have almost led to *me* suffering that fate. So I will tell you something very useful." He reached out, pulled open a drawer, and dropped an envelope on the desk.

I opened it; the negative was inside. "How ..." I began, then thought a moment. "Never mind."

Verne Domingo pointed to the photo. "That is the key, you see. Not in the way you thought, of course. It is the fact of its existence."

"How do you mean?"

"I have been well aware of my effect, or lack thereof, on photographic film for many years. Therefore, I do not permit myself to be photographed. Moreover, I am always aware of all mortals in my vicinity. If I concentrate—and I always do when outside—I know who is about me, within a large radius." He shifted his gaze to me. "The only beings I cannot sense—and thus the only beings who could photograph me without my knowledge—are my own or similar kind."

My appetite vanished and my stomach knotted. It was suddenly as clear as the crystal glass in front of me. Who had taken the picture? Who liked nightshifts? Who had argued with me until I realized I had a photo of a vampire? Who had handed over a phone number and practically pushed me toward Verne Domingo?

Lieutenant Elias Klein.

I stood and crossed the room to the desk, reached out. Verne Domingo's dark-skinned hand came down on mine, effortlessly forced the telephone receiver back to its base. "No calls, Mr. Wood, please."

"I have to at least let Sylvie know I'm all right."

"You do not have to do anything of the kind."

"But—"

"Will you *listen* to yourself! Think, mortal, use that mind of yours! Why are you here?"

That was a silly question. "Because three thugs with Uzis dragged me out of my bedroom and brought me here."

He closed his eyes and drew a breath. "That is a simplistic answer, Mr. Wood. It is nearing dawn and I am tired. Now please think about your situation."

Okay, what did he mean? I thought about it, piecing together causes, effects, Klein... "I'm here because Klein wanted you to come after me; he wanted me out of the way, or maybe if I got lucky, *you* out of the way."

Domingo opened his eyes and smiled. "Light begins to dawn. So what will happen if you call?"

"Sylvie wouldn't tell."

"Perhaps not; I lack the pleasure of the young lady's acquaintance, so I am ill-equipped to judge. However, she would very likely not show an appropriate level of worry. Why should you risk your present position when her authentic emotions can serve a better purpose?"

Finally, the idea clicked. *God, I am slow sometimes.* "You mean, let Klein think you got me...that I'm dead or removed."

"Precisely."

"But then what? I can't prove a thing against him without coming back out, and even then I'd have to expose you, and I assume you wouldn't..." I looked at him and his eyes answered the question. "No, you wouldn't."

Domingo drained a wineglass of red liquid; I tried not to watch, but it had a horrid fascination about it. He set the glass down and looked at me. "I shall have to help you, Mr. Wood. There are certain things—'loose ends,' as you would say—which Elias must clear up in order to secure his position. One is this negative. He must find it and destroy it; he can ill-afford to let evidence of vampires remain. I am, of course, another."

"Loose ends...Sylvie!"

He nodded slowly. "Yes, she is certainly one. She knows far too much for him to be safe, and moreover she believes...and has psychic resources as well."

I started to stand, then looked at him suspiciously. "How do *you* know that Syl's...psychic? I didn't think you even knew her!"

Domingo chuckled slightly. "Personally, I do not. However, it is in my best interests to determine what people of Talent exist in my vicinity, and it was not long at all before my people had compiled a considerable dossier on the young lady. Your own reaction, skeptic though you are, merely confirms my impression; she is one of the few who truly possesses what she claims to have."

This time I did stand, and started for the door. "Then I have to go! Her safety's more important than mine or even than nailing Elias."

Without so much as a flicker, Verne Domingo suddenly stood between me and the door. "Not more important to *me,* young man. This Elias has dared to use me—*me*—as a pawn in his games." For a moment, I saw, not a vampire of the modern world, but a man of a far more ancient time, a lord whose honor had suffered a mortal insult. "He will regret that."

"I don't give a damn about your stupid ego, Domingo! He could be going after Syl this minute!"

He spread his hands, yielding a point. "Well spoken; if I do not respect your reasons, I cannot expect you to respect mine. But he will make no move until tomorrow night; or rather, tonight, since we are well into the morning. He must have the police—probably through your young lady—discover that you have been taken. He believes me ruthless and willing to kill to protect myself, and will assume you dead. Only tonight will he search your quarters and deal with your Sylvia."

An idea occurred to me. "Is it true that vampires cannot enter a dwelling unbidden?"

He hesitated a moment. "Yes. It is true."

"Then Syl should be safe if she stays home."

"Indeed? Elias Klein, respected lieutenant of police, friend of yours, shows up on her doorstep with news of you; do you truly believe she would have him stay on the porch?"

I shook my head reluctantly. "I guess not." I thought that Syl's... Talent might warn her, but it might not. Syl had been in an accident or two, so while her power might be a hundred percent accurate, it was far from a hundred percent reliable.

"I guess not as well! No, there is only one way to handle Mr. Elias Klein, and this is the way it shall be done..."

CHAPTER 6

Fright and Flight

I ejected the magazine from the .45, checked it, returned it to the gun.

"Believe me, Mr. Wood. I have no reason to tamper with your weapon. Your captors were instructed to bring any weapons they might find; not to interfere with them."

I clicked off the safety. "It isn't that; it's just always wise to recheck your weapon before you might need it."

"Indeed." Verne Domingo touched my arm suddenly, and pointed.

From our concealment to one side of Tamara's Tanning, I saw the tall, angular figure of Elias Klein emerge from the Silver Stake. There was no mistaking the long black hair of the person with him. "Sylvie! He's got her!"

Domingo's hand almost crushed my bicep. "Wait! Can you not see that *she* is leading *him*? Obviously he has not yet revealed himself to her; she is probably trying to aid him. When they enter your office, then will be your time."

"My time? What about you?"

For a moment, I thought I saw conflict on his face, a shadow of a feeling of responsibility. But then his face hardened. "I have done all I intend to. If you fail, then I may have to act more directly. I prefer, however, to let you finish the job at hand."

I glared at him, but he simply gazed back with expressionless eyes. "Are you sure he can't sense me?"

"Quite. Any vampire can cloak a limited number of mortals from the senses of other vampires; undoubtedly, our friend Klein used that to conceal whatever partners he worked with. Mr. Klein

35

will not notice you until he actually sees you. At that point, my protection will be gone." He glanced outward. "They have entered. Good luck, Jason Wood."

I gave his hand a quick shake. "I wouldn't say it's been fun... but it has been interesting."

Carefully, I started for my front door. I slipped inside and walked with great care along one side of the hallway. As I approached my office, I heard Klein's voice:

"Where else? Think, Sylvie! That negative may be the only thing keeping Jason alive now!"

Sylvie's voice trembled faintly. "I don't know, Elias—wait. He kept really important data in a safe, over there behind the wall panels."

Footsteps as they went from the upstairs towards my workstation; then a rattle as the panel was pushed open. I peeked around the corner from the den.

Sylvie was standing behind Elias, who was bent down over the small safe.

"Sylvie, do you know the combination?"

"I don't know if I should tell you that."

He turned towards her; I ducked back just in time. "Sylvie, please! Domingo knows that negative is the only hard evidence we have! Without it, we don't have a thing to bargain with."

She sighed. "All right. It's thirty-one, forty-one, fifty-nine, twenty-six."

He snickered a bit. "Of course. Pi." I heard the rustle of his clothes as he turned back to the safe.

My only chance. As quietly as I could, I stepped through the door and snaked an arm around Sylvie, clamping my hand over her mouth and nose so she couldn't make a sound and pulling her head toward me enough so she could see me. Her eyes widened, then narrowed when I put a finger to my lips. I could see her glance towards Klein as I let go. One nod told me she'd figured out the situation. She slowly started back out the door.

"Sylvie, it's not there! Where else—you?!" As Elias turned, he caught sight of me. I'd never seen someone's jaw literally drop before. He stood there for several seconds, just staring.

"Hello, Elias." I raised the gun.

"Wood? Wood, what the hell are you doing? How did you get away from Domingo? We were worried to death about you!" He started forward.

I gestured with the gun; he stopped. "No, I don't think you were worried at all, Elias. You were sure that after I called Domingo he'd cancel my ticket for you. Save you the trouble."

"What are you talking about?"

"Don't try it, Elias; I can see you thinking about moving. It must've been a shock to you when you came in and saw all those vampire books on my desk. You knew right then that I was closing in on you. You also saw your one chance to send me on a one-way chase after the wrong guy: that negative. All you had to do was call my attention to it; you could rely on me to imagine the rest."

I shook my head. "Even then, you almost blew it entirely by pointing out that SLR—Single Lens Reflex—cameras show exactly what's in the picture. You see, SLRs use *mirrors* to send that image to the viewfinder. I knew that, but with everything else I didn't think of it at the time. Anyone taking snapshots of a vampire through an SLR would've known something was funny...if, of course, he wasn't a vampire himself.

"I don't know if you even realized you'd made a mistake there, but whether you did or didn't the whole thing was fantastic control on your part; you must've noticed the books as soon as you came in, and you never gave a sign. And your shock at seeing them—only after you'd made sure I knew the significance of the photo—oh, that was perfect. But Domingo isn't quite the ruthless guy you think he is." I clicked the safety twice, so he knew it was ready to fire. "There's only one thing that puzzles me, Elias."

He dropped the pretense. "What, Jason?"

"Well, two, really. How'd it happen?"

Klein shrugged. "I don't really know, to tell the truth. I was on a job a while back, got jumped, put into the hospital, remember?"

Now that he mentioned it, I did. About half a year ago; he'd been taken out of a regular hospital to some rehab facility.

"Yeah," he said, still watching my hand with the gun. "So I actually don't remember much for a while after the accident. And when I came back, I knew what I was, and that there was another one here. One that I couldn't afford to have around. But if I took the right course, I could get rid of Domingo *and* clean up the streets. Get the drug traffic shut down, and at the same time make sure Morgantown's undesirable population went...down."

Undesirable population? I couldn't believe what I was hearing.

Klein hadn't ever talked that way before. "What the hell, Elias? Why?"

He sneered. "It just seemed a lot clearer. People like Lewis, and that Corrigan woman—wastes of space. And since I needed *something* to eat..."

"But you didn't...I mean, does it have to be *human* blood? And do you have to *kill*?"

His hands twitched aimlessly. "Human blood has...more of a kick to it, I guess. And when they die, you get this incredible *rush*, a feeling of such *power*..." He'd been looking at his hands. When he raised his face, my guts turned to ice. Deep in his eyes was a hellish red glow. And as he spoke, I saw lengthening fangs. "Besides," he continued, and now his voice had an edge of hysteria, "besides, they had to die. They saw me, you see. And it wasn't as if they were anyone important."

"Not anyone...Elias, they were human beings!"

"You always did take the liberal view, Jason." His face was distorting, somehow shifting before my eyes. "I really liked you, Jason...But now you have to die, too." He smiled, and there was very little of the old Elias in that deadly smile.

"Don't, Elias. I don't want to kill you."

He started forward slowly. "Let's not pretend, Jason. You can't arrest me, and I need blood."

I backed away, trying to make myself pull the trigger. But, Jesus, Elias was my friend! "Stop, Elias! For God's sake, you're... addicted, that's what you're talking about! Think about it! A big rush, something you *need*, something that you're going after for that rush..."

He laughed. "That's funny, Jason. Should I go to AA? 'Hello, my name is Elias, and I'm a vampire'?" He shook his head. "I don't *want* to kill you, but I have no choice. Neither have you. It's a shame that you can't do anything about it." He was barely human now, a Hollywood vampire straight out of *Fright Night*. "Good-bye, Jason." He rose straight off the floor, a nightmare of fangs and talons.

My finger spasmed on the trigger.

There was a roar of thunder.

Elias was hit in mid-descent. The force of the round, as it mushroomed within him, hurled him back over my desk. He rose, only a scorched bullet hole in his suit showing he'd been hit.

"So much for silver," I said as I sprinted out the door. I almost bowled over Sylvie as she came running back. "Go, Syl, go!" I heard jarring footsteps behind me, whirled and fired the second bullet.

The bullet caught him square in the chest; Elias' scream shook the windows as white flame exploded from the incendiary bullet.

"Wood! You bastard! That hurt!" As I backpedaled away, I could see the burns healing. "I think I'll break a few things before I kill you!" He ducked away before I could get another clear bead on him.

"Crap. Anne Rice failed me too. I should have known better than to trust a book with a punk vampire." I glanced around nervously.

If I were a vampire, where would I come from next...?

I whirled in time to see Elias coming through the wall like a ghost. I leapt through the doorway to the kitchen, but Elias' hand caught me just as I reached the side door. "Gotcha!"

I tried to pull away, but I might as well have been pushing on a vault door. He bent his head toward my neck. I screamed.

Then it was *Elias* who screamed, a yell of utter shock and agony. I fell to the floor and rolled heavily away, looked up.

Sylvie stood there, holding a large ankh before her. "Back, Undead! By the power of Earth and Life, back!"

The incantation sounded silly; Elias obviously saw no humor in it. As he turned away, trying to get around the looped cross, I saw a black imprint on his back where the ankh had hit him. I raised the .45, fired the third bullet.

The heavy shell hit him like a sledgehammer, spinning him completely around, smashing him into the stove. He put a hand to his chest, where a red stain was beginning to spread. His expression was utter disbelief. Then he fell.

"What did you *shoot* him with?" Syl demanded, her face pale.

I looked at the body. "A wooden bullet. Thank you, Fred Saberhagen."

"Who's he?"

"He wrote *The Holmes-Dracula File*; that's where I got the idea." I holstered the gun and started out of the kitchen—I didn't want to look at the body while I tried to figure out what I was going to say to the cops.

Elias' hand shot out and grabbed my ankle.

I felt myself lifted like a toy, smashed into Syl, sending her ankh flying. Then there was a crash and I felt slivers of glass as I was hurled out of the window. I remember thinking vaguely that I'd gotten the genre wrong. It wasn't a mystery novel; it was *Friday the 13th,* where the psycho never dies.

I landed badly, barely rolling. I heard the gun skid out of the holster. I scrabbled after it; but then a leather-skinned hand closed clawed fingers around it. "You almost had me, Jason," said the thing that had been Elias Klein. "Too bad you missed the heart. It still might have worked, but you must've used an *awfully* tough wood; most of the bullet went right on through." He squeezed. The barrel of my gun bent.

I got up and ran.

I didn't get twenty feet.

Talons ripped my shirt; he pitched me the rest of the way across the street and through a storefront. A shard of glass ripped my arm, and my ankle smashed into the edge of the window. I looked up, seeing Elias approach me, the inverted neon letters above lending a hellish cast to his distorted features.

Neon letters?

I scrambled away from the window, limped towards the back of the store, grabbed the doorknob, ducked inside.

It was a tiny room with no other exit. I was trapped. The door opened. "A dead end. How appropriate." Elias smiled. No reluctance now, he was happy to kill.

I tried to duck past him; his hands lashed out like whips, lifting me clear of the ground. He turned while holding me. "Trying to get out the door?" He shoved me through the doorway, pulled me back. "It's over, Wood...and I am hungry." He bent his head again.

Suddenly, the crystal hammer went warm against my chest. Elias cursed and dropped me. "*Damn* that bitch! She made that, didn't she?"

I didn't answer. I hurled myself towards the switch by the door.

Elias caught me with one hand. But I swung my body and kicked the switch up.

The tanning booth blazed to life, uncountable rows of sun-lamps flooding the air with concentrated sunshine. Elias shrieked, dropped me, threw his arms across his face. "Shut it off! Oh, God, shut it off!"

I took a limping step back.

"Please, Jason, please!" Elias stumbled blindly towards me.

I swung my right fist as hard as I could.

He was off balance already. He fell backward onto the tanning bed. "Oh God oh God I'm burning alive Jason *please*!!"

Blisters popped across his flesh. There was a stench like burning meat. I felt my stomach convulse and I turned away.

"Oh I'm sorry I'm sorry oh just help me Jason!"

"I'm sorry too, Elias," I choked out. I put my hands over my ears but I couldn't drown out the sound of frying fat.

"*HELP MEEEeeeee . . .*"

Slowly I uncovered my ears. Then I opened them and turned around.

On the tanning pallet lay a blackened, scorched mummy, mouth gaping wide, revealing razor-sharp fangs. One hand was frozen above the clouded eyes, clawing the air in a vain attempt to fend off the radiance, blistered skin drawn tight over bone. As I watched, the skin began to peel away and turn to oily smoke.

I managed to make it just outside the door before I was violently sick.

CHAPTER 7

Unwrapped Wrap-Up

"So what are the police going to do about this?" asked Sylvie.

It was the next evening. I was lying on my bed with my left ankle's cast propped on a pillow. "I was lucky. It was Renee Reisman who got there first. Between us and the ME, we faked up a story that should hold."

"So what's the official line?"

"Klein was running a sideline of drugs and protection and was going to set Domingo up to take the fall. The victims like Lewis were connections who knew too much. When I was called in, I got suspicious. Klein decided I had to be removed too, came after me. In the fight, we ended up in the salon, where he swung his gun into one of the lights and electrocuted the crap out of himself."

Sylvie looked at me like I was crazy. "Are you nuts? No one will swallow that yarn for a second! One look at that body and any layman would know there was something fishy . . . once he stopped tossing his cookies."

"First, no one is going to see that body. Second, most of that department are hard-nosed realists. They don't want to believe in vampires and are not going to reopen the case if that is the direction the investigation will take them."

"Is that all?"

"Nope, there is one more thing." I nodded my head in the direction of the door.

Verne Domingo stepped into the room.

Sylvie's eyes widened.

"Greetings, Ms. Stake. Thank you for inviting me into your home, Jason."

I shrugged. "I figured I should return your favor."

"I am the final reason the ruse will work, Ms. Stake...or can I call you Sylvia?"

"Uh...call me Sylvie; you can understand why." She looked at me. "Jason, are you sure this is safe?"

"Syl, if Mr. Domingo wants my ass, he doesn't have to do it himself."

"Exactly, Mr. Wood."

"So just exactly what are you doing to make this silly story work?"

"Beings such as myself have many talents, Sylvie. One of them is a degree of mental control. I have exerted this ability so as to make the people involved believe the story as presented."

"You hypnotized them?"

"Something a bit less crude and far more reliable, Sylvie. It is obviously in my interest to make this story work, as you put it." He bowed to me. "An excellent bit of work last night, Mr. Wood. Congratulations." With that, he simply...faded...away.

It was several seconds before we stopped staring. "Wow," Sylvie said finally.

"Yeah," I agreed. I blushed a little. "Uh, Syl...I didn't say thanks. You saved my life twice last night. First with that crazy stunt with the ankh, then with the hammer charm." I pulled it out and looked at it. "These things are only supposed to work with faith. I don't have much of that. Yours must have been enough for us both."

She flushed to the roots of her hair. "Don't sell yourself short, Jason. It was made for you; any strength it showed came equally from your own spirit."

"Okay. But still, I didn't make it, and you were the one who insisted I wear it."

She smiled. "All right, Jason. I'll take the credit. And you're very, very welcome. I just wanted you to come back in one piece."

"Which I pretty much did, if a little cracked," I agreed, looking at my cast. Syl laughed.

I looked at the thin air into which Verne Domingo had vanished. "So tell me something, Syl..."

"What, Jason?"

"Do you think...it's over?"

She smiled...and then her face suddenly went serious, her

eyes got that strange distant look as though they were look-ing through everything around her. "No," she said after a long moment, and the tone in her voice sent a faint chill down my spine. "No, Jason, it's not over.

"This isn't the end; it's the beginning."

Part II

Lawyers, Ghouls, and Mummies

May 1999

CHAPTER 8

New Client, Closed Case

For some reason, Syl's words echoed back to me at odd hours in the next few weeks. I did find myself glancing at shadows out of the corner of my eye more often, looking at mist-fogged streets with a different perception, but for quite a while nothing of any note happened.

The only real reminder of the strangeness in my life was the lack of strangeness when I talked to Renee Reisman. She had volunteered to forget the truth—it would make the deception easier and more convincing—but that meant that she had literally no recollection of the most frightening and bizarre episode in both our lives. It was difficult, at first, to go to our usual Thursday bowling night without expecting the subject to come up, and to not *bring* it up. But after a couple of weeks I adapted to it, and things were back on track.

I glanced at the clock. *Four-fifteen*. I keep WIS open until five every day, but a lot of the time no one comes in for hours. More than half my clients I hardly ever see, just hear over a telephone or get e-mail or faxes from. I had just looked back down to the package I was preparing for IntraScience Technologies—prior art research on a patent they thought they could get, but probably wouldn't if they couldn't get around the prior art I'd found—when the door chimed.

The boy coming in looked vaguely familiar; about five-foot-seven, maybe fifteen, skin with the dark complexion of the Middle East, a narrow face that Syl would have described as hawklike, a slender build, and eyes of a startlingly clear gray I could see from my desk.

I could also see even darker circles under his eyes, and he was walking with the heaviness I associated with someone near the limit of exhaustion. "Mr. Wood?" he asked.

"That's me, yes. Welcome to Wood's Information Service, Mr. . . . ?"

"Ross. Xavier Ross."

Oh, that poor kid. Once he said his name, I knew who he was. I'd actually seen him a couple of times in the news before the lastest disaster—he was a star of the local martial arts scene and had just come back from an overseas tournament of some kind with medals. But the big news hadn't been nearly so cheery. "My sympathies, Mr. Ross. I was familiar with a lot of your brother's work."

"Th . . . thanks." He hesitated, then sat down on the red leather chair I had in front of my desk for clients. "Um . . . how much would it cost me to have you do something for me?"

I grinned. "Depends on the something, I'd say. What do you want me to do?"

He looked embarrassed. "Sorry, that *was* stupid. I . . ." Xavier sighed, looked down. "You work with the cops, right?"

"Sometimes. I can't talk about or give you any information on whatever they give me to do. Just to warn you."

"Oh, no, I don't want that. But you're not part of the police *yourself*?"

Well, this is an interesting conversation already. "No. But if you want me to do anything criminal, I don't do that."

He shook his head violently, long black hair twitching in the ponytail he wore. "No, no, I wouldn't ask you to do anything like that, Mr. Wood. I just . . . you know they've closed the case?"

I started to get some idea of what he might want. "I'd heard. Drug-related killing. Your brother was a freelance investigative reporter and photographer; he must have seen the wrong thing at the wrong time."

"I don't *think* so," Xavier said, and I was startled by the *venom* in his voice. The conviction in those words was also impressive. "Sorry. Not your fault. But . . . they sent back my brother's laptop." He reached into a bag he was carrying and brought out a Lumiere ToughScreen 97E—a *very* nice computer for anyone on the go. "I'd like you to check it out for me."

I raised an eyebrow. "I'm sure the police went over all the

files, and if it boots it should be in good shape. What do you want me to check?"

He looked suspiciously at me, then his gaze dropped. "For anything that might have been wiped. I've heard you're really good." He rolled his eyes, obviously annoyed with himself. "Okay, look, I'm not... I've never done this kind of thing before. My brother, M... Michael, he used this to take notes. He took notes on everything he did and kept it in a very exact format. Like this." He opened the laptop and showed me a series of files with names that told me the location and date. "The cops didn't find anything that showed he was in any kind of..." he hesitated.

I decided to wait, see what he had to say.

"Any kind of... strange investigation," he finally finished. "Something different than the ordinary. They didn't find anything *specifically* about drug running either, but they figured he'd run into his problem while on one of the other jobs. But I *knew* Mike, you know?" I nodded when he looked at me. "So I knew what his workload was like and how he did things. It just doesn't look like there's enough on the computer for those weeks."

"All right. You want me to see if there's anything showing that someone erased files in this format, and recover anything I can. Is that it?"

"Yes! That's exactly it."

I frowned. Lumiere PCs were pretty good about their erasure procedures, and bringing up stuff someone tried to delete... Maybe. But it'd be a bear. "That's going to be very expensive, Xavier, and I don't know if I should be doing this at all. Who owns this?"

"I do. Once they released Michael's stuff, my mom gave me pretty much everything." His tone wavered and I could see the effort it took for him to not begin crying.

Well, if the cops closed the case there's nothing stopping me from poking around in it. "You want this done the way I'd do it for a top police investigation, I'm going to have to charge you what I would charge them. That's about three thousand dollars, Xavier." Actually, for an official investigation it'd be about *six* thousand, but I was willing to cut him a break—just not too much of a break, because this *would* take some work.

He didn't hesitate; his eyes might have widened a bit, but he reached into another pocket of the backpack and pulled out a debit card. "You take Virtuoso cards?"

Man, I wish I'd had that much money to spend when I was his age. "You're allowed to do this?"

"Mom said I can spend the money in that account any way I want."

"If you say so." I worked up the job on one of my standard forms with a clear, short statement of work, had him sign it, and ran the card. It cleared that amount without a problem. "All right, Mr. Ross, I'll get to work on this. It will take some time, and I have other clients, but you can expect to hear something back from me no later than two weeks from now, and possibly as early as one week."

He stood stiffly and nodded. "Okay." Xavier stuck out his hand and we shook hands. "Thanks, Mr. Wood."

I watched him leave, wondering. Then I took the laptop and put it back in my main work area.

"Time to start closing up," I said to myself.

CHAPTER 9

Join Me for a Bite?

It is an immutable law of nature in any business that *just* as you go to hang up the CLOSED sign, the phone will ring or a customer walk in. It gets to the point that you automatically hesitate for a few seconds before finally turning the lock and setting the security system, not because you've forgotten anything, but because you're giving the inevitable a chance to make its appearance less painful through preparation.

This does not fool the gods, however, so just as I stopped hesitating and turned the key, the phone rang. I gave my usual mild curse and picked up the phone. "Wood's Information Service, Jason Wood speaking."

"Ah, Mr. Wood. It is good to hear your voice again."

There was no way I could forget that deep, resonant voice with its undefinable accent.

"Mr. Domingo! This is...a surprise."

I hadn't heard from Domingo in several weeks, ever since we'd finished the Great Vampire Coverup, and hadn't expected to ever hear from the blood-drinking gentleman again.

"No doubt. I was wondering if you would do me the honor of joining me for dinner—in the purely normal sense—sometime this week."

Well, now, there was a poser of a question. And given that he had more than enough people to arrange his schedule, it must be important, especially if he was calling me personally. "Ummm," I said smoothly. "Might I ask why?"

To my surprise, he also hesitated for a moment. "There are several matters I would like to discuss, but at least one of them was touched on during your first visit to my home. In a sense, you might consider this a business meeting."

"I'm aware of certain elements of your business, Mr. Domingo," I said, trying not to sound overly cold despite my distaste for drug-runners. "Without meaning any undue offense, I don't think that I could be of much assistance, given certain preconditions of my own." Such as wanting to stay on the right side of the law, for instance.

I was startled to hear a soft chuckle. "Would you be willing to take my word for it that you will find any business proposal I make to be neither overly onerous nor morally reprehensible to you?"

I considered that. "As a matter of fact . . . yes, I guess I would. All other things aside, you strike me as a man who takes his word very seriously."

"Your perceptions are accurate. Can I take that to mean you will accept my invitation?"

"Now that you've piqued my curiosity, you'd have a hard time keeping me away. I can't manage it tonight, but tomorrow night or Friday would do."

"Excellent. Tomorrow night it is, then. I shall tell Morgan to expect you at eight o'clock. Have you a preference for a menu?"

What the hell, I knew he wasn't hurting for money. "Since you're buying, I have a fondness for fresh lobster and shrimp."

"Noted. My chef rarely has a chance to show off; I shall let him know someone will be coming who can appreciate his work, as he has himself a preference for seafood dishes."

"Great. Um, should I bring anything with me, this being partly business?"

"For this meeting, I think just your mind will suffice. If we reach a significant agreement, then we shall go into the more formal details."

"Gotcha. Okay, see you at eight then."

"I shall be looking forward to it. Good-bye, Mr. Wood."

"Good-bye, Mr. Domingo."

I stared at the phone for several minutes afterwards. "It appears I have an interview with a vampire."

CHAPTER 10

Career Counseling

It was somewhat more comforting to be pulling into the huge, curving driveway in my own car under my own control.

The door opened as I reached the landing, and I saw the impeccably elegant butler/majordomo I remembered from the last visit. "Thank you . . . um, Morgan, wasn't it?"

"Indeed, sir," Morgan replied, with a small bow. "Your coat, sir? Thank you." I handed him my overcoat, which he took and handed to another servant. "If you will be good enough to follow me, sir, Master Verne is waiting for you in the dining room."

The manners in the Domingo household, I had to admit, had never given me room for complaint, at least aside from the initial threats. I followed Morgan to an absolutely magnificent dining room, with a genuine cut-crystal chandelier that shed a sparkling light over a huge elongated dinner table which could have easily seated fifty people. The paneling was elegant, real wood I was sure, and there were small oil paintings tastefully set along the walls.

Verne Domingo, resplendent in an archaic outfit, rose upon my entry and bowed. "Welcome to my home, Mr. Wood. Enter freely and of your own will."

I couldn't manage to keep a straight face, though I tried. After I stopped laughing, I spread my hands. "Okay, okay, enough. I see you have a sense of humor, too. At least you have the looks to carry it off."

"I thank you. Please, sit down and tell me how my chef has done his work. Alas, I am unable to directly appreciate such talents anymore."

It was a shellfish dream—seven different dishes, small enough that I could eat something of each of them without feeling like I was going to put a large number of crustaceans to waste. As it turned out, small enough so that if I felt like a pig—and I did—I could make sure no crustacean went untouched. I sat back finally, realizing I'd overeaten and not regretting it one bit. "Magnificent, sir. I haven't eaten that well since...um...I don't think I've ever eaten that well, actually. Seven dishes, four cuisines, the spices perfect, neither over- nor underdone...I'm going to miss this when I go home, I can tell you that."

Domingo smiled broadly, giving a view of slightly-too-long canines. "Excellent!" He glanced to the side. "Did you hear that, Hitoshi?"

A middle-aged Japanese man came in and bowed. "I did. Many thanks for your kind words, Mr. Wood."

"Jason—may I call you Jason?—this is Hitoshi Mori. He has been my chef for several decades now, but rarely has he had a chance for a personal command performance. I am sure he finds it good to know his skills have not faded."

"They certainly haven't. *Domo arigato*, Mori-*san*." That was admittedly the limit of my Japanese, and I suspected that both Verne and Chef Mori knew it, because the chef simply bowed and thanked me again.

I glanced at Verne. "I'd guess then that your entire staff isn't made up of vampires? I mean, Hitoshi-*san* must have people to cook for?"

Hitoshi bowed. "It is true that, aside from Domingo-*sama*, his household needs to eat. But it is also unfortunately true that a man can become too accustomed to a routine—either the chef to the tastes of the household, or the household to the work of the chef. Only one who is new can truly permit the chef to measure his skill."

"Well, you have my vote. I've eaten in top-flight restaurants that served far worse. And I'm sure that at least one—the grilled lobster with the citrus and soy sauce—was an original."

Hitoshi looked gratified. "You are correct, Mr. Wood. I am glad that my efforts meet with your approval." He bowed again to Verne and me, and left.

"Okay," I said, leaning back to let my somewhat overstressed stomach relax, "let's cut to the chase, Verne. What, exactly, did you want to talk to me about?"

For the first time, I saw Verne Domingo look...uncomfortable. Almost as though he was embarrassed. "As I mentioned, it has to do with a discussion we began the first time we met. You described your objections to my profession, I dismissed them.

"I have...reconsidered some of my statements."

I raised an eyebrow at him. "Oh? You no longer want to argue about whether drug-pushing is an acceptable profession?"

He cast a faintly annoyed glance at me, then nodded, conceding that I had the right to phrase it that way. "Philosophically, I remain of the opinion that your government is committing an act of extreme idiocy in criminalizing these substances. In terms of morals and practicality, however, I have considered your words and realized that there is far more truth to them than I was originally willing to grant.

"While, ideally, I sold only to those who were both wealthy and foolish, I discovered that this was, in practice, virtually impossible to maintain; some of my...products were inevitably being sold down an ever-branching hierarchy of smaller and smaller distributors, eventually to be marketed to the very unfortunates I would never have intended to ensnare. Moreover..."

He trailed off, then rose from his chair, walked over to a window, and looked out into the darkness.

I waited a bit. Finally, I said, "Yes?"

He took a breath—I noticed that he didn't seem to do that habitually, which was a subtle but definite clue to his nature—and forced himself to continue. "...moreover, I found that I was not pleased with my own behavior, when I compared it with yours, or—in truth—that which I would perhaps have expected of myself in times past. I do not think my own people—those bound to me by oaths and by the power that makes them able to share my journey through time—could ever complain of their treatment at my hands, but outside of this isolated and self-contained circle, I have not been the sort of man I originally meant to be, not in...a very, very long time."

He gripped the windowsill, tight enough that I heard faint crackling sounds and was sure that if I went there later, I'd find dents the shape of fingers in the wood. "Many things happened in the past centuries which soured me, made me less than I had been in many ways. I do not think, were I to talk with my self of ages past, that he would be proud of what I have become;

in truth, I think he would pity me. I have had no true friends outside of these, my people, for a very long time indeed. I was, despite my unchanging appearance, becoming a bitter, cynical old man. I had...and still have...enemies who would consider that a triumph and amusement." He turned to me. "I wish to try to change that. I would abandon this peddling of illegal substances, find some other venture to provide for myself and my people, and perhaps, find a way of, in some small manner, rejoining humanity."

Other people might make a speech like that for effect; but in the way he spoke, I could hear pain under the restrained and dignified words. In my business, you often make a living by guessing who you can and can't trust. Verne Domingo, vampire and drug-runner, struck me as a man whose word was inviolate and who would never say things like this unless they came from his heart.

I nodded. "For what it's worth, Mr. Domingo, I agree with your philosophical position. I think people have the right to be fools, and that the criminalization of things like drugs was proven to be a failure during Prohibition. The same market forces that eliminated booze as a profitable black-market item here would pretty much eliminate the crime caused by drugs if we just stopped making it illegal to sell them. Doesn't mean that this wouldn't create other problems, but I think the new problems would be a lot more manageable than the old ones." I studied him. "But I think you called me here for another reason—although I immensely appreciate your decision, and find it pretty darn gratifying that you decided to tell me this personally. So...what do you want from me?"

"In a sense...little more than you have already given, Jason."

"Excuse me?"

"Aside from the words you have already spoken, which eventually led to this revelation, the fact that you have known what I am, and have nonetheless chosen to leave me to myself—and have even trusted me, to assist in hiding what happened here, and to come here and speak with me, on nothing more than my word." He was looking at me very gravely. "I have trusted no mortal with my secret for a long time, save those who have become a part of my household. You have taken that trust and already repaid it.

"Yet I confess that there is another, more practical need I have of you." He sat down again, looking slightly less formal than he had moments earlier. "As you can see, I live quite well; this involves the expenditure of money, for which I would prefer to have a visible source. It is undoubtedly true, however, that I am hardly a man of these times, and I have no idea what professions I could do well in."

I blinked at that. "Mr. Domingo—"

"Call me Verne, if you would."

"Okay. Verne, I'm not an employment agent or counselor."

"This I understand, Jason. Yet it is true, is it not, that finding jobs or evaluating people could be construed as something involving finding and analyzing information?"

I chuckled. "Well, yeah, I guess you could put it that way. I could probably do a half-assed job at those kind of things, but a professional advisor would be a lot more effective."

"This I cannot argue with," Verne conceded. "However, to do their job to the best of their ability, such people would need to understand many things about me—including what makes my situation unique."

I saw what he was getting at now. "In other words, they'd have to be able to understand why you are in the position you are—most likely, they would have to know there is something weird about you, at the least, and may learn exactly what you are."

"Precisely. Now, I have already confessed that I have been a sour old man for far too long, but that does not mean that I have decided it would be wise to spread the secrets of my existence far and wide. In fact, I suspect that this is one area in which I must remain as careful as I have ever been."

I nodded slowly. "Can't argue that. Despite *The X-Files* and other similar shows, the world is not ready for real vampires as standard citizens. And the angry mob these days carries automatic weapons, Molotov cocktails, and explosives." I dropped into my professional mode and started analyzing the problem.

"Okay, Verne, let's take this a step at a time. I find it hard to believe that you don't have scads of money stashed away somewhere—you've had centuries, and it's pretty obvious to me, just from your mannerisms, that you've been in the upper crust for a long time. So I guess the first question is, why do you need a job at all?"

He looked pleased. "Indeed, you cut to the heart of the matter. I do, as you surmise, have quite considerable wealth in various locations and institutions around the world. However, this is not as simple to access as you might think. Until recently, you see, there was little ability to examine the flow of funds from one country to another, and thus it was relatively easy for a man such as myself to move from one place to another and bring my fortune with me, needing only a rather simple cover story to explain why I had so much."

"Gotcha. Transferring significant sums around, making formerly inactive-for-a-century accounts active, dragging in large quantities of gold or whatever, tends to draw the notice of the IRS and other agencies interested in potentially shady activities." Having grown up in an era where the government was already well in place with computers monitoring any significant transaction, this was an issue I hadn't previously considered. Oh, it had become more pervasive in areas since I was born, but the basic idea that income was watched by the IRS had been taken as a given. Someone like Verne, who had been living for hundreds of years in civilizations which didn't communicate much between countries and who had, at best, spotty ways of tracing assets, would indeed find the new higher-tech and higher-monitoring civilizations a bit daunting, to say the least.

"As you say. In addition . . . I am accustomed to doing some form of work. I have been many things in my time, but even as a nobleman, I tried to busy myself with the responsibilities such a position entailed. I would feel quite at a loss if I had nothing at all to do." He waited for me to acknowledge this second point, then continued. "Now, my former profession, while illegal, has the advantage of being paradoxically expected. When the government sees large sums of unexplained cash, it expects drugs are the source. If it finds what it expects, then it digs no farther. And if I can deny the government admissible evidence and have . . . connections who pay the right people, it is unlikely to do more than try to harass the suppliers. Supplying drugs also, as I understand you deduced, has the advantage of no set hours. If I wish to be eccentric and meet people only at night, well, this is no more strange than some of the other people involved in this business."

I rubbed my chin, thinking. "Uh-huh. You have this double problem. Not only do you have money of unknown provenance— and thus, from the point of view of any cop, probably crooked somewhere—you can't afford to have people look at you *too* closely because there's some aspects of your own existence that you have to keep hidden.

"So what you need is a job or profession which permits you to communicate with people exclusively, or nearly exclusively, during darkness hours, which has the potential to earn very large sums of money, and which you can at least fake having the talents for. Either that, or you need a way to get a huge sum of money here where you can use it openly and have an ironclad reason for getting that money."

"I think you have summed it up admirably, yes. I also have something of a philosophical objection to the rates of taxation applied to certain sources of income, but that's a different matter."

"And way out of my league; finding more acceptable employment is one thing, convincing the federal government that it shouldn't tax income is another." Verne smiled in acknowledgement. I went on to the next item of business.

"And what are you doing about your soon-to-be-former business associates?" At a glance from him, I hastily added, "No, no, I'm not asking if you're going to turn them in or anything. Just when and how you're going to get out of the business, so to speak."

"I have, in point of fact, already informed the relevant persons of my decision. I will, of course, clarify my position to them if any of them desire it."

I looked at him questioningly. "You do realize that some of these people may not think of retirement as an option?"

He smiled, but this smile was colder somehow, less the smile of a gracious host and more the bared-fang expression of a predator. "I am sure I can...persuade anyone who might think otherwise, Jason. Do not concern yourself with that side of the equation."

I gave an inward shiver, remembering what Elias Klein—barely a baby by Verne's standards—had been capable of. No, I didn't suppose Verne would have much trouble there.

"Okay," I said. "I guess I can give it a shot. I'll have to think about it a bit, and of course we're going to have to go into your skills and knowledge areas. I'd feel kinda silly giving you a standard questionnaire, so I'll just have to talk to you for a while on that—get a feel for what you would enjoy, what you'd hate to do, what you've already got the skills and knowledge for, and what you'd learn easily. Also, you'll have to confirm or deny the various limitations I guessed for your people, and how they apply to you, so I know what things are definite no-nos and which ones are 'sometimes, but only rarely,' if you know what I mean."

"I grasp your meaning, yes. Would you like to start tonight?"

I ran over my schedule in my head. "Unfortunately, no. I'd have to leave here in about another hour anyway—I have some early clients to see—and I'd like time to let the concept percolate through my brain. How about Thursday—day after tomorrow? I know that one was clear, since I checked on it yesterday."

"Thursday will be eminently satisfactory. I shall expect you at the same time, then?"

"Fine with me." I got up and extended my hand.

He shook it with a firm but not oppressively strong grip. "You have neglected to mention your fee, Jason."

I shrugged. "This isn't a normal job—I have no idea what to charge at this point. We'll cross that bridge when we come to it. In fact, I have a better idea. When I bring over the work-for-hire agreement, the price will be left open to your discretion. You can decide after the fact what the work was worth to you."

"Are you not concerned I might take advantage of this option?"

I shook my head. "You're a man of honor. You'd feel too guilty. In fact, I will probably come out ahead, since you're likely to charge yourself more than I would."

He laughed. "You are indeed wiser than your years would make you, Jason. Good night, then, and have a pleasant journey home."

"After that dinner, I certainly will. Thank you, Verne."

CHAPTER 11

Personal History

"All right," I said, "you *can* meet people in the daytime if necessary. Just not a good thing to do often. That's great—there are a lot of things, like signing papers, getting permits, and so on, that are close to impossible to manage if you can't get the principal to make himself available when other people are."

I was going over the notes I'd gotten that night, while Verne answered my questions and read the work-for-hire agreement. "Yes, I understand that," Verne confirmed. "I will certainly make myself available for official meetings in the daytime, but would strongly prefer such things be very few and far between. By the way, I admire your wording in this agreement—making it clear that part of your job is to take into consideration my special requirements, while being so utterly generic that someone getting a look at this agreement wouldn't think anything of it."

I grinned. "Wish I could take credit for that one, but I stole most of the wording from similar agreements for people with disabilities." I stood up. "Okay, let's take a look around your house here. Sometimes what you see in a man's home gives you ideas—I'm assuming you keep at least some things around because you like them, not just for show."

"Indeed I do. Most things are for my enjoyment, or that of my people." Verne rose also and began to lead me on a tour of the house.

Verne Domingo's "house" was one of the only ones I'd ever visited that deserved the appellation "mansion." It rose a full three stories, sprawled across a huge area of land, and had at least one basement level (given my host's nature, I was not at all sure that there weren't parts of the house, above or below ground, that were being concealed). His staff numbered twelve; thirteen, if you counted Morgan. He seemed wryly amused at the coincidence of the number, and noted to me that it had been that way for at least three hundred years. "Therefore," he said, "you must forgive me for putting little stock in triskaidekaphobia."

"So none of your staff is less than three hundred years old?" I asked, trying to get my brain around the concept.

"Not precisely. What has happened is that, on the occasions I have lost a member of my household over the past few centuries, I have quickly found a replacement. This number seems to be suited to my requirements for efficiency, comfort, and security. My youngest, in fact, you have met—Hitoshi Mori is scarcely seventy-five years old, and has been in my service for forty-two years."

"Morgan, I know, can work during the day. So they aren't vampires like yourself, right?"

Verne nodded, pausing to point out the engravings that were spaced evenly around the walls of this room. "It is possible for someone such as myself to bind others to my essence—allowing them to partake of the power that makes me what I am—without giving them all the limitations of the life I follow. Naturally, they do not gain all the advantages, either."

"No blood-drinking?"

Morgan shook his head, opening the next door for us. "No, sir. We do have a preference for meat, given a choice—our metabolism, to use the modern term, seems to use more protein and so on. We gain immortality, some additional strengths and resistances, but nothing like the powers accorded to Master Verne."

"This is my library, Jason," Verne said as we entered another large room, with tall windows that admitted moonlight in stripes across the carpet before it was banished by Morgan's finger on the switch for the overhead lights. "One of them, to be more precise. This contains those works that might be commonly consulted, or read for pleasure, and which are not so unusual or valuable as to require special treatment."

The other three walls were covered with bookshelves—long, very tall bookshelves. A runner for one of the moving bookladders I'd seen in some bookstores ran the entire circumference of the room, aside from the one window-covered wall. Other tall shelves stood at intervals across the room, with a large central space for tables and chairs. Two people were there now, one taking notes from a large volume in front of him, the other leaning back in her chair, reading a newspaper. "Ah, Camillus, Meta, good evening."

The two rose to their feet. Camillus was the one who'd led the three-man assault team that had kidnapped me; a man of average height, slightly graying brown hair, brown eyes, and the wide shoulders and bearing of a career soldier; despite a strongly hooked nose, I was sure that Syl would have rated the tanned, square-faced Camillus highly on looks. Meta was a young lady—or, I amended, a young-looking lady—whose height matched Camillus', but whose long, inky-black hair very nearly matched her skin shade. Despite that, her eyes were a startling gray-blue, and her features were sharp and even, giving her a look of aristocratic elegance that made questions of beauty almost inconsequential.

"No need to rise," Verne said with a smile. "But since you are up, please say hello to Jason Wood."

"Mr. Wood." Camillus' grip was as strong as I would have expected. "Domingo's spoken of you quite a bit of late. My apologies for a certain . . . comment on our prior meeting?"

I grinned. "As long as the threat's withdrawn, sure."

"It is forgotten, then. Let me know if there's anything I can do to assist."

"Sure," I said. "What exactly do you do?"

"I'm the master-at-arms and in charge of security here," he responded.

I noted the nature of the material scattered around his side of the table and grinned. "And how do you feel about that?"

He understood exactly what I meant and grinned back. "You have me there. By all the gods, security has changed in the past century! At least in the old days the common man didn't have access to sorcery; nowadays, you can pick up one of these," he gestured at several home electronics catalogs, "and order up something with the eyes of an eagle and the hearing of a bat that will send all it sees and hears right back to you."

"Well, I noticed the security setup you have here; it's not bad for a man who seems to still be playing catch-up on the century."

He acknowledged the comment with a bow. "Mostly done on contractor recommendations. I'm not comfortable, though, with having anything in the house that I don't understand."

"Then ask me. Once I've got Verne's problem out of the way,

I'll be glad to bring you up to speed. I've got plenty of resources in the security area."

"I'll do that," he said, smiling. "Oh, sir," he said, looking at Verne, "Carmichael sent a pretty pissed-off message to you. I don't like the tone of it."

The two of them went off a ways to discuss Carmichael. I turned to Meta and shook her hand. "And your position here is...?"

"I suppose you might call me...librarian? Archivist? Something of that sort." Her grip was gentle, though not a limp fish by any means.

"Ah, so I'm in your territory here."

She smiled. "It is of course Master Domingo's, but I have jurisdiction as he allows."

Meta and Verne let me wander the library for a few minutes; it was rather instructive, I thought, to see just what Verne thought of as "not unusual or valuable enough" to warrant being kept elsewhere. Even with my relatively limited knowledge of books, I noted several items on the shelves that would easily bring in several hundred dollars if sold.

The next hour of the tour passed without notable event—the other staff might have been sleeping or out for the evening, but whatever the reason I didn't run into any more.

Finally, Verne led me down a wide flight of stairs into the basement, which was as high-ceilinged and opulently furnished as the downstairs, but had clearly greater security. "And here is my bedroom."

"Wait a minute. I thought you said that room on the second floor was your bedroom?"

"My show bedroom—the one that visitors of most sorts will be told is my bedroom, if they have any occasion to ask or discover it. I can rest there, if necessary, but here, enclosed in the earth itself, I am better protected."

The room was very large; I was vaguely disappointed not to see a classic pedestal supporting an open, velvet-lined coffin; instead there was a huge four-poster bed with heavy curtains about it. Several small bookshelves stood at intervals along the walls, along with some large and oddly elaborate frames for paintings, a desk and chairs, a fair-sized entertainment center, and two wardrobes. Besides the paintings, there were a few other objects on the wall, most of them weapons of one kind or another. I wandered around the room, studying these things carefully. The oddity of the painting frames became clear when I realized they were double-sealed frames—museum quality, for preserving fragile materials against the ravages of time. Probably nitrogen-filled.

"So, Jason," Verne said finally, "does anything occur to you?"

I rubbed my chin. "I'm getting something of an idea, it's just being stubborn and refusing to gel. I need just one more thing to trigger it. Unfortunately, I haven't got any idea what that one more thing is."

"Well, I have saved the part I believe you will find most entertaining for last," Verne said. "It is, of course, natural that I would place those things I value most in the most secure area. Here is the entry to my vault—a small museum, if you will." He led the way to another room, relatively small and undecorated, whose far wall was dominated by a no-nonsense, massive door suitable for use in banks and government secure areas. Verne placed his hand on a polished area near the door, then punched in a number on a keypad and turned the large handle. The door opened onto another set of stairs going down to a landing which ended in another door—also clearly strong, though nothing like the several-foot-thick monster Verne had just swung open. I paused, but he gestured me down. "Go first, Jason. I think you will find it more effective to see it without my leading the way."

I shrugged, then went down the steps. As I reached for the door handle, I saw it turn and push inward, as though grasped by an invisible hand. I felt the prickle of gooseflesh as I realized this wasn't any cute gadgetry, but a subtle demonstration of Verne Domingo's powers, clearly for the effect. I felt myself momentarily immersed in something mystical, standing at the edge of ancient mysteries. The black door swung open, into inky darkness. Then the same unseen force switched on the lights.

I can't remember what I said; I think I may have gasped something incomprehensible. What I do know is that I stood for what seemed an eternity, staring.

In that first instant, the room was ablaze with the sunlight sheen of gold, the glitter of gems, the glow of inlay and paint so fresh it might have been finished only yesterday. At first I couldn't even grasp the sheer size of the vault's collection; it wasn't possible, simply wasn't even imaginable that so many artifacts and treasures could be here, beneath a mansion in upstate New York.

Once more, a quote from long-ago years surfaced: Lord Carnevon to Howard Carter as Carter took the first look into the tomb of Tutankhamen: "What do you see?"

And Howard's response: "Wonderful things."

There were statues of animal-headed gods, resplendent in ebony and gold, bedecked with jeweled inlay. A wall filled with incised hieroglyphics provided a sufficient backdrop to set off coffers of jewelry, ceremonial urns, royal chariots. Farther down, beyond what was obviously the Egyptian collection, were carefully hung paintings, marble statues, books and scrolls in glass cases, something at the far end that shimmered like a blown-glass rainbow...

I stepped slowly forward, almost afraid that the entire fantastic scene would disappear like smoke. I reached out, very hesitantly, and touched a finger to the golden nose of a sitting dog.

"From the chambers of Ramses II," Verne said from behind me, almost making me jump. "His tomb was looted quite early, as things go; I managed to procure a large number of the artifacts, which was fortunate since otherwise they would have been melted down or defaced for valuable inlay and so on."

I just shook my head, trying to take it in. Ramses... II? "That's the one they associate with Moses?"

"Indeed."

I walked cautiously around this first incredible chamber, stopping at a huge sarcophagus. The golden face rang a faint bell, which was odd because I'd seen very few statues or busts of Egyptian nobles. What...I studied some of the symbology, not that I was an authority or even much of an amateur in the field, but because maybe something would trigger a memory. As an information expert, it's a matter of pride to get the answers yourself, even if it's by luck.

There! That disc, the rays...

My head snapped up and I looked at Verne in disbelief. "No. It can't be."

He inclined his own. "Can't be...what?"

"Ahkenaten. That's the Aten, and it's all over here. And I've seen a couple of busts supposedly of him. But I thought they found his mummy."

He smiled faintly. "I did hear that someone had found something they believed to be Akhenaten's mummy. Since this has never been out of my, or my people's, possession since shortly after finding out that the Sun Pharaoh's tomb was being looted, I must incline to doubt that what they found was indeed Akhenaten."

It was then that the idea finally crystallized. "Good God, Verne, I've got it."

He looked at me. "What is it?"

"Art, of course!" I waved my hands around at the treasures that surrounded us. "The art world can be tolerant of strange hours and stranger habits. You've already *got* stuff to sell or donate—no, wait, hear me out. You speak many languages, you certainly have various connections around the world, and, well, you appear to have taste and style which I don't have. You could deal in rare artworks, maybe be a patron to newer artists, and so on."

Verne looked thoughtful. "True. I have in fact been a student of the arts, off and on through the centuries; I could determine authenticity in many ways, not the least being first-hand experience of how many things were actually done. Even though I would not, of course, wish to reveal the source of that information, simply knowing the correct from the incorrect is something that I could justify with the proper scholarly logic."

"Yep. It's always easier to write the impeccable logical chain to prove your point if you already know where you're going."

"But selling these masterworks... I have kept them safe for thousands of years, Jason. Do not speak lightly of this."

"I'm not speaking lightly, not at all," I said earnestly. "Verne, these things would rock the archaeological world—and I haven't even looked in the rest of this vault; to be honest, I'm almost afraid of what I'll find. Stuff of this historical and cultural value should be out there for other people to appreciate. Hell, just the aesthetic value would justify putting it out there on the proper market. Okay, it's impolite at the least to go around breaking into someone's tomb and ripping off their stuff, but since it was done long ago, shouldn't the work of those ancient artists at least have the chance to be fully appreciated?"

Verne's expression was pained; a man listening to someone trying to tell him to give up his children wouldn't have looked much more upset. Then Morgan spoke:

"Begging your pardon, sir, but I think Master Jason is correct."

Verne just looked at him, silent but questioning.

"If you truly wish to open yourself up, as you once were, sir, I think this means not keeping everything locked away. Not just your feelings, sir, but those things of beauty which we treasure. We have guarded them long enough, sir." He gave another look that I had trouble interpreting; it seemed filled with more meaning than I could easily interpret, something from their past. "We already know of someone whose love of beauty and fear for its fate transformed him ... in ways that I would not wish to see happen to you."

Those last words got through to Verne; he gave a momentary shiver, as of a man doused with cold water. "Yes ... yes, Morgan. Perhaps you are right." He turned back to me, speaking in a more normal tone. "Your idea certainly has merit, Jason. I shall consider it carefully, and discuss it with my household. I would appreciate it if you would be so kind as to examine the best ways for me to begin on such a course of action."

"Sure," I said, wondering if I'd ever quite know what was going on there. "I suppose I'll leave you to it, then."

I cast a last, incredulous glance over my shoulder at that vault of wonders, then headed up the stairs.

CHAPTER 12

Mystery of a Brother

"Sure, Syl—I'd love to go out tomorrow. You want a movie or something else?"

"How about *Sabers of Twilight*? I've heard that one's a lot of fun and just up your alley, Jason."

I grinned into the phone. "Because of the pretty girls in interesting costumes? Sounds fine. Odd how you don't mention the pretty *boys* in tight leather outfits."

"I didn't say it wasn't up *my* alley too," she said with a laugh. "All right, after we lock up tomorrow then."

"See you!"

I turned back to the pictures on my screen. *This is a real possibility.*

Verne had given me the go-ahead to both start figuring out how to put select pieces of his collection onto the market, and how to start helping him find proper clients that he could patron. The first part was not terribly hard; it was more a matter of deciding how much should be *sold* and how much should be donated, since a lot of the really valuable stuff was considered national treasure by places like Egypt. While Verne's possession of these treasures was (obviously) far before the cut-off date at which such possession would be considered theft, it was still a matter of political delicacy and publicity; *giving* the treasures, at least the most high-profile ones, back to their original owners for display would earn Verne a lot of respect.

If, of course, we could keep people from asking too many of the wrong questions.

Finding clients was somewhat more difficult. In the long run,

Verne would probably do the selecting himself—he was, after all, the guy who was supposed to be the patron and knew a lot more about art than I ever would. But he was also busy... rebuilding himself, I guess would be the way to put it. The Verne Domingo I now spoke to was rather different than the one I'd first met, and I knew part of that was through making an effort to reconnect with his older self, and with the people who had followed him through history.

I'd remembered an art show I'd gone to with Syl some time back, and seeing the paintings online confirmed my memory. There was something special there, even to my casual eye. This Sky Hashima was a good candidate, and even better, he was local.

The door chimed, and I glanced at the clock in surprise. *It is that time already.*

Xavier Ross sat down nervously. "So... did you..."

"You were right, Xavier," I said without beating around the bush. Taking the laptop from the drawer where I'd kept it, I handed it back to the young man. "There *were* other entries during that period of time. Someone deliberately erased them, and a large amount of other data too, before the police got their hands on the machine."

He leaned forward. "Is there... anything that tells us what he was doing?"

I shook my head. "Not much. There were quite a few missing entries—looks like he was on the trail of whatever-it-was for at least three months. A couple of earlier entries had been modified after their apparent date, so probably there were hints even as long as five months ago, but from what you said, your brother knew how to keep a secret.

"What's *in* those entries, though... I can't get much of anything. Whoever did the erasure knew what they were doing. I only got a few cryptic phrases out of dozens of entries. I've collected them here." I handed him an envelope. "And one last interesting point."

"Well?"

"I managed to get enough out of the most recently tampered-with files to see that they were written in the format he used as a tickler file for travel. He had apparently bought himself a ticket to JFK Airport in New York City—he was supposed to be leaving within a few hours of the time he died. Since the police didn't seem to look into it, I'd guess he'd purchased the ticket with cash, under another identity."

"Really? Where do you think he was going?" Xavier blinked. "Wait, another identity?"

"Not entirely unheard of for people looking into dangerous stuff. He probably had used this other ID several times."

"Can you...find out more about what he was doing? Track him, now that you know something?"

I frowned. "I...guess I could do a little more searching. If I can figure out his alternate ID or IDs, that'd make it a lot easier. But that's way out of the work we'd already agreed on."

"I'll pay for it."

I hesitated. *He's really...obsessing over this.* I could tell by the intensity in his gaze that this was desperately important to him. I'd also checked with Renee about the case, so I knew that Xavier simply didn't agree with their conclusions.

I also was aware that *Renee* wasn't entirely happy with the way the Los Angeles police had closed the file, either, but she had no say in the matter. It was their jurisdiction; this was just where the victim's family lived.

"All right," I said after a moment. "I'll see if I can trace where he went and what he did. That'll be a one-thousand-dollar retainer, though; I have no idea how hard this will be."

After I ran his card and he left, holding the laptop tightly to him, I stared out the window for a while. I didn't have whatever weird sense Syl used, but I was very used to trusting my instincts. Most of the time, when the police investigate a case and close it, it's because they've actually found the perpetrator and the case *is* closed.

But my gut said that in *this* case, Xavier Ross was right to be uncertain; it wasn't just what I'd found on that machine, but what Renee had said. If Lieutenant Renee Reisman wasn't happy with the way a case had been solved, that was enough for me; *something* wasn't right. Unfortunately, while the answers the police had given Xavier didn't take into account this evidence, getting them to reopen the case based on what amounted to stuff that wasn't there would be a tough, tough call.

Okay, Jason. Let's see if we can trail someone who didn't want to be found.

CHAPTER 13

Interview With the Artist

The apartment door opened in front of me, at least to the limit that the chain on it would permit. Two bright blue eyes looked up at me, framed by blue-black hair and set in a pretty, well-defined face. "Hi. Can I help you?"

"I'm Jason Wood."

"Oh, right, Dad's expecting you! Hold on, I'll get the chain off here." The door closed. I heard rattling, and "Dad! Your guest's here!"

When the door opened, I saw Sky Hashima walking towards me, wiping his hands on a towel. "Mr. Wood, please come in." He shook my hand. "This is my daughter, Star," he said, and I shook hands with the girl who had greeted me. "Star, we'll be in my studio—this probably won't take long, but please don't disturb us."

"Okay, Dad. You want anything to drink, Dad, Mr. Wood?"

I smiled at her; she obviously knew my visit was important. "A soda would be nice—ginger ale?"

"We've got that. Dad? Water for you?"

"For now, yes. Thank you, Star."

Sky led the way into his studio; his hair was longer than his daughter's, but other than traces of silver here and there, was just as night-dark. Their features were also similar enough; there wasn't any doubt about who his daughter was, and in this case, that was a good thing for Star. "A very polite young lady."

Sky gave a small chuckle. "Ahh, that's because she thinks you might be a good thing for her dad. If she thought you were trouble, you'd have needed a crowbar to get inside the house."

"And when she's old enough to date, I'm sure you'll be just as protective."

"Star will be old enough to date when she's ninety. I've told her that already." We shared another chuckle at that. "I recall meeting you at that little show I did at one of the libraries, Mr. Wood, but I didn't think you were really interested in art."

"I'm not, really," I confessed. "Thanks, Star," I said, as she came in, handed us each a glass, and left. "I came to that show with Sylvie, who is interested in art and found some of your pieces quite fascinating. But I do have a few other acquaintances who have more than a passing interest in art."

"And...?"

"And it so happens that one of them is looking to find people to sponsor—to be a sort of patron of the arts. I remembered you and wanted to see what kind of work you were doing, and (a) if you are serious about it, and (b) if you are willing to meet with him to discuss it." I studied some of the canvases set around the studio. One thing that impressed me was Sky's versatility. I saw paintings that were, to my uneducated gaze, random blots of colors, shapes, and streaks; others which were landscapes or scenes of such sharp realism that you almost thought they were windows rather than paintings; and still others that fell some-where in-between—didn't follow the accurate shapes or lines yet somehow conveyed the essence of the thing he was depicting.

Sky had an expression that was almost disbelieving; I realized that this must sound like that classic Hollywood myth: working in a restaurant and being discovered by the famous director who stops in for a cup of coffee. "You're joking."

"Not at all. Would you like to meet him, then?"

"If he's ready, I'll go right now."

I laughed. "Not *quite* that fast—I have to let him know, then he'll either set up the meeting, or have me do it. He's a bit eccentric—"

"That's almost a requirement for being a private patron these days. Patronage used to be standard practice, back in Leonardo's day, but those days...long gone." He took a gulp from his glass and looked at me. "The answer to the first question is yes, I am serious about it. I make an okay living from my framing work, but if you look around, you must realize that the stuff I'm pro-ducing represents a major investment of time and effort. I could do an awful lot of other things with the money I spend on my art, but my art's worth it to me." He smiled again. "That doesn't mean I'm at all averse to start seeing my art make money rather than take money, however."

I grinned back. "Excellent. Now, why don't you just show me a few of your favorites here and explain to me what you're doing, so I can give my friend a capsule overview and he'll know what to expect."

Sky was only too pleased to do that, and I spent a good half-hour listening to him describe his intentions and techniques in several of his works. I noticed that he, like almost all artists I've ever met, mentioned all the myriad ways in which his works failed to live up to his expectations. It's always been a source of frustration that someone can produce something that's clearly amazing, and all they can think about is how it is flawed—often in ways that no one but they themselves can see. It does however seem to be an almost required characteristic for an artist.

Finally, I shook hands with him again and left. "Thank you, Sky. I'll be getting back to you very soon. Nice meeting you, Star."

A short time later, I pulled up into the curved driveway which was becoming increasingly familiar to me, and smiled to Morgan as he opened the door. "Good evening, sir. Master Verne is in the study."

"Morgan, do you ever get tired of playing the butler?"

He gave me a raised eyebrow and slightly miffed expression in reply. "Playing, sir? This is my place in the household, and I assure you it is precisely what I wanted. I have, with some varia-tion in regional standards of propriety, been performing these duties for considerably longer than the Pharaohs endured, sir, and had I found the task overall onerous or distasteful, I assure you I would have asked Master Verne for a change."

People like Morgan gave the phrase "faithful retainer" an entirely new, and impressive, meaning. "Sorry. It's just that it sometimes strikes me you're too good to be true."

He smiled with a proper level of reserve. "I strive to be good at my job, sir. I feel that a gentleman such as Master Verne deserves to have a household worthy of his age and bloodline, and therefore I shall endeavor to maintain his home at a proper level of respectability."

"And you succeed admirably, old friend," Verne said as we

entered. "Jason, every member of my household has chosen their lifestyle and I would never hold them to me, if any of them chose to leave. It has been a great pleasure, and immense vindication, that not one of my personal staff has ever made that choice...though on occasion, as of my recent descent into less-than-respectable business, they have made clear some of their personal fears and objections." He put away a book that he had been reading and gestured for me to sit down as Morgan left. "I have been taking up some considerable portion of your time, Jason. I hope I am not interfering in your personal life—your friends Sylvia and Renee, for instance, are not suffering your absence overly much?"

I laughed. "No, no. Syl's off on some kind of convention for people in her line of work and isn't coming back for something like a week from now, and I only get together with Renee once in a while. Most of my other friends, sad to say, aren't in this area—they've gone off to college, moved, and so on, so I only talk with them via phone or email. Really. So have no fear, I'm at your disposal for at least the next week or so; the only other big job I have at the moment I can work on during the day."

"Excellent." Morgan came in with his usual sinfully tempting tray of hors d'oeuvres and snacks. "By the way, Morgan, have there been any further problems from my erstwhile business associates?"

"No, sir. They have found that it is not easy to intrude here and have apparently given up after I was forced to injure the one gentleman at the store."

"Very good. I shall send another message to Carmichael emphasizing that I will be extremely displeased if any more such incidents happen, but it does appear he has learned something about futility." He turned back to me. "And how did your meeting go?"

"I think he'd be a great choice, Verne. He's clearly serious about his work, and with my limited grasp of art I think his stuff is really, really good. If you want to meet with him, he's willing to meet any time you name."

"Then let us not keep him waiting overlong. Tomorrow evening, at about seven, let us say."

"I'll give him a call now." Suiting actions to words, I picked up a phone and called Sky Hashima. As he'd implied, he was more than willing to meet then, and assured me that he'd be able to assemble a reasonable portfolio by that time.

"I'm glad you're going to check him over yourself," I confessed. "I know just enough about art to know that I really don't know the difference between 'illustration' and 'art,' and that the latter is what you are interested in."

Verne smiled. I was, at least, getting used to seeing the fangs at various moments, although I also had to admit that they weren't *that* obvious; someone who didn't know what he was would quite probably just assume he had oddly long canines. "You may be confident, my friend, that I would still wish to see for myself even were you an expert in all things artistic. If I will sponsor anyone, it will be because I am convinced the person deserves my support. Now that that is settled," he said, pulling out a chessboard, "would you care for a game?"

I pulled my chair up to the table. "Sure...if you take black and a queen handicap. You've got a few years on me."

"A *queen*? A rook."

"You're on."

CHAPTER 14

A Sudden Trip Downstate

I opened the trunk and helped Sky get out his portfolio. Innocent that I was, I thought a "portfolio" would be a notebook-sized collection of pictures—reproductions, etc. Artists, as I found out, do not do things that way. Reproductions are often used, but they're done as near as possible to full size as can be managed, and Sky had a lot of samples. He was trying to show a number of things about his work (most of which I could only vaguely understand) and accordingly had put together a very large collection of material.

Morgan bowed us in the door, and Verne came forward. "Mr. Hashima, it is a great pleasure to meet you."

Sky smiled back and shook his hand. "The pleasure's all mine."

I nodded at Verne. "I'll be off, then. I know you people have plenty to discuss and I won't have a clue as to what you're talking about."

"Of course, Jason. Thank you for bringing Sky over; Morgan will arrange his transport home once we are done here, so do not trouble yourself further."

I waved, said "Good luck!" to Sky, got back into Mjölnir, turned down the driveway and headed home.

It was only when I turned the key in the office door that I was bothered. I felt it click . . . but at the wrong time. The door had already been opened. Not having expected any trouble, I wasn't carrying my gun. Then again, I supposed it was possible, though unlikely, that I'd forgotten to lock it. I pushed the door open, letting it swing all the way around to make sure no one was hiding behind it. Nothing seemed out of place. I went in and locked the door behind me.

   With the lights switched on, I still didn't see anything disturbed
in the office—which was what I'd be mainly concerned with. I
checked the secure room at the back; nothing. That left only my
living quarters upstairs. I went through the connecting door.

   Something exploded against my head. I went down, almost
completely unconscious, unable to see anything except vague
blurs. Rough hands grabbed me, dragged me out the back door,
threw me into a car, and then shoved something over my mouth
and nose.

   By then I was focused enough to fight back, but these people
were stronger than me and had the advantage. Eventually I had
to breathe, and whatever they'd put in that cloth finished bringing down the curtain.

   I came slowly awake, my head pounding like a pie pan in the
hands of a toddler. With difficulty, I concentrated on evaluating
myself. I could feel a focused ache on the side of my skull, where
I'd been conked. My stomach was protesting, an interesting but
unpleasant combination of hunger and nausea; some hours had
gone by, I figured. There was the generalized headache, of course.
Chloroform? Halothane? I supposed that the specific chemical
didn't matter, though it had felt too fast for classic chloroform.
I'd been in too much pain to notice the smell clearly. I was sitting upright—tied up in a chair or something similar, because I
could feel some kind of bindings on my arms, legs, and chest.

   Now, if this was a proper adventure novel or TV episode,
they'd have inadvertently left my Swiss Army knife for me to
attempt an escape, but I could, in fact, feel that, while I was
still dressed, there wasn't a damn thing left in my pockets except
possibly some lint. Not being an escape expert, martial artist,
or superhero, I decided I'd gotten all I could out of sitting and
thinking, so I slowly raised my head and opened my eyes.

   The pain only increased slightly and then started to ebb.
Leaving aside the niceties of being tied up and with a knot on
my head, I was in a rather pleasant room, large and airy, with a
big picture window looking out on a driveway somewhat remi-
niscent of Verne's own, although this one was a wide drive that
turned into a circle at the end rather than a drive shaped like
a teardrop. The landscaping was also different, more sculpted
and controlled, less wild; Verne liked a more natural look, while

whoever owned this clearly preferred symmetry and precision. The trees and fountains and bushes were all laid out in a smoothly rolling but still almost mathematically precise manner.

I was facing the picture window; off to my right were some cases of books—which I was fairly sure were chosen for show rather than actual reading material, judging from what I could see—as well as some pictures, an in-wall television screen, and some chairs and low tables. Off to my left was a very large desk. The person behind the desk, however, made the desk look small. He was as blond as I was, but tanned, wearing a suit that had to be custom-made because he was large enough to be a pro wrestler—six foot eight standing was my guess, maybe even bigger—but the suit fit him perfectly, making him look simply like a well-dressed adult in a room made for twelve-year-olds. His hair was fairly long, pulled back in a smooth ponytail, and his face had the same square, rough look that many boxers get, complete with a previously broken nose.

He had been reading a newspaper, but when I turned my head to look at him, the movement apparently caught his eye. "He's awake," he said in a deep, slightly rough voice.

I heard a chair or two scrape back behind me, and heavy footsteps approached. Twisting my neck around, I was able to see two large men—though neither of them quite the size of the guy behind the desk—walking over. They picked up my chair and turned it to face the desk.

"Good morning," I said. "Mr. Carmichael, I presume?"

He didn't exactly smile, but something in his expression acknowledged my feeble sally. "That's right."

"I was afraid of that. As far as I knew, I didn't have anyone who disliked me enough to use a blackjack to introduce themselves, and I haven't been on any really nasty cases lately."

"Since you know who I am, we can get to business." He nodded, and one of the silent thugs pulled up one of the small tables with a telephone on it. "I'm going to call Domingo. You'll listen in on that extension. You say nothing—and I mean nothing—until I tell you. When I tell you, you will confirm to Domingo that I do indeed have you here, and that I'm going to have you painfully killed if he doesn't cooperate."

I nodded. There wasn't much point in arguing with him; in my current position, what was I going to do?

He gave a small smile. "Good. I hate people who don't cooperate. You might actually get out of this alive, if Domingo doesn't screw up." He punched in the numbers, and one goon picked up the extension and held the receiver to my hear.

"Domingo residence, Morgan speaking."

"Morgan, buddy, this is Carmichael. I need to talk to Domingo right now."

Morgan paused. I could see that it was, in fact, morning, so Verne was doubtless sleeping. "Master Verne is not available at the moment—"

"Listen up. I know for a fact he hasn't left that mansion—my people were watching yesterday. So okay, he went to bed. Get him up. Now. I'll guarantee you he'll be the one regretting it if you don't."

Morgan sighed. "If you insist, sir. Please hold the line."

Faint strains of classical music came on; apparently Verne or whoever ran the phone system agreed that dead air was no fun to listen to. Carmichael made a face. "'Please hold the line.' Jeez, I still can't figure this clown. He thinks he's in a goddamn *Masterpiece Theatre* show or something?"

I didn't say anything; I figured silence was my best policy right now.

Several minutes later, the music cut off and Verne's voice spoke. "Mr. Carmichael."

"Verne! Good to hear you, buddy. Look, if you want to cut out of the business personally, I want you to know, that's okay with me, so long as you aren't going to rat. But your leaving like this is causing me a problem, and I'm not okay with that."

"What you are 'okay' with, Mr. Carmichael, is not really much of my concern."

Carmichael gave a nasty laugh. "I think I got an argument about why it is, Verne old buddy. Take a listen and then tell me." He nodded at me.

"Hello, Verne," I said. I at least managed to sound casual.

There was silence for a moment, then, "Jason? Is that you?"

"I'm afraid so. Mr. Carmichael made me an offer I couldn't refuse and invited me to visit him. He's instructed me to tell you that if you don't go along with what he wants, he's going to have me killed. Painfully."

I could envision the offended shock on the other end. "Carmichael. What do you want?"

The nasty laugh again, combined with a nastier grin. "I thought you might want to ask about that now. I want your contacts, Verne. You had some seriously smooth pipelines to bring stuff in from various places. No matter how hard I tried, I never could quite figure out who was doing it, and you never lost a goddamn shipment. I admire that, really. That's art. But I was depending on those pipelines, and suddenly you cut me off? Where the hell do you get off thinking you can just tell me to go screw? What is that crap? You wanna go play with your English butler in teatime land, hell, I don't care, but without a replacement I'm eating into my reserves and I ain't got supply for my customers to last more than a couple weeks. And I ain't going to go for a supplier that's gonna cost me more or give me lower quality. So, if you ain't doing the supply end, I'll take your place. You just hand me your contacts, whoever ran the pipelines, and I'll do it from there. Your friend here goes home, we all end up happy. Get stupid with me and I'll send him to you in pieces."

Verne's voice, when it finally answered, was as calm as usual; but now that I was familiar with it, I detected a hint of iron anger I'd never heard before. "Mr. Carmichael, my . . . contacts would be useless to you. When I stopped, they stopped. They no longer trade in the same merchandise."

"Well, baby, that sounds just too bad. You'd better tell 'em to start trading in it again, and give me the names double-quick. I ain't got too much time, so my patience is totally gone." He pointed at the other thug, who stepped up and kicked me hard in the shin.

I know I screamed or shouted something, in pain, then cursed. The surprise of the kick prevented me from keeping quiet.

"Hear that? That wasn't much, Domingo. Right now he's just got a couple bruises."

"I will need some time."

"You never needed much, buddy, so don't you even think about stalling me. I'll give you to midnight tonight, Domingo, to start coming through. Either you start the supply back up yourself, or you hand me the people who were doing the job for you, or I'll finish your friend here off."

There were a few moments of silence. "Domingo, do you hear me? I need an answer, buddy, or do I have to make your friend uncomfortable again?"

"I hear you," Verne answered. "I will have something for you before midnight, Carmichael. But if you harm Jason again, you will be exceedingly sorry. That I promise you."

"Not another touch, Domingo, unless you try something cute. His safety's all in your hands. I'll call you later tonight. Be ready." He hung up, and so did the thug holding the receiver.

"You did that good, Mr. Wood," Carmichael said. "Now, boys, you can untie him, take him to the bathroom if he needs to go, and we'll get him some food. You're not going to do anything stupid, are you?" he asked me.

"Nope," I said honestly. "I don't know exactly where we are, and I'm sure you've got lots more where these guys come from."

"Great. Y'know, I grabbed another guy once, few years ago, thought he was a frickin' action hero. Busted up a few of my guys, tried to get out, ended up shot. Nice to see not everyone's that stupid."

Privately, I wondered. Verne was an honorable guy; he'd probably see it as his obligation to get me out of this, but it would really suck if a bastard like Carmichael got access to his drugs again.

But no point in worrying now. Using the bathroom sounded good, and now that my stomach was settling, so did food. I figured I'd just try to be a good Boy Scout and be prepared.

CHAPTER 15

Enter Freely and of Your Own Will

"Ten o'clock," Carmichael said. "Jeez, will you look at that stuff come down!"

Even as worried as I was, I had to admit it was an impressive storm. Gusts of gale-force winds battered the house, blue-white lightning shattered the night, torrents of rain came down so heavily that they obscured our sight of the front gate, even with all the lights of the estate on. An occasional rattling spatter indicated that there was some hail as well.

"Man, did the weatherman ever screw up this one. Forecast said clear and calm all night. Boy, that put the crimp in some party plans, I can tell you." Carmichael picked up the phone and dialed. "Yo, Morgan, put Verne on the line." He listened and his brows came together. "What do you mean, 'not available at the moment'? Listen, you just tell him he's got two goddamn hours... Yeah, well, he damn well better be 'planning to discuss it with me momentarily.'" He slammed the phone down. "I dunno, bud, maybe Domingo doesn't give a crap about you."

I glanced outside. *Could it be...?* "I wouldn't bet on that if I were you."

He looked out speculatively. "He couldn't be *that* dumb, could he?" I heard him mutter. Then he pushed a button on his desk—looked like one of several, probably security—and said, "Hey, Jay, look, I know it's a dog's night out, but pass the word to the boys—Domingo and his gang might try something on us tonight. Yeah, yeah, I know, they'd be morons to try, especially in this crap, but people do dumb things sometimes."

He leaned back. "If he does try, I'll make sure he gets to see you shot, you do know that, right?"

I looked back at him. A faint hope was rising, along with the shriek of the suddenly redoubled wind. "Yeah, I guess you will."

The intercom buzzed. "Mr. Carmichael, Jimmy and Double-T don't answer."

His relaxed demeanor vanished. "What? Which post were they on?"

"Number one—the private road entrance."

"The line down?"

"No, sir, it's ringing; they just aren't answering."

He glared at me, then flicked his gaze to the window, as did I. So we were both watching when it happened.

The huge gates were barely visible, distorted shapes through the wind-lashed storm; but even with that, there was no way to miss it when the twin iron barriers suddenly blew inward, torn from their hinges by some immense force.

"What the hell—" Carmichael stared.

Slowly, emerging from the howling maelstrom, a single figure became visible. Dressed in black, some kind of cloak or cape streaming from its shoulders, it walked forward through the storm, seemingly untouched by the tempest. I felt a chill of awe start down my spine, gooseflesh sprang out across my arms.

Battling their way through the gale, six men half-ran, half-staggered up to defensive positions. Stroboscopic flashes of light, accompanied by faint rattling noises, showed they were trying to cut the intruder down with a hail of bullets. Even in this storm, there was no way that six men with fully automatic weaponry could possibly miss their target, especially when it continued walking towards them, unhurried, making no attempt to dodge or shield itself, and keeping a measured pace towards the mansion's front doors.

The figure twitched as gunfire hit, slowed its pace for a moment, and staggered backwards as all six concentrated their fire in a hail of bullets that could have stopped a bull elephant in its tracks. But the figure didn't go down. I heard an incredulous curse from Carmichael.

The figure raised one arm, and the three men on that side were suddenly slapped aside, sent spinning through the air as though hit by a runaway train. The other arm lifted, the other three men flew away like rag dolls. The intruder came forward, into the light at the stairway that led up to the front door, and now there was no mistaking it.

Verne Domingo had come calling.

He glanced up and seemed to see us even though the sheeting rain and flashing lightning should have made that impossible. The winds curled down, tore one of the trees up by the roots, and the massive bole smashed into the picture window, showering us both with fragments of glass.

I felt Carmichael's immense arm wrap around me and a gun press into my temple. Verne came into view, walking slowly up the tree that now formed a ramp to our room. He stopped just outside of the window. "Put the gun down, Carmichael," he said, softly.

"You...whatever the hell you're doing, you just cut it out, or you can scrape up Wood's brains with a spatula!" Carmichael shouted.

I wondered why the heck Verne wasn't doing something more. Then it clicked for me. "Come on inside, Verne," I said. "We were just talking about you."

With my invitation, I saw a deadly cold smile cross his face, one that showed sharper, whiter teeth than I'd seen before. "Why, thank you, Jason. I do believe I shall."

The two thugs charged Verne; with a single backhanded blow, he sent them tumbling across the floor, fetching up unconscious against the back wall.

Carmichael's hand spasmed on the gun.

Nothing happened. I felt, rather than saw, him straining to pull a trigger that had become as immovable as a mountain. Verne continued towards me. "Put my friend down now, Carmichael," he said, in that same dangerously soft tone.

Carmichael, completely unnerved, tried to break my neck. But he found that his arms wouldn't cooperate. I squirmed, managed to extricate myself from his frozen grip, and backed away.

Now Verne allowed Carmichael to move. Deprived of me as a hostage, the huge man grabbed up the solid mahogany chair and swung it with all his might.

Made of wood, the chair was one of the few weapons he could've chosen that might have been able to hurt Verne. But to make it work, he had to hit the ancient vampire, and Verne was quite aware of what he was doing.

One of the aristocratic hands came up, caught the chair and

stopped it as easily as if it had been a pillow swung by a child. The other hand whipped out and grasped Carmichael by the neck, lifting him from the ground with negligible effort.

"You utter fool. Were you not warned to leave me and mine alone? I would have ignored you, Carmichael. I would have allowed you to live out your squalid little life without interference, if only you had the sense to let go. Now what shall I do? If I release you, doubtless you shall try something even more foolish, will you not?"

Purple in the face, Carmichael struggled with that grip, finding it as solid as though cast in iron. He shook his head desperately.

"Oh? And should I trust you? The world would be better off with you dead. Certainly for daring to strike in such a cowardly fashion I should have you killed."

"No, Verne."

He looked at me. "You would have me spare him?"

"Killing him will force the cops to investigate. You haven't killed anyone yet, have you?"

He shook his head. "No. Battered, unconscious, and so on, but none of his people are dead, as of now."

"Then leave it. I think he's got the point. It's not like he'd be believed if he told this one, and he can't afford the cops to come in anyway; even if they tied something to you, they'd also get stuff on him."

Verne gave an elaborate shrug, done as smoothly as though he was not actually holding three hundred pounds of drug lord in one hand. "As you will, then. I, also, prefer not to kill, even such scum as this." He let Carmichael drop. "But remember this well, Carmichael. I never wish to hear your name again. I do not ever want to know you *exist* again. If you, or anyone in your control or working for you in any way, interferes with my life or that of my friends again, I shall kill you . . . in such a manner that you will wish that you had killed yourself first. Believe me. I shall not warn you again. This is your final chance."

Carmichael was ashen. "I gotcha. I won't. You won't ever hear from me again, Domingo, I promise."

"Good." Verne turned to me. "My apologies, Jason. It never occurred to me that you might be in danger. Let me get you home."

Outside, the storm was already fading away, as though it had never been.

CHAPTER 16

The Only Thing He has to Fear...

"How did you find me?"

Verne and I were comfortably seated in his study. He smiled slightly. "I have always known roughly where Carmichael lived, just as he knows where I live. Once I arrived in the general area, it was simple to sense your presence and follow it."

"Thanks."

"No need to thank me, Jason. It was my fault entirely that you were involved. I should have realized that once he found my household impenetrable, he would look for anyone outside who was connected to me."

"Maybe you should have, but so should I. Heck, you hadn't *had* anyone 'outside' connected to you for so long that I'm not surprised you sorta forgot."

"For far too long, but I thank you for your understanding."

"You think he'll keep his hands off from now on?"

Verne gave that cold smile again. "Oh, yes, I assure you. I was not concerned with the niceties of civilized behavior at that point, Jason. I made sure that he was, shall we say, thinking very clearly. He knows precisely what will happen to him if he ever crosses me again. And as you pointed out, the authorities won't believe him even if he tells his story, nor would it do him much good if they did."

"So how did your interview with Sky go?"

"Excellently well," he replied, offering me a refill on the champagne, which I declined. "Your casual evaluation was, as far as it went, accurate. Mr. Hashima is a true artist, a dedicated one, and highly talented in several ways. I will have no qualms about supporting him fully. He is naturally a bit cautious—I do seem to him to be a bit too good to be true—but I am sure that we shall get past this minor difficulty."

I sipped, appreciating the unique taste that a real champagne offers. "And the antiquities?"

Verne grinned, a warm smile that lit the room. "As usual, you and Morgan are right. I shall be donating, or selling, many of the items in question to people who will both appreciate them and be willing to place them on proper display. Some discreet inquiries have already elicited several interested responses, and I expect several archaeologists to visit in a few weeks in order to authenticate, insofar as is possible, the artifacts and prepare a preliminary assessment. I have already decided to send Akhenaten, at least, directly to Egypt. Let the Sun Pharaoh return to his home." He raised his own red-glinting glass in salute. "My thanks, Jason, again. You have indeed found something that I shall enjoy doing, something which will contribute to the world as well. And you have given me your friendship, which I value perhaps even more."

I managed, I think, to keep from blushing, something I tend to do when praised extravagantly. "It was my pleasure, really. Well, aside from being kidnapped, but that wasn't completely in your control. I just hope Carmichael has bad dreams about you whenever he goes to sleep."

"I assure you, your hope will be more than adequately fulfilled, Jason," Verne said, with the expression of someone with a small secret.

"Why?"

"As I implied, I was quite capable of hearing his thoughts when I extorted certain promises from him, and discovered one quite serendipitous fact." He paused for me to urge him to finish, and then said, "Many people are afraid of various things, real and otherwise.

"It turns out that Mr. Carmichael's greatest and most secret fear . . . is vampires."

I laughed out loud. "Well, I'll drink to that!"

CHAPTER 17

Laughing Assassin

I really don't like this one.

I'd done plenty of work for the police, and other people. I may not have been very old, but I'd already done everything from enhance photos and research prior art on patents to, well, finding out that vampires are real. Sometimes you get feelings about things, and right now, I had a very strong, very bad feeling about the job I was doing for Xavier Ross.

Not that I felt there was anything wrong with *doing* the job; I didn't think there was anything shady about the kid himself. But I was finding way too many questions for a case that had been closed by police. *Way* too many. Oh, a lot of them were circumstantial, but the fact was that most good cops pay attention to stuff like that, and this case had been closed up so quick and neat...

The door chimed as someone came through, and I looked up from my monitor. *Damn. Well, I knew he was coming soon.* "Hello, Mr. Ross. Please, sit down."

Xavier looked hopeful. "Did you..."

"I found some things, yes." I picked up a file and handed it to him.

"For a fairly well-known figure, your brother was good at losing people. He turned out to be pretty hard to track. The bill for this is not going to be cheap."

He was already glancing through the file. "I know. Will seven thousand dollars cut it?"

That's about what I'd charge the cops, but... he's serious. "I'd find that acceptable, perhaps overgenerous, but Mr. Ross, you *are* a minor. I'm starting to get very *very* uncomfortable with this. I find it extremely hard to believe that your mother would approve of your spending ten thousand dollars on an investigation that may not even *go* anywhere."

"Look," he said, "can we discuss that afterward? I'd really like to hear what you found."

I sighed. "Okay. But I'm not forgetting this subject." I turned to the monitor. "I started trying to trace his movements around the time that we first found indications that his records had been altered. At that point he was working on an article for *Time* on the nightclub revival in New York City.

"Now, that assignment finished up a little before Christmas; he came back up here for the holidays but then went back to New York for several days. He got an assignment that flew him out to Costa Rica, but as soon as that was done he came back to New York and again spent several days there before he came up to visit you."

Xavier looked up, startled. "But...I remember him saying he'd flown straight back from Costa Rica."

"Not unless he was letting someone use his ID and credit cards, he didn't."

"Wait...you're not the police, how could you...?"

"Let's say that while what I did is technically probably legal, I don't want to discuss the details and the police would take a very dim view of it." I couldn't get direct access to such information without police authority, but there were indirect methods to get people to *give* you that information.

"All right," the boy said, settling back into his chair. "I didn't want you to do anything to get yourself in trouble."

I shrugged. "I'm not in trouble. Not now, anyway. If you *talk* about this to too many people, I might be, so it's up to you whether I'm in trouble."

"Hey, I won't talk about this."

"Okay. Your brother then went to the West Coast and got a couple of assignments in the Los Angeles vicinity. Note that the *order* there is important. He'd already *flown* to Los Angeles when *National Geographic* asked him to do a photo article on modern filmmaking and another for current earthquake research at the universities."

"So...he wanted to go to Los Angeles and found jobs to keep himself there?"

"That's my guess. What I *can't* figure out without further

research is where he went exactly. I can show you the hotels where he stayed and some of the restaurants where he ate, but where he went when he was on his own . . . I really don't know. There were a couple of locations that I got lucky and made a hit on—Thanation Research and Development apparently hired him during his visit as a photographer for a big release event, for instance—but for the most part? No clue. I'd have to hire some *real* talent to do gumshoe work through the city, and the trail's already pretty cold."

Xavier rolled his eyes skyward. "Damn. What about those pictures?"

"The girl?" I shrugged. "I did quite a bit of looking through various file references but I haven't turned up an ID yet. Now, if you could *wait* a few months . . ."

He started to shake his head violently, then controlled himself with a visible effort. "Why a few months?"

"Because I might be able to get access to an online image comparator that can access a *very* large database of photos, if I ask the right people nicely. Something I'd really like to have but it's way out of my price range, unfortunately."

"What about hiring those . . . people you mentioned to do the work to find out—"

No. "Xavier, that would start to get *very* expensive. Very, *very* expensive. I don't care how much your . . . bank account has in it, this is going too far outside of my comfort zone. This is something much more for the police than for someone like me. I've given you some circumstantial evidence; maybe they'll reopen the case. But at this point, I think I have to stop. If you were an adult . . . maybe. Probably. But honestly? It sounds like you're obsessing over this."

Xavier glared at me with those startling gray eyes.

"I understand you cared about your brother very much—"

"She *laughed*," he said suddenly.

"What?"

"The bi . . . girl that killed him. She killed him, and he was screaming, and then she picked the phone up and *laughed about it.*"

Crap. I could see the anger—very cold, very hard—in his eyes, and hear it in his voice. Xavier Ross might be a kid, but he was apparently old enough to have an adult's desire for justice . . . or revenge. "You *heard* this?"

"He was . . ." his voice caught, then he managed to control it. "He was talking to me when she did it."

"Sure it was a 'she'?"

His smile was tight, without much humor. "Yeah. I can't prove it, but I'm sure. Real sure. Almost sounded like a little girl, and the way my brother reacted before . . . before she did it, he didn't think she was a threat, just someone who wanted to use the phone."

That was surprising on multiple levels. His brother had obviously called him from a public phone—not a hotel room, not using a cell phone. And then he'd been apparently killed quickly and savagely by someone he didn't think of as threatening. Given that my research had shown Michael Ross as a survivor of dangerous situations around the world, and an expert in both armed and unarmed combat . . . *whoever took him down had to be something special.* "And she laughed?"

"Oh, yeah." His teeth clenched so hard I could see the muscles jump at his temples before he relaxed. "I . . ." He swallowed. "I heard Mike scream, and then . . . she laughed. Like a . . . like a happy little girl. And she said 'Oh, so pretty, so pretty, the patterns in the moonlight. But oh, such a waste of blood.' And then she whispered 'Michael's quiet now. He says good-bye,' and hung up on me."

Jesus H. Christ. I couldn't blame Xavier for his anger. That was one of the most macabre stories I'd ever heard. "I'm sorry, Xavier. That's . . . hideous."

He looked at me. "But you're still not going to help me anymore."

I shook my head reluctantly. "No. This is clearly police business. Take the evidence I've got, bring it to Lieutenant Reisman—you know her?"

He nodded. "She interviewed me."

"Okay, take it to her, tell her you got it from me. I'm sure they'll have to reopen the case, especially if you and your family push for it."

He looked unconvinced, but apparently the expression on my face convinced him I wasn't going to change my mind. "Okay."

He got out his credit card, but I waved it away. "Not taking any more from you, not after that story. Consider it a public service. Someone like that shouldn't get away with it."

His expression brightened, just a hair. "Thanks. I mean it."

"You're welcome." I shook his hand. "Good luck, Xavier."

I watched him go out the door. *They damn well better reopen that case, because he's not taking "no" for an answer.*

Part III

Photo Finish

August 1999

CHAPTER 18

Action and Reaction

"But I thought we would be seeing *The Thirteenth Floor* tomorrow night," Syl said.

I winced. Truth be told, I'd forgotten all about our movie plans in the past few weeks, and Verne had made an appointment—after hours, naturally—to discuss several interesting opportunities he was looking into. I hadn't yet let Syl in on the situation with Verne, and if her unique... sensitivity had clued her in, she hadn't let me know about it. "Sorry, Syl. How about Saturday evening?"

She shook her head, miffed. "You *know* my reading group meets on Saturday evening. And Sunday I'm visiting my parents." She looked at me with a sudden sly smile. "You know, this is the third set of plans we've had to cancel in the last couple of months. Are you going out on a *date* tomorrow, Jase?"

Though there had been a few times I had dated in the last few years, the thought of going on a date with *Verne* made me laugh out loud. "No, no. It's a business meeting, I just forgot about our plans. And of course, tonight's bowling night." I went bowling with Renee Reisman and not Syl because Syl found bowling *utterly* boring. "Sorry. Really. How about Monday then?"

"I'll forgive you... *this* time," she said, tossing her long black hair, making her assortment of beads and bracelets jingle with the motion. "But only if you pay for it *all* this time. Even the snacks."

I grinned. "It's a deal."

"All right." She glanced at her watch. "Oh! I'd better get moving. Witan and Sherry are going to be waiting for me!"

I went back to work, which right now was mostly research for people trying to finish up their degrees and a bunch of patent stuff. That made the time both crawl and fly by, a paradox that I didn't find as amusing as it sounds.

The door jingled and I looked up, relieved to have a distraction. "Hi, Renee—" I caught the expression on her face and changed out *relieved* for *worried* at the same time I changed my mode of address. "I mean, hello, Lieutenant Reisman."

She was even grimmer than I thought as she got closer. "Mr. Wood, do you know a person named Xavier Ross?"

What the hell? "I did some work for a Xavier Ross, yes," I said, cautiously. "Why?"

"I need to know everything you said to him, everything you told him."

I shook my head. "That's client information. You know I won't give you any of that without—"

She shoved a piece of paper under my nose.

"—a...warrant. Which this apparently is." I glanced it over; this wasn't the first time I'd seen one, but it *was* the first time I'd had one served on *me*. "Okay, I'll get that stuff out. But why?"

"Xavier Uriel Ross disappeared from home—apparently deliberately, as there were signs he'd carefully accumulated both cash and supplies for traveling—a few days ago."

I swore, something I generally reserved for serious situations. "I told him to go to *you*."

"He did," she said, and if possible her face looked even *more* grim, set in stone. "LA wouldn't reopen the case, no matter how hard I kicked them. And I kicked them plenty hard."

That's...not good. I started burning a disc containing all the information I'd given Xavier. "Do you think they should?"

For a moment, I didn't think she'd answer; she might be here alone but she was still in her "official" mode. But then she shrugged. "Wasn't up to me. But...yeah, I would have thought so. That was some real interesting evidence you turned up, especially with the erased hard drive and hidden pictures. Usually that *does* get people to sit up and take notice, and when I talked to the main detective in charge he *sounded* interested...but after that things just got shut down."

The disc finished burning; I put it in a case and handed it to her. "Here you go, Lieutenant. This is everything."

"Mr. Ross paid you three thousand dollars, right?"

"Because I gave him a bunch free. I could have charged him another seven easy, and he acted like he had it to spend."

"He did. Personal bank account worth over twenty thousand—I have *no* idea where he was supposed to have gotten that much, but his mother was apparently aware of it—and he'd just about emptied it before he left. Withdrawals in cash, too."

"Jesus. So this kid went missing with over fifteen thousand in cash on him?"

"Yep. You have any idea where he's gone?"

I grimaced. "You know just as well as I do where he's probably headed."

She nodded. "Los Angeles."

"Where else?"

"All right. You'd better come with me to give a statement, too. You don't *have* to," she emphasized, "but you probably should."

"Okay, okay." I started shutting down for the day. "But since I don't *have* to do this yet, at least keep me updated on what happens?"

Renee looked at me, then flashed a momentary smile. "You got it. Now come on, Wood."

I followed her out, locking the door behind me. *Not what I was planning for this evening.*

CHAPTER 19

Blood and Moonlight

When I can't talk and can't act and can't work... I drive. I cruised down various highways—the Northway, then part of the Thruway, 787, back to I-90—the windows wide open and the wind roaring at sixty-five. Even so, I barely felt any cooler; for sheer miserable muggy heat, it's hard to beat the worst summer days of Albany, New York, and its environs, which unfortunately include Morgantown. It was days like this that made me think an air conditioner retrofit would be a really, really good idea; there were a few drawbacks to driving a 1970s vintage car.

How long I was out driving I wasn't sure. For a while, I just tried to follow the moon as it rose slowly, round and white. It was the flashing red lights that finally drew my attention back to earth.

No, they weren't chasing me—I wasn't speeding; there were two police cars up ahead and flares in the road. I slowed and started to go around them; then I saw a familiar, slender figure standing at one car. That made me wince; it was that same person's voice who'd caused part of my major upset earlier, and *she* couldn't be feeling great about it, either. I pulled up just ahead of the squad car. "What's up, Renee?" I asked.

She jumped and her hand twitched towards her gun. "Jesus! I didn't even hear you come up."

That was weird in itself. "Must be something pretty heavy if you didn't notice Mjölnir pulling in."

She gestured. "Take a look if you want. Just don't go beyond the tape. We're still working here."

I went down the steep, grassy embankment carefully, finally pulling out my penlight to pick my way down. Despite the moon, it was pitchy dark, and the high, jagged pines blocked out what feeble light there was; at least it was cooler under the trees. The slope leveled out, and the light from the crime scene started brightening. The police had set up several portable floods and the area was almost bright as day. I stopped just at the tape.

At first, it looked like someone had stood near the middle of the clearing and spun around while holding a can of red-brown paint. Then one of the investigators moved to one side.

A body was sprawled, spread-eagle, in the center of the clearing. The green eyes stared sightlessly upward and the mouth hung open in a frozen scream. His throat had been torn out. The charcoal-gray suit was flung wide open, the white shirt now soaked in red-brown clotting blood where his gut was ripped open. My stomach gave a sudden twist as my gaze reached his waist.

Something had torn his legs, still in the pant legs, off at the hip; then that something had stripped every ounce of meat off the bones and laid the bones carefully back, to gleam whitely where the legs had been.

I got my stomach under control. A few months ago, I might have lost it, but having watched Elias Klein fry under a hundred sunlamps had been a couple steps worse.

Still, it was an ugly sight, and I felt pretty shaky as I climbed back up the hill. "Jesus Christ, Renee! What kind of a sicko does things like that?"

She shook her head. "That's what we'd like to know."

"Who was the vic?" I asked.

"ID found on him says he's a Gerald Brandeis of Albany, New York. ID *also* says he's Morgan Steinbeck of Hartford, Connecticut. His last ID says he's Hamilton Fredericks of Washington, DC; also says he's a fed."

That got my attention. "Fed? What kind of fed?"

She glanced hard at me. I made a zipped-lips motion. She nodded. "Okay, but make sure you keep it zipped. His ID says he's NSA, Special Division. Occupation is just Special Agent. His Hartford ID makes him an insurance investigator for Aetna; the one for Brandeis gives him IRS status."

I whistled. "From the No Such Agency?" It was a cinch that one was the real deal; no one sane would fake that. "One heavy hitter, that's for sure. Was he carrying, and if so did he get off any shots?"

"Answer is yes to both." She pointed inside her squad car. I glanced in, could just make out a nine-millimeter pistol. "Smell indicates it was fired just recently and we found three shell casings. With all the blood around we haven't been able to tell if he hit anything. We're trying to find the bullets, but in that sandy-soiled forest, the chance of getting all three is slim."

A vehicle with a flashing blue light pulled up; the medical examiner's office. The ME got out and nodded to me, turned to Renee. "Your people done?"

"With the body, yeah. But ask the other officers to direct you; we're nowhere near finished with the site yet and we don't want anything here messed up." The ME gestured and he and his assistants started down the hill.

"How'd you get on to this?" I asked Renee.

She looked uncomfortable. "Someone called us."

I could tell there was something bothering her. "Someone who found the body?"

She shook her head.

"Then what? Come on, Renee."

She shrugged. "The station got a call from someone at 7:40 p.m. who claimed to have left a body at this location. The operator said it sounded male, but kind of deep and strange. He didn't stay on long enough to trace."

"That is weird. I'd assume he didn't give a name."

"You'd assume wrong." Her face was grim. "He gave a name, all right.

"The name was Vlad Dracul."

CHAPTER 20

An Unusual Consultant

Red liquid swirled warmly in the crystal glass, throwing off crimson highlights. Verne Domingo sipped. I swallowed some of my ginger ale, noticing how little I was affected these days by the knowledge that Verne was drinking blood.

"Why doesn't it clot?" I asked idly.

"Heparin, my friend. A standard anticoagulant."

"Doesn't that give you any problems?"

His warm chuckle rolled out. "Not in the least, Jason. Nor does anything else within the blood. Disease and toxins cannot harm me. It does change the taste somewhat, and on occasion I do need some fresh blood; but that, too, can be arranged."

"How's things going?" I asked, realizing I was evading what had brought me here...but now that I was here, I found myself a little nervous. "Your new business and all?"

"Oh, well enough. Sky Hashima was to have visited either this evening or the next, but he had a family emergency; his daughter apparently managed to break her leg *and* develop appendicitis at the same time."

"What?"

"The description was a bit...disjointed, but I gather that the infection came on quickly, and when she was trying to come down the stairs the pain hit, she tripped, and fell. So she is now in the hospital, having surgery for a ruptured appendix *and* a complex fracture."

"Holy crap. I'd better send them a card or something. I hope she'll be okay."

"I believe she will be, and am sure they would appreciate it."

101

He gazed at me levelly. "Enough of these pleasantries, Jason. Tell me what is bothering you."

Okay, I can't hide much from him, can I? "An awful lot of things, really. This has been the kind of day that makes me think I should have just slept on to tomorrow." I put the glass down and fiddled with my keys. "I really don't want to bother you, either. I guess any problems I have would seem pretty insignificant to you anyway."

"Perhaps not, my friend." He took another sip. "I am many centuries old, that is true, and such a perspective makes many mortal concerns seem at best amusing conceits. But the affairs of the heart, and the concerns of a friend, these things are eternal. Those... immortals who lose sight of their basic humanity become as was your friend Elias Klein. Something I was myself in danger of becoming, and had come very close to becoming more than once in the past."

He put the glass down. "Truly, Jason. I am interested. It is a rare thing for me, remember, to again think of, and take part in, the ordinary things of humanity."

That much was true. "Well, first there was a call from Renee," I said finally. "This kid, Xavier Ross... well, long story short, his brother was murdered in a nasty way, cops closed the case awfully fast, Xavier had reason to think they were wrong, he came to me. I found some other evidence, he took it to the police but they wouldn't reopen the case, so he waits a few weeks and then takes off on his own—best guess is that he's heading for LA like he's some kind of hero."

Verne nodded. "And..."

"Renee called again today; they managed to track him to Chicago, and he just disappears. Some kind of gang fight right in his last vicinity, and they found a *lot* of blood and a couple traces of clothing that matched his."

"So," Verne said seriously, "then you blame yourself?"

"I should've cut him off from the start. Damn, Verne, he was *fifteen*. He shouldn't have been..."

"Understandable, indeed. Yet... I feel there is more. You must have ways of letting go, so to speak."

I sighed. "Yeah. Yeah, I do, and mostly I know he made his choices on his own, and it's not my fault. But still, that took me a few hours to dig my brain out from under, so to speak, and then I get out of work and Sylvie wants to... talk to me." I hesitated.

He smiled. He probably meant it to comfort me, but the kindly effect was slightly offset by the sight of his fangs. "I can guess, my friend. The *affaire d'amour*, eh? And you are, I have noticed, a bit uncomfortable with the subject."

I stared carefully at my drink. "That obvious, huh?"

"Quite." He raised his glass and drank. "A word of advice, if you will take it? Women are indeed different from men in many ways—even as they are much the same in many others; but both sides like things that are certain and predictable. If you do not intend a romantic involvement with the young lady, then comport yourself accordingly. I know you, my young friend. You are attracted to her, but at the same time I can sense that you are, to put it bluntly, petrified at the thought of such an involvement. When she demands a decision, she is not telling you to either become involved with her or she will leave; she is telling you to treat her as either lover or simple friend, not something of each. It may be easy for you to behave as your impulses lead; it is hard on her."

I stared intently at my glass. That was a cutting analysis. I hate having to see myself like that. But he was right. "Sylvie... she's different from everyone else. It's strange, really. You intimidate me a lot less than she does."

Verne laughed. "Now that *is* odd, my friend. I agree, most certainly, that the lady is different. She has a Power which is rare, rarer even than you or she realize, especially in this day and age. But for a man who has dueled one of the Undead and emerged the victor, a talented young lady should hardly be a great threat." His smile softened. "It seems to me that, just perhaps, the reason is that she is more precious to you than any others because of this talent—she sees within the souls of those about her, and thus you know she accepts what you are more fully than anyone else living could. To a bachelor such as yourself, she is a grave threat indeed."

I couldn't restrain a nervous laugh of my own. "I couldn't be that clichéd, could I?"

The old vampire smiled again. "I am afraid, my friend, that we are all too often the clichés of our times. I am only unusual because I have outlived all those who would recognize me. Yet, in your own fiction, I have found myself being stereotyped once more." He finished the glass of blood and set it down. "Was there anything else, Jason? Though I will admit that a young life in jeopardy due to perceived responsibility on your part, followed by friendship troubles, is quite enough to make a bad day, I suspect something worse would be needed to make you come here."

I nodded. "You could say that." In a few sentences I outlined the horror in the clearing. "So, you see, I had to come here."

He raised an eyebrow. "I don't quite see that you *had* to come here."

"Reisman may be thinking 'psycho' right now, but that's because your little hypnotism job, or whatever you call it, keeps her from remembering that there's a local vampire who could do that to someone a heckuva lot easier than an ordinary nut. And since the guy was a Fed...I had to find out from you if you did have him killed."

His lips tightened. "You offend me, Jason. Once before you suspected me of being a murderer, but then I had been well-framed for the part. Now you know me, and yet you would think I would kill someone in such a grotesque way?"

"Look, I'm sorry, Verne. It's not that *I* suspect it. It's a question I have to ask because Reisman *can't* ask it. I don't believe it. But Elias knew you were a drug-runner, and though we conveniently made that disappear when we did the Great Vampire Coverup, Renee Reisman could easily find it out again, and then she would be up here grilling you. Even though you've changed your profession since, the fact that you were ever involved in that kind of thing won't look good."

He sat back slowly, and I relaxed a bit. Pissing a vampire off isn't the way to ensure a long life—what he'd done to Carmichael's estate had shown that all too well. "I did have another couple of reasons. I thought you might know something, maybe about another vampire that for some ungodly reason decided to move here."

He shook his head, hesitated a moment, then spoke. "As you know, vampires are one of the few sorts of beings that I cannot sense automatically. Unless your hypothetical newcomer were to introduce himself, I'm afraid that I would have no better idea than you of his presence.

"Besides that, it stretches the bounds of reason to suppose that three vampires would be found in such close proximity." He chuckled slightly. "We are a rare race; were the environmentalists aware of us, I would not be surprised to find us on an endangered species list. I am still somewhat puzzled by Klein's presence; he obviously became a vampire relatively recently, yet his maker seemed unconcerned with either Klein's behavior or survival."

I raised an eyebrow. "You mean his maker might have objected to what he did?"

Verne nodded. "His maker *should* have objected, or in fact have *controlled* him. As a general rule, they try not to make waves, so to speak, for other beings that live in the twilight world between your civilization's 'reality' and the lands of myth. And, not to sound overly egotistical, I am an extremely well-known member of that group. I would have expected his maker to be extremely concerned about annoying me by involving me in the manner Klein did. And, indeed, if I discover who was responsible for making him and leaving him uncontrolled, I will...have a talk with that person."

"We never did find out how or why Klein became a vampire; couldn't this killing be due to whoever Klein's maker was?"

Verne rubbed his chin thoughtfully. "It is possible, of course. It *would* eliminate that element of coincidence; if this was the case, then Klein's behavior might even have been precisely what his maker wanted. But still...a vampire who had decided on such a bizarre and savage method of killing...I find it difficult to believe such a creature would waste so much of the *essence* of the living. But you said 'a couple' of other reasons. What was the other?"

"The murderer apparently phoned headquarters...and he gave his name as Vlad Dracul."

I would never have believed it possible, but the blood drained straight out of Verne's face, leaving him literally white as paper. "*Vlad Dracul*...that is not possible. It *must* not be possible." His voice was a whisper. I felt gooseflesh rising on my arms; Verne sounded *afraid*.

I didn't want to imagine what could scare him. "Of course, it's impossible. Vlad Tepes, the Dracula of legend, died a long, long time ago." Another thought occurred to me. "Unless...given the initials...you *were* him."

He made a cutting gesture with his hand, his ruby ring flashing like a warning. He stepped to the window; for several minutes he stared out at the moonlit landscape. "No. I was not...him. But that name has...meaning..." He paused. "I'd rather not discuss this now, Jason. I must make some inquiries." He turned back to me. "I'm sorry to cut this short, but you'll have to leave now."

One look was enough to convince me not to argue. "Okay, Verne. Can you just tell me one thing?"

"Perhaps."

"Is it another vampire? Is that what you think?"

A very faint, eerie smile crossed his face. My skin prickled anew. "A vampire? Oh, no, not a vampire."

That smile stayed with me all the way home.

CHAPTER 21

Admissions and Evidence

The door opened. "Jason!" Sylvie said, looking surprised.

"Hi, Syl. Can I come in?"

"Sure. Watch out for the books on the floor; I'm rearranging the library."

I stepped in. I noticed again the odd, warm smell of her house; the dusty, comfortable scent of old books blended with a faint tinge of kitchen spices and old-fashioned perfume, a smell that didn't fit someone as young and gorgeous as Syl—except that, somehow, it did fit, because it was Sylvie's house. Sylvie stepped ahead of me and carefully lifted a stack of books off a large chair.

"I suppose I should apologize, Jason. I was pretty hard on you."

"No, Syl, you were right." I sat down; she took the arm of the couch right next to me. "I've been trying to have it both ways and it doesn't work. I can't flirt with you half the time and then expect you to act like just a friend the other half. You can't switch your behavior to match whatever my mood is, and even if you could, it's wrong for me to expect you to."

"I know, Jason," she said gently. She put her hand on my shoulder. "I'm the person you've told practically your life story to, remember? I'm only a little surprised that you've understood yourself so quickly."

"It wasn't me, really. Someone who has better perception than I do held a mirror to my face."

"Now who would..." she trailed off, staring at me. "My *God*, Jason. Not... *him*?"

I *had* kept my interactions with Verne quiet, so I wasn't too surprised by her surprise, but... "Verne Domingo, yes."

She shuddered slightly, then studied me intensely; I almost expected her to start doing some kind of crystal ritual or something. "Are you...all right?"

"What? Of course I'm all right. What's the matter?"

She stared at me, wide-eyed. "What's the *matter*? He's a *vampire*! The question *should* be why you have anything to do with him! I know you worked together with him but...you've gone from turning up your nose at the drug-runner to, it seems, being his best buddy! For that matter," she frowned, "why does he have anything to do with you? I still don't understand why he allowed us to remember. It sure would have been simpler for him to make *all* of us forget."

"He let us remember because, well, he needs *me* to remember if I'm going to be of any use, and he knows that part of the price of *my* cooperation is that he keeps his hands off *you*. Not that I'm worried about that so much, now. I've gotten to know him since. He's *lonely*, Syl! Just think about it for a minute. Here you are, immortal, for most purposes invulnerable, with all these superhuman powers, and at the same time you don't dare mention it to anyone! I think he got to the point that, when he realized I wasn't all that scared of him, he just couldn't make himself wipe my memory away and shut me out of his life. He needs someone he can talk to, someone who knows what he is and still will treat him like a person.

"Also, he *smuggled* drugs, not *smuggles*. Those stories aren't just for show—he really has become an art and artifact expert." I hadn't gone over the entire story before with Syl, and didn't want to muddy the waters right now.

Syl's face was serious now. She's very empathic; I could see that she understood. "So why did he wipe Renee's memory?"

"Because Renee *told* him to do it. She said that she would be better off not knowing, and it would help her carry conviction in the story we cooked up."

"I see." She looked thoughtful now.

"I also think he hopes you will visit him. He speaks very highly of you."

She looked surprised at that, but then her gaze sharpened. "Jason, why were you there yesterday evening? I know it wasn't just to talk about your love life."

"You're right." I gave her the whole story along with everything

Verne had said. Just as I finished, the phone rang. It was Lieutenant Reisman. She'd guessed where I had to be tonight. She was calling from a pay phone, so I took the number and called her back. "What's up, Renee?"

"Remember our federal friend? Well, his business associates showed up. We've been told to butt out; national security and all that."

"Well, we could have predicted that. SOP."

Renee snorted. "Bullcrap, Wood. Usually the feds cooperate with the locals; they don't want to piss us off. When they go into a total stonewall like this, they're not kidding around, and there's something big involved."

"So why call me?"

"Because I know you, Wood. You dropped into the middle of it and you never give up on anything. I haven't told them you're in the picture. No one else on the site really saw you except the ME, and he's so close-mouthed he wouldn't say if he saw his own mother at her funeral unless he was under oath. I'm just warning you about what kind of trouble you could be in if you keep poking into this."

"What about you?"

There was a pause, then an explosive, short laugh. "Yeah, you know me, too."

"Can you get me the ME's report?"

She thought for a moment. "I'll have to figure out some way to weasel it out of him without alerting the feds, but yeah, I think I can. So what are you going to do for me?"

"My job. Get you information." I smiled slowly. "Don't you think it might help if we can find out why they're so worried?"

She hesitated. "It sure would. But I don't want to know how you get it."

"Right. Look, why don't you come over for dinner tomorrow, if you're not too busy? I should have something by then, and hopefully they won't try to listen in. We can set up some way to talk safely then."

"Okay. And, Jason," her tone shifted, "be careful. This is dangerous stuff we're playing with."

"I know. Bye."

I looked up at Syl. One glance froze me. She had that deep-eyed, deadly serious look again. Her "feeling" look. After the last few times, I'd learned to trust those feelings with my life. "What is it, Syl?"

"It's bad, Jason. Very bad." She shivered. "More people are going to die before this is over."

CHAPTER 22

Three Conversations, One Problem

I got back to my house, opened the door, and went to the kitchen. A few minutes later, sandwich and soda next to me, I booted up my terminal program. I needed to contact Manuel Garcia O'Kelly Davis. Manuel was actually a fairly high-placed military intelligence analyst. I thought he was Air Force, but there was no way to be sure. I sent him a secured e-mail, asking for a conference. He promptly agreed, and we set up the doubly secured relay, with me supplying a few bells and whistles that would make anyone trying to trace us end up chasing their own tails through the telecommunications network. As per our long-established habits, neither of us used the other's real name; to him, I was "Mentor of Arisia," and he remained "Manuel."

>>Hello, Mentor. You ready for the apocalypse? Less than six months to go!<<

I snorted. We often joked around about the "Y2K" problem, but it hadn't been a joke for a lot of people I knew. It was a costly problem that people had put off for years; as a result, in the last few months, people were scrambling to put the last patches in. Not that the disasters predicted were likely to happen, but it *was* a major pain in the butt. I typed back:

>>*MY* computer software is up to date. It's you guys in the government that have to worry about your antiquated systems with two-digit date fields.<<

>>True dat. What's up?<<

>>Got a problem. You have time?<<

>>Two hours enough?<<

>>Should be.<<

I filled him in on the situation, leaving out the gory details and concentrating on the NSA factors.

>>Can you find out what their angle is?<<

>>Christ. You don't ask for much, do you. Look, I can check into it, but you'd do better to just drop out, you know?<<

>>I can't. It'd nag at me forever.<<

>>I know the feeling. :) Just remember, anything I tell you, I didn't tell you. Right?<<

>>Right.<<

I signed off, then finally got on to one of the underground boards; one run by a pirate and hacker that I knew pretty well.

>>Hello, Demon? You there?<<

>>Readin' you loud and clear, Mentor old buddy. You slumming?<<

>>Looking for info, as usual. You still keep up on the doings of the rich and infamous?<<

>>Best I can, you can bet on it.<<

The Demon was a damn good hacker—almost on a par with the legendary Jammer—and very well informed. He kept an eye on criminal doings not merely on the Net, but throughout the world. He viewed his piracy as a matter of free information distribution; since I make my living by distributing information and getting paid for that service, I found myself simultaneously agreeing and disagreeing with him. Nonetheless, we got along pretty well since the Demon absolutely *hated* the real Darksiders—people who destroyed others' work. To his mind, copying information was one thing. Destroying or corrupting it was another thing entirely.

>>Demon, what's going on now that might be bothering the feds?<<

>>You talking big or little?<<

>>Big, but not like countries going to war; NSA stuff.<<

>>Hold on. Lemme think.<<

I waited.

>>Okay, there are about three things I can think of; but lemme ask, did something happen in your area?<<

>>Yes, that's how I got interested.<<

>>Got you. That only leaves one. NSA and the other agencies have been checking your general area trying to locate a real nasty Darksider who calls himself Gorthaur. He's a total sleaze. None of the respectable hackers or crackers will deal with him, but no

one's really got the guts to tell him to kiss off. There are a lot of ugly rumors about him. Or her, no one's really sure either way. Gorthaur's been heavy into espionage and industrial spying and sabotage. A real prize.<<

>>He ever sign on your board?<<

>>He did until I found out who he was. Far as I know, I'm the only one to tell him what I thought of him. I told him that he'd better not log back on 'cuz if I ever got anything on him I'd turn him over to the cops so fast it'd make his chips spin.<<

>>Bet he didn't like that.<<

>>He told me it wasn't healthy to get in his way. I told him to save the threats for the kiddies.<<

I frowned at that.

>>Look, Demon, if it turns out that this Gorthaur is part of what I'm involved in, you'd better take his warning seriously. There's already one corpse and the place is crawling with NSA.<<

>>I'll be careful then.<<

I logged off, shut the system down, and sat back. Then I got up. I turned around. A tall, angular, dark figure loomed over me, scarcely a foot away.

"Holy CRAP!" I jumped back, tripped over the chair, dropped my glass, fell. My head smacked into the edge of the table and I flopped to the floor and just lay there as the red mist cleared.

"My apologies, Jason. Let me help you up." Verne Domingo pulled me to my feet as though I were a doll.

I pushed him away; he let go. "Christ! What in *hell* did you think you were doing? You scared me into next week!" I rubbed the already growing lump on my skull.

"I have said I was sorry. I did not wish to call you via phone; the government has ears, after all. And coming in person would call just as much attention. I had only just materialized when you turned, and I had no chance to warn you."

"Okay, Okay. Sorry I yelled." I started for the kitchen, towards the freezer.

"Sit, Jason. I will take care of that." He took the hand towel from the countertop, rinsed it, dumped several ice cubes into it. Then he folded the towel into a bundle and squeezed. I heard splintering noises as the ice was crushed. "There. Put that on the swelling."

I did. The cold helped, even when it started to ache. "What'd you want to see me for?"

"To explain, my friend." He stood with his back to the refrigerator, stiff and somehow sad. "The story you told me last night... it had very disturbing elements in it, very disturbing indeed. I had to check them before I could believe what my heart knew was the truth. Now I must tell you what is happening here, and for you to understand, you must hear a little history.

"Vampires are among the most powerful of what you would call the supernatural races, but—as I am sure you have guessed—we are not the only such. Most have..." he hesitated, then went on, "...either long since died out or else found some way to leave this world that is no longer congenial to them, but a few, either through preference or necessity, still live on. My people are, on the whole, cautious not to arouse the awareness of you mortals, and this suits us. Bound as we are to the world in which we are born, we cannot leave, and so we live as best we can without doing that which could rouse you who now rule it to pursue us.

"There was another race of beings, however, which was not so circumspect. They did not reproduce as we do—by converting mortals; they reproduced themselves as do most races, and this is perhaps why they had less sympathy for your people. But more likely, they lacked sympathy because it was not in their nature; for they preyed on us as well." He looked at me steadily. "Your people call them werewolves."

I blinked. "Oh, no. Not again."

"I am afraid so. You have stumbled into the realm of the paranormal once more."

Vaguely, I had the feeling that there was something missing— something Verne was not telling me. But it wasn't central; the main points, I was sure, were the real thing. But something else wasn't quite... right. Well, maybe he'd clear that up later. I grimaced. "What was that line from *Die Hard 2*? 'How can the same shit happen to the same guy twice?' Look, how could werewolves prey on you? I mean, you guys are awfully hard to kill and once you die, well, you go to dust, at least the older ones. Klein took several days. Not much to eat there. Besides, couldn't you just turn around and eat them?"

"We are not as invulnerable as you think." He hesitated. "The truth is that it is not merely wood which can harm us. Wood harms us because it was once living. Any object composed of living or formerly living matter can harm us. Thus, werewolves could kill us with their formidable natural weaponry. As for the feeding... your writers have often glimpsed the truth. They did indeed consume flesh; but more, they fed on raw emotions. Fear and despair, terror and rage, these things strengthened them; and when their victims finally died, they fed, directly, on the life force, the soul if you will, as it passed from the body. Nor could we return the favor. Their blood-scent was enticing, true; but any attempt to drain them only succeeded in slaying both parties. We immortals were a rare delicacy to them. We hid ourselves well, but they eventually found ways to locate us. We fought them off on occasion, but they became ever more devious and effective over the centuries, leaving us alone for long enough that we began to feel safe, then returning to feast upon those who did not know their peril and were unready to defend themselves against the monsters.

"That threat accomplished what none of our talking had managed before; all the different... groups of vampires united against the lycanthropes, and waged a long and bitter war. In the end we destroyed them. I myself confronted the last, and greatest, of the breed, and I slew him with great pleasure. He had been terrorizing the city of London while using a name which he knew would taunt me."

"Vlad Dracul."

He nodded.

"And now you wonder if you really killed him at all."

"No." He sat slowly. "I do not wonder at all. I know now that I did *not* kill him; that somehow he survived what I had believed were mortal wounds."

"You'd better tell me everything about these things. Especially how to kill them."

"Silver is the only way—at least the only way that you could make use of. I do not know in what manner, but the metal somehow disrupts their internal balance. Both teeth and claws, in their lupine form, are a crystalline substance of great toughness. Their strength is immense, their cunning formidable, and their ability to shift shape, though confined to a vaguely wolflike monstrous form on the one hand, is unlimited in the human range; they can be anyone at all. They do not fear night or day, nor does the phase of the moon have any effect upon them. They also have a talent similar to my own to charm and cloud other minds. They do not have my people's ability to dematerialize, but they can prevent us from using it if they get a hold on us."

"Ugh. Tell me, do they become stronger with age like you vampires?"

"I am afraid so."

"And this one was the biggest, oldest, baddest of the were-wolves when you fought him?"

"Quite. I was not alone, however."

"Not alone? You mean you couldn't handle him by yourself?" The thought was terrifying. I knew how strong Klein had been, how hard he was to kill, and since then I'd seen what Verne was capable of; trying to imagine something powerful enough to beat a vampire as ancient as Verne...

He showed his fangs in a humorless grin. "I will admit that we never found out. I had two companions..." he hesitated again before continuing, "...both of them...leaders of their own clans or families of vampires. Though normally enemies, we realized that these creatures were more of a threat to us all. We ambushed him, all striking at once with silver knives I had prepared, and threw his body in the Thames, the knives embedded in the corpse so that his people would not find him in time to have any chance to save him. So swift were we that he never had a chance to strike back."

"Marvelous." I shook my head. "Well, at least you've eased my mind on one thing."

"That being...?"

"I hate coincidences. I don't believe in them. Now I know why he's ended up here." I looked across the table. "He's been tracking you. And he's going to kill you if he can."

Verne Domingo nodded slowly.

CHAPTER 23

Remembering Old Times

"Okay, Jason, what've you got?"

That was Renee, straight to the point. "A whole lot. But first, come here; there's someone I want you to meet."

She followed me to the living room. Verne rose from the red chair, bowed as I introduced them. "Renee Reisman, Verne Domingo."

She didn't shake hands. "Jason, we've had our eye on this man for some time. I'd like to know just what his connection is with you."

"I shall explain, my lady," Verne said. "Look at me," he continued in a low but commanding voice.

Reflexively she shot a glance into his eyes—and froze.

He stepped closer, touched her temple gently with his right hand. He gazed intensely at her for several seconds. "Remember," he said.

Renee's eyes widened. A choked scream burst from her lips, and she staggered back, sagged, pale and shaking, onto my couch. "Oh dear God . . ." She closed her eyes, massaged her temples, and took several ragged breaths. Finally she raised her head. "I . . . I remember now. But until now, it was like those memories didn't exist." She stared at Verne, still shaking.

"My sincerest apologies, Renee—may I call you Renee? Those memories were still there; merely locked away, as you requested. But Jason has convinced me that we need your aid, and we both knew that you must have your full memory to help us."

The old Renee was reasserting herself, albeit slowly. "That bad, huh?" She raised an eyebrow at me. "I assume that his being here means that he isn't our killer."

117

"You're right."

She turned back to Verne. "Okay, Domingo. Now that my brain is back, this had better be real good. Because," she shivered again, "I don't think I'll be able to go through that again. Having my memory switched on and off like a light..."

Verne smiled, the gentlest expression I'd ever seen him use; his fangs didn't show. "Milady, you showed courage far greater than mine to undergo that treatment once; neither of us either desired or expected that you would once more ask to forget."

"Damn straight." She ran her fingers through her hair, took a deep breath, and crossed her legs. "All right, let's have it."

CHAPTER 24

Gone and Dead

I logged on and checked; I had a secured e-mail waiting. I pulled it up onscreen.

The message decoded just as though Manuel had sent it... but it wasn't from Mannie at all. That was so close to impossible that, for a moment, I couldn't do anything except gape. Then I reread the signature at the bottom, and understood.

Mentor (or should I say, Jason?): I'm sorry to tell you that Manuel has gotten himself into a bit of trouble by poking his nose into this. He doesn't have anywhere near the necessary clearance. He's being debriefed right now, but I'd suggest you not contact him for a while; not only is he more than slightly peeved at you, but any more contact from the outside might be seen as seriously amiss by his superiors.

Since he emphatically assured me that you're too stubborn to be frightened off, and because we happen to be kindred spirits in a way, I'll give you what information I can. But let me warn you: this is dangerous. You and everyone you know could get killed if you play these games. So give serious consideration to just dropping it.

"Vlad Dracul" is apparently another alias being used by an independent operator called "Gorthaur." Gorthaur plays no favorites; he's been bypassing security and penetrating installations on five continents. Very rarely does he take direct credit for his actions except for those which he perpetrates on the Net—that's where he gets his name.

What tells us that Gorthaur's involved is the sheer perfection of his work. In every case, he penetrates the installation in the guise of a high-clearance individual who is well-known to the personnel. Fingerprints, retinals, passwords, everything checks out perfectly. These individuals vary in age, height, weight, and even gender to such a degree that we are utterly unable to imagine—much less determine—how one person can pull off all of these impersonations. Yet, subtle indicators tell us that it is just one person.

So far, three agents have been killed in particularly savage ways while trying to locate Gorthaur. The one killed in Morgantown thought he had found a hot trail. Apparently, he had. Gorthaur exhibits psychopathic strength and savagery, and has killed several other people who apparently offended him at one point or another. Our best psych profile makes him out to be a complete sociopath with a megalomaniac complex, but there are enough anomalies that we can't begin to classify him. He's unique.

Watch your back. If he can disguise himself this well, he could be anyone.

The Jammer

The Jammer: hacker legend, thief, one of the few completely nonviolent criminals to make the ten-most-wanted list, and maybe the only one who never had a picture to go with his "wanted" poster. No one knows anything about him—even the "him" was in question. He'd disappeared a couple of years ago, and everyone thought he'd retired. Now, it was clear that he'd been caught and recruited. But someone with his talent couldn't be forced to work, so they must have shown him something so important that he chose to work for them rather than against them.

I erased the message and sat back, sweating. Who knew what this werewolf wanted, really? Vengeance against Verne Domingo, yes, but that wasn't enough for him to go breaking into top-secret vaults here and around the world. He had to have some other, larger agenda. And how in the name of God could you catch something that could change sex, fingerprints, and genetics at will?

There *wasn't* any way, I realized. The only chance to catch Gorthaur was to get him to come to us, and only one thing was keeping him here: Verne Domingo. Once he settled with Verne, he'd vanish forever.

I logged off that system, got on to the Demon's board. He hadn't responded to my query; probably at dinner, which was where I should be. Then I noticed one of my status tags:

Email: Waiting: 0 Old: 3

The last time I'd been on, there'd only been two old messages. I called up the last one:

>>From System Operator Demon<<

Okay, if it's that important, we can meet in person. Be here at six; we'll have dinner. I don't like it, Mentor; this had better be worth it.

THE DEMON

```
   (____)
  \* */
   \#/
```

What the hell? I hadn't written him lately! Who...?

Suddenly it hit me. If even the Jammer couldn't catch this guy...I shut the computer off and sprinted for Mjölnir.

I had a sickening feeling that I was too late.

I'd been there only once before, but that I remembered every turn. The lights were with me, and it was only fourteen minutes before I slammed on the brakes and skidded into place in front of the Demon's house. I was out the door before the engine finished dying, my S&W ten-millimeter out and ready. I rang the bell. No answer. I tried the door. Already unlatched, it swung open quietly at my touch. The hallway was dim and silent. "Yo! Demon!" I called.

No answer.

My heart was hammering too damn fast; I'd swear it was audible a hundred feet away. I stepped cautiously into the house. In the faint light, I could see the hallway, the stairs to the second floor, and two entryways. I knew that one led to the living room, the one on the left, and past that was the den where the computer was. Slowly, I took my coat off and threw it through the entry. It hit the rug; nothing moved. I dove into the living room, rolled as I hit, and landed with my back to the far corner, gun up.

Nothing. Just furniture.

A faint creaking noise came from ahead of me. I stood stock-still, listening. The wind outside moaned. The creak came again. It was emanating from the den. The door to the den was ajar, and I could see the white glow of a monitor screen.

I went forward one step at a time, trying to watch all directions at once. My ears would have pricked up if they could. The only sounds I heard were the whistle of the wind and that faint, periodic creaking.

I reached the door. Taking a deep, shaky breath, I flung it wide.

A horrid red-splotched face swung toward me. I almost fired, but stopped and lowered the gun. "Jesus Christ..." I muttered.

Jerome Sumner, aka the Demon, hung head-down from one of the big beams of his old house. The rope that was tied around his ankles creaked as he swung slowly in the wind from the open window. His eyes stared blankly at me; his mouth was jammed open with a crumpled floppy disk. The room was filled with the faint metallic scent of the blood on his face, on his clothes, and on the floor. I glanced away, saw his computer.

It was covered with spatters of blood. Lying on top of the keyboard was a shapeless dark object. I moved closer.

It was the Demon's tongue. I swallowed bile, looked at the screen.

The BBS was off, but there was a banner-making program on. Four giant words blazed on the screen:

HE TALKED TOO MUCH

I was still staring a few minutes later when the NSA arrived.

CHAPTER 25

Ways to Make You Talk

I looked up as the cell door opened. Renee entered. She walked over and took my hand without a word. After a moment, she said, "You okay?"

"I guess," I said finally. "Am I getting out of here?"

"Hell if I know," Renee said. "Jason, what were you doing over at Jerome Sumner's?"

"Bending over and getting screwed by the bastard who killed him." The fury overwhelmed me for a moment; I slammed my fist into the wall, then nursed my bruised hand. "I was set up perfectly. He was killed by this 'Vlad' guy you're looking for, and I'm supposed to take the fall."

She might have been in uniform, but she was here as a friend. Her hand on my shoulder told me that. "You won't. No one who knows you will believe it."

"But the NSA doesn't know me. How does the evidence look?"

Renee Reisman screwed up her face. "Not good. You were found there. Your fingerprints were all over the place, including on the keyboard . . . on just the keys necessary to put up that banner."

Jesus Christ. Of course they were. The bastard was imitating *me*! "But the way he was killed—I don't think I *could* do that, even if I wanted to."

She shook her head. "You know the answer to that. Besides, you're a smart guy, Jase. Always have been. Prosecution wouldn't have any problem convincing people that you could figure out how to do it." She hugged me suddenly. "I just came to let you know I'm with you. I could pull strings and get myself here. Sylvie's pulling for you too."

I hugged her back, feeling suddenly scared. If the NSA followed the evidence . . . and Gorthaur was as good at this as he seemed to be . . . I could end up put away for life. "Thanks, Renee. I mean it."

"We should get together more often. Not in a jail cell, either." She smiled faintly, and for a moment she looked like the same girl I'd first met in junior high. "You aren't going to prison. I promise you."

"Exceeding our authority a bit, Lieutenant?" a precise voice said from the doorway.

We both jumped slightly. The woman who entered was in her mid to late thirties, sharp-featured, with red hair and a tall, athletic frame. She was followed by a somewhat younger sandy-haired man carrying a brown paper sack and a briefcase. The woman continued, "Fortunately, I don't like to make liars out of my professional associates. You aren't going to prison, Mr. Wood. Jeri Winthrope, Special Agent, at your service; this is my assistant and second pair of hands, Agent Steve Dellarocca." She extended her hand.

I shook it, then waited while Steve put down the stuff he was carrying and shook his, too. "Thanks. Glad to meet you. These have been the longest hours I've ever spent waiting anywhere."

"Couldn't be helped, I'm afraid. We didn't think you were the responsible party, but the evidence didn't look good. We had to check everything out thoroughly." She looked at Renee. "I'll have to talk to Mr. Wood alone now, Lieutenant Reisman."

Renee nodded. I gave her a smile and said, "Thanks, Renee."

"Don't mention it." The door closed behind her.

"Me, too, Jeri?" asked Steve.

"For now," Jeri said. "I want you to keep tabs on the rest of the operation."

"Gotcha. You know where to find me."

I became aware of the aroma of Chinese food coming from the bag Dellarocca had brought with him.

"Hope you like pork lo mein." Jeri said. "I thought you'd be hungry, and lord knows I never get a chance to eat on this job."

"Thanks." I started unpacking the food. "How did you people get to Demon's place so fast? I only ended up there out of sheer luck."

"We got a call. Person said he heard screams from that house and saw a car pulling out fast."

"You got a call? That sounds more like police business."

She nodded. "We're manning the police phones. Mostly we just pass the stuff on, but it gives us the chance to keep sensitive material to ourselves."

"But what made that call sensitive?"

"The address. Your friend Jerome, the Demon, was on our little list of Gorthaur's potential targets."

So she wasn't going to pretend that I didn't know what was going on. That made it easier. "Why did he go after the Demon?"

"Several reasons. The major one is that Gorthaur hates to be laughed at or threatened; he's an utter psycho when it comes to insults. The Demon had thrown Gorthaur off his board and threatened him with exposure."

Nodding, I started to dig into the pork lo mein. Poor Demon. An image of him hanging head-down flashed in my mind. I put my fork down quickly; all of a sudden I wasn't hungry. "Okay, you seem to assume Gorthaur did him in. So what in the evidence keeps me from being Gorthaur?"

Winthrope gave a snort, which I interpreted as a chuckle. "Gorthaur may be able to do a lot of things we don't understand, but he's not omnipotent or omniscient. He's good at planting evidence, but apparently he either doesn't understand or neglected to remember what modern technology can do. Despite the caller's description matching your car, we were able to determine that your vehicle hadn't been there previously. We could tell how long it had been standing there—not long at all. Also, if you were calm enough to put up the banner program, you were very unlikely to have forgotten anything...and thus you'd never have come back." She smiled. "Interesting car, by the way. In your profession, I suppose the electronic gadgetry should be expected, but I don't recall ever seeing an armored Dodge Dart before. Made us wonder if you were in our line of work for real, except that most of the other work seemed homemade rather than professional."

I grinned back. "Picked it up at one of those seized-property auctions. I think it belonged to a mid-level drug-runner. It was the silver and black colors that caught my attention. That and the fact that I'd been shot at twice made an armored car sound like a good investment."

"I can understand that." She finished off an egg roll, then sat back. "Okay, let's get working. Everything here's being recorded, of course. We've got some questions for you and I hope you'll cooperate."

"Hey, I want this twit caught as much as you do. Maybe more; he killed my friend and tried to get me sent up."

"Right." She pulled out a laptop computer from a case slung over her shoulder, and opened it up. "First, tell me how you got into this and what you know so far."

I told the whole story, starting with my arrival on the scene in the woods, leaving out certain small points—like vampires and werewolves—and finishing with finding Jerome dead. "That's about it."

"I don't suppose you'd like to tell me who your contact was that spilled the beans on Gorthaur and his particularly annoying technique?"

"Don't even think about it. Confidentiality is a large part of my business. If the police can't trust me to keep my mouth shut, they wouldn't hire me. Nor would a lot of other people."

"Thought not." She glanced at a few papers. "Okay, Mr. Wood, now let's have the whole story, shall we?"

Uh-oh. "What do you mean?"

"Give me some credit for brains, please. Interrogation is my business. I've been doing this for sixteen years now, and I assure you, I know when I'm not getting everything. So far, you haven't lied to me...but I know damn well that you're hiding something. So let's try specific questions and answers, shall we?"

"Go ahead," I said, trying to look confused. "I'll tell you what I can."

"First, what was your part in the death of Elias Klein?"

What the hell had put her on that track? "He was trying to kill me and accidentally electrocuted himself; you can look that up in the records."

"Funny thing about those records," Winthrope said with a nasty smile. "It is written up as you describe it...but the coroner's report is about as vague as I've ever seen. In fact, our analysis department has a ninety-percent certainty that the report was totally fabricated."

Oh crap. "I'm not the coroner; you'd have to ask him."

"Oh, I intend to. But let's go on. What was Elias Klein working on before his unfortunate demise?"

"I'm not exactly sure. I wasn't always up on everything he did."

"Now, that's very odd, Mr. Wood, since according to this receipt, he used your services just days prior to his death. Also very odd is that the files for his last investigation are not to be found."

Damn, damn, damn! Renee must've forgotten the accounting office files. Either that or, more likely, some of the stuff had been misfiled and was found and properly filed some months later.

"And finally, it's very interesting that neither of Mr. Klein's partners can give a detailed account of his investigations. However, we are fortunate that the wife of one partner recalled a name that her husband had mentioned during the time in question: Verne Domingo."

That tore it. The Great Vampire Coverup was full of more holes than a colander. "Okay, Ms. Winthrope. I'd like to tell you a story. But I can't do it without permission—it affects more people than just me, and like I said, confidentiality is my business."

She studied me a moment. "Sure. Here, use my phone. I'll wait right here, of course."

I grimaced. "Naturally." I took her cell phone and punched in Verne's number.

"Domingo residence, Morgan speaking."

"Hey, Morgan, this is Jason. I have to talk to Verne."

"Of course, sir." A few moments went by, and then that well-known deep voice came on the line. "Jason! I heard you were arrested! Are you all right?"

"Physically, I'm fine, but we have a serious issue. I'm being interrogated by an NSA agent named Jeri Winthrope, and she's been asking some pretty pointed questions. In particular, she's been looking into the past history of certain people, and she wants the truth about Elias Klein."

Verne was silent for a few moments. "You do not believe you can, as you would put it, 'scam' her?"

"I wouldn't want to try. I tried tapdancing around the whole subject and she yanked my chain but good. They've found some remaining files and gotten a few clues that give them you as a lead."

I could sense the consternation on the other end. Finally, he sighed. "Jason, I trust you. I have to, in this instance, for you have had it in your power to bring me down for months now, had you wished, and instead you have proven to be a friend. Tell her what you must. I will prepare my household to move, if things become impossible."

"I don't want you to—"

"I know. But also, if you do not tell her the truth—about me and about what is behind this entire series of murders—we may be condemning her to death. Do as you must."

I swallowed. "Thanks, Verne. Maybe it won't come to that. Bye."

I turned back to the agent. "Okay, Ms. Winthrope, you win. I'll tell you everything. But I'm not going to argue it out with you. If you don't believe what I tell you, it's going to be your loss, not mine."

CHAPTER 26

Special Guest Appearance By . . .

"What was her reaction?"

"About what you'd expect." Verne raised an eyebrow. "Well, she didn't believe me, that's for sure. But she also wasn't comfortable not believing, either; the stuff Gorthaur's been up to has got them spooked."

"And she let you go rather than have you examined by a specialist? Isn't that a bit odd?"

"Not really. She'd already admitted she knew I hadn't killed Jerome, and she wanted to trace me and find out who I met with and who I knew."

"How do you know that, Jason?" asked Syl. Her high boots with shining metal inlay rapped loudly on the wood as she crossed the floor with the coffeepot.

"Simple." I held up a small, silvery object that looked like a button. "Someone stuck this inside Mjölnir's front bumper." I dropped a few other tiny gadgets of varying color on the kitchen table where we were all seated. "And these were planted around the house."

Verne reached out and picked one up, examining it carefully. "Monitoring devices? How very rude. I presume you have deactivated them?"

"No."

They all stared at me. "Why in the world not?"

"Because I've already told Winthrope everything we know, so I don't have a thing to hide from her, and if I shut these off, she could just put in others that I'd never find. Right, Winthrope?" I said, addressing my words to the audio bug I'd removed from the business phone. "Besides, if Gorthaur tries to nail me, he'll be doing it on prime-time with the NSA watching. That should make the bastard think twice."

"Perhaps," conceded Verne. "But perhaps not. Have you not realized the most important part of your latest adventure?"

I thought for a moment. "I guess not. What is it?"

"Our opponent was able to imitate you perfectly. While his powers are vast, they still do have certain limitations. In order to imitate anyone, he must have seen them at close range. That means that you have been close to him in the past few days."

That made my skin prickle. "How close?"

Verne considered. "I would say no more than five feet. Werewolves can assume any form they can visualize, but to pick up on details as explicit as fingerprints would require them to be close enough for their aura to interact with yours."

"And the Demon's death shows he's aware of your involvement," Renee added.

I frowned. "So who . . . no, that question won't work either. He doesn't have to be a single person. He could have been a hacker watching the local boards and that's how he got on to me. Then all he had to do was go out on the street and bump into me. Or he could be a customer."

The doorbell rang. I went to the door, looked out the peephole. "Agent Winthrope? Come in. I've been expecting you."

"I rather thought so," she said. Her assistant Steve followed her in. "Since you made it clear you want us to hear things, it seemed a waste of comfortable seating to hang around in a van trying to eavesdrop." She glanced at Renee. "I thought we told you and the entire police department to stay out of this. Oh, never mind. I've been known to ignore orders on occasion myself."

With two more people in my house, it was too crowded. We all moved next door to Sylvie's shop, which had a big conference-room-style table in one room. Syl rented the room to various groups, usually psychic types for seances.

"So *all* of you people are in on this? What in hell happened to security, Lieutenant Reisman?" Winthrope demanded, her faint smile taking the edge off her question.

"Wood showed up before you classified the operation, ma'am," she answered. "And the only way to get him to drop anything is to put him in jail, or shoot him."

"Not practical solutions as a general rule, I'll admit," she said. "Okay. I know why *you're* in on this, Domingo. I'm not sure I believe in it, but I know why. And I see why Jason had to brief Ms. Stake—"

"Sylvia, or Syl, please," she broke in. "You understand why."

"Hm. Yes." She shifted in her chair, glancing around at the dark-panelled walls. "The important question is, how many others know about all this?"

Verne spoke first. "I assure you that I, at least, have told no one else. It would be a generally futile effort, and I need no advice on this subject."

Renee gave Winthrope a look. "I'd like to continue a career. If I mentioned this to anyone else, my career'd be inside padded walls."

"I've consulted with the Wizard—you remember him, don't you, Jason?—on how to deal with werewolves," Sylvie said.

"Really? And what did he say?" Winthrope asked. Her assistant looked uncomfortable; he was probably bored or wondering if he was trapped in a room full of lunatics.

Syl made a face. "Not much. He said that most spirits can be controlled only if you know their origin, that is, what religious or spiritual discipline they belong to; otherwise you're limited to whatever their classic weaknesses are."

Verne agreed. "It is true. Vampires who believe in the Christian faith can perhaps be turned away by crosses or bound by a daemonic pentacle; but an enlightened nosferatu cares little for such things. There are certain mystical methods which work on all such...but even those are of no use against a Great Wolf. Silver, and silver alone, will suffice."

"Just what did you tell this Wizard character?"

"Actually not that much; I didn't want to get him involved, so I just asked about werewolves."

"And you, Mr. Wood?"

I shrugged. "No one outside of this room knows any of the weird stuff. A couple of the BBS users know I'm poking around in a classified investigation, but no more."

Steve smiled suddenly. "Thanks. That's all we needed to know."

His teeth glinted sharply as he lunged.

Winthrope moved faster than anyone I'd ever seen, even Elias Klein. Her hand blurred and came up holding a nine-millimeter automatic. Before she could fire, though, the werewolf's hand grabbed her arm and pitched her like a horseshoe straight into Verne. "Steve" was no longer human at all, but a shaggy, lupine nightmare with crystal-sharp claws and razor-sharp fangs. If the monster hadn't been delayed in its attack on Agent Winthrope, we all would have been lost to the momentary paralysis of shock. Chairs crashed to the floor as we all rolled, sprang, or ducked away from the huge, monstrous thing that had appeared in the place of Steve Dellarocca.

Verne caught Winthrope, set her aside. "You must be a fool, Virigar. Though this mortal was not expecting you, the rest of us are prepared to deal with your sort. And our prior duel seems to have rendered you less than what you were. Against us you stand little chance."

It smiled, showing glittering rows of crystal teeth. "Not so. My name is Shirrith. I am honored that you mistake me, even for a moment, for the Great King, yet I am but His servant. And we are not unprepared." It gave an eerie howl.

In a shower of glass, two werewolves crashed through the large windows. One sank its claws into Verne's shoulder, but Verne smashed it aside with a tremendous backhand blow that sent it back through the wall into the night. Verne shoved Winthrope towards me. "Run!" he shouted. His face showed shock and, chillingly, the same fear I'd seen before.

Shirrith began to come after us, but Verne dove across the room and caught him. The third werewolf almost reached Renee, but she had her gun out and pumped three shots into him. The .357 magnum slugs drove the creature back far enough for her to run out and slam the door between the conference room and the Silver Stake's main floor. The werewolf tore the door off its hinges and threw it at us. The impact knocked Renee and me down, and sent the ten-millimeter with its silver bullets skittering out of my hand. The creature lashed out, caught Sylvie, and bent its muzzle towards her throat.

Silver inlay flashed as the toe of her right boot slammed into the werewolf's groin. Its eyes bulged; a ludicrously tiny whine escaped its lips, and it staggered backward. As it folded in pain, Sylvie grabbed a large silver candlestick from a shelf and clobbered the werewolf over the head; it crumpled to the floor.

A tremendous crash shook the building as the battle in the conference room escalated. The second werewolf crashed through the broken doorway; it rolled and came up, slashing at Sylvie. She swung the candlestick but it glanced off the thing's arm; the claws left long trails of crimson across her dress. I had my pistol now; before the creature could lunge again, I put three shots into it. The wolflike face snapped back, glaring at me in astonishment. Then it sagged and fell.

"Syl! Jesus, are you okay?" I ran to her. Blood was soaking her dress, spreading quickly.

"I'm fine," she said weakly. "Help Verne!"

I hesitated, looking around. Renee had hit her head when the door knocked us over; she was still dazed. Winthrope was backed up against the wall, staring at the two bodies and repeating, "Oh crap...oh crap..." She cradled her right arm, which hung limply; Shirrith's grip had crushed it like a paper cup.

Another crash echoed through the Silver Stake. I heard Verne cursing in some Central European tongue. With one more agonized look at Sylvie, I charged back into the conference room.

I had the gun ready; then I stopped. "Son of a bitch!"

Verne Domingo looked back at me...twice.

Two Vernes were locked together, straining against each other. They were identical, down to the tears on their clothing.

The damn thing can even emulate clothing? That really sucks.

There was no way to tell them apart; even their cursing sounded the same, and each was calling the other "Shirrith." One was faking...but which?

I could have kicked myself. How stupid can you be? I raised the gun and fired twice.

The one on the left twitched as the bullet hit; the one on the right screamed and tore itself away from the real Verne Domingo, its disguise fading away.

There was a *clack* as the gun jammed, trying to eject the last shell. "You *bugger*!" I said, as the werewolf dove out the window, a perfect target if I could only have fired.

I cleared the jam, but it was too late. Shirrith was gone.

Verne gazed out the broken window, then turned away.

I shoved past Winthrope, who was muttering apologies, ran to Syl. "How're you doing, Syl?"

She tried to smile but failed miserably. "Not so good."

Blood was pooling on the floor.

"Verne, call the hospital, quick! Get an ambulance!"

CHAPTER 27

Empathy and Electronics

"Jason, you need your rest. It's been twenty-seven hours. Go to bed."

I was too tired to jump at the sudden voice from a formerly empty space. "Verne, I've got work to do. I'm going to find that bastard and silver him like a goddam mirror. I don't have time to sleep. You heard what Winthrope said."

"About her assistant being found dead? Yes."

"Then don't talk to me about sleep. Every hour I sleep could get someone else killed." I rubbed my throbbing forehead. "Besides, every time I close my eyes, I see Syl getting slashed by that other werewolf." Fury took over. "That *other* werewolf, dammit!" I shouted at Verne, feeling my eyes sting. "You said there was only one, the last one, and all of a sudden it's *The Howling III* around here!"

Suddenly, Verne looked tired himself; tired and very, very old. "I know, my friend. It was my arrogance and stupidity that led to that mistake. I should have realized that to exterminate an intelligent race is well-nigh impossible. These are not passenger pigeons or dodos. Virigar survived and must have sought out the few that remained; for the past century, they have increased their numbers, awaiting the time of revenge."

My anger evaporated. "Damn. Sorry, Verne. I shouldn't take it out on you. We *all* should have realized that where there was one, there might be more." I wiped my eyes, half-noticing how damp they were. "It's just that Syl . . . of all of us, Syl should have been the last to get hurt. She saved Renee and me—did you know that?"

He bowed his head. "I had not known. But I would have expected no less from her."

"She did. Then the last one got her. Now..."

"She will make it, Jason. I give you my word on that. Sylvia will not die for my mistakes." His dark eyes held mine, lent his words conviction.

"Thanks," I said. "I hope you're right."

"I have never broken my word yet."

"Why didn't you go after Shirrith when he ran?"

"Because..." He hesitated, staring down at his hands. "Because, I am ashamed to admit, my past centuries of soft existence have made me slow and not as adept in combat as I was in years past. Even the small strikes they managed caused pain to my soul, and with weakness and pain come fear. I must remedy that. Also, it would have done no good. Shirrith would never have led me to Virigar, unless that was his plan... in which case, I would be dead." He sighed, and glanced at the odd tubular object on my workbench. "Since you will not rest, perhaps you can explain what you are doing?"

"Sure." I picked up the tube, showing the lens at one end with the eyepiece on the other. "This viewer fits onto this little headband, like this."

"I see that, yes. But what function does this device perform?"

"Well, it..." I broke off, thinking for a minute. "How well-versed are you in the sciences?"

He made a modest gesture. "I am sufficiently educated that I consider myself a well-read layman."

"Good enough. Then you know that visible light is just one small part of the electromagnetic spectrum, right?" He nodded. "Well, I've thought for a long time about how to find a hiding werewolf. Normal methods can't work. Their physical imitation seems to be so perfect that they can duplicate the DNA of the subject. But if that were true, then they must be more than merely material beings—you follow me?"

He thought for a moment, then nodded again. "I believe so. You are saying that if they were purely physical beings, once they assumed a perfect duplicate form, they would then become that person... and lose their special powers."

"You've got it. So if they aren't just matter, that leaves some additional energy component. A werewolf has to be surrounded, permeated, with a special energy field." I locked the viewer into the holder, checked the fit. "That's where this comes in. That field has to radiate somehow, in some wavelength outside the visible."

He raised an eyebrow. "I see. But what wavelength? And would psychic powers, or mystic ones if you prefer, radiate in such mundane ways?"

"At some point I'd think they would," I answered, clipping on a power lead. "If these fields interact with matter, matter will produce certain emissions. As to what wavelength, I'm betting on infrared. In the end, all energy decays to waste heat, you see. But I've also added an ultraviolet switch to this viewer, and these two little gadgets cover other areas—magnetic fields and radio waves, respectively."

He smiled. "I am impressed, Jason. I had thought you proficient solely with your computers and databases; I had no idea you were adept with technical devices as well."

"Any real hacker has to have some skill with a soldering iron and circuitry," I answered. "But I just happen to like gadgets. The Edmund Scientific catalog is some of my favorite bedtime reading. Heck, most people think I named my car Mjölnir because I'm weird. Actually, I've put thousands of dollars into gadgetizing the hell out of it. Mjölnir doesn't fly and if you drive it into water, it stalls like any other car, but it's got some optional features that no major manufacturer never thought of installing." The phone rang; I grabbed it fast.

"Hello? Doctor Millson?" I said.

"No." The voice was deep and resonant in a peculiar way; it sounded like a man in a tin closet. "We met earlier, though you did not realize it at the time. I am Virigar, Mr. Wood."

Adrenaline stabbed my chest with icy slivers. "What do you want?"

"To deliver an ultimatum, Mr. Wood. You know why I am here. I presume that you care for the young lady, Sylvia? If you wish her to survive the night, you will do one of two things: either you kill Verne Domingo for me . . . or you deliver him to me that I might kill him myself. Do this, and my people—who even now walk that hospital's corridors—shall spare the lady's life."

"You bastard." I barely recognized my own voice. "If I'd known—"

"Yes, well, we all have things we'd have done differently 'if only,' do we not, Mr. Wood? You are worthy prey; it makes the chase and the kill sweeter. But for Domingo I will let you and your mortal friends live. Bring him, or the ruby ring he wears, to the old warehouse on Lovell Avenue within the next six hours. Any trickery or failure on your part, and the lady shall die... painfully." The line went dead.

I put the phone down slowly and looked up. Verne looked grimly back at me.

"I heard it all, my friend," he said softly.

CHAPTER 28

A Nice Evening Drive, with Gunfire

"Why the hell not?"

I gestured at the ornate ruby-and-gold ring. "Why not, Verne? If he's going to be satisfied with the ring, just *give* it to him! Then we hit him later."

Verne rubbed the ring gently, turning it about his finger and making the ruby send out sparks of crimson. "The reason he would be satisfied with the ring, Jason, is because he knows that I will never remove this ring. *Never.* I gave my word many, many years ago to one who meant more than life itself to me that I would wear her ring until the final death claimed me." He looked up; his eyes were black ice, cold and hard. "I value my honor, Jason. Nothing, not even God himself, shall compel me to break my word."

"That's asinine, Verne! We're talking Sylvie's life here, and you're worried about honor! Whoever your lady was, I'm sure she'd understand!"

"You are probably right," Verne said, his eyes unchanged. "But I cannot decide on the basis of what might be. She and she alone could release me from my vow, and unless she is born again and regains that which she was, she cannot. I do not expect you to understand; honor is not valued here as it was when I was young."

"Where is the honor in letting a friend die?" I hurled the question at him.

He closed his eyes, drew one of his rare deep breaths. "There is none in that, my friend. I have no intention of letting Sylvia be killed; did I not also give my word that she would not die?" He opened one of my drawers, looked inside.

"Then you are going to give me the ring," I said, relieved.

"No," he said, taking something out of the drawer and handing it to me. "You will take it from me."

I looked down. In my hand was a magazine loaded with wooden bullets for my automatic; a vampire special.

It took a minute for that to sink in. Then I threw the magazine against the wall so hard it left a dent. "Christ, no! Kill you?"

"It seems the only way. I would rather die by your hand than his, and only my death will satisfy him; else Sylvia dies."

"Look," I said, glancing back at the pistol magazine, "maybe if... well, I could shoot your finger off, I guess."

He made the dismissing gesture I'd come to know so well. "Impossible. It matters not how the ring leaves my possession. My word will still have been broken if it leaves my possession with my connivance and I yet live."

I couldn't believe this. "You want to die?"

"Of course not, Jason! I have spent many centuries trying to ensure my safety. But I will not break my word to her whose ring I wear, nor shall I break my word to you. That leaves me little choice."

"Bull!" I didn't understand this; how the hell could someone take a promise *that* seriously? But I could see he was deadly serious. "You only made that promise to make me feel better. Forget it, okay? I release you from that obligation. Whatever the formula is. You know as well as I do that Virigar has no intention of letting *any* of us go. For all I know, he's got a hit squad waiting outside."

He relaxed slightly. "I thank you, my friend. Yes, I also doubt Virigar's benign intent, but I had to make the offer. None of you would be imperiled were I not here... and were you not my friends."

"Bull," I said again. "Maybe we wouldn't be on today's hit list, but we'd sure as hell be on tomorrow's menu." I looked at him again. "Is this the same Verne Domingo who sent me out to take on Elias Klein with nothing more than a mental shield and moral support?"

For the first time, I saw his features soften, and for once, his smile held nothing unsettling. "No, my friend. For you are my friend now. I have had no true friends, save those in my household, since... well, since before your country was born. In the past few months, you have shown me what a precious thing I was missing. More; you have given back to me the faith I lost, oh . . . more centuries ago than I care to remember. That, Jason, is a debt I shall be long in repaying."

I couldn't think of anything to say; I guess I didn't need to.

As quickly as it had come, Verne's gentle expression faded and his face returned to its usual aristocratic detachment. "We are agreed that Virigar's offer is without honor; thus we cannot follow that course of action. So what do you suggest?"

I stared at the ring again. "Well, even if he isn't trustworthy, if I *did* deliver the ring it might give us *some* advantage."

"I have already explained to you that I cannot—"

"I know that," I said, cutting off his protest. "I'm not saying take it off."

"Then what do you mean?"

"For guys as rich as you, jewelers make house calls. Surely one could make a duplicate in a few hours?"

That stopped him. He looked very thoughtful for several minutes, but then shook his head. "I'm afraid it would never work. The time element aside—and we would be cutting it extremely close—you are underestimating Virigar. He would undoubtedly check the authenticity of the ring; I would not be surprised if he were himself an expert in jewelry. Moreover, we have no way of ascertaining if he has watchers about our residences; a visiting jeweler would tell him all he needed to know." He shrugged. "In any case, it is irrelevant. He would know that ring in an instant, for it is more than mere jewelry."

"Seriously, Verne, could he really spare that many to watch us? I mean, we killed one and injured another; how many more could there be?"

He gave me a look reserved for idiots. "You are the expert in mathematics, my friend. Calculate how many descendants a single pair could have in one hundred years, assuming a twenty-year maturity age."

I winced. "Sorry, so I'm slow. That'd be eighty from the original pair alone that'd be full-grown."

"That, of course," Verne admitted, "assumes that they maintain normal human birthrates and take no 'breaks,' so to speak, from parenting. In reality, this will not be the case, but even so, I would be surprised if there were less than a hundred all told."

A hundred! Christ! I didn't even have that many silver bullets! "Outnumbered and outgunned..." Suddenly, one of my favorite, if crazy, quotes came to mind: "It's you and me against the world... When do we *attack*?"

I put the viewer's headband on, fitted the straps, then took it off and packed it carefully in a foam-lined bag. "We're both targets as it is; the only chance we have is to attack. Get him off-balance, surprise the crap out of him. I've got to hope that one of the gadgets I've got can spot the buggers; I'm going to get to the hospital and protect Syl."

"And I...?"

I grinned nastily, remembering what Verne had done to a drug lord's estate and his thugs. I pulled out another drawer and handed him the rings inside. "All silver rings. I got them because I liked the look of them but I never wear any of them. You are going to put those on and go down and beat Virigar's door in. Any werewolf that jumps at you then, just give him a left hook and keep going."

He put the rings on slowly. "I cannot enter a dwelling without permission of the residents, you remember."

"I didn't say enter; I said beat his door in... and his walls, and everything else. We have to disorganize him."

Now he smiled coldly, the fangs lending the right predatory look. "Precisely so. Shall we...?"

"After you."

We left by the back door; Mjölnir was parked in that alley.

I got into the car, locked the doors, and nodded to Verne. He faded into a cloud of mist, and then disappeared. I still stared at that; I don't think I'll ever get used to vampires. I started the engine, put Mjölnir in gear, began to pull out of the alley.

With a shuddering *thump*, a shaggy, glittering-fanged nightmare landed on the car's hood. The car jolted to a stop; in my mirror, I could see the werewolf that had grabbed the rear bumper and lifted the wheels clear of the ground. I swear my heart stopped for a second; then it gave a huge leap and tried to pound its way out of my chest. I yanked the gun out and pointed it at the one on the hood; the glass was bulletproof, but hopefully it didn't know that.

It didn't; the werewolf rolled off the hood and to the side. I shoved the pistol into the gunport the previous owner had thoughtfully installed and fired twice. Neither shot hit the beast, but it must've decided that retreat was a good idea. I hit the hidden release and part of the dashboard flopped out and locked, revealing the small control panel. As the one in back began to yank harder on the bumper, trying to tip the car over, I pressed the second button.

Mjölnir's engine revs rose to a thundering shriek as the nitro supercharger kicked in. Blue flame shot two feet from the tailpipe, and what I'd hoped for happened: the werewolf, in startlement and pain, dropped the bumper.

I mashed the pedal to the floor. The V8-318 engine spun the wheels, throwing rubber smoke in the things' faces, and Mjölnir hurtled onto the street. By the time I passed Denny's, I was doing fifty. A glance in the rearview almost made me lose control; three hairy killers were in hot pursuit, and they were closing in!

I searched the panel for any other tricks I might play, wishing I had James Bond's armamentarium...or even Maxwell Smart's. I triggered the rear spotlight, blinding them momentarily and gaining maybe a hundred feet before they recovered.

Mjölnir shuddered as I hit a series of potholes at sixty-two miles per hour. I wrenched the wheel around, skidded onto the interstate entrance ramp. Behind me, I could see my pursuers catching up fast. On the straightaway, I hammered the gas again, watched the speedometer climb towards triple digits. I heard myself talking: "That's right, come on, come on you little bastards, let's see how fast you really are!"

At seventy-five, they started to fall back; the largest made a final desperate dive and hooked onto the rear bumper. I tried to bounce it off by running off and on the shoulder, but the creature just snarled and held on tighter. It started to claw its way up the back.

If Mjölnir had been an ordinary car, those crystal claws would've torn straight through and the thing would've climbed right into my lap. Instead, its talons made long gouges in the armor but failed to get any real purchase as I swerved the car back and forth. The werewolf scrabbled desperately at the trunk, but there was nothing for it to grab. With an indignant glare, it pitched off the rear bumper and somersaulted to a defeated halt. I gave it a salute with my middle finger as it disappeared in the darkness. Then I turned down an off-ramp and headed Mjölnir towards St. Michael's Hospital.

CHAPTER 29

Intensive Combat Unit

The hospital was quiet; at three-thirty, only the emergency crews were around. I parked, checked my gun, and put the viewer on. I looked weird but that didn't worry me; the only thing that concerned me was that the werewolves could hide from anything technology could think up. I didn't believe that . . . but what if I was wrong?

I went in through the side entrance. I got some strange looks but no one asked me what I was doing. I've noticed that if you look like you know where you're going, people don't ask questions. And once you get past them, they're too embarrassed by their hesitation to go after you.

I got to the fifth floor, where the ICU was set up. Outside sat a familiar figure.

Renee raised her head, looked, and then looked again, a startled expression on her face. Then she smiled. "Hello, Wood. I thought you'd be home getting some shut-eye."

"I thought the same about you. Why are you here?"

"Winthrope and I both agreed that Sylvie should have some kind of watch over her. I took this shift." Renee glanced inside; Sylvie was sleeping. Renee turned back to me. "What the hell is that on your head?"

"An idea that doesn't seem to be working out." I'd looked through it at everyone I'd passed, and even glanced at the patients. I could tell when someone had a fever, but if there were any werewolves around, the viewer didn't spot them. I looked at the magnetic indicator and the radio meter; neither showed anything helpful. Hell, with the MRI unit in this building, likely neither one would pick up anything.

"Well, it's been quiet as hell here. You might as well go home. I'll call you if there's any change." She gave my shoulder a tentative pat.

I noticed a movement behind her.

Sylvie opened her eyes suddenly. She turned her head weakly towards me; her eyes widened, and it felt like icewater was running down my spine as I saw her face—her "feeling" face.

I nodded my head sharply; the viewer dropped down, and I looked through it.

Renee Reisman's face sparkled in infrared, a network of tiny sparks and lines rippling across it.

Everything froze. I had never looked at anyone through the viewer at this range. What I was seeing could simply be what moving muscle looked like close up. If I was wrong, I'd be killing a police lieutenant and a friend.

But if I was right . . .

It only seemed to take a long time; my body made the decision even as I glanced down. Before I was sure what I should do, I had fired the ten-millimeter twice.

Renee staggered back, shock written on every line of her face, and I realized I'd made a horrible mistake—it wasn't a werewolf at all! I started forward . . . just as claws and fangs sprouted like deadly weeds from her twisting form. But the werewolf was dead even as it lunged for me; only one claw caught me, leaving a thin red trail across my left cheek.

Screams and shouts echoed through the hospital. Three figures appeared around the corner. When they saw my gun, they dodged back. "Who are you?" one called out. "What do you want? This is a hospital, for Christ's sake!"

"I'm not here to hurt anyone," I said and then realized how utterly asinine that sounded coming from a man holding a pistol in front of the ICU. "I'm just trying to protect my friend in here." I could imagine their thoughts: a homicidal paranoid is holding ICU patients as hostages.

"Look," said one, very quietly, reasonably, "I'm going to just step around the corner, okay? I just want to talk with you, is that all right?"

I heard another voice mutter something in a heated undertone; it sounded like: "Are you nuts? Don't do it!"

"Sure," I said. "Just do it slowly."

A young orderly, my age or a little younger, eased carefully around the corner. His hands were raised. "See, I'm not going to hurt you."

"I know what you're thinking, but I'm not crazy." I gestured to the body. "Just look at that; you'll see what I'm up against."

He walked forward slowly, hands over his head. As he got closer, the viewer image started to sparkle.

"Hold it right there. You're one of them."

The expression of sudden terror, the pleading look—they were perfect and caused me another stab of doubt.

The claws nearly took my head off before I fired. The werewolf howled in agony and died quickly. I saw two pairs of eyes staring widely in shock as the creature that had been playing their friend expired.

"Friggin' *Nightmare on Elm Street*, man! What is going down here?"

"Werewolves," I answered, "and if you're smart, you'll get out of the hospital."

"I'm history," one said. "But I've gotta go through where you are."

"If you aren't one of them, go ahead. Otherwise you'll be number one with a bullet."

He had more guts than I would have. He walked out, crossed the hallway to the closest door, and started down the stairs. Another followed, his hands up, and bolted down the stairs.

Just then, I heard a window shatter. A tall blond man, rather like a young Robert Redford, dropped lithely into the hall from outside. He straightened and looked at me. "You are most extraordinarily annoying, Mr. Wood. I have been considering how best to kill you." The deep, warm, yet strangely resonant voice was chillingly familiar.

I raised the pistol, centered it on his jacket. "Virigar, I presume."

He bowed. "At your service."

If Virigar was here... God, had he already killed Verne? "What are you doing here? I thought—"

"Yes, you *thought* I would be at the warehouse." For a moment, the good-humored mask dropped. My blood froze at the sheer malevolence in his face. Had he attacked then, I couldn't have moved a muscle to stop him. "In point of fact, I was. Then that thrice-damned vampire began his attack and I knew precisely what you had planned. I also believe in keeping my word, so I came to make sure the young lady was killed." He glanced around at the two bodies. "A wise choice, it would seem."

He inclined his head. "You have been lucky and resourceful so far. I look forward to tasting your soul; it should be a strong and, ah, heady vintage. Then I will finish with Domingo. Your interference has been really quite intolerable."

"Aren't you overlooking something?" I asked.

"Such as ... ?"

"The fact that I'm going to blow you away in the next two steps?"

He laughed. "I doubt you could hit me. I am not one of these younglings."

I wasn't going to dick around with him. Before he could react, I put three shots in the bullseye where most people keep their hearts.

His eyes flew open wide. He stared at me, then down at the three neat holes in his suit. He sank to his knees, muttered something like, "Impressive aim ..." Then his eyes rolled and he fell.

I waited a few minutes, keeping the gun on him; he didn't move. I went forward a few feet just to check.

Something hit my hand so hard it went numb, picked me up and hurled me down the hallway. I fetched up against the far wall, disoriented. When I could focus my eyes, I saw Virigar standing there with my gun dangling from his hand. Grinning pleasantly, he shrugged off his coat, revealing the bullet-proof vest beneath.

"I should have blown your head off." I shook my hand, trying to get feeling back into it.

He nodded cheerfully. "Yes indeed, but I depended both on myth and training. The myth of three silver bullets to the heart for a Great Werewolf, and the fact that most people are taught to shoot for the body rather than the smaller target of the head." He tossed the gun aside. "Your friend Renee lasted for a few minutes, Mr. Wood. Let us see how well you do."

He began to change. I froze. I had seen another werewolf change ... but this was not just another werewolf.

This was Virigar.

This was no transformation like a morphing—it was more: a manifestation of the truth behind the facade. The air thickened and condensed, becoming black-brown shaggy fur. Virigar's eyes blazed with ravenous malevolence, flickering between blood red and poisonous yellow. His head reared up, seven feet, eight, nine towering, hideous feet above the floor, the marble sheeting cracking and spitting powder from the energies that crackled about Virigar like black lightning. It drew a breath and roared, a shrieking, bellowing, rumbling impossible sound that shattered every remaining window on the floor and deafened me. The head wasn't really wolflike...wasn't like anything that had ever lived. It was dominated by the terrible mouth, opening to a cavernous diameter, unhinging like a snake's, wide enough to sever a man in one bite, armed with impossibly long, sparkling diamond fangs like an array of razor-sharp knives...

For a moment, all thought fled; all I had was terror. I ran.

Virigar let me get some distance before he began following. I remembered what Verne had told me: they fed on fear. Obviously, Virigar wanted a square meal. I ran down the steps, taking them two, three at a time...but I could hear his clawed footsteps closing in on me.

I remembered a trick I'd first read about in the Stainless Steel Rat series. If I could do it, I might gain a few seconds.

I jumped as I reached the next flight of stairs and hit them sideways, one foot raised above and behind the other, both slightly tilted. My ankles protested as the stairs hammered underneath me like a giant washboard. I hit the landing, spun, and repeated it, then banged out the doorway, sprinted down the hall, ignoring the ache in my feet. *It worked!*

My heart jumped in panic as Virigar smashed out of the stairwell fifty feet behind me, the metal fire door tearing from its hinges and embedding in the opposite wall. Nurses and orderlies scattered before us, screaming. *Oh, the bastard must be gorging himself now.*

Somewhere in the distance, I thought I heard gunshots. Too far away to make any difference now though...

Around the corner, trying to find another stairwell. Oh, Christ, I'd found the pediatric wing!

A young girl with dark hair in two ponytails blinked bright blue eyes at me in surprise as I raced past her wheelchair, her attention on her late-night sundae momentarily distracted. With horror I recognized her: Star Hashima, Sky's daughter, just recovering from double surgery. Virigar skidded around the corner after me, growling in a grotesquely cheerful way. I faltered momentarily, realizing that the monster was already trailing blood; he wouldn't hesitate to kill again.

Her face paled, but at the same time I could swear there was an almost *interested* expression in her face as she saw the huge thing bearing down on her. Star calmly and accurately pitched her sundae into the King Wolf's face.

The laughter in its growl transformed instantly into startled rage and agony; blinded, Virigar stumbled and cannonballed into a wall, smashing a hole halfway through and clawing at his face. Star spun her chair around and rolled into one of the rooms, slamming the door behind her.

Virigar roared again, shaking the floor. "*Bitch!* I'll have your *soul* for that!"

I ran, praying this was the right decision. Would Virigar waste time taking care of Star right now, or would he chase me first because of what I knew? And what in the name of God had that girl *done*? As I half-ran, half-fell down the back stairs, I suddenly recalled a faint sparkle from the ice-cream bowl. Silver-coated decorations.

No, Virigar couldn't afford to waste time now. If I got out to Mjölnir, I could draw him off, outrun him probably, and then too many people would know too much. I shoved open a door, ran out.

Oh no. I'd come down one floor too many. This was the basement! Ammonia and other chemical smells from the labs filled the air. Above me, I heard the stairwell door smash open.

I ran.

Technicians and maintenance workers gaped at me. Signs flashed by: Hematology, Micro Lab, Urinalysis, Radiology...

At Radiology, I screeched to a halt, dove inside. A last-chance plan was forming. Behind me, screams sounded as Virigar charged after me.

I shoved the technician there aside. "Get the hell out of here!"

Hearing the screams, and the approaching snarls, the tech didn't argue. I ducked into the next room, grabbing a bucket that stood nearby, slammed and locked the door. I worked fast.

Heavy breathing suddenly sounded from the other side of the door. "Dear me, Jason; you seem to have cornered yourself."

I didn't have to fake terror; I knew my chances were hanging by a thread.

The door disappeared, ripped to splinters. "It's over, Mr. Wood!" Virigar leapt for me.

That leap almost finished me, but the door had slowed him just enough. With all the strength in my arms, I slung the contents of the pail straight into Virigar's open mouth. The sharp-smelling liquid splashed down the monster's throat, over his face, across his body, soaking the fur. Even as that pailful struck, I was plunging the bucket into the tank for a second load.

Virigar bellowed, a ragged-sounding gurgling noise of equal parts incredulity and agony. He was still moving too fast to stop; one shaggy arm brushed me as I leapt aside and he smashed into the tank itself, tripping and falling to his knees, one arm plunging into the liquid. The metal bent, but then tore as he scrambled blindly and disgorged the tank's remaining contents in a wave across his thighs and lower legs. Behind him, I doused him with my second pailful, soaking him from head to toe.

The Werewolf King's second scream was a steam-whistle shriek that pierced my head, but lacked the awesome force of the roar that had shivered hospital windows to splinters. Foul vapors like smoke were pouring from him, obscuring the hideous bubbling, dissolving effects the liquid was causing. The monstrous form staggered past me, mewling and screaming. Incredibly, I felt the earth itself heave as Virigar wailed wetly, and a flash of yellow-green light followed. Lamplight poured in through a ragged gap in the far wall and was momentary eclipsed by the horrific silhouette of something half-eaten as Virigar clawed his way to the outside...and disappeared into the night.

Slowly, a small dot of light approached. The beam of a flashlight found me, then the tank, which had been broken into pieces, leaving its sharp-smelling contents flowing harmlessly across the floor. The light showed me the way out, its beam illuminating the wall just enough to show the sign painted there:

X-RAY

DEVELOPER, FIXER, SILVER RECOVERY

CHAPTER 30

Endings and Beginnings

Winthrope waved me past the yellow barricade. I pulled up another one hundred fifty feet, got out, and went around to help Sylvie into the wheelchair. She still looked pale and weak, but it was good to see her out and moving. She smiled at me, then looked up and gave a little gasp. "Verne did *that*?"

I felt as awed as she looked. The hundred-foot-long, three-story warehouse was nothing more than a pile of charred boards and twisted steel, still smoking after several days. The last rays of the setting sun covered it with a cast of blood. From the tangled mass of wreckage, two I-beams jutted up, corroded fangs, mute testimony to the power of an ancient vampire's fury.

"You still haven't heard from him, have you?"

"No. It's hard to believe, but . . . there were dozens of them in there. Winthrope's still finding bodies. They must've gotten him somehow, maybe by sheer numbers." I felt stinging in my eyes, blinked it away. "And Renee . . ." This time I couldn't blink away the tears. Syl said nothing, just held my hand.

It was hard to believe I'd never see her again. Renee had been found in her house, her body in a chair and her head on the table in front of her.

"I'm so sorry," Syl said finally. "When I looked over and saw her, I knew it wasn't her at all. What about Star?"

"I got to see her the next day. She made me promise not to say anything about her helping me; her dad was already throwing a fit that she'd even been in the hospital when it happened. She thinks her father is the greatest thing in the world and doesn't want to worry him. I just hope she'll be all right. It was quick thinking on her part, but I don't believe any kid that age could see that monster coming and not have nightmares from it."

Syl started to say something, but suddenly choked off; her hand gripped my arm painfully. I turned quickly.

A man was standing next to Syl. He looked at me.

I knew that face, with the dark eyebrows, crooked grin, streaky-blond hair, and green eyes. I should know it; it looked at me every day in my mirror.

I went for my gun, found to my surprise that it wasn't there. The man before me smiled, his face shifting to the Robert Redford lookalike I remembered all too well. He held up his hand with my gun in it.

"Good evening, Mr. Wood. I believe we have some unfinished business."

"Never mind the dramatics," I choked out, hoping he'd prolong them. "Finish your business, then. Nothing much I can do."

"Dear me. No respect for tradition? I must congratulate you; I haven't been hurt that badly in centuries. Even our mutual acquaintance, Verne, failed to injure me as grievously. Why, I'm genuinely weakened. A clever, clever improvisation, Mr. Wood. I'm minded to let you live for a while."

I blinked. "Umm...thanks. But why?"

The urbane smile shifted to a psychotic snarl. "So you will suffer all the more while everything you value is destroyed before your very eyes!"

I read the intention in his eyes and leapt hopelessly for his arm; he tossed me aside like a doll. His hand came up and the fingers lengthened, changed to diamond-glittering blades. Sylvie stared upward, immobile with terror.

Something *smashed* into Virigar, an impact that flung him a hundred feet to smack with an echoing *clang* into one of the two standing girders. The girder bent nearly double.

Virigar snarled in an unknown tongue. "Who dares..."

"I dare, Virigar. Will you try me, now that I am prepared?"

Between us, in a streaming black cloak, stood a tall figure that seemed to have materialized from the gathering shadows of night.

"*Verne!*" I heard Sylvie gasp.

Virigar snarled, wrenching himself from the girder. Then he stopped, straightened, and laughed. "Very well! Far be it from me to argue points with Destiny." He bowed to Verne, who made no sign of acknowledgment. "You have won a battle against me, Mr. Wood. And your friend here has surprised me. This game is yours. Your souls are still mine, and shall be claimed in time. But for now, I shall leave you. One day, I shall return. But no other of my people shall touch you, for that which is claimed for the King is death for any other who would dare to take it." He turned and began to stride off.

"Freeze! Hold it right there!" Jeri Winthrope had the Werewolf King in her gunsights, and I had no doubt that, this time, the gun was loaded with silver bullets. Even with the cast on her arm, I was sure she wouldn't miss.

Virigar turned his head slightly, but he ignored Jeri and looked at Verne. "My patience is being tried. Tell the child to put her weapon away now."

"Do it," Verne said.

Jeri glanced at him, startled. "But—"

"*Do it!*" Verne's voice was filled with a mixture of loathing, fury, and a touch of fear.

Slowly, Winthrope lowered her gun. Virigar smiled, though the expression was barely visible. "Wiser than I thought. Until later." He turned the corner around a large chunk of warehouse.

"Why?" Jeri demanded after a moment of silence. "I had him right there!"

Verne glared at her. "Think you that something as ancient as he didn't know of your approach? I heard you as soon as you turned from your post. Your bullet would never have found its mark, and he would have killed us all. Even the fact that he spared us was a whim. Something to *amuse* him," Verne spat the word out as though he could barely tolerate the taste, "until he devises an artistic way to destroy us."

"I thought," I said, "he spared us because he wasn't sure he could win against us."

Verne shook his head. "If he appeared here, he was ready. Perhaps I could have defeated him." I noticed that he didn't say "we." "But I believe he left because..." Verne seemed to be searching for the proper way to describe something "...because he had 'lost the game,' as he himself put it. This battle, even your injuring him, was to him nothing more than a game. The object was vengeance against me, and then against you once you became an impediment of note. But we managed to meet some...

standard he set for his opposition. You injured him; I reappeared from the dead. He is as immortal as I, and older; he must find his own amusement where he can. But where I find mine in the elegance of art, in friendship, in more ordinary games, he finds his in the dance of destruction and death, in evil versus good." Verne shuddered, a movement so uncharacteristic of him that it sent chills down my spine. "Perhaps I could have defeated him," he repeated softly. "But I very much wish never to find out."

Jeri shrugged. "Not my problem now. Okay. We'll talk later." She walked off.

I grasped Verne's hand, realizing how much it would have meant to lose him, especially after having just lost Renee. "Jesus, it's good to see you. We thought you were dead!"

"Hardly, my friend." He looked even stronger, more assured and powerful than he had ever been. "Though not for want of trying on their part, I assure you. How does it feel to have changed the world?"

Sylvie spoke up. "Verne, pardon me, but I don't understand why any of them died in there. I thought—"

"That only silver could harm them? Quite so, my lady." He gazed at the wreckage. "Once I knew the werewolves had returned, I laid in a supply of diverse forms of silver—although I must confess," he bowed slightly to me, "it never occurred to me that *preparations*—compounds—of silver would be efficacious as well. Part of my armament was a large supply of silver dust, which I hurled into the warehouse from several different points with sufficient force so as to disperse it throughout the interior rather like a gas."

I winced at the mental picture. "Instant asthma attack. Ugh."

"Precisely. In addition, since nearly all surfaces then had silver upon them, even falling beams became capable of causing harm."

"That still doesn't explain where you've been the past few days."

"Ah, yes." He looked somewhat embarrassed. "Well, in the end, the battle degenerated so that I was reduced to physical confrontation. By the time the last of them came for me, I found myself without silver of any kind. Your rings, I am afraid, were not meant for combat. They...ah...came apart. So when the last one attacked, I was unarmed against her great natural weaponry. I was thus forced to a course of action the results of which I could not foresee."

"Well?" I said when he hesitated.

He coughed and examined the ruby ring studiously. "I . . . drained her."

"You mean you bit her? But you said that was fatal!"

He nodded. "Other vampires had tried it; they all died along with their intended prey. I found out why." He shook his head slowly. "The power was . . . incredible. No younger vampire could have survived it."

I thought about that for a moment. "Then, in a way, you also drain souls?"

"Yes and no. There is usually a link and exchange of energies. However, in the case of something like combat, it can become a direct drain, and against a werewolf or something of similar nature, it must be. As it was, my body fell into what you would call a coma for several days as my system adjusted. I was fortunate; we were underground in one of these abandoned buildings' basements. Had that not been the case, I would have faced the irony of dying in sunshine on the morning of my triumph. But survive I did, and I find that I am stronger for it." He smiled, the predatory grin of the hunter. "It is fitting that their attempt to destroy me would only strengthen me; it is . . . justice."

We nodded, then Sylvie spoke. "What did you mean when you said Jason had changed the world?"

"Is it not obvious, my lady?" He gestured at the lights of the city, silhouetted against the darkening sky. "For centuries, humanity has wondered if there were others out there, beyond the sky; but always they were secure in their science and civilization, knowing that here, at least, they ruled supreme. The Others—vampires, werewolves, and so on—hid themselves away, not to be found by scientists who sought to chart the limits of reality, and so became known as legend, myth, tales to frighten children and nothing more. On this world, at least, humanity knew that it was the sole and total ruler of all they could survey.

"But now, they know that is not true; that other beings walk among them. And this is not one of their stories, a book to be read and then closed, to disappear with the morning light." Verne shot a glance at me. "You recall, my friend, how you spoke about the horror stories, the Kings and Straubs and Koontzes?"

I thought for a moment, then I remembered the conversation he meant. "I think I see."

"Yes. You were disturbed by their stories showing such titanic struggles, and yet no subsequent stories ever referred to them; as though such power could ever be concealed. But this is the true world. The genie cannot be replaced in the bottle. Even your government has realized the futility of a coverup. Winthrope speaks on the news of these events to an incredulous nation, and scientists gather to study that which is left. The world changes; we have changed it. For good or ill, the world shall never be the same."

He fell quiet, and we gazed upward; watching as the stars began to spread—like silver dust—across the sky.

Part IV

Viewed in a Harsh Light

June 2000

CHAPTER 31

Presentations in High Places

"This is ridiculous," I said. "Considering that werewolves weren't even seriously considered to *exist* until a few weeks ago, how exactly would it be 'obvious for anyone skilled in the art' to combine these elements to detect a werewolf?"

"Hey, I'm on your side, remember?" my patent attorney, John Huffman, said. "The examiner's pointing to prior art that involves combining infrared and visible to detect living creatures and discriminate them from non-living objects. The argument is that anyone presented with the existence of werewolves and who was skilled in the art would have tried the same thing."

I snorted. "So what are our options?"

"Well, we can try to modify the claims slightly to include some of the dependent claims; he indicates some of the other work might be innovative."

"I'm not weakening this basic patent. What's the other option?"

"We have to file a formal challenge of his evaluation, specifically obviousness. That's going to be an uphill battle, though."

"I've fought uphill battles before; I'm not backing down on this one. It was *not* 'obvious.' I had to get information about them—from sources most people wouldn't have—and make shrewd deductions or wild-ass guesses, depending on how you look at it, to come up with that design. Either way, it's not 'obvious.'"

He grinned. "I agree. And to be honest, I don't get to try this kind of fight very often."

I saw a blinking light on my desktop monitor. "Okay, John, thanks. Sorry to cut you off, but I've got to go catch a plane."

✧　　✧　　✧

I wasn't unfamiliar with flying, but the VIP treatment—and the fact that someone else was footing the bill—made this flight a little more pleasant. I was disconcerted, however, by seeing a mob of reporters waiting at the gate when I deplaned. *I was able to dodge them in Albany—I know the right people—but no chance here.*

I ignored the barrage of questions, which ranged from the inanely obvious "Are you here for the Werewolf Hearings?" to one guy from one of the fringe outlets asking if I'd heard anything from the Vampire Council, and made my way past them.

Three men in suits seemed to materialize from the crowd; two of them flanked me and slowed the pursuit of the press as the third nodded to me and said, "Mr. Wood? Please follow me. We've got a car waiting."

"I kinda assumed you would. Good coordination with your friends there, Mr. . . . ?"

"Special Agent Colin Marsh," he said, guiding me through the maze of the airport. "Thanks. I approve of the free press, I just wish they'd be free where it didn't hold up traffic." He glanced at me. "Of course, if you kept a lower profile . . ."

I shrugged. "I guess I *could* turn down large sums of money for television appearances to tell people about something that's totally blown their minds, but while I wasn't ever *broke* before, I wasn't rich, either."

"Can't say I blame you," he conceded.

The waiting vehicle was a classic black limousine—though not quite as posh as one of Verne's—that pulled away from the curb smoothly with only a purring hum of the engine. "So, we're headed to the Capitol?"

"Not really," said one of the others. "Agent Jake Finn, Mr. Wood."

"Glad to meet you, Agent Finn. But I thought—"

"Oh, the public info says that's where the meeting is, and we're sure letting it *look* that way, but completely securing the Capitol Building the way it is? That's a bitch and a half—sorry for the language—and it'd really interfere with other operations. So we're actually meeting somewhere else."

That made sense. "So, we'll appear to drive to the Capitol, but then, what, switch cars?"

He grinned. "Not that complicated. We can go into an

underground garage, then take an exit to a different street and continue on."

It was, in fact, that easy, and about fifteen minutes later, we pulled into another underground parking garage across the river in the Crystal City area near Alexandria. We then walked to one of several relatively nondescript-looking buildings and entered.

A security and guard post was set up just past the main entrance to prevent anyone from getting into the building proper without permission. A familiar face was waiting there. "Hey, Jeri."

Agent Jeri Winthrope nodded. "Mr. Wood, glad you made it. You'll have to go through the security screening before you go any farther, though."

I went towards the security archway, which looked like a metal detector. Three MPs stepped forward. Two aimed rifles directly at my head, one on either side. I noticed my escorts clear the line of fire. The third man stepped up. "Hold up your hands, Mr. Wood."

I blinked, but did so. Faced with rifles ready to blow your brains out encourages compliance with simple instructions. The MP took each hand, examined it carefully front and back and scraped it with something that looked like an emery board—it probably *was* an emery board—and then stepped back. "On your left and right, you will see a metal cylinder. Please pick up each cylinder and hold it tightly. It is *very* important that you make good contact with both cylinders, sir."

The way he said *very*, the way he now raised *his* weapon, and the way his companions each took a breath and steadied their stances, made me suspect that *I* was the one it was most important to.

The silver cylinders were each attached to a retractable cable that went into the booth walls. I grinned suddenly. "Oh, I get it. Very clever." I squeezed both tightly. "That should work, and be pretty hard to get around."

After about ten seconds, someone to the side gestured and the MPs moved to "at ease" stance. "All clear, sir. Welcome to the conference, Mr. Wood."

"Thanks," I said, not without some considerable relief. "So why that particular test, Jeri? I mean, you could've used some silver-based drops or something."

She gestured for me to follow. "Yes, we could have, but if

you add other substances to the mix, there's the chance of it reacting to those substances; exposure to the chemical mess you hit Virigar with would poison a human being anyway and potentially cause a rash. We wanted pure silver since there's no documented cases of allergic reaction to it—as opposed to silver alloy. That way, if the person holding it reacted at all, we could be pretty sure we had a wolf."

I nodded. "And the cables there mean you've got it hooked to something—resistivity, capacitance, something—that tells you whether the person's actually making contact with the metal. You use the emery board to take a sample and to scratch any coatings on the hands. Nice." I glanced back, made out the logo above the rear side of the booth. "Oh, of course. Shadowgard Tech. Smart outfit. It's a good stopgap, though you need something better in the long run. I can figure ways to scam this."

She grimaced. "You're kidding. That fast?"

"I've been thinking about this problem longer than anyone else. Maybe I'll give Shadowgard a call. I'll need someone with experience in the security industry to market my solution and if we improve their design a bit, it'll be a good supporting solution for mine." I looked at her. "Now, *everyone* who comes into the building goes through that procedure?"

"Including the people manning that barricade, yes."

I whistled. "And some of the people coming in here are awfully...high up, I'd bet. Caught any?"

She grimaced. "Three so far. Fortunately, after Morgantown, it looks like they're trying to be a *little* circumspect; all of the human beings they were duplicating are alive. A couple of the guards who were there when they were unmasked...weren't so lucky." She nodded to the guards at a set of double doors and ushered me in. "Still, it provided a *lot* of urgency to the meeting—"

"Especially," said a *very* familiar voice with a Texan twang, "since one of them was my friend Sal Battaglia, the Speaker of the House."

I stared for a moment. I'm not normally prone to stage fright, and I'd been interviewed a lot in the last couple of weeks, but this was something way out of my normal league. At the head of the meeting table was the President of the United States, Rexford Aisley Ash II, and seated near him were most of his cabinet, enough military men—some from other countries—that the room held, as a friend of mine might have put it, "More stars than Hollywood and more scrambled eggs than a truckstop diner."

Not being a military man, I didn't salute, but I did immediately approach the president. "A great honor to meet you, Mr. President."

His grip was firm but not too tight—a classic handclasp in the political world. "Oh, much more my honor, Mr. Wood. You've managed to turn this country more upside down than I have yet. Please, take your seat—it's down at the far end, opposite me."

As I did so, I realized everyone was continuing to look at me, and the president stood again. "Well, everyone, our guest of honor's here, and I'm sure we're all ready to hear what he has to say. Mr. Wood, you read the briefing materials?"

I swallowed and took a breath. *I thought I'd just be* one *person they were talking to, not the star of the darn show.* "Yes, sir. You're working on how we respond to a threat we never realized existed, and so you want me to give my views on the situation. I've prepared a presentation, and I can answer questions afterwards."

He nodded. "All right, then—let's get started."

I gave a quick summary of who I was—before all this mess, at least—and reviewed the events that led to what the papers and newscasts were calling "the Morgantown Incident." This was a careful blend of fact and fiction, but I was reasonably confident it would hold up because Jeri Winthrope had worked with me and Verne to make the story hold water a lot better than our previous vampire coverup.

"So," one of the military, a General Jean Bravaias, a woman with gray-streaked sandy hair, said after some questioning, "you were able to see these creatures? Sort them out from regular people by using this viewer you built, right? What's the range?"

I waggled my hand from side to side. "Hard to say, General. What little field experience I got showed that my jury-rigged gadget gave me fifteen, maybe twenty feet, but the real limit's a combination of imager resolution and sensitivity through atmosphere. I'd already *gotten* that particular infrared camera heavily customized for absolute minimum noise, so I don't know if you could really improve on it all that much. You're looking for patterns of heat that are very, very small in scale and intensity combined with some emissions on the UV band, but those are *really* small. Maybe thirty, thirty-five feet at the outside."

"Still," she said, "that's one hell of a lot better than what we've got now, which is somehow getting the target to be in contact with silver directly, then observing the reaction. If we don't have people right there, watching, a smart man—or ..." she hesitated "... werewolf, could figure out ways to *look* like they were carrying out the instructions and actually avoid it. But *with* people that close ... they get killed."

"Well," said another person—someone from the CIA, I thought, "couldn't we just give the guards better armor? I'd think—"

"Mr ..." I squinted "... Rosedale, have you ever actually *seen* a werewolf?"

"Well, I've seen the pictures, but ... no."

I looked around. "How many people here *have* actually seen one in person?"

Besides my hand and Jeri's, only one other hand went up out of fifty other people in the room. I guessed that was someone who'd been there when they caught one of the three trying to get into this building. "Then you—all of you—need to really get into your heads what you're dealing with." I reached into my bag and found the slender sheath, grasped what was inside carefully. "The average wolf—when not pretending to be human—stands eight feet high and weighs over five hundred pounds. As my experience shows, they are capable of sprinting at speeds in excess of sixty miles per hour—almost as fast as the fastest land animal known.

"As for armor," I continued, and with a practiced flick of my hand, sent something sparkling through the air to land with a *chunk!* in the conference table, "take a look at that."

Standing up at an angle from the shining wood of the table, vibrating slightly with a faint, chiming hum that was fading away, was a sparkling, transparent, curved form measuring nearly nine inches long. "*That* is one claw—a hand, I think—from an average werewolf. As you can see, I threw that thing very gently, just a flick of my wrist, and it buried itself about two inches into the hardwood of the table. I mentioned that my car is armored. After my encounter with Virigar, I found that the one that grabbed onto my car had cut nearly through the armor in four separate places. And this was with almost no chance to grab and establish purchase."

I clicked my presentation back to the sketch of a werewolf. "Unfortunately, I don't have any good *photos* of these things.

But I want you to look at that claw, then realize that these," I pointed to the claws on the sketch, "are what you're looking at. This is a creature that can outrace a car on anything except a straightaway, has claws that can cut like butter through almost anything, is strong enough to lift one end of an armored car clear off the ground, and that likely has other tricks it didn't show us.

"And they can transform themselves to look and act *exactly* like anyone else on Earth."

Faces were noticeably paler around the table. General Bravaias reached out and carefully pulled the claw free, studying it. "What is this thing *made* of?"

"We don't really know. It's something like diamond in that it's mostly carbon, but it doesn't shatter like diamond can. It's almost unbreakable, whether we're talking impacts, compression, tension, or torque. Right now, the guess is it's some form of carbon with an unknown microstructure, but exactly what that microstructure is we won't know until we get a detailed X-ray crystallographic scan on it. And even that might not work."

The general nodded, then passed the claw back down to me. "In any case, it is clear that we *really* need your sensing devices. Yes, I know that's slightly outside of this meeting's purpose—"

"Don't you worry about that, Jean," said the president. "This is definitely a high priority. Mr. Wood, I'd like to make sure our major installations are protected by these, er..."

"CryWolf sensors," I said with a grin. "That's the name I want to call them, anyway."

He laughed. "Let's hope they *don't* 'cry wolf' too often, huh? Anyway, I'd like to make sure that happens as soon as possible."

Hmm, that gives me an idea. "Well, sir, I'd be glad to give the government a license on the technology and all, but right now I'm getting held up in the patent office..."

CHAPTER 32

Upgrades and Relationships

"I must thank you, Jason," Verne said, surveying the mound of equipment assembled in his dining room. "The advice of an expert is always appreciated."

Verne had decided to fully enter the fast-approaching twenty-first century, adding telecommunications and computers to his formidable range of resources. I grinned. "No thanks needed. Advising someone on what to buy is always fun, especially when you know that the person in question doesn't have a limited budget." One of the workmen looked at me with a question in his eyes. "Oh, yeah. Verne, how many places are you going to want to be able to plug in a computer? I mean to the Ethernet lines." Extra jacks were a good idea; cable didn't yet run out to Verne's house, so we were going with a dedicated satellite hookup and a LAN on Ethernet through the house.

"Ah, yes. I would say...Hmm. Morgan?"

"Yes, sir?"

"Are any of the staff likely to need such access?"

Morgan smiled slightly. "I would say most of them, sir." While Verne was modernizing, he was not quite grasping the change it was going to bring to his household.

Verne sighed theatrically. "Very well, then." He turned to the workman. "You might as well rewire the entire house—first, second, and third floors—and put two of these Ethernet jacks in every bedroom and study, as well as one here in the living room," he pointed, "and another three in my office, marked there. Make sure there are also enough phone connections for everyone; several of my staff would like their own private lines."

Ed Sommer, the head contractor, smiled broadly, obviously thinking of the money involved, and glanced at the plans. "We'll write up a work order. What about the basement?"

"No need for anything there."

"Gotcha."

Sommer cut the work order quickly; I'd recommended his company because of their efficiency, despite the fact that they were the new kids on the block. Verne signed it, and we left the rest of the work in Morgan's hands. "Coming, Verne? Syl's out of town on a convention and I'm up for a game of chess if you're interested."

He hesitated, the light glinting off the ruby ring he never removed. "Perhaps tomorrow, Jason. Having all these strangers in the house is upsetting."

"Then get away from them for a while. Morgan can handle things here. Besides, how could anything upset *you*?" This was partly a reference to his vampire nature—I expected a man who's umpteen thousands of years old to be comfortable everywhere—but also to his constant old-world-calm approach, which was rarely disturbed by anything except major disasters.

"You may be right. Very well, Jason, let us go."

The night was still fairly young as we got into my new Infiniti. Verne nodded appreciatively. "Moving up a bit in the world, my friend?"

"The only advantage of being attacked by ancient werewolves is that the interview fees alone become impressive. And the publicity for WIS has made sure I've got more work than I can handle, even if I do have to turn down about a thousand screwballs a day who want me to investigate their alien abduction cases. Not to mention that the government groups involved in the Morgantown Incident investigation would rather use me as a researcher than an outsider." I gave a slightly sad smile. "And age, plus being hacked at by werewolves, finally caught up with old Mjölnir."

"He served you well. Have you named this one yet?"

"Nope. I was thinking of Hugin or Munin—it's black and shiny like raven feathers." We pulled out of his driveway and onto the main road into town. We drove for a few minutes in silence.

"I was not deliberately changing the subject," Verne said finally. "I understand how you would find it hard to imagine me being disturbed by anything. I was thinking about how to answer you."

I was momentarily confused, then remembered my earlier comment. At times, it was disconcerting to talk to Verne; his long life made time compress from his point of view, so a conversation that seemed distant to me was recent for him. Sometimes he forgot that the rest of us don't have his manner of thinking.

"You have to remember that one with my...peculiarities rarely can have an actual long-lasting home." Verne continued. "So instead, one attempts to bring one's life *with* one in each move. Rather like a hermit crab, we move from one shell to another, none of them actually being our own, yet being for that time, a place of safety. Anything that enters your house, then, has the ability to encroach on all those things you bring with you—both physical and spiritual. Workmen are things beyond my direct control, especially in a society such as this one."

"Are you afraid they'll find out about you?"

Verne shrugged, then smiled slightly, his large dark eyes twinkling momentarily in the lights of a passing car. "Not really. Besides the fact that Morgan would be unlikely to miss anyone trying to enter the basement, the basement itself contains little of value for those seeking the unusual. The entrance to the vault and my true *sanctum sanctorum* is hidden very carefully indeed, and it's quite difficult to open even if found. And my personal refrigerator upstairs is secured very carefully, as you know well." Verne referred to the fact that I'd installed the security there myself. "No, Jason. It is simply that my home is the last fading remnant of my own world, even if all that remains there are my memory and a few truly ancient relics. The mass entry of so many people of this world...somehow, it reminds me how alone I am."

I pulled into my new garage, built after werewolves nearly whacked me on the way to my car, and shut off the engine. "I understand. But now you're reaching out to this world, Verne. You're not alone. If something in your house concerns you, come to mine. I mean it. You were willing to die to protect me and Syl."

"And you revived my spirit, Jason. In a sense, I had let myself die a long time ago; only now am I becoming what I once was."

The kitchen was warm and well-lighted—I like leaving those lights on—and the aroma of baking Ten Spice Chicken filled the room. I was slightly embarrassed by Verne's words, but at the same time, I knew he meant them. Our first meeting had struck a long-dead chord in him and during our apocalyptic confrontation with Virigar, I'd discovered just how much he valued friendship...and how much I valued him. "I'd offer you dinner, but it's not quite to your taste."

"Indeed, though I assure you I appreciate both the thought and the scent. I may be unable to eat ordinary food without pain, but my sense of smell is undiminished. Do you still have some of my stock here?"

"Yep." I reached into the fridge and pitched him a bottle, which he caught easily. "I never imagined I would overlook a bottle of blood in my fridge any more than I would a can of beer." Sliding on a potholder, I reached into the oven and pulled out the chicken, which was coated in honey with a touch of Inner Beauty and worcestershire sauce, garlic, cilantro, pepper, cardamom, cumin, red pepper, oregano, basil, turmeric, and a pinch of saffron. I put that on the stovetop, pulled out two baked potatoes (crunchy the way I like 'em) and set the microwave to heat up the formerly frozen vegetables I'd put in before leaving for Verne's.

By the time I had my place set, my water glass filled, and the chicken and potatoes on the plate, the veggies were done and I sat down to eat. Verne had poured his scarlet meal into the crystal glass reserved for him and he sat across from me, dressed as one might expect a genteel vampire to dress: evening clothes, immaculately pressed, with a sharp contrast between the midnight black of his hair and jacket and the blinding white of his teeth and shirt.

"I haven't asked you lately—how's the art business going?"

Verne smiled. "Very well indeed. Expect an invitation from our friend Mr. Hashima in the mail soon, in fact; young Star is recovering nicely, and he will be having an exhibition in New York in a month or so."

"Great!" I said. "I'm looking forward to it. I was a bit concerned, to be honest—it seemed that he was hemming and hawing about doing anything with you for a while."

Verne nodded, momentarily pensive. "True. There were some oddities, some reluctance which I do not entirely understand... but it is none of our business, really. What is important is that he and I are now enjoying our work together." He leaned back. "In other related areas, I'm sure you saw the news about Akhenaten being returned to Egypt, but thus far the archaeological world is keeping the other treasures quiet while they're examining them. Most of the truly unique artworks are already elsewhere, and I confess to feeling quite some relief. As their custodian, it was something of a strain, I came to realize, to ensure their preservation along with my own whenever I was forced to move."

"You can't tell me you've emptied that vault?" I asked in surprise.

He laughed. "Hardly, my friend. There are pieces there I keep for beauty's sake alone, others for historical value, ones which are personally important, and so on. And even of those I would consider selling or donating there remain quite some number; it would be unwise for me to either flood the market or to eliminate one of my major reserves of wealth in case some disaster occurs."

I couldn't argue with that. "Let's hope there are no more disasters. I've had enough of 'em."

"To that, I can wholeheartedly agree."

We finished dinner and went to my living room, where I set up the chessboard. Playing chess was fun, but it was more an excuse for us to get together and talk. Neither Verne nor I were comfortable with just *talking*; we had to be *doing* something.

"So," I said after we began, "what did you mean about 'letting yourself die' a while back?"

Verne took a deep breath and moved his pawn. As I considered that position, he answered. "I should clarify something, which I should have done some time ago. I am not a vampire."

"Huh?"

"Or, perhaps, I should say not a vampire in any ordinary sense of the term. True, I drink blood and have a number of supernatural abilities and weaknesses. But these are not the result of being infected by a vampire. For me, my abilities are a blessing, a gift—not a curse. I am not driven by those impulses that 'traditional' vampires must follow."

"So why didn't you tell me this before?" I decided to continue with the standard opening strategy. Getting fancy with Verne usually resulted in my getting roundly trounced in fifteen or twenty moves. "It does explain a few things—I remember thinking that you seemed to hesitate at times when talking about vampires. But why dance around the subject?"

Verne smiled. "It was much easier to go with the obvious assumptions, Jason. And by doing so, I minimized the chance of anything being learned that I wished kept secret. And it was *much* simpler. The word 'vampire' can be applied to any one of several sorts of beings, not merely one, and—for the most basic purposes—calling me a 'vampire' was and, to some extent still is, sufficient to the moment." His smile faded. "Your friend Elias… he was of a type that typically go mad as they gain their power, until they have grown used to it. They were made in mockery of what I am."

"And what is that?"

He hesitated, not seeming to see the board. When he finally answered, his voice was softer, and touched with a faint musical accent unlike any I had heard. "A remnant of the greatest days of this world, my friend. In the ending of that time, I was wounded unto death, but I refused to die. I would *not* die, for there were those who needed me and I would not betray them by failing to reach them, even if that failure was through death itself.

"Perhaps there was something different about me even then, or it was something about the difference between the world that was and the world that is now for, certainly, I cannot have been the only man to ever attempt to hold Death at bay with pure will. I did not die; I rose and staggered onward only to find that my solitary triumph had been in vain." I heard echoes of pain and rage in his voice, tears he'd shed long ago still bringing a phantom stinging to the eye, a hoarseness to his words.

"Of those who had been my charges, none remained; and all was in ruins. But in the moment I would have despaired… *She* came." He moved again.

I could hear the capital "S" in "She" when he spoke. "*She?*"

"The Lady Herself." The accent was stronger now, and I was certain I'd never heard anything like it. Not even close to it. The accent was of a language whose very echoes were gone from this world. Then it was as though a door suddenly closed in his mind, for he glanced up quickly. When he spoke again, the accent was gone, replaced by the faint trace of Central European lilt I was used to. "I'm sorry, Jason. No more."

"Too painful?"

He looked at me narrowly, his eyes unfathomable. "Too dangerous."

"To you?"

"To you."

CHAPTER 33

Who's Your Daddy?

The man sitting across from me was small. Oriental, handsome (at least that's what Syl told me later; I'm not much of a judge), average-length hair just a bit shaggy. He was dressed casually, but that wasn't much indication of his job or resources; people come to WIS in guises that are different from what people normally see.

"Okay, Mr., um, Xiang—right?—okay, what can I help you with?"

Tai Lee Xiang shifted uncomfortably in his chair, obviously ill-at-ease. "I'm trying to locate someone."

Locate someone? That didn't sound particularly promising. There is some work that I do once in a while, but that I don't find interesting, such as locating old girlfriends, enemies, and so. "What kind of a someone?"

"My father."

Okay, that was more interesting, maybe. "Your father? Okay. How do you know he needs finding? A family argument?"

He shifted again, then stood up and began pacing in the small space available. "It's . . . hard to explain. I didn't have any argument with him. It's . . . I've just not seen him in a long time." His voice was heavily accented—Vietnamese, if what he told me was true—but the word "long" was clearly emphasized.

"Why do you need to find him?"

"Why do you need to know?" he countered, slightly annoyed.

"I don't *need* to know, as long as there's nothing illegal involved, but any information can help." I always toss in the word "illegal" with potential clients—it wasn't unusual for people to try using Wood's Information Service to get info they had no business getting.

He frowned at me, then shrugged. "I am new in this country, and he is my only living relative, aside from my children."

"Fair enough." This actually sounded interesting. Finding a man can be a relatively easy thing, or almost impossible, depending on how much information you have to go on. "I'll need to know everything you can tell me about your father. The more I know, the easier it will be to find him."

He looked somewhat embarrassed and uncomfortable again. "I...I can't tell you too much. I have...memory trouble."

"Amnesia?" I was surprised by this little twist.

"Um, yes, I think that's what they called it. I remember some things well, other things not so well."

This was getting interesting. "Okay. Can I ask why you chose WIS for this job?"

"I saw the reports on the werewolves..." he began. I already knew the rest; the "Morgantown Incident" was a great piece of advertisement. I was wrong.

"...and of all the investigators out there, only you seemed ready to search for someone...unusual."

I raised an eyebrow. "Are you telling me there's something out of the ordinary about your father?"

"Yes."

"Tell me."

Tai Lee looked at me. "I can't tell you any more unless you agree to take the job. You...seem like an honorable man, which means if you agree to do the job, you won't talk about it to other people if I don't want you to."

He had me pegged right. I thought a moment. "Nothing illegal involved in this job?"

"I know of nothing that would be illegal in finding my father, no."

"Very well, then. I agree. I'll find your father, if it's at all possible."

His nervous fidgeting subsided almost instantly and he visibly relaxed. "Thank you."

"So what can you tell me about your father? Skip the description for now—I've got a computer program we'll use later to construct the best picture. Tell me some facts I wouldn't gather from his appearance."

"That is where my memory is weak. I can only tell you five things about Father."

"Shoot."

"Excuse me?"

"That means, 'go ahead, let me have them.'"

"First, he is not my natural father. I was adopted. He is not of Oriental blood, but I think is a Westerner instead."

Well, that weakened one approach. Obviously, there'd be no link in appearance between father and son, and not necessarily one of immigration, either. "Next?"

"Father is a priest. Priest of ... um ... nature? I'm not sure the term ... ?"

This was interesting. "You mean of the Earth itself? Not Shinto or something of that nature?"

"Yes. The world's spirit?"

"Our word for that is generally 'Gaia.'"

"Yes! That is it." He nodded, recognizing the word. "Father also had a ring that he wore, which he would never remove."

"A ring?"

"A big, wide, heavy gold ring, with a very large red stone— a ruby I think—set in it."

I blinked for a moment. "O ... kay."

"Something wrong?"

"No, nothing. Go on."

He hesitated. "This is the ... weird part."

"I'm ready."

"No, I mean, really strange. Please believe me when I tell you this is not a joke, okay?"

I studied him carefully. "I believe you're not playing a joke on me. You seem too serious to be able to joke about it at all."

"Thank you." He had tensed up again; with my assurance he relaxed once more. "All right ... my father didn't eat; instead, he drank blood."

I stopped dead in mid-keystroke. What were the odds? Drinking *blood*? A red ruby ring that never came off?

Tai could tell I was shocked. "Mr. Wood?"

"What was the fifth thing?"

"What?"

"You just recounted four facts about your father. What's the fifth?"

"His name ... the name he was using then. His name was V'ierna Dhomienkha a Atla'a Alandar."

It was impossible. But it had *to be.* I stood up. "Excuse me for a minute; I'm going to check something."

"What? Mr. Wood, what is it?"

"I'll be back in a moment."

I stepped into the back office, grabbed the phone off the hook, and punched in Verne's number.

"Domingo Residence, Morgan speaking."

"Morgan, this is Jason. I need to speak with Verne."

Morgan's voice was puzzled. "But, Jason, you know that Master Verne is never awake at this time. It's barely two o'clock."

"Then wake him. This is important!"

There was a long pause—even longer to me, sitting on the other end of the phone waiting. Finally I heard the familiar voice pick up at the other end. "Jason? What is the emergency?" Tired though he was, what I heard most in his voice was worry. "It isn't the Wolf, is it?"

Jesus, I should have realized that was the first thing he'd think of. "No, no. Nothing that bad. Maybe...not bad...really...at all. There is a guy here looking for his father."

His tone was slightly nettled. "And how does this concern me?"

"Because of what he told me about his father: that he wore a ruby-colored crystal and gold ring, which he never took off, and that he drank blood."

There was dead silence for several moments. "Interesting coincidence to say the least, Jason. But I have no children."

"He said he wasn't a natural child of this man—he is adopted. He also said that his father was some kind of priest of nature, and he gave his father's name. I'm not sure quite how to spell it, but it sounded a lot like yours..."

In a whisper almost inaudible, I heard, "V'ierna Dhomienkha a Atla'a Alandar i Sh'ekatha..."

"Holy crap," I heard my own whisper.

"That name? He spoke *that* name? But...that is impossible." Verne's voice was at the edge of anger, laughter, or tears—I couldn't tell which—and hearing the strain in his voice was more upsetting than I'd imagined. "I am on my way, sun or no sun."

I hung up and stepped back into the office. Tai Lee Xiang looked up at me. "Mr. Wood?"

"If what you've told me is accurate, Mr. Xiang...I think I've located your father already."

As his jaw dropped, a chill wind blew through the closed office, and from my back room stepped Verne Domingo, dark eyes fixed on my visitor.

There was no recognition in Verne's eyes, but there was no doubt about Tai Lee's reaction. He leapt to his feet, eyes wide. "Father!"

Verne fixed him with a cold glare. "Who are you? Who, that you know that name unspoken for generations unnumbered, that you would claim to be son to me?" That alien accent was back and emphasized by his anger.

There was no mistaking the shocked, wounded look in Tai Lee Xiang's eyes. "Father? Don't you recognize me? The boy in the temple?"

Verne's mouth opened for a bitter retort, but with the last words, slowly closed. He stared at the young man intensely, as though he would burn a hole through him by gaze alone. I felt a faint power stir in the room. Then Verne's face went even paler than usual and he stepped forward, reaching out slowly to touch the young man's face. "The scent is wrong... but the soul. I know that soul. Is it really you, Raiakafan?"

Tai jerked as Verne spoke the name, as though slapped in the face, then nodded. "Y... yes. Yes. That was my name."

For the first time since I'd known him, Verne was too overcome to speak. He simply stepped forward, around the desk, and stared straight into the young man's eyes. "Even with what I feel... I must have proof. For you disappeared..."

Tai—Raiakafan?—looked at me, and suddenly I had a completely different impression of him. The uncertain, nervous young man was gone; instead, I saw a black, polished-stone gaze as cold as ebony. I found myself stepping backward involuntarily; only once before had I gotten the sense of such total lethality, and that had been in the hallway at the hospital when I witnessed Virigar assume his true form. That same feeling carried the utter conviction that Tai was not merely trained in the art of killing, but a killer to his very core. "In front of him?" he asked coldly.

I could see that Verne was surprised by the tone, but apparently not by the question. "It may be necessary later... but you are quite correct. We shall speak in private. But I would ask that you moderate your tone of address to one who is not only my friend, but who has reunited us."

The cold gaze softened abruptly and was replaced by an apologetic look. "I'm sorry, Father. You are right. Mr. Wood, forgive me. It has been a difficult time for me. But I am very grateful ... and amazed."

I shrugged. "Don't mention it. Not as much a coincidence as I first thought; anyone who was Verne's friend would have been around during the last dust-up. The only *real* coincidence is that one of those friends happens to be an info specialist. No," I said as I saw him reaching for a wallet, "no charge. Not only is Verne a friend, but I hardly had to do any work on this one."

"Still, I thank you, Jason," Verne said.

His hand on Tai's arm, the two disappeared into thin air. I jumped at that, but my mind was distracted by the fact that I'd seen a new and different sparkle in Verne's eyes.

Vampire tears are just like ours.

CHAPTER 34

Reunion Jitters

"Guess who!"

Two soft hands covered my eyes in time with the words. To my credit, I managed not to jump, though she probably knew how much she'd startled me anyway.

"Madame Blavatsky?"

She giggled. "Nope."

"Nostradamus?"

"Do you feel a beard against your neck? Try again!"

"Then it must be the great Medium of the Mohawk Valley herself, Sylvia Stake!"

The hands came away as I turned around.

"You guessed!"

"No one else has a key to this place, and Verne's voice is two octaves lower and his hands are five sizes bigger."

Sylvie was looking good this evening: her black hair was styled in tight ringlet curls pulled back by several colorful scarves, and she was wearing a low-cut dress with a long skirt—one of her gypsy outfits—and a big over-the-shoulder bag that was hand-woven with enough colors to supply a dozen rainbows. "Oh, is *that* the only difference?" she said, leaning forward.

Sylvie makes me nervous. She's not the only woman I've ever dated, but I never got this nervous around any of them, or anyone else for that matter. Syl has always assumed that *all* women make me nervous, and she has always enjoyed flustering me. Leaning forward in *that* dress did not help matters. "C'mon, Syl, cut it out. I can't take the games today."

She switched gears immediately. "Sorry, Jason. You seem tense;

I thought a little joking around might help alleviate that. Plus I've been away so long."

"It's not like I fall apart when you go away, you know."

"Then what's bothering you?"

I turned back to the computer screen. "Sorta business, sorta personal."

"Verne." It was a statement, not a question.

"How did you know?"

"Just a feeling."

"You know, it's tough to hide anything from you. A guy came in the other day and asked me to find his father who he'd been separated from for years. It turned out that his father is Verne."

"Well, that's wonderful . . . isn't it?"

"I dunno." I pointed at the screen. "Verne didn't recognize his face, but said something about recognizing his 'soul,' and then the two of them went off to talk together. Verne seemed to think he's bona fide, but I have to wonder. Even if he *is* the real McCoy, that doesn't mean he couldn't have something nasty up his sleeve."

"Jason, it's not like you to be this paranoid."

I told her about the cold gaze. "That started me thinking. I wouldn't worry if that was all, but because of that, I decided to run a background check on this guy, and I don't like what came up."

Syl looked at the screen. It showed a front-page story and two photos in a Vietnamese newspaper from several months ago. The first photo was of a Vietnamese wearing a business suit and standing in one of those typical "ID Photo" poses; the other showed a blond-haired, sharp-featured young man with a cold, angry expression.

"If you color the hair black," I said, hitting the command as I spoke, "that guy's a twin for 'Tai Lee Xiang,' the man who is claiming that Verne is his father."

"What does the story say?"

"Says that the unnamed subject—the blond guy—here killed the man in the picture while escaping from a maximum-security hospital for the criminally insane. Doctor Ping Xi, the dead man, was very important, apparently." I hit a few more controls and another newspaper headline appeared. "A couple of days later, the blond guy killed a colonel in their army, and he's been hunted ever since. International warrants, the whole nine yards."

"You don't really think even a madman would be a threat to Verne, do you?"

I chuckled slightly in spite of myself. If I looked out the right-hand window, I could see out one of the two girders left standing from the warehouse that Verne single-handedly demolished while killing Virigar's brood of werewolves. "It does sound a little silly, doesn't it? But this guy isn't an ordinary killer. According to this story, the colonel was practically torn apart." I felt a spike of ice form in my chest as I spoke, and remembered a particular clearing in the woods.

Sylvie paled suddenly. "You don't think…"

"…Yes, I do think. We'd better get over there."

Neither one of us had to voice the thought that had simultaneously occurred to us. Werewolves. If Virigar knew something about Verne's background…how very easy to have one of his people change into some form with a good background story.

Pausing only to grab a few pieces of equipment, we headed for the car at a dead run.

CHAPTER 35

A Test of Trust

"Good evening, Master Jason," Morgan said, opening the door.

"Evening, Morgan," I answered, glancing around. There was still lots of clutter around from the work that was being done on the house. "Verne around?"

"He and Master Kafan are in the library at the moment, sir."

I opened my mouth to ask who Master Kafan was, then remembered Verne calling Tai Lee Xiang "Raiakafan." "Thanks, Morgan."

"Your coats, sir, Lady Sylvia?"

Though impatient, I didn't show sign of our concern. Neither did Syl; we both knew that if Tai Lee *were* a werewolf, giving any hint that we suspected him could be fatal.

The library was much neater than the other areas of the house. I remembered that Verne pushed the contractors to finish that room first and to clean it up each day; he valued the library more than just about any other room. Verne and Tai were sitting together, bent over what looked like an atlas, with other books scattered about the table. Both looked up as we entered.

"Jason!" Verne rose. "I did not expect you. And Lady Sylvie." He took her hand and bowed deeply over it.

I felt a tinge of jealousy as Syl developed a slight blush and thanked Verne for his courtesy. She once was scared stiff of Verne, but that seemed to be a thing of the past now.

Tai nodded to me and stood up at a gesture from Verne. "Tai, please meet my good friend, Sylvia Stake," Verne said.

We'd hoped for a setup like this. As he reached out, his attention focused on Syl, I pulled my hand out of my pocket and flung what was in it at him.

Neither of us saw everything that happened. From Syl's point of view, Tai suddenly disappeared. I, on the other hand, saw a blur move toward me and felt myself lifted into the air and slammed into a wall so hard that the breath left me with an explosive *whoosh* and red haze fogged my vision. I struggled feebly, trying to force some air back into my lungs.

The pressure on my windpipe vanished as my attacker was yanked backwards. "Raiakafan! Jason! What is the meaning of this?" Verne demanded.

"I saw him move and the characteristics of his motion strongly implied an attack." Tai's voice was level, cold, and flat, like a robot rather than a living being. "I moved to neutralize him."

"No one 'neutralizes' a member of my household or my friends." Verne stated flatly. "As to Jason's action, I am sure he will explain himself... immediately." The last word carried considerable coldness with it.

"Urrg..." I gurgled, then managed to gasp, pulling precious air back into my lungs. "Sorry... Verne." I studied Tai carefully. Yes... I could see traces of the stuff. It had definitely hit him. Hell, he'd charged straight into it. Obviously, he didn't realize what kind of an "attack" it had been. "In a way, Tai is correct. Under the right circumstances, what I did would have been considered an attack. A lethal one."

Verne's eyes narrowed, fortunately showing more puzzlement than anger; we'd been through enough together that he knew I'd never do anything like this without good reason. "And just what circumstances would those have been?"

Syl answered. "If Tai had been a werewolf, he'd be dead now."

Tai blinked, brushing away the silver dust I'd thrown in his face.

Verne's expression softened in comprehension. "Ahh. Of course. You could hardly be blamed for such a suspicion, Jason. Without knowledge of the extent of my senses, you had no way of realizing that I *know* this is the real Raiakafan, no matter what his outward seeming. And he has confirmed his identity in other ways."

"According to what you told me," I said, "a werewolf can foil even your senses."

"True," Verne admitted. "But there are other things that mere duplication of the soul and body cannot achieve, such as the memories that would have to be derived from... well, from someone supposedly dead a very, very long time. You still seem unsure, Jason. Please, tell me what troubles you."

Without a word, I pulled out a printed copy of the pictures and articles I'd located and handed it to Verne, who read them in silence, then closely studied the picture, carefully comparing it with Tai. Finally, he handed them back.

"As we expected, Raiakafan," he said. "I am of the opinion that we must tell them everything."

That dead-black gaze returned; I saw Syl shrink back from it and it took some effort not to do so myself. "Are we sure?"

Verne waited until the strange young man was looking at him, then answered. "Jason has risked his life to protect me. He has rekindled the Faith that was lost. And the Lady Sylvia is his best companion, a Mistress of Crystal, and born with the Sight. If I cannot trust them, then I cannot trust you, and if you cannot trust them, then I am not who you believe." His words were very strange, half-explanation, half-ritual, spoken in a measured, formal manner that sent a shiver up my spine; that alien accent had returned once more.

Tai studied me again with less iciness than before. Finally, he nodded. "As you wish, Father."

Verne relaxed, and so did we. The last thing any of us wanted was conflict. Whatever was going on here, it was obvious that Raiakafan, or Tai—whatever his name was—had some real problems in his life, and these might affect Verne.

"Morgan!" Verne called. "Send in refreshments for everyone." He turned to us. "Make yourselves comfortable, Jason, Lady Sylvie. This will be a long and difficult story, but a necessary one, for I see no other way around it but that I—that both Raiaka-fan and I—will need your help to solve the difficulties that face us." Morgan came in, bearing a tray of drinks, and returned a moment later with two trays of hors d'oeuvres. Verne took a sip of his usual and frowned faintly. "How to begin though...?"

"How about using the White King's approach?" I suggested. "Start at the beginning. Go on to the end. And then stop."

Syl and Verne chuckled at that; Kafan (I'd decided to use Verne's name for him) just looked puzzled. Verne smiled sadly, his eyes distant. "Ahh. The beginning. But it's always hard to mark the beginning, is it not? For whatever beginning you choose, there is always a cause that predates it. But it is true that for most great things, there is a point at which you can say, 'Here. At this point, all that went before was different.' Perhaps I should start there . . ."

"No, Father! It is too dangerous—for them."

Verne sighed. "It would be too dangerous *not* to tell them, Raiakafan. Jason works best with maximum information. But you are correct, as well." He turned to us. "Before I proceed . . . Jason, Sylvia, I must impress upon you these facts.

"First, that much of what I am going to tell you contradicts that which is accepted as scientific fact.

"Second, that these contradictions—though they be global in scale—were nonetheless *designed*; that it was intended by certain parties that the information I possess would never again be known to a living soul. My own continued existence is due as much to blind luck as it is to my own skill and power.

"Third, once you have been told these things, you potentially become a target for the forces that would keep these things secret . . . and so will anyone to whom you reveal these things. And the forces behind this are of such magnitude as to give even Virigar pause, so powerful that the mightiest nations of this world are as nothing to them." He gazed solemnly at us. "So think carefully; do you still wish to involve yourselves in these matters? I will think no less of you either way, I assure you. But once I speak, there is no going back. Ever. Even my ability to hide memories will not save you. These forces will never trust that a memory is completely gone; instead they will ensure it by killing the one who has the memory."

Verne's deadly serious warning made me hesitate. He had shown similar concern when Virigar had come, but at that time, there was no doubt that the Great Wolf's forces were directed exclusively towards him. Now, he was speaking of forces about which he had little knowledge and, yet, were so fearsome as to warrant the most frightening warning he could give me. Not a reassuring thought.

I remembered our recent conversation when Verne had abruptly changed the subject. "What we discussed once before—who you were, where you came from . . . the fact you're not, exactly, a vampire . . . that's part of it?"

"It is," he said.

Syl replied first. "I want to hear the truth, Verne. I believe we were *meant* to hear it. If not, I would not be here."

I nodded. "I didn't think I'd be able to befriend a vampire and never get into trouble. We might as well know what's really going on. Seriously, Verne...if you have troubles on that scale, you're going to need all the help you can get someday."

Kafan studied us for a moment, and then smiled very slightly. "They are strong friends, Father."

"They are indeed." Verne leaned back in his red-cushioned chair. Light the color of blood flashed from his ring as he folded his hands. "Then, my friends, I start...or, rather, Raiakafan, would you begin? For what I must tell them, although more dangerous, is less immediate. Your story comes first. Mine is important to explain your own."

Kafan nodded. Turning to us, he began.

CHAPTER 36

Fleeing From Frankenstein

He looked around and smiled, satisfied. Despite his oddities, the village accepted him. His children were growing up strong and healthy. His wife took care of them all. In a country torn apart by civil war, his village had managed to keep itself isolated and secure. Untouched by the strange devices of the outside world, unimportant in the political maneuverings that dictated rule in one part of the land or another, the village looked much the same as it did two hundred years ago.

He shivered, suddenly, as though chilled, despite the bright sunlight streaming down on him. The village and his home seemed to him now like a veneer, a fragile layer of paint laid over something of unspeakable horror. But he knew that the real horror was what lay in his past. He had escaped that, hadn't he? Years gone by now...he must be safe, forgotten, thought dead and lost forever. Surely, they would have come for him long ago had they known...wouldn't they?

The wail of a child demanding attention came from within the house, a sound that could simultaneously raise frustration, warmth, and concern in a parent. But he could hear something else in the cry, as could any who knew what to listen for: the sound of the past. It was the reason he could never, ever be sure they were not watching and waiting, though with his utmost skill and caution he had stalked the dense mountain forests and found not a single trace of intrusion. Genshi, his sister, and two brothers were reason enough for them to wait.

Kay put a hand on his shoulder. "Tai...you aren't thinking about *that* again, are you?"

186

Tai turned and gazed at his wife. Several inches taller than he, willowy, with skin the color of heartwood, she was the only proof (aside from himself and his children) that there *was* an "outside world," different from the one the village knew. Kay was a strange woman by anyone's standards, which was fortunate, because no other woman could possibly have accepted what he was, let alone married him. He had long thought that her arrival to this village had been more than coincidence; it had felt like destiny. She had belonged to an organization she called "Peace Corps." The aircraft carrying her and a number of other workers had crashed in the mountains. Kay had become separated from the other survivors in a storm and wandered for a long time in the wilderness. Had she not been trained in survival, she would have died. Instead, when Tai found her, she was using a stream as a mirror, cutting her hair in a ruler-straight line as though working in a beauty salon. Her civilized, calm, utterly *human* demeanor even in the midst of a complete wilderness captured Tai instantly. He brought her to the village and by the time she had recovered from her ordeal, she didn't want to leave. She had no relatives or friends elsewhere; it was here that she felt she belonged.

"What else?" he answered finally. "I can't help it, Kay. You weren't part of it; little Tai is too young to remember it. Only Seb remembers. Seb and me."

"We've been over this again and again, Tai. They've had all the time in the world to find you. If they wanted you back and thought you were alive, they'd have gotten you long ago. They have no reason in the world to believe you'd be able to survive out here and fit in; you'd either have died on your own or been killed by a frenzied mob from their point of view. Stop worrying. Maybe someone caught up with them and they don't even exist anymore."

Oh, all the gods of all the world, let that be true. Please let that be true, he thought.

"Maybe," he said aloud.

He followed her inside, feeling better. Kay had been sent to him from the skies above; surely that was a sign in itself.

The children were inside—the two youngest, Genshi and Kei, on one side of the table; the two others, Seb and little Tai, opposite them. Not for the first time, it struck Tai as a strange coincidence that even though the older children had a different mother, all four were much darker-skinned than their father. Tai and Genshi, in particular, looked very similar ... if you ignored the *difference* that Genshi, unlike his older siblings, could not hide. Kei had been born without it, looking very much like a copy of her mother.

Kay began serving the food, beginning with Tai and ending with the toddlers. As they began to eat, Seb suddenly stiffened. "Father—"

A single sound ... of a metal catch being released.

The coldness returned, became a lump of ice in his gut. "I heard, Seb. Kay, get down. Everyone, on the floor, now!"

He moved stealthily towards the side door, caught a faint scent and heard movement. Then a voice boomed out, impossibly loud: "Attention! This house is surrounded. Surrender quietly and none of you will be harmed!"

"Go away!" he shouted hopelessly. "I don't want to go back! Leave us alone!"

The unfamiliar voice was replaced by the oily, ingratiating tone of the Colonel. "Now, now, let's not be that way ... Tai, is it? There's been an enormous amount of investment involved in you and your children. You can't expect us to just throw it all away. If you'll come back quietly, I promise that you can even keep your whole family with you. Just cooperate and you will find yourself living a lavish life."

"I like the life I have here!" He saw that Seb and Tai had crawled over and pulled up the floorboards to get at the weapons. He nodded. Good boys. Kay was pale, tears running down her face.

"I am sorry I was wrong," she whispered.

"It's all right," he said, knowing nothing was going to be "all right" again. "You made us feel better while it lasted. I love you."

"I love you."

The Colonel spoke again, no longer trying to be friendly. This time his voice was precisely reflective of what he was: a military commander, ruthless, amoral, determined, efficient, and pitiless. "All right, Alpha. Give up. You are surrounded. There is no way to escape. The less trouble you give us, the less pain your children and your wife will suffer. We know very well that you don't give a damn about pain for yourself, but how about your family? Surrender immediately, or all of them go the the labs along with you!"

"With all respect, Colonel, you and your ancestors were all sheep-screwing perverts. Shove your offer up your ass!"

The Colonel didn't respond verbally; suddenly a volley of canisters flew through the leaf-shuttered windows, hissing yellow vapor.

Holding her breath, Kay dove out the largest window with the infants, who immediately began screaming. Tai was too busy to worry about that; they had to win. And there was only one way to do that.

He leapt out the window nearest the Colonel's booming voice. A soldier tried to strike him, but Tai was too fast. Seb and little Tai followed momentarily; the soldier blocked Seb's escape. Tai continued on, nodding to himself as he heard the man scream and then the sound of a head being separated from a body.

There was no more need for subtlety here. Concealment was useless. As the men ahead raised their weapons, he *changed*.

Horror paralyzed the soldiers. Though they must have been warned, there's an infinite difference between being told about something impossible and seeing it come for you, savage and hungry, in real life. Using his claws, Tai ripped the armor off the first soldier, sent him staggering back. He was the lucky one. The other two fell dead, one fountaining blood from the throat, the other with a broken neck. He tore through their ranks, closing on the Colonel. If he could just reach the man...

Several small explosions erupted through the clearing and Tai caught an odd odor. He tried to hold his breath, but droplets dotted his skin. He found himself slowing even as he tried desperately to force himself forward. As his vision began to fade into blackness, the last thing he saw was the sardonic smile of the Colonel, merely twenty feet away.

Tai slowly blinked his way back to consciousness. He wished he hadn't. The sterile white walls...the thick, one-way glass... the ordinary-looking door that was locked and armored like a vault...

He was back at the Project.

He'd barely come to that bleak conclusion when the wall screen lit up. The Colonel looked back at him. The figure next to him sent shivers up Tai's spine, causing his light fur to ruffle. Ping Xi. Doctor Ping Xi. The Colonel might have the financing and the facilities, but it was this man, with his narrow eyes, white hair, long pianist's hands, and cold, calculating brilliance who ruled the Project.

"Congratulations, Alpha," the Colonel said. "A fine group of youngsters. Dr. Xi was just telling me how useful they're going to be."

With difficulty, Tai choked back his rage. Once he started fighting, even verbally, it would be impossible to stop, and any intelligent thinking would be lost. "Leave them alone. I'll cooperate. Just leave my family out of this."

The Colonel shook his head. "I gave you the chance for that, but you insisted on the hard way. Now that you're caught, of course you'll try singing a different tune. I'm afraid not."

"At least let Kay go!" he said, fighting to keep the killing fury under control. "She's not one of us!"

This time it was Ping Xi who answered. "Impossible. The most important information we will get will be to determine the results of cross-breeding. This would be impossible without having both of the parents available for study. It is particularly interesting that the children represent a dichotomous birth in both ways—fraternal twins of different sex, one showing all the Project characteristics and the other showing none. It will take a great deal of study to determine just what caused such a fascinatingly clear division of genetic expression."

It was no use. With an inarticulate roar of anger, Tai launched himself at the wall screen. As if from a great distance, he heard the Colonel calmly remark, "Just as usual. Some things never change."

✧   ✧   ✧

He fought them after that. But, he wondered, had he been fully human, would he have continued to fight? Why bother? For years they'd been watching him. Waiting. The level of their patience was frightening; not what he considered the norm for military and government but, rather, as though they had all the time in the world.

And once more they drugged him. Days melted into weeks of sluggish thought and dulled senses, which sharpened only when they needed him unimpaired for some test. Sometimes he thought he could sense Seb or little Tai or even Genshi, but he never saw them.

Time passed. Where had he come from? He wasn't sure. Had the labs really made him? It was all he really knew...and yet... and yet...

In the depths of his rage, something broke through. A memory...

Tall twoleg thing. My territory! Kill!

Pain! Hit me! Where? How? Fast twoleg!

Brightsharp metal! Cut! No. No cut! Hit! Why no cut?

Claw twoleg! Miss? Bite twoleg! Miss? Miss? How miss?

Pain! Hit again! Twoleg growl! Leap! Not hit ground???

Twoleg hold up! Stop in air! Twoleg too fast!

Idea Twoleg holding me...Can't get away! Claw!

???MISS??? PAIN! Blackness....Death coming...

Wake up. Not-dead? Twoleg here!

Twoleg...Twoleg stronger. Twoleg still not kill.

Not able kill Twoleg? Twoleg not kill?

Stop. Wait...

Tai's eyes snapped open. He could see the face from the final scene of that frighteningly disjointed, animalistic memory. A face. Dark-skinned, human, sharp-edged, with the look of a hawk. Clothing that would be considered strange in any place he had ever heard of. And eyes...eyes the color of stormclouds and steel, huge gray eyes filled with calm certainty.

That is a real memory, he thought. *Impossible though it is, that is real.*

At night, when he slept, the drugs loosened their hold. He dreamed...

Standing in a strange pose, the Master nodded. Tai launched himself at the tall, angular figure, claws outstretched. The Master moved the slightest bit, and Tai's claws caught nothing but air. Again. And again. No matter how fast, no matter what direction or technique he tried, he could never touch the strange man. Finally, he stopped and waited, wishing he could express what he felt to the figure before him. The figure made sounds...he stopped and thought. Those sounds...they were...a way to...tell other people things.

The Master's sounds fell into regular, recognizable patterns. Though it would be a while before he understood words, the sounds remained: "Well done, little one. You have learned the concept of practice and of when to stop practicing. When you begin to speak, then truly your training can start."

More days passed. More dreams. Pain. Tests. Most of the dreams faded before waking, but one, finally, remained.

Revelation.

Tai stood in the center of his room. Drugs fogged his thoughts, made clear thinking nearly impossible. So much easier to just lie down, sleep. Anger burned away the fog, but replaced it with the smoke of fury. No, anger was no good now. They knew what he could do when driven by rage. Only with discipline, only with the power of his mind could he hope to surprise them.

The Master studied him as he practiced. "There is a Power in the soul, little one. The mind and the body are one, and yet each has its own strengths and weaknesses. One trained sufficiently in both can never be defeated, or so it is said. You have a special strength, a power that enough training will bring to its peak. That path I can show you how to begin."

He brought his arms up and parallel, in the stance that his Master had taught. He looked in the one-way mirror, and then closed his eyes, focusing on himself. Tai visualized himself in every detail, every hair, the way the faint air currents in the room moved his clothing in infinitesimal patterns. The fog began to recede from his mind, pushed back by the extremity of what he was doing, by the focus in his soul. He trembled, forcing his body to obey. He needed more. A way out. But panic and fear would do him no good. He remembered the last dream, the last lesson of the Master:

"When your body betrays you, it must be disciplined by the spirit, by the mind. Only the mind matters. Think upon water, little one. Water. It is all but the smallest part of what you are. All but the veriest fraction of the world. And all but indestructible, infinitely adaptable, nothing you can grasp in your hand, yet able to become something irresistible, unstoppable, infinitely fast like a flood, infinitely slow like a glacier, yielding to the smallest object, yet able to wear down the mountains themselves; in fact, all but the very essence of life itself. You have learned the Hand Center. You have seen the Wind Vision. You have found in yourself the High Center. Now, take into yourself the Water Vision."

He thought of water. A droplet, condensing in a cloud. The droplet, a single thought. Droplets coalescing, becoming a raindrop; the raindrop, a single idea. The rain falling, becoming a puddle, a thousand puddles, a downpour; a day in the life of a man, a thousand thousand thousand thoughts moving as one. The downpour, still made of a trillion trillion droplets, pouring into rivers, the rivers into a mighty ocean that covered the world; the ocean, a man. Infinite in complexity, yet united in the substance of the soul.

Tai didn't understand the nature of what he was doing. It was an art, a technique, a skill taught to him so long ago that only in his dreams would he remember the teaching. Yet, in his bones he understood it. He would not fail the Master, even now.

The ocean was his soul. How, then, could anything withstand it? How could a drug, however potent, have any effect when diluted unnumbered times in the waters of his mind? It could not. And so it did not.

Tai felt his mind clearing. Yet, just by noticing that, he trembled at the edge of this transcendent moment. He knew he might not reach this point again; it required the desperation and, perhaps, the paradox of the drugged calmness to reach it.

But the very instability was the key. Like the shaken ocean, his soul gathered into a roiling wave. He spun and gathered the force of the oceans into his movements, a fluid lunge at a wall of armored, tempered glass that could withstand explosive shells.

But what is anything next to the power of a tsunami? What use armor plate against the relentless pressure of a glacier?

The wall bulged outward like cardboard, bulged and then shattered into a billion fragments that glittered in the laboratory lights like diamonds. In that moment, he saw the shocked faces of the scientists in the lab, and the calmness evaporated. Berserker fury took him.

Breathing hard, Tai slowly came back to sanity. He was splattered with blood from head to toe. He chose not to look at what he had left behind him. In front of him was a door, and behind that door...

"FATHER!"

He hugged Seb and Tai fiercely for a moment, then pulled away. "Go. The way out is clear. Run."

"But what about you?" Seb asked, fighting to keep from crying.

Tai shook his head. "I have to go after Genshi, Kei, and Kay. But I won't have you stay here any longer. Go. And keep going. As far away from here as you can get, to another country if you can. Don't look back. I will find you. If it takes a year or a dozen years, I will find you. Just make sure that you're safe."

Seb was torn, but then looked at little Tai and realized what his father meant. It was his time to be a protector. "Yes, Father."

Tai watched until the two were out of sight, then he loped down the corridor. Turning the corner, he backpedaled to a halt.

Dr. Ping Xi was there, holding a black box. "Tsk. Are you forgetting something, Alpha?"

"I AM NOT ALPHA!" Loathing and fear held him where he was. Dr. Xi was the only thing that frightened him.

"Do you think I left everything to chance? The coded transmissions this sends out will detonate a small implant in your brain. A hideous waste, one I would rather avoid. But your children will serve well enough in the lab. You have become, as the Colonel would say, a far too expensive luxury."

The black box pulled his gaze like an evil magnet. One button, and he would cease to exist. He didn't doubt Dr. Xi. The doctor never lied; it wasn't in his nature.

But was it better to live in the grip of the Project?

That thought decided him. He would win either way. But his children...

He had to succeed. He remembered his Master's movements. He had to combine his own speed with the Master's inhuman accuracy. And only one chance to get it right.

He let his shoulders sag, as though realizing he was hopelessly trapped. Then he lunged forward, leaping like a missile across the forty feet separating them.

He saw Xi's eyes widen, and knew in that instant that he was too late; the bastard had more than enough time to press the button.

But he saw the finger hesitate; perhaps, in the end, it was too hard for the doctor to destroy his greatest work. And then he was on Dr. Ping Xi, and his blood tasted like freedom.

CHAPTER 37

Six Impossible Things Before Breakfast

I rubbed my temples, trying to take all of this in. "Okay, let's see if I have this straight. You are some kind of genetic experiment? And this wanted poster stuff about you is all lies made up by the Evil Government Conspiracy?"

If Kafan had been a cat, his fur would have bristled; as it was, he did a pretty good imitation by glaring at me. "I don't like your tone of voice."

"Gently, Raiakafan," Verne said sternly. "The story is not one to be accepted easily. Jason has a mind that is open...but not so open that he is utterly credulous."

Kafan snorted, but turned back to me. "It's not the government, except a few key people. At least that is the impression I got. The group that...made...me is a self-contained organization. There were references to a prior group to which they belonged, but I never heard much. Educating me did not interest them." He stood up, as he had many times during his story, and paced a circle around the room like a caged lion. "Why do you find this so hard to believe? I haven't been here that long, but I know that genetic engineering *is* part of your civilization, while magic is not, yet you accept Verne..."

"That's why," I answered. "First, I've seen Verne and other things like him in action. I don't ignore the things I actually see. But I know a fair amount about genetic engineering, at least for a layman, and I *do* know that we haven't gotten *close* to the level of technology we'd need to make something like you claim to be. And other elements—this 'super martial arts' or whatever it is you say got you out of their holding cells..." I chuckled, then looked apologetic. "...Sorry, but that kind of stuff comes out of video games and bad Hong Kong flicks. Accepting it as 'real' just isn't easy."

Kafan shrugged helplessly. "I can't help what you believe. I know what I am."

"What happened after you killed Dr. Xi?" Sylvie asked.

Kafan's gaze dropped to the floor. He stood still for a moment, and the slow sagging of his shoulders told us more than we wanted to know. "I failed.

"I found where they were keeping Gen, Kei, and Kay. And I got in. But by then, the Colonel had organized a counterattack. I was separated from them...I had Gen, but Kay and our daughter..."

Syl put her hand on his shoulder. He turned his back, but didn't pull away; he shook for a moment with silent sobs. Then he turned around. "They were back in *their* hands."

"And the Colonel?"

The iron-cold expression returned. "I tracked him all the way to Greece, where he had a secondary headquarters. But he'd tricked me. Even as I killed him, he laughed at me. I'd come all the way across the continent and all that time, Kay and Kei were back in another part of the lab complex!"

I winced; Sylvie looked sympathetic. "So what brought you here?"

"In my travels across the continent...I started remembering other things from my past. The few things I told you, Mr. Wood. And I thought that America was the best place to begin looking, especially once I saw the news about the werewolves and realized that there was someone here who was able to deal with such things."

"So can you prove this story of yours?" I asked.

Kafan narrowed his eyes, then smiled—an expression that held very little humor. "I think so." He turned and looked out the archway, towards the entrance hall where the stairs went to the second floor. "Gen? Genshi! Come in now, Gen."

There was a scuffling noise with little scratching sounds, like a dog running on a wooden floor, followed by a thump and a high-pitched grunt. Then a small head peeked around the edge of the doorway, followed by an equally small body crawling along on all fours.

The little boy had a mane of tousled blond hair, bright green eyes... and a layer of honey-colored fur on his face. His hands were clawed, as were his feet, and canine teeth that were much too long and sharp showed when he gave us a little smile and giggle, and crawled faster towards his father. His long, fur-covered tail wagged in time to his determined crawl.

"Genshi! Walk, don't crawl."

Genshi pouted slightly at his father, but pushed himself up onto two legs and ran over to Kafan, jumping into his arms and babbling something in what I presumed was a toddler's version of Vietnamese. Kafan replied and hugged him, then looked at us.

Sylvie was smiling. I was just speechless. "Can I see him, Kafan?" Sylvie asked.

Kafan frowned a moment, but relented. "All right. But be careful. He's very, very strong and those claws are sharp." He said something in a warning tone to Genshi, who blinked solemnly and nodded.

Sylvie picked up the little furry boy, who blinked at her and then wrapped his arms around her neck and hugged her. Syl broke into a delighted grin. "What a little darling you are. Now, now, don't dig those claws in... there's a good boy..." she continued in the usual limited conversation adults have with babies.

I finally found my voice. "All right. Can't argue with the evidence there. I find it hard to believe, though, that you were the only product of their research. They couldn't have built a whole complex around you alone."

Kafan's smile became once again as cold as ice. "They didn't. When I went to kill him, I found that the Colonel was no more human than I am. Some kind of monster."

"Crap." I didn't elaborate out loud, but to me it was obvious: if Kafan was telling the truth, these people were not only more technologically advanced than anyone I'd ever heard of, but they were also crazier than anyone I'd ever heard of. Attempting experimental genetic modifications on yourself? Jesus! I thought for a moment. "But... something's funny about your story. If you were a lab product, what's this about Verne being your father? And what about your training under this whoever-he-was?"

"That," said Verne, "is indeed the question. For there is no doubt, Jason, that I did, indeed, have a foster son named Raiakafan Ularion—Thornhair Fallenstar as he would be called in English—and there is no doubt in my mind that, changed though he may be, this is indeed the Raiakafan I raised from the time he was a small boy. I knew Raiakafan for many years indeed; he could never have been the subject of genetic experiments. Yet here he is, and there is much evidence that these people he speaks of exist.

"These two things, seeming impossible, tell me that vast powers are on the move, and grave matters afoot. For this reason, I must tell you of the ancient days.

"I must speak...of Atla'a Alandar."

CHAPTER 38

It was an Age Undreamed of...

The Sh'ekatha, or Highest Speaker, gazed in bemused wonder at the tiny figure before him. Beneath the tangled mass of hair, filled with sticks and briar thorns, two serious, emerald-green eyes regarded him. Across the back was strapped a gigantic (for such a small traveller) sword, three feet long with a blade over five inches wide. A bright golden tail twitched proudly behind the boy, who was dressed raggedly in skins.

Yet ... yet, despite his appearance, there was something special about this boy, more than merely his strange race. The way he stood ... and that sword. Surely ... it was workmanship of the old days.

"Yes, boy? What do you wish?"

The boy studied him. "You are ... in command here?" he asked in a halting, uncertain fashion. The voice was rough, like a suppressed growl, but just as high-pitched as any child's.

V'ierna smiled slightly. "I am the Sh'ekatha. I am the highest authority that you may speak with at this time, yes."

The boy frowned, trying to decide if that met with whatever requirements he might have. Then his brow unfurrowed and he nodded. "My Master sent me to you."

V'ierna understood what he meant; he had been being taught by a Master of some craft, and now this Master wished the Temple to continue and expand his education. "But there is no certainty that there will be an opening here, young one. We select only a small number of willing youngsters, and then only when there is proper room for them."

The boy shook his head. "You have to take me. You have to

teach me. That is what he said." He blinked as though remembering something. "Oh, I was supposed to show you this." He reached over his back and unsheathed the monstrous blade. Holding it with entirely too much ease for such a tiny boy, he extended the weapon to the Sh'ekatha.

Puzzled, V'ierna studied the weapon. Old workmanship, yes, and very good. But that didn't...

It was then that he saw the symbol etched at the very base of the sword: Seven towers between two parallel blades.

His head snapped up involuntarily. He scrutinized the child more carefully now. Yes...now that he knew what to look for...

He gave the blade back. "Have you a name, young one?"

"Master said that you would give me one."

"Did he, now?" V'ierna contemplated the scruffy figure before him. Certainly born of no race in this world. He smiled. "Then your name is Raiakafan." He reached out and gently pulled a briar free of its tangled nest. "Raiakafan Ularion." He turned. "Follow me, Raiakafan. Your Master was correct. There is indeed a place for you."

"It has never been done!"

V'ierna shook his head. "In the ancient days, there were no such distinctions made, milady. None of these separations of duty or of privilege. I am not at all sure that the comfort brought about by such clear divisions is worth the price paid in inflexibility. Be that as it may," he raised a hand to forestall the First Guardian's retort, "in this case, it *will* be so. The Lady Herself has so decreed it. If Raiakafan can pass the requirements, he is to be trained for the Guardianship."

Melenae closed her mouth, the argument dying on her lips. If the Lady decreed it and the Sh'ekatha concurred, there was nothing more to be said. "As the Founder decrees, so will it be," she said woodenly, and turned to leave.

"Melenae."

She looked back. "Yes, Sh'ekatha?"

"I will not tolerate any manipulation of the testing. If he is held to either a higher or lower standard than any other trainee, I will be *most* displeased. And so will the Lady."

Her mouth tightened, but she nodded. "Understood."

V'ierna watched her leave. He sighed, and began walking in

the opposite direction, down the corridor that was open only to himself, the corridor that led to the Heart. How long had it been? Three thousand years? Four? Ten, perhaps? More? Long enough for mortal memory to fade, and for cultures to change even when the one who founded them tried to retain that which had been lost. Even the name of the city was, to them, little more than a name. To him, it was so much more; Atla'a Alandar; *Atlantaea Alandarion* it had been, "Star of Atlantaea's Memory." But he was one man. Highest Speaker, yes. Blessed in his own way, noted in ritual and in action. But even his longevity was nothing more than a faded echo of the Eternal King, and he had no Eternal Queen, save the Lady Herself.

He emerged into the Heart. The Mirror of the Sky glinted as a wind ruffled the sacred pool's surface. V'ierna knelt by the Heartstone and closed his eyes.

Time changes all things, V'ierna.

I know that, Lady. As always, he felt warmed by the silent voice within his mind. Her limitless compassion and energy lightened the world simply by existing. *But is it so necessary that I see loss as well as change? Have we not lost enough already? Atlantaea—*

—was as near perfect as a society of humanity shall ever be, V'ierna. But that very perfection was its destruction. If your people are to attain such heights again, they must work themselves through all the difficulties, all the perils and hatreds and disputes, that are part of growing up. You are all part of nature; I am loving, but a stern teacher as well. Even to my most favored, I am not without requirements or price, as you know well.

V'ierna knew. *I understand, Lady.*

He could see her now—night-dark hair enveloping the heavens in a warm blanket, her face simultaneously reflecting the hardness of the mountains and the softness of the fields; beautiful and terrifying and comforting all at once. *And Raiakafan? What is his place in this?*

She smiled. *He has a higher destiny than he knows. His people are filled with violence, a race of savage killers; yet by being born here—his mother landing here, on this world, and giving birth to a child—it was permitted that I touch upon him. He is a part of me, a part of the Earth for all time. He will become my Guardian, as you are my Speaker, and Seirgei my Priest . . .*

It will not be easy.

The arguments of the Guardians will be overcome by his ability. Jealousy cannot be helped. Evil will come of it. But no choice worth making comes easily. The Power fades, my love; those who destroyed Atlantaea bent all their power to sealing it away, and Zarathan, our sister world, now lies beyond our reach. Without something truly extraordinary, even I shall fade from the world, and then... her phantom face looked forlornly into the distance... *then only a miracle will restore that which was gone. And you will have to provide that miracle.*

V'ierna's heart froze within him. This was the first time the Lady had spoken so clearly about the possibility of her own death. *I? What can I possibly do? If you go, Lady, will I, too, not pass from this world? For I am nothing but a man blessed by your powers.*

Her smile lit the world again, driving away the ice in his heart. *V'ierna, to the one who held to me beyond death itself I have given all that I can. You are tied to this world more strongly than I, and by the Ring that symbolizes the Blood of Life, you carry my blessing. You are a part of Earth's life, and so long as this world lives, so shall you, though the quality of that life may well change. Through you, some part of me will survive though all other magic be sealed away from the world by the actions of the ones who destroyed Atlantaea. If the worst comes to pass, still will there be you, to find the path to the miracle that will bring the Spirit of the Earth back and let Eönae, the Lady, be reborn.*

He stood, feeling her presence fade. But he felt ready now. The Lady was right; he could do no more for these people than he had already done. To force them into a mold of his own vision would deprive them of the full understanding of the reasons behind that mold. Better a return to barbarism than the iron dictatorship he would have to create.

CHAPTER 39

But Wait, There's MORE!

"I wonder if I would have thought that," Verne concluded, "had I known what would come to pass."

For the second time that night, I was speechless. After battling vampires and werewolves, I'd thought I was ready for anything. Even Kafan's story was, well... *modern*. Elias Klein had been a twentieth-century vampire. Virigar, the Werewolf King, was at home in this world of computers and automobiles. Kafan's mad scientist and secret labs were just a part of the more paranoid tabloid headlines.

But this was like opening the door to my house and finding Gandalf and Conan the Barbarian in a fight to the finish with Cthulhu and Morgan le Fay.

Syl, of course, was in her element. Lost civilizations, Eönae the Earth Goddess, magic, no problem. "So what happened?"

Verne explained, "Raiakafan, naturally, was perfect to fulfill the role of Guardian—one of the warriors whose job it was to protect the Temple and the priests and lead the defense of the city. The fact that he wasn't a woman caused great opposition, but even his worst enemies had to admit that in pure fighting spirit and skill, he had no equal. He had difficulty with the more diplomatic and intellectual demands of the position, but he was by no means inept and he passed those requirements as well. In the end, not only did he become the High Guardian, but he married Kaylarea, daughter to the High Priest Seirgei. Kaylarea, in turn, became the High Priestess, chosen vessel of the Lady, so that, in truth, one could say that Raiakafan married the Lady Herself."

I could see Kafan blinking. Obviously, much of this was as much news to him as it was to us.

Verne stared off into the distance, seeing something in his distant past. He looked slightly more pale and worn than usual. "Then came the demons. The same ones, I thought, who had destroyed Atlantaea so long ago. In the fighting, Kaylarea was killed, Raiakafan and his children, Sev'erantean and Taiminashi, disappeared, and Atla'a Alandar was devastated. Five years later, just as we were finishing the reconstruction, the Curse fell upon us."

"Curse?"

Verne nodded. "An enemy of mine devised a . . . punishment . . . for my daring to oppose him long ago. The curse he placed upon my people was what produced the race of vampires of which Elias Klein was born. It was a mockery of the Blessing of Eönae; I drink blood to remind me of the intimate ties between all living things; I partake on occasion of the life force, freely given, of others because that life-energy is what separates the world of matter from that of spirit. I am, or was in the beginning, harmed by the Sun because I am tied wholly to the Earth and other powers are excluded from me; only when I grew into my strength, could I face the power from which other life drew its strength. And only things living or formerly living things can harm me, because only life may touch that which draws upon its very essence. All these aspects and more were twisted and mocked in the Curse. My people . . ."

He closed his eyes and clenched his jaw for some moments before he continued. "My people, for the most part, destroyed themselves in the madness of the Curse; the few who 'survived' were twisted by the magic into becoming something else. The Curse sustains itself by life-energy, so even when virtually all magic disappeared, it continued, though its sufferers were weakened. And, in the end, I myself became so embittered that for a long time, I very nearly became the same as those made in my twisted image. A diabolical and, yes, most fitting vengeance."

I shook my head and looked up. "Okay, so let me see if I get *this* story straight. You were the high Priest . . . er, Speaker for Eönae, what we'd call Gaia. The spirit of the Earth itself. And Eönae talked to you, for real. That's where you get your power. And Kafan, here, was a little boy who trained to become palace guard. *How* long ago?"

"Approximately five hundred thousand years."

I gagged. "*What?* Half a *million* years?! Are you completely out of your mind, Verne? *People* didn't *exist* back then—at least not human beings like we know today!"

"I told you," Verne said calmly. "Much of what science knows about that era is wrong. Not because your scientists are stupid or, as so many foolish cultists would have it, are looking in the wrong places or 'covering up' the truth. No, the truth is far, far more frightening, Jason. Your scientists are looking at falsified evidence. The geological record ... the traces of the greatest civilization ever to exist ... all of that was erased and rewritten to make it as though they never existed at all, to expunge from all memory the knowledge of what was."

I tried to imagine a power capable of such a thing; to wipe out every trace of a civilization, to remove fossil traces of one sort, replacing them with another ... I couldn't do it. "Impossible. Verne, you've flipped your vampiric lid."

"If only it were so. Do you understand now, Jason, why even after all this time, I must be terribly, terribly careful not to reveal the truth to any save those who absolutely must know it? Power such as that is beyond simple comprehension. Although much of that power would now be useless here, with magic closed off from this world, still there remains the potential for unimaginable destruction."

I searched Verne's face, desperately hoping for some trace of uncertainty, insanity, self-delusion. But there was no trace of any of those; just a grim and haunted certainty that this was truth, truth known by one who had lived through it. With a delayed blow, another fact slammed into my head: this meant that *Verne* was that old—older not just than any civilization we knew of, but older than the very species *Homo sapiens* should ever have been. Old enough to have seen the mammoths come and go, to have watched glaciers flow from the north to invade the southern plains and retreat again. He became more powerful with each passing year ... and yet remained terrified of the powers that had destroyed the world he knew.

I shook my head and leaned back. "This ... this is awfully hard to take in, Verne."

"I understand. Do *you* understand why it was necessary to tell you these things?"

I rubbed my jaw. "Not entirely. I see the connection—that is, that you've got two separate histories here for the same man, each incompatible with the other. But why it's necessary that I be made aware of both of these histories... no, I'm not quite clear on that."

"Neither am I," Kafan said.

Verne sighed. "Because we need you immediately for something having to do with the first, and because the very existence of the second means that anyone involved in this may have to face the legacy of that past. Jason, think on what I've told you. Five hundred millennia ago, my adopted son and his two children vanished from the face of the Earth. Even with all my powers and those of the Lady, we could not tell where they had gone, or why. Kafan's people are long-lived, but they age. Yet Raiakafan is scarcely older now than when he disappeared. His presence here is utterly impossible, as is this other life, but somehow he was returned here. And, if my son can return, I cannot help but worry that the enemies against which he guarded us have also returned. So I cannot, in good conscience, bring you into this without making you aware of what dangers you may face."

"It's simpler than that," I said after a pause. "If these people were willing to wipe out entire civilizations, surely they're the kind that prefer to be 'better safe than sorry.' Because I know you, they'd likely kill me anyway, just to be sure."

"Indeed." Verne nodded. "And to be honest... my friends... I lost my faith—in myself, in the Lady—long ago. In great part, Jason, your friendship has allowed me to start accepting myself again. In the past, between the time of the Sh'ekatha and the time we met, I did things that now repel me, which were the very antithesis of what I am. Yet... yet the Lady's blessing was never truly withdrawn from me, though it could well have been. Her last Speaker survives still... and that which was lost may now be regained, as she wished. But I will need friends. And those friends must know that which they face."

"I'm warning you: I'm not religious, and despite all this paranormal wierdness going on around me, I don't believe in gods of any kind," I replied.

Verne smiled. "Raiakafan claims the same thing these days. It does not matter if you believe in the gods; it only matters to those who *do* believe... and whether the gods believe in themselves."

He sat back, the light emphasizing the vampiric pallor that lay beneath his naturally darker skin. Despite his smile, I could see how tired he was. It was clear that no matter how uplifting the resurrection of his son had been, he was under an awful strain.

"Okay, Verne," I said as I glanced at the time; damn, there went any chance of opening the shop at a reasonable hour. Oh, well... cosmic revelations don't happen every day. "If I have any questions on this... I'll ask later. What can I do for you?"

"A simple question with a simple answer. Two answers, actually. First, Raiakafan needs an identity—a safe one. While I have contacts that can provide such things for me, I'd rather that our identities not share that kind of tie; that is, if either of us is found out, I'd rather it didn't bring the other one down with the first."

"Faking an ID isn't exactly in WIS rules... but you're right, I know people who can arrange it. Jeri might, too. And the second thing?"

Kafan answered. "Find my children. Find Seb and Tai. And Kay and Kei."

I smiled slightly. "So, we're back to the thing you originally hired me for: to find someone. At least *this* is something I'm ready to deal with. Since we're obviously not going to be asleep at a reasonable hour, why don't you come down to WIS now? We'll get full descriptions set up in the machine so I can start my searches."

"Father?"

"If you want to, Raiakafan, go ahead. Jason wouldn't offer if he didn't mean it."

Kafan looked at me. "You are sure you don't need to sleep first?"

I snorted. "I probably *should* sleep, but after all this? I don't think I'll be ready to go to bed until tomorrow night. Come on; the sooner we locate your kids and get you settled in, the more *all* of us will sleep."

CHAPTER 40

Solve One Problem, Get Two Free

I frowned at the faces on my screen. One was definitely non-human: Tai as he might look if he changed. Seb's inhumanity was less obvious, though it was there in subtle ways. The other two faces were composites of how the children looked in their human guise. This was my first look at the pictures with a clear head. After going over the details with Kafan several times, I'd wandered around my house in a daze before finally going to bed. I hadn't opened WIS today; it was evening now, and I was finally able to take a look at the pictures and think about them.

This search wasn't going to be routine. Assuming the truth of Kafan's story and seeing his furry child, I really couldn't doubt it, I wasn't the only one looking for them. I also had to be very careful with my searches so that I didn't tip off anyone else. The last thing we wanted was to alert the government that there was a genetic experiment living in Morgantown.

For that reason, I'd decided not to involve Jeri Winthrope. She'd taken a job as police liaison here, though it was pretty certain that her *real* employers were still in Washington somewhere. I couldn't ask her to set up a phony ID without a lot of questions. Since she tried to keep an eye on Verne, she'd be poking around and asking questions soon enough anyway.

Well, I thought, *might as well run the composites through the simple stuff.* An influx of money resulting from my involvement in the Morgantown Incident had allowed me to purchase a lot of the new toys I'd wanted, including SearchlightSoft's photo-comparator suite. I'd customized the hell out of it, and I was pretty sure that I had one of the most advanced photo-search programs in the world. I set up a search with various parameters to locate pictures of children from that general geographic area who were within the correct age range, and then to compare those pictures with the two pictures on my screen. As a programmer, I'm so-so, but I'm damned good at pattern logic problems, and that is what information retrieval and photo comparison rely on. I didn't expect much out of this first run; after all, it would be virtually impossible for the kids to be easily visible without a good searcher finding them quick. But it would be stupid of me to pass up any chance. My search parameters might be different than the opposition's, or I might have access to pictures they don't.

I leaned back and sorted through my mail. Bills...damn NiMo bill got higher every month; this bulky one...oh, the pictures from the State Police they wanted me to look at; invoices from Ed Sommer for the electrical work he was doing for Verne. Verne wanted me to look them over to make sure everything was okay. I wondered for a moment how he'd managed to hide Genshi and Kafan from Ed and his team. I glanced over Ed's invoices...damn, even with the money I was making these days, I couldn't pay these without selling everything I owned. Complete rewiring, lights...the works. I marked a couple of borderline entries—I didn't know if all these things were needed, but if they had already been installed, we wouldn't gripe, so I scribbled "tell Verne check if installed" on them and put them aside.

The next letter brought a grin. Mom and Dad had written again. I opened the envelope and scanned the contents. Dad had gone to a jeweler's convention—he made jewelry as a sort of hobby—and was working on some new stuff. He was about to retire from the college (Professor of Chemistry). Mom had retired from teaching a couple of years ago and we had a continual exchange of ideas going. I was going to have to read *that* section in more detail later. There was no way to just dash off a reply to Mom; she was too deep for that. They'd also included a Dilbert cartoon they thought I'd appreciate. I'd have to write back soon. It was a little difficult to write these days, though; they knew about Virigar, but I was trying to keep a lid on Verne. But Mom was an *awfully* sharp cookie and she'd know if I was hiding something.

The rest of the stuff was junk mail, which I consigned to the permanent circular file. I stretched, went to the kitchen and reheated some of the taco meat I'd made earlier that week. Fortified with a couple of tacos sprinkled with onions, cheese, lettuce, and homemade salsa, I sat down at my second terminal and started downloading my e-mail. I flagged one immediately—it came from a remote drop which was a remote drop for a remote drop for...well, you get the picture. Only one person used that route: the Jammer.

Probably the best hacker/cracker in the world, the Jammer had taken a sort of brotherly interest in protecting my butt when Virigar first showed up. Since then, we'd had occasional correspondence. Once I'd started thinking about false ID, he'd been at the top of my mind. However, the way he'd disappeared a while back had indicated to me that, like Slippery Jim DiGriz, he'd gotten "recruited" by some bigger agency. So I'd had to tiptoe around the subject to see what his reaction was.

TO:{Jason Wood}wisdom@wis.com
FROM:{The Jammer}
SUBJECT:RE: Old days

You're not bad yourself, JW. I particularly liked the triple-loop trick you set up to make people trying to track this down follow the message in circles. But you really need to relax. Trust me, there isn't anyone on the planet who can trace or decode a message *I* want kept secret except God himself, and even He'd have to do some serious work first.

It was hard to decide if I should laugh or growl at that. The problem with the Jammer was that he had an ego the size of the solar system. I was tempted to write back something like, "If you're that good, who was it that caught you?" but impulses like that are stupid. If stroking his ego got good results, why should it bother me? I laughed. At least he had a sense of humor, which was more than a lot of geeks.

What you're asking is if I still do some non-legit work? Normally no, but for you...as long as it's not aiding and abetting a real crime, no problem. I've been itching for an excuse to hack something on my own lately anyway. My, um, friends don't like to let me out to play very often except "on duty." Not that that isn't challenging work in itself, but...Doing an analysis of your prior inquiries, I'll bet you need an ID.

I blinked. Thinking about it, and glancing through my messages again...yeah, I suppose he might have been able to assume that...but it took a pattern sense as good or better than mine to do it dead cold. Maybe I shouldn't call it "ego."

If it's one for yourself, I've got everything I need already; if it's for someone else, I need all the info you can give me—blood type, fingerprints, photos, the works. The more I can work with, the more I can give you. Drop me a line and let me know.
The JAMMER

Not bad. One major problem probably solved. I glanced over at the comparison program, sorting through picture after picture...no hits. I didn't expect any. Picking up the phone, I called Verne. As usual, Morgan answered and called Verne to the phone. "Hello, Jason."

"Got a couple marks on those invoices—you just have to make sure he installed all the stuff he says he installed. I'll come over and do that now, if you like. I've got the machines running on something that doesn't need my attention right now. I'm going to stop by the mini-mart for a couple things, then I'll be right over."

"By all means. Thank you, Jason."

The mini-mart wasn't too busy. I noted the security camera with its odd bulbous attachment. Nothing brought home the profound changes that were happening more than this prosaic addition: that attachment was, with slight changes, the same headpiece I'd worn while searching out werewolves in the hospital hallways. *Except that this one wasn't made by me, or under my license. Which means I'd give a better than fifty-percent chance it's useless.* I pulled out my pocket camera and snapped a pic of it; the gadget wasn't a brand I recognized. *One more to hit up for infringement claims.*

I paid for my items and headed back out.

There were unaccustomed faint lines of concern on Morgan's usually impassive, English-butler face. I saw the reason immediately. "Verne!"

Nothing essential had changed in him; he still had the dark, wide eyes that could hold you with a magnetic presence and the distant and aristocratic stance, but beneath the dusky olive color natural to his skin, his paleness had become something beyond mere vampiric pallor; he was washed out, diminished, as though being slowly leached of his color and his strength. The way he stood was unnaturally stiff. And in his dark hair, I thought I could see a few strands of white and gray. "Jesus, Verne, you look like crap."

A tired smile crossed his face. "As usual, your diplomacy is staggering, Jason. You are not the first to inform me of this. And your face said all that needed to be said."

"What's wrong?"

Verne shrugged. "I am not sure. There have been a few, a very few, cases in which I felt similarly, aside from the one time I was forced to cross desert plains with little to no shelter—that was infinitely worse. I suspect all the changes in my life, from finding Raiakafan to simply trying to become more human again, have made me overwork. For if I lie down to rest, and my mind does not enter the proper state, I do not gain the proper amount of rest; those of my sort do not sleep in truth, any more than the Earth sleeps, but there is a difference between activity and rest even so."

I couldn't keep the concern from my voice. "I hope that's all it is. Look, just take it easy. Anyone would be a little punchy after all the stuff that's happened, but you're the only one who can take care of *you*. I mean, what would I do if you collapsed? Call 911 and tell the paramedics I have a sick vampire here?"

"Indeed." Verne straightened with visible effort. "But let me see these invoices... Ah, I see. I believe those sockets were installed, but let us check."

We went through the huge mansion, checking off the items. Personally, I'd've rather seen Verne go to bed, but his tone and manner indicated that, weak or not, he wasn't going to listen to me or any other mortal doing a mother hen imitation.

I figured he was a lot more worried than he let on. In his room, we stopped and he grabbed a bottle of AB+, draining the entire thing without letting it warm first. This made him visibly less pale, but something about it struck me as vaguely false, like the temporarily alert feeling you might get from amphetamines or a lot of coffee. Still, he moved more easily and the gray strands were no longer visible in his hair. Maybe he just hadn't been eating right. Was there such a thing as vitamin deficiency for a vampire . . . nature priest, whatever?

"Very good, Jason," Verne said finally. "All seems to be in order. I will pay these invoices, then. Thank you for checking them."

"No problem. Where's Kafan?"

"Sleeping. He tends to keep to Gen's schedule, and we don't want Gen to become habitually nocturnal."

As good a chance as any. "Verne, there's one thing that's been bothering me about Kafan." I grinned momentarily. "Well, one *new* thing. I know his story now, but . . . there have been a few times when he has seemed to *change* his whole personality, going from someone who's as normal as you could expect with his background, to . . . well, I don't know how to say it. Almost a machine—a *killing* machine."

Verne's expression was *too* carefully neutral, so I raised an eyebrow. "Well? What's going on?"

He shook his head. "You are correct in your observation, Jason. There is some other trigger, some other mystery associated with him, and I have talked about it with him as much as I am able. It is not associated with the Project, that much I have learned; but it *does* have the sort of . . . programmed reactions one might have expected from such an organization if they were to have tried to make use of him. But Raiakafan is adamant about two things: first, it has nothing to do with the Project from which he escaped, and second, that no one must pry too far into this mystery or he will be forced to kill them, or die trying."

"Even *you*?"

"He implied that he would try to resist any impulses associated with me . . . he was sworn to my service in ancient days, and that oath still has the force of the Lady behind it. But anyone else would have no protection at all."

Great. A mystery within a mystery. "I'd bet, if we knew what it was, we'd know how he can be here, today, when he disappeared completely from your city half a million years back."

Verne nodded. "I, too, believe that is the case. Wherever he went in that time . . . it made him into something else. Something he mostly represses, unless it threatens to probe into that particular secret, or threatens his life."

I shrugged. This was a problem for later; I had more than enough on my plate for now. "Well, say hi to him and Genshi for me. I don't know how long this search is going to take me, but I've already started on it. Might as well get home and try to get *my* schedule back on track."

"An excellent idea. I will see you later, then."

I stopped and turned in the doorway. "Verne, take care of yourself, okay?"

"Of course, Jason."

I drove back to my house slowly. If Verne really was sick, I didn't see how anyone could do anything. Other than Morgan, presumably, and Kafan, maybe. *Was* there anything like first aid for Verne's kind, or was that like thinking of stocking bandages for God?

I really should have started work on those state police photos, but my heart just wasn't in it tonight. I put in *Casablanca* and let it run while I ate a late-night snack. Finally, as Rick and Louis walked off through the rain, I headed upstairs to bed. I wasn't that tired, but if I didn't get back on track...I glanced over at the search station. It had stopped the comparisons, finally. I reached out to shut it off when the message on the screen hit me with delayed impact:

Matches: 10

Ten matches? I hadn't expected even *one*! Bedtime forgotten, I sat down at the keyboard and called up the ten matching pictures.

As they appeared onscreen, I heard myself say, "Oh, crap."

I'd had a vague feeling that the boys' faces were familiar, but I'd put it down to having seen their father and talked over their appearance for hours. But as soon as the photos with their headlines appeared, I remembered all too well where I'd seen them:

SENATOR MACLAIN ADOPTS TWO VIET CHILDREN.

CHAPTER 41

Worries and Joys

Verne and Kafan stared at the reprinted articles, while Sylvie peeked over their shoulders. "*H'alate,*" muttered Verne. "This is most inconvenient."

"Maybe not quite as bad as it seems," I said. Verne had looked like death warmed over when he came in, but that might have been the yellow street lights. He looked a little better, here in the office, than he had yesterday. I hoped that meant he was taking it easy. "With that kind of high profile, yeah, it's certain that your enemies know where the kids are. But the good thing is that the high profile also makes it virtually impossible to kidnap them. Doing a snatch-and-grab on some random runaway is one thing; kidnapping the children of a United States senator—especially one like Paula MacLain, who's one of the most outspoken and uncompromising people I've ever heard—is very, very different."

"True," Verne said. "But it will be difficult to convince the lady to return her children to their father when that father is wanted across the globe. Giving him a new identity would work for ordinary situations, but you can be sure that if we ask her to hand over her children to us, she will have us investigated to the full extent of her powers, which are quite considerable. She would most certainly discover your internationally known identity, Kafan, and might find out some rather unwelcome facts about myself as well."

Syl nodded. "And...didn't she have a son before? One about Tai's age? He was killed somehow. She's going to hold on to those kids like grim death."

I winced. I'd forgotten about that—it had happened about

ten years ago, before I started reading about politics, since in high school things like that seem pretty unimportant. But now that Syl mentioned it, I remembered: her husband and son were killed in a plane crash, and it had something to do with her job so she might have blamed herself somehow. "We'll have to think about this."

"What is there to think about?" Kafan demanded. "I am their father. They belong with me."

"I'd tend to agree," I said, "but the rest of the world knows you as a psycho killer, wanted by an international task force. Not exactly the kind of parent people want for children, you know."

"Then we'll tell her the truth."

"Which truth? The one about genetic experiments? Kafan, that'd be a quick way to end up in yet another lab. The one about ancient civilizations for which there are no signs of existence? *That* would be a good way to get us *all* locked up. No, I'm sure there's an angle here, but I'm going to have to work on it. At least relax some; we know where they are, and they're being treated very well. They're not suffering, and it's for damn sure this organization won't dare touch them as long as they're in the senator's custody."

Kafan's lips tightened, showing faint hints of the fangs underneath, until he got his temper under control. Then he shrank back, depressed even though the news was at least partly good. "You are correct. I cannot fight this whole world if I wish to live here." He brooded for a moment, then asked, "What about Kay and Kei?"

I shook my head. "Sorry. Nothing yet. If they were captured again as you said, I'm not going to find anything quickly, even if they did move them. Most likely, they're still in the lab compound you mentioned, if they managed to keep it hidden this long. You can't tell us where it is?"

"No." The short, blunt monosyllable carried a world of frustration. "Showing me where I was on a map was never something they did. And I merely ran when I escaped. I had no time to mark bearings. Oh, put me physically back in the general area and I'll find it, that I promise you, but I can't show you where it is."

"Too bad. But if we're even going to *think* about finding a way to go back and get them, we absolutely *have* to find out where the compound is, and, to be honest, a whole lot more."

This was getting more and more difficult. I wasn't James Bond, and I didn't know anyone who qualified for the part, either. Jeri Winthrope was about as close as I got, and I sure didn't like the idea of involving her in this—both because of the problems it could cause for us and the problems it would cause for her. There was a serious threat hanging over anyone who got too close to this mess. "Guess I'll have to work on that too."

Verne, still pale but looking definitely better than he had yesterday, sat up. "Jason, at this point I insist on paying you. This may require a great deal of your time and resources, and perhaps more than you can easily afford."

I opened my mouth to protest, then shut it. It grated on me to charge a friend for something so important to him, but Verne was right. If I followed this thing to its logical conclusion, I might have to do everything from paying out bribes to masterminding and equipping a commando raid! I shook my head at that; I didn't know anyone who even *knew* anyone who could do that. Oh well, one thing at a time. "Thanks, Verne. You're right. This is going to get expensive no matter how I slice it."

Taking out his checkbook, Verne wrote quickly and tore out the paper. I boggled at the amount. "Verne—"

"Don't protest, Jason. Better to be overpaid than underpaid. You have no idea how little such a sum means to me, nor how highly I value your services."

I nodded. "Okay." I gestured at the pile of newspaper copies. "Take those if you want. I'd better get back to work. Besides this snafu, I've got three other regular jobs on the burner."

Sylvie remained behind after Verne, Kafan, and Gen left. "Verne isn't well, Jason."

"Tell me something I don't know," I said. "He looks better than he did yesterday, though."

She frowned, a distant and, unfortunately, familiar look on her face. "Maybe...but I have a bad feeling about that."

I sighed. "Syl, sweetheart, maybe you can do something. It's for sure that I've got enough to do here. I'm no vampire medic. He regards you very highly and talks about your being a 'Mistress of Crystal,' whatever that means. Maybe you can do something to help him."

Her expression lightened. "Why, thank you, Jason! For calling me 'sweetheart,' that is."

I blushed; I could feel the heat on my cheeks. "So maybe it wasn't ever a secret. Syl, you're the only woman that makes me feel like I'm still fourteen, clumsy, and tongue-tied. Maybe that's a good thing." She started to say something—I could tell it would be something that embarrassed me more—but then stopped. "Thanks. I don't need to blush more than once a day."

She smiled, a very gentle smile. "It doesn't hurt your looks at all, you know. And that clumsy approach of yours makes me feel like *I'm* still in my teens, too, so I'd say it's a good thing."

I smiled back. "I guess you make me nervous because you're the only woman I'm serious about."

"Are you?"

I swallowed. "I've been in love with you for years, Syl. I just wasn't ready to admit it."

You can insert your own experience of a happy first kiss here; I'm pretty sure they're similar for the lucky people involved: time stops, or passes, but it certainly doesn't behave the same, and the rest of the world doesn't exist. I'd kissed Syl before, quick pecks here and there, and I'd kissed a girl or two once I was out of my geek stage, but there just wasn't any comparison. I'd been waiting to do this since I met her, and from her response, I guessed she'd been waiting just as long.

When lack of air finally signaled the end of eternity, I pulled back from her for a moment, looking into those deep blue eyes. "Whew."

"So what was it you were so afraid of, Jason?"

"This. I like having control over my own life, and there's no control over this."

That smile again. "Do you want to change your mind?"

"Don't you even *think* about it. After all the courage I had to work up to say that four-letter word 'love,' you're not getting a chance to get away." I wanted to spend the rest of the night—maybe the rest of the week—continuing what we'd started, but I couldn't ignore business, either.

Especially when business also involved a friend. "Syl, can we make a date for tomorrow night? Right now, I'd better keep working—I've already lost a couple of days. And do you think you can do anything for Verne?"

She grinned. "Not jealous of him anymore?"

"What?!"

"I can sense things, you know that. And I could see your little pout every time Verne put on the charm and I smiled back at him."

I gave a sour look. "Well, he does have a kind of overwhelming presence, not to mention that perfect sense of style."

"Jealous, like I said. Don't worry, Jason. I knew you were the one for me as soon as I saw you. I had a feeling about it."

Now that *really* made me wince. "I don't believe in destiny."

"Then call it a self-fulfilling prophecy. I'll head over to Verne's. Maybe I can't do anything, but then again maybe I can."

"Thanks, Syl."

Even after she left, it took a while to start concentrating on the work at hand.

Perfume stays with you.

CHAPTER 42

Reaching Limits

TO:{Jason Wood}wisdom@wis.com
FROM:{The Jammer}
SUBJECT:EXCUSE ME????

Do you have ANY idea what kind of mess you were trying to get me into? No, let me revise that. Do you have ANY idea what THAT kind of mess can do to me?

Dammit, Wood. This guy's an international fugitive and you want me to give him a bulletproof ID? What are you mixed up in THIS time?

So there *were* limits to what the Jammer would take casually. Nice to know, but I wished he'd have stayed in his omnipotent mode for a while longer.

Look, I know enough about you to know that you know perfectly well who this guy is, at least on the public-international level. So, since I also know you're not into helping criminals, I'll assume you know something I don't, hard as that is to believe, which makes this guy worth helping. But for this little bit of work, I'm charging. Not money, naturally. You'll make available a writable CD-ROM on a dial-in line at 2:15 Tuesday evening. When it's finished, you'll take the disk—without reading it, and believe you me I'll know—to a secure locale of your choosing. In a separate letter, you tell me the location. Once that's done, I'll deliver your IDs.

Oh, man. What was I getting myself into? He could be down-loading anything from recipes to top secret documents into the drive, and I had no doubt that if I made a single attempt to read the contents, he *would* find out; he was that good.

But then again, what was I asking him to do? Create an ID for a known international criminal. And if my guess was right, he was working for an organization that was tasked with finding Kafan. No, the Jammer had the right to ask for something like this; I was asking him to put his ass on the line for me, so I would stick my neck out for him.

I typed a very short reply—"Terms accepted"—and sent it off.

❖   ❖   ❖

A week into my work and I wasn't any closer to figuring out how to approach Senator MacLain without opening about a dozen cans of worms that were better left closed. On the other hand, I was starting, I thought, to close in on the location of this mysterious Project. The break had come a few days ago, when a search program had highlighted the Organization for Scientific Research. A check showed that not only had the OSR always been heavily involved in biological research, but it previously had a couple of branches in the far East—one in or very near Vietnam. During the '70s, those labs were closed. A bit of digging on my part, however, showed that the discontinuance had actually been a transfer of ownership to interested parties, probably in the Viet government. Details on the site were vague; the OSR files from the '70s were hard to access, since it had begun as a UN venture but had separated from the UN and become a private corporation, so it was possible all the old records not directly relevant to operation had been purged. And stuff that old often wasn't online anywhere in any case.

It might be possible, however, to take the vague info I had gathered and combine it with a careful modeling of the layout as Kafan remembered it to see if a pattern-recognition program could come up with anything using satellite photos of the area. There were probably records of the installation on one of the intelligence computers—NSA, CIA—but I wasn't about to try hacking one of those. This had to be an independent operation. With Verne's backing, at least we didn't need to worry about whether we could afford it.

That brought up the next problem: Verne. Syl had tried a

number of things with him regarding his health, and though it appeared to have helped some, within a few days, he had deteriorated again. He was visibly older.

I closed my eyes. Genetically engineered people, ancient civilizations, vampires, priests.... damn, it was a wonder my head didn't explode. All that stuff combined was enough to...

All that stuff combined?

I straightened. Reaching out, I grabbed the phone. "Verne? Sorry to disturb you, but I just thought of something."

Verne's weariness was now evident in his voice. It was still as rich as ever, but the underlying tone lacked the measured certainty that was usually there. "And what is that, Jason?"

"Verne, you talked about how certain forces might have returned, right? Isn't it possible that what's happening to you is an attack? Maybe even carried out—unconsciously—by Kafan?"

The silence on the other end was very long. Then:

"Not merely possible..." Verne said slowly, "...but even probable. In all these thousands of years, nothing like this has ever happened to me. Can it be coincidence that it happens now, of all times? Most unlikely. My brain has been affected as well, if I did not think of this myself."

"Is there a way to find out?"

"There is," Verne said. "With Sylvie's help, Morgan and I should be able to determine if any outside mystical forces are operating here."

"What about biological? You did say that living things could affect you."

Verne hesitated a moment, considering. His voice, given hope, was stronger now. "I do not believe any disease, howsoever virulent, could affect me without some small mystical component. This was one of the Lady's blessings, and it is not within the power of ordinary science to gainsay that, even in this era. My metabolism differs so greatly from that of anything else on this world that I doubt it would be recognized by most tests. No, if this is an attack, it must be a magical one. Thank you, Jason."

"No problem. Will you need me for anything?"

"No, my friend. You have given all that was necessary. We will endeavor to make this as short as possible, that your lady be not unduly inconvenienced."

"Is it that obvious to everyone?"

Verne's laugh was the first genuinely cheerful response I had heard from him in a week. "Jason, such things are always obvious. And welcome, I assure you. You have finally accepted that which was always in your heart."

"Don't you start. I may have been slow and dumb, but I don't have to be reminded every day."

He chuckled. "Good night, Jason."

CHAPTER 43

Beware of Spooks Leaving Gifts

I stared down at the disk in my hand. The fact that it contained potentially treasonous information made it feel as heavy as lead. Unfortunately, it wasn't the worst thing I had to deal with. My date with Sylvie last night, our third "real" date, had been bittersweet at best. We were happy to be together finally, but our enjoyment was overshadowed. Despite three days of careful work, Syl, Verne, Morgan, and their few other trusted contacts had turned up precisely nothing. My "brilliant idea" was a washout, and Verne was worse than ever. He would improve slightly for a few hours, but the mysterious illness always came back. No mystical influences alien to the house. No mental controls on Kafan that they could find. Nothing.

I sighed. Syl wasn't coming over today—the Silver Stake had three shipments that needed to be classified, and she didn't want to be faced with Verne right now anyway.

I glanced at an envelope on my desk—one which, under any other circumstances, would have me calling Syl for champagne and a very, very expensive dinner out. But it barely gave me a momentary smile. I sighed; putting the CD into a protective case, I put the case into my backpack. Time to send it off for delivery.

As I opened the front door, I saw a package lying on the doorstep. I picked it up, noting that it had no mailing stamps, return address, or postal marks of any kind.

Belatedly, it occurred to me that I might expect to start getting mail bombs soon. Well, if it was a bomb, it wasn't motion-activated. I hefted it a couple of times. It was light; *not much more than paper in here*, I thought. There could be enough plastique in it to do serious damage, though. It didn't take much high explosive to do a number on you.

I shrugged. *Not likely to be a bomb, what the hell.* I ripped it open.

No explosions. Looking inside, I saw an envelope and a sheet of paper. It was a note:

Jason, you have the goddamned devil's luck. Here are the IDs. Destroy the disk. Since I know you're too damn curious for your own good, I'll let you in on this latest development: somehow, whatever you're up to got the attention of one of my bosses and he caught me. Instead of shutting us down, he told me to make the IDs. Must be personal—he told me not to mention this to the other members of our group. So this one's free. But I'd worry, if I were you. If HE thinks you're involved in something important enough to let you off a felony charge without so much as a warning, you're playing with nukes, not fire.

The Jammer

I stared at the package, then opened the envelope. Birth certificate...passport...driver's license...Jesus, even documents showing he was proficient in woodworking and construction, as well as a Black Belt certification from Budoukai Tai Kwan Do in California. I looked closer. The passport was genuine—seal and all.

Who *were* these people? And what the hell had I gotten myself into *now*?

CHAPTER 44

Paternity and Possibility

"Senator MacLain?"

"This is Paula MacLain. Mr. Jason Wood?" The voice on the other end was as distinctive over the phone as it was in public address or on television: precise, educated, pleasant yet cool, that carried both authority and intelligence; it reminded me of Katharine Hepburn.

"Yes, ma'am. I don't know if you know who I am—"

"Young man, if I didn't, I wouldn't be speaking to you." There was a tinge of humor that took any sting out of the words. "In any case, a United States senator who isn't aware of the recent events in Morgantown would be a sad example of a legislator, don't you agree?"

"I certainly do, Senator. And I certainly didn't mean to imply—"

"Don't concern yourself with my feelings, Mr. Wood. I know when offense is intended and when it isn't. Now that you and I have finally managed to connect, let's waste no more time. What can I do for you? You were intriguingly uninformative to my staff."

I took a deep breath. I'd decided to go for the most honest route I could, while tapdancing around the more dangerous areas. "Senator, a few weeks ago, a man walked into my office asking me for help in locating his family. To make a long story short, he originally comes from Vietnam. And the descriptions of his two children, and pictures made from those descriptions, match those of your adopted children in great detail."

There was a long silence. I'd expected as much, given her history. Finally, "That . . . is quite remarkable, Mr. Wood. Am I to presume that you would like to find a way to confirm that they are, or are not, your client's children? And that he would subsequently want to obtain custody of them, if they are indeed his children?" Her voice was carefully controlled, but not perfectly so; she wasn't taking this as calmly as she'd like me to think.

"Basically correct, Senator. But we also don't wish to distress the children, either by giving them false hopes or by forcing them to leave a stable home. What I was hoping was that we could permit someone you trust to take a sample for genetic comparison and do a paternity test."

Senator MacLain was known for her quick decisions. "That much I will certainly do. But I must warn you and your client, Mr. Wood: I will never relinquish custody of my children unless I am absolutely certain that they will be happy and well-cared for, regardless of who is the blood parent. I love them both very much."

I nodded, though she couldn't see it. "Senator . . . we expected no less, and to be honest if you felt any differently you wouldn't be a fit mother for them. It's not going to be easy either way, but I assure you, I feel the same way. I'll make that clear to my client."

"I appreciate that, Mr. Wood. And I appreciate, now, the trouble you went to to keep this all confidential. Let me see . . ." I heard the sounds of tapping on a computer keyboard. "Ah. If you would be so kind as to have the sample sent to Dr. Julian Gray, 101 Main Street, Carmel, New York, he will see to the comparisons. I have no trouble with your obtaining the samples for him; falsifying genetic evidence would seem a bit beyond anyone's capacities at the present time."

"Indeed. Thank you very much for your time, Senator. Good-bye."

Maybe not beyond anyone's *capacities,* I thought as I hung up the phone, *but certainly beyond mine.*

The invoice for the State Police job finished printing. I stuffed it into the package along with the originals and enhanced versions. Sealing it up, I affixed the prewritten label and dumped it into my outbox.

So much for the simple part of my current life.

It had taken a couple of days to install my newest machine, a Lumiere Industries' TERA-5. Without Verne's money, I'd still be looking at the catalog, drooling, and thinking "maybe next decade." Now that it was up and running, I'd given it the biggest assignment I had: sorting through all the recent satellite data that

I'd been able to find, beg, borrow, or...acquire, and looking for various indications of hidden installations. So far, it had given me at least twenty positives, none of which had turned out promising. I was starting to wonder if there was a bug in the program; some of the positives were pretty far outside of the parameters of the installation as described by Kafan. There was one that might be a hidden POW camp—I'd forwarded that to one of the MIA-POW groups I knew about. I didn't think those camps existed anymore, but maybe there was more than hearsay behind the rumors.

The TERA-5 was chugging away, meter by detailed meter on the map; this was going to take a while, even for the fastest commercially available general-purpose machine ever made. Although a machine specifically designed for map-comparison searching would be far faster, it be a lot more expensive, and next to useless for anything else; there's always a catch somewhere. I preferred to wait a little longer and have a use for the machine later on as well. My only consolation was that only an intelligence agency likely had better equipment and programs for the job.

I thought about Verne. Given the situation with his health, I didn't know what good this was going to do. Without Verne, we were helpless, even if I could locate the installation. I looked sadly down at the thick document on my desk. Verne's will. Morgan as executor, Kafan and his family as major heirs, and, maybe not so surprisingly, me and Sylvie figuring prominently in it as well. There were also bequests to his efficient and often nearly invisible staff. The sight of the will told me more than I needed to know. Verne knew his time was up.

My friend was dying. It hit me hard all of a sudden. I collapsed into my chair, angry, sad, and frustrated all at once. He'd been the gateway through which a whole world of wonder opened up for me, and he said I'd helped him regain his faith. It wasn't *fair* that it end like this, with him wasting away to nothing for no explainable reason.

And there was nothing I could do. Last night, he'd taken us through his house to show us all of its secrets. "Just in case," he said, but we knew there was no doubt in his mind. The place he called "the Heart," built out of habit and tradition, only recently having been used by him for the purposes that it had existed... once more to become an unused cave when he died. All his papers, books, and tablets, here and elsewhere.

He'd found his lost son, I'd found his son's children, and for what? He wouldn't live long enough to see them reunited. Dammit! I slapped at the wall switch, killing the lights as I turned to leave.

Then I froze.

I remembered what I'd said to Verne months ago, when Virigar first arrived: "I don't like coincidences. I don't believe in them."

What if my idea was still basically true?

There was just one possibility. I switched the lights back on, spun the chair around, and rebooted the terminal. It was a crazy idea... but no crazier than anything else that had been happening. Just a few things to check, and I'd know.

It took several hours—the data was hard to find—but finally my screen lit up with some critical pieces of information. I grabbed my gun, spare magazines, a small toolbox, and a large flashlight and sprinted out the door.

CHAPTER 45

That Future is Past

Morgan opened the door, startled as I pushed past him without so much as a "hello." "Master Jason...?"

I looked around, shrugged, jogged into the living room and climbed up on a chair. Verne was in that room, staring at me curiously out of hollow eyes set in a leathery, lined face and framed by pure white hair. "J...Jason," he said slowly, as I mumbled a curse to myself and dragged the chair over a bit, "what...are you doing?"

"Maybe making a fool of myself."

I reached up and unscrewed one of the bulbs from the fixture and pulled the fixture itself towards me. It looked normal...

The other lights on the fixture went out. Morgan stood near the switch. "Perhaps, if you are intending on tinkering with the lighting, you may wish the electricity off, sir."

"Thanks, Morgan," I said absently. Pulling out a small screwdriver, I unfastened the interior baseplate of the fixture.

There. Underneath the base. "Morgan, you said it. Kill the electricity—*all* the electricity in the house! *Now!*"

"Sir...?" Morgan hesitated for a moment, then hurried off towards the basement and the main breakers. I switched on the flashlight; a moment later the house was plunged into darkness.

"What...what is going on, Jason?" Verne asked.

"I was right all along, Verne," I said. Morgan entered; he had a much larger portable light. "Unless you bought that light in the last few days, you might even want to shut off that light. Go with candles." I turned back to Verne. "It wasn't magic. It was technology that was killing you. Every one of your lights—and

230

maybe even some other devices—is fitted with a gadget that turns ordinary light into the kind of light that hurts you. My guess is it's managing to get filaments to spike high enough temperatures to radiate UV somehow, along with everything else; cuts their lifetime down a *lot*, but they only need this to work for a few months. In the short term, it can't damage you, but with enough exposure..."

"...yes," Verne said slowly. "It...it becomes like a slow cancer, eating away at me. But even in the day, when I sleep in darkness?"

"Probably a device in your rooms does the same thing. If, as I suspect, it's not just one wavelength of light but a combination of them, it probably can't do enough in darkness to continue *hurting* you during the day, but it could slow your recovery so that you'd always be getting damaged more than you were healing during your rest, especially if the really critical wavelengths are combinations of ultraviolet and infrared."

"How did you know?"

"There were a lot of clues, but the biggest one—which didn't register until almost too late—was that the few times you were *outside* of your house, you actually started to look a tiny bit better. But when you and Sylvie couldn't find anything, I was stumped...until I realized that coincidence is damn unlikely."

We both thought for a moment. "I must confess, Jason, that I don't quite understand," Verne said finally. His voice was slightly steadier already, testament to the tremendous recuperative powers that were his, and I started to relax slightly. It looked like I might be right. I *knew* I was.

"Well, to kill you, someone would have to know what you are, exactly. Maybe one of your old enemies, right? Who else would know precisely how to kill you subtly, without alerting everyone you are close too? But this started just as Kafan showed up, so, to me, that's not a coincidence.

"What if the lab that Raiakafan escaped from was being run *by the same people* who were *your* enemies, Verne?"

"Impossible," Verne breathed. "After all this time..."

"But it would explain everything. And there's evidence for it. Consider Raiakafan himself—if your enemies didn't have a hand in this, how else? You survived all these years, they certainly could have. And another thing, one that's bothered us both for quite a while: Klein. Where the hell did he come from? Only another

vampire—of the kind made by one of your enemies—could create him. And what did he do? He *set you up*, that's what—tried
to get you killed off! Somebody knew where you were, and what
you were! Somebody who knew that converting Klein would give
them a weapon to trap you, and they damn near succeeded. If
Virigar hadn't shown up, I suspect there would have been another
attack on your life." I took another breath, then continued, "And
look at the timing. Klein showed up sporting a new set of fangs,
if my calendar's right, a few weeks after Kafan whacked the good
doctor. *They knew who Kafan really was, and they knew where
he was going.*"

"Very good, Mr. Wood."

I knew that voice. "And Ed Sommer's business started about
the same time. Funny thing, that, Ed. Digging into your background produced some fascinating blanks."

Ed was holding a large-caliber gun—a .44, I guessed. While
ordinary bullets wouldn't hurt Verne and probably not Morgan,
I suspected that he would not be using ordinary bullets. For me,
of course, the point was moot; if you fired a wad of gum at the
speed of a bullet it'd probably kill me. "I've gotta hand it to you,
Mr. Wood. If we hadn't been watching the house constantly over
the past couple of days, you might have blown the whole thing.
We wanted him," he nodded at Verne, "to be unconscious before
we actually moved."

"How very convenient for you that I happened to decide on
remodeling at just the right time." Verne tried to deliver the lines
in his usual measured, sure manner, but his weakening had gone
far past the point where iron will could banish it.

"Convenient, but hardly necessary. Morgan, down on the floor.
Once we'd tested to make sure that our precautions rendered us
invisible to your casual inspection, the installation could have
been made at any time. More dangerous, but no major enterprise
is without risk. And after we began remodeling, the whole house
was wired in more than one way. It would have been a *lot* easier
if our . . . subcontract that sent Klein over had worked out, but hey,
measure once, cut twice, right?" He smiled. "We learned a great
deal recently. It does bother me about Kafan's new identity. Why
anyone would take that much interest in this case is a matter for
concern. But not for you." Ed shifted his aim directly to Morgan
and, to my horror, began to squeeze the trigger.

Weakened and sick Verne might have been, but when it came to the life of his friend and oldest retainer all his supernal speed must have come back. There was movement, a blur that fogged the darkened air between Ed and Morgan for a split second; then Ed Sommer was hurled backwards into the front stairwell with an impact that shook the house. The gun vanished somewhere in the darkness.

The lights came back on; there must have been some of Ed's people in the house. Caught in the light again, I could see Verne sag slightly.

From the stairwell came a curse, but it wasn't the voice of a human being. A monstrous figure tore its way out of the wreckage, a hideous cross between man, lizard, and insect. Humanoid in form, scaled and clawed and with patches of spiked, glistening armor from which hung the tattered remains of Ed's clothing. "A good final effort, Sh'ekatha," the Ed-thing hissed. "But foredoomed to failure."

While it was focused on Verne, I had time to draw my own gun. Its gaze shifted towards me just as I got a bead on it.

BlamBlamBlamBlamBlamBlamBlamBlamBlamBlam! I emptied the full ten rounds into the monstrosity. It staggered with the impact, and toppled backwards. "Run!" I shouted. Verne and Morgan were already moving. I ejected the empty magazine and slammed in a fresh one as I sprinted after them. A single glance had sufficed to show me that the bullets hadn't done any notable damage. "Just *once* I'd like to find something I can shoot and *kill*, like any normal person!"

Verne staggered down the basement steps to be caught by something indescribable that tried to rip him apart. Morgan intervened, shoving the interloper through a nearby wall with unexpected strength. "Keep going, sir!" he said over his shoulder as he kept his attention on his adversary. Distantly, we could hear other things smashing; the rest of the household must be under attack now as well!

"Damn you, Jason!" I heard a voice roar as we pried open the door to the Heart. "This was supposed to be a subtle operation!" Massive feet thundered down the stairs behind us.

The door swung open; I shoved Verne through it and then stepped through myself, pulling the door shut as a huge shadow rushed towards us. I pulled the door shut and twisted the lock.

The impact on the other side shook rock dust from the tunnel ceiling.

"It will not stop him for long, Jason," Verne forced out.

"A little time's better than none," I gasped.

I'd seen the Heart a few days before, as a sort of postscript to Verne's story. Here, things seemed quieter, like a summer forest in midafternoon; lazy, sleepy, silent. In the center of the large cavern, a perfectly circular pool of pure water shimmered in the light, blue as the vault of heaven. At the far side, a squat obelisk of black obsidian. The Mirror of the Sky and the Heartstone. Hanging on the far wall was some kind of sheath or casing.

I became aware I was gasping for breath, realizing only then that Verne hadn't really been running; that I'd been dragging him along instead. Even here, in the place most sacred to him, he had no strength. Technology was winning the battle.

A rending, shattering sound echoed down the corridor as I dragged Verne to the pool's far side and dropped him to rest against the obelisk. Slow, measured footfalls clicked down the tunnel. The snake-headed monster that called itself "Ed Sommer" entered the room, smiling at me. "Too bad about you, Jason. You just happened to be in the wrong place at the wrong time."

I didn't say anything; I couldn't afford to waste my breath.

"Tired?" it asked cheerfully as it continued towards me. "Well, it will be over soon enough."

As long as he was moving slowly, with full control, I didn't have a chance. "At least I know you're not going to survive me by much, Ed or whatever your name is."

The slit-pupiled eyes narrowed. "What do you mean?"

"I mean that I found the location of your laboratory tonight. My TERA-5 got lucky and matched patterns. And if I don't send the 'no-go' code soon, the system storing my data will dump the location and all the info I have on the lab's operations into every intelligence agency and scientific forum on the planet. It'll be a lot easier to pry the kid and the mother away from a bunch of squabbling agencies than from one group of demonic crossbreeds with a unified purpose."

The lie worked; it fit perfectly with what they knew of my capabilities, was precisely what I would've done if I *had* found the location and had no other choice. The giant figure charged forward. "I'll have that code out of you if I have to rip it out of your heart!"

Jesus, he was fast! Fast as Klein! But with him charging, everything changed. I jumped up onto the Heartstone and lunged to meet the Ed-thing just as he leapt towards us across the Mirror of the Sky.

The impact stunned me, and I felt at least three armored spikes go deep into my arms, but I held on. My momentum had mostly canceled his, and the two of us plummeted directly into the deceptively deep pool below.

A detonation of leaf-green light nearly blinded me as the entire pool lit up like an emerald spotlight; surges of energy whipped through me and I came close to blacking out. Boiling water fountained up and I was flung outward to strike with numbing force on the altar, shocked, parboiled, and aching. Electrical arcs danced around the edge of the water, then spat outwards, shattering the lightbulbs across half the room. A roar of agony echoed from the depths of the Mirror of the Sky. Then the boiling subsided, the eerie green light faded away. Blinking away spots, I looked down. A few pieces of spiky armor, bubbling and dissolving away like Easter egg dye pellets, were all that remained.

"One more guess confirmed." My voice, not surprisingly, shook. I reached down and retrieved my gun from where I'd dropped it near the Heartstone.

Verne gave a very weak chuckle. "If they were my enemies, they would be the very antithesis of the power I wielded. Yes?"

"I hope so."

Another voice spoke from the entranceway. "And you were quite correct."

I felt my jaw go slack as I looked across. "Oh...oh damn. You're dead."

In the bright lights that remained, the Colonel, resplendent in his uniform, walked towards us. "As is oft-quoted, reports of my death were greatly exaggerated. Kafan, poor boy, didn't realize precisely what I was, so he only damaged my body. As you learned," and suddenly, without any visible pause, he was there, taking the gun from my hand with irresistible force, "ordinary weapons are rather useless against us. Tearing out my throat was an inconvenience, easily remedied. But it was more convenient to appear to die and hope he'd lead us to the other two children, than to keep fighting him."

Despite my struggles, he picked me up and tied me up with

rope he had slung over his shoulder. A casual kick from him sent Verne sprawling. "Now we can fix things. Pity about Ed, though. Rather promising in some ways, but a trifle dense. If only I'd been a moment sooner... good bluff, boy. But your mind is a bit transparent." He set me down on the Heartstone and groped under his uniform. "Now where... ah, there it is." His hand came back into view, holding a long, sharp, crystalline knife. He smiled.

I couldn't maintain my usual facade of confidence here. I swallowed, tried to speak, found that my throat had gone completely dry.

"Don't bother trying to speak. You see, a ritual sacrifice on this stone will negate its very nature, ending the power of this shrine, which is quite painful to me, and in his weakened condition it should also destroy the priest. So you, by virtue of your very bad fortune, shall be the one through which we cleanse the world of the last trace of Eönae and her nauseating priests."

"So why are you bothering to tell me?" I managed to get out. "Just a melodramatic villain with a long-winded streak?"

He laughed at that, a cheerful sound all the more macabre because it was so unforced and honest. "Why, not at all; a purely practical reason, I assure you. You see, fear, despair, and the anticipation of death are part of what strengthens the ritual. They are antidotes to life and endurance and all the other things that this shrine represents. The more I allow you to muse upon your end, the more you see your friends weakened and destroyed, and the stronger my final sacrifice will be. If it were just a matter of killing you, I'd have had you shot weeks ago." The blade rested on my Adam's apple, pricking my skin coldly. He drew a line down my throat. I felt a warm trickle of blood. "And your little seer friend, the girl... she, too, has a part to play in this."

"She'll see you for what you are, and get away."

"I think not. We caught her earlier this evening, actually. I was anticipating the priest's incapacitation this morning." He raised the knife, brought it towards my right wrist.

A blurred motion swept past me, pushing the Colonel away in that instant. A confused set of motions later, the Colonel and the blur separated and stopped.

The Colonel regarded Kafan with tight-lipped amusement. "I must confess I didn't expect you quite yet."

Kafan answered in Vietnamese; the two squared off. "What

do you hope to accomplish, boy?" the Colonel asked. "You failed the last time. What is the point of fighting me again?"

I began wiggling my hand towards my Swiss Army knife. If I could just get it out...

"This time you're not coming back," Kafan growled. He and the Colonel exchanged a blinding flurry of blows and blocks, neither of them touching the other.

"Really?" the Colonel said. He swept Kafan's feet out from under him and hammered the smaller man's face with his elbow. Kafan barely evaded the next strike and rolled up, throwing a punch at the Colonel that left a dent in the wall. They circled each other, Kafan spitting out blood as the Colonel's grin widened, the teeth sharpening. "And why is that?"

"Because now I know what I am."

The Colonel hesitated fractionally. Not quite as much as Kafan obviously hoped for, but even so Kafan's instantaneous lunge nearly decapitated him. As it was, the Colonel's preternatural speed pulled his head aside barely in time; Kafan's claws scored his cheek with five parallel scratches. "Feh! *Kr'lm akh!* What difference is that, boy? So you were meant to be a Guardian! Without the Goddess behind your power, what are you but a simple thug, one whose blows are nothing more than stinging sand?" I'd hoped his words were boasting, but seeing how those five cuts were already healing, I realized that the Colonel was speaking the truth.

Kafan returned the Colonel's grin, with interest, his form fully changed into a tailed, fanged humanoid. He straightened slightly and brought his arms into a strange, formal stance. "I don't need the Goddess behind my power. All I need are two words, given to me by the Master who taught me."

The Colonel tensed.

"*Tor.*"

At that word, the Colonel stepped back.

Not fast enough. Two slashing movements of Kafan's hands, too fast to follow, ripped aside blocking arms and a third strike against the uniformed chest sent the Colonel flying into the wall with a combined sound of shattering stone and breaking bone.

While the Colonel slowly rose, bones forcing themselves back to their proper positions and healing in moments, Raiakafan sprinted to the section of the wall nearest me. "And *Shevazherana*," he said. He pulled the sheath from the wall and drew out the immense, squat-bladed sword.

The Colonel's eyes widened. His form began to shift and he leapt away, towards the exit.

Raiakafan stood there, impossibly having crossed the room in the blink of an eye. "No escape for you, monster. For my father—*this!*"

The first slash took off the changing form's right arm. What was formerly the Colonel screeched and tried to stumble backwards. It ran into something, spun around to find itself facing... Raiakafan again. "For my children—*this!*"

The other arm flew off in a fountain of red-black blood. Screeching in terror, not a trace of humanity left on its bony, angular form, the thing flapped feeble wings and flew upwards, away from the implacable hunter. A hunter who disappeared from view while both the monster and I stared.

And once more, the creature that had been the Colonel rebounded from something that had appeared in its path. Falling along with the stunned demon, Raiakafan shoved it downwards so it landed prone on the grassy floor of the cavern. "And for my wife."

The great sword came down once more. In a flash of black light, a flicker of shadow that momentarily erased all illumination, the thing dispersed.

A pile of noisome dust sifted away from Kafan's sword, dust that slowly evaporated and turned into a smell of death and decay...and faded away to nothing.

"Get up, Father," Kafan said, helping Verne. "It's over now."

I staggered wearily to my feet, feeling the warm trickle of blood down my arms. "No. Not yet. They've got Sylvie!"

Kafan cursed in that ancient tongue. "But where?"

"Only one guess. She's got to be at Ed's place. At least, I hope so, because without the Colonel to tell us, it'll be a long hard search if she isn't." And I couldn't afford to think about that.

"Is it not...possible that he was bluffing?" Verne said weakly.

"Do you think he was?"

Verne didn't answer; his expression was enough.

"Neither did I. He wouldn't bluff that way. He was smart enough to set things up ahead of time."

Kafan looked at me. "You're not in any condition to fight."

"Don't even *think* about keeping me out of this. Who else are we going to call?"

Somehow we got to the top of the stairs. Morgan, with his usual imperturbable expression denying the very existence of his torn clothing and bloodied form, smiled slightly as we emerged. "I'm glad to see you're all still alive."

"Can you drive, Morgan?"

Morgan raised an eyebrow. "Certainly, Master Jason. I presume there is some urgency?"

"If any of these monsters are left, they've got Syl."

Morgan snatched the keys from my hand and half-dragged me along. Verne was moving easier, but it was plain that neither of us was up to a fight with a half-dead Chihuahua, let alone a group of demonic assassins. The fact that neither Morgan or Kafan said anything told us that they knew that we'd never allow ourselves to be left behind.

The drive across town was excruciatingly slow. It seemed that every block was ten times longer than I remembered. We entered Morgantown's main district, crossed through, and continued. Though only fifteen minutes had passed, I felt as though precious days were passing. Syl. How *could* we have left her unguarded?

Ed Sommer's house was lit up like a full-blown party was going on inside. The fence around it looked normal, but I could tell it was stronger than it appeared ... and electrified, too. A contractor like Ed wouldn't have had trouble installing all sorts of bad news for intruders.

"Hang on, gentlemen," Morgan said.

"What are you doing?" I asked.

"Going through the gate, of course," he said calmly, as the engine on Verne's limousine roared and we were pressed back by acceleration. "Without being in suitable combat condition, our best chance is ..."

With a rending crash, the limo shuddered but tore through the gateway.

"... total surprise and uncompromising speed. Prepare to attack."

Expecting a counterattack, we dove out of the limo. The front door of the house popped open. Arms screaming in pain, I still managed to bring the gun up, sighted on the target—

—and immediately dropped the gun. "Don't shoot! It's SYL!"

Sylvia emerged from the doorway, stepping gingerly over the

limp body of a demonoid as she did so. As I raced up the steps and embraced her, she smiled and said, "I see you missed me."

"We should hurry, Master Jason," Morgan said. "There may be others pursuing her."

"There aren't," Syl said with calm certainty.

CHAPTER 46

Explanations

"I must confess, Jason, that there are a few things which remain unclear to me."

Rebuilding Verne's mansion was taking some time. It had also taken a lot of fast talking to keep Jeri from poking her nose too far in; even though the mansion was relatively isolated, the battle between the Colonel's half-demons and Verne's household had been more than loud enough to draw a lot of attention. Now, a week later, we were meeting in the repaired living room.

Verne was back to his old, debonair self: black hair glistening sleekly in the lamplight, dark eyes as intense and deep as they ever were. "Firstly, Jason, how did all the people gain entrance without us knowing of them?"

"Since the house was bugged," I answered, reaching out for an *hors d'oeuvre* and wincing slightly from the pain in my arms, "Ed and the others heard me come in. When I said to shut down *all* the electrical power in the house, that took out the alarm systems. Your own personal alarms—the mystical ones—were weakened along with you, of course. I'd presume that they had some ability to subvert magical wards as well. And, of course, once the shooting started, none of us would've noticed an alarm much anyways."

Verne nodded. "True enough. In my condition, I wouldn't have noticed much, nor cared, I admit. Now, second . . . Lady Sylvia."

Syl grinned from ear to ear. "It was almost worth being kidnapped by those things to see the expressions on your faces. Jason, dear, you try to take me seriously, but like so many people—men and women—you see my gypsy facade and my crystal earrings and pendants and forget what I really am." She paused. "So did they. They didn't search me at all; I didn't resist except to scream and struggle a bit. Then when they had me locked away"—for a moment her face had a grim expression on it, one I'd never seen before; I wasn't sure I liked it—"I prepared myself, and then I . . . *left*."

"Indeed, milady. But *how*?"

"You trust my visions. So do I. That's because I'm not a fake."

I remembered Elias Klein dropping me in agony because the touch of a rock-crystal amulet burned him. I thought about what that meant.

So did Verne. "My apologies, milady."

"No apologies needed, Verne. You saw me as I prefer to be seen; a somewhat airheaded, gentle mystic with no taste for war and a hint of the Talent. But when my friends are in danger, I'm not as gentle as I look. The truth is that they weren't ready for a real magician, even a very minor one. And that was fatal." She looked ill for a moment.

"It's okay, Syl," I said.

She looked up at me. "You're not too shocked?"

"It'll take a little readjustment, I guess. But not that much. You carry a gun. I've known that you're smart enough not to carry something unless you were sure you could use it if you had to. So I shouldn't have been surprised that you'd be able to fight in other ways, too. I'm glad it still bothers you, though. As long as we're both bothered by it, we're still human."

Verne nodded solemnly. "Killing is a part of life at times. But it is when we come to accept it as a matter of course that we give up a part of our souls."

"I have a few questions of my own," I said. "Kafan, what were those words you said that made the Colonel back up?"

Kafan glanced at Verne, who inclined his head slightly. "Well, 'Shevazherana' is the name of that sword my Master gave me, the one Verne kept after I disappeared. It means . . . Dragontooth, Dragon Fang, something like that. The other word, 'Tor' . . . it is the name for the method of combat that I was taught. Why, exactly, it scares demons, I don't know, but it does."

Verne shrugged. "It was the technique of combat used by the Royal Family of Atlantaea and their guardians. And demons had good reason to fear that family's vengeance after the fall of

Atlantaea. And the one who taught you ... oh, there are excellent reasons for them to fear anyone who knows that word."

All of us could see that Verne might know more, but wasn't going to continue. I decided I'd delved into more than enough unspeakable mysteries in the past few weeks. This one I'd leave alone. "When you were fighting the Colonel, you ..." I paused, "you seemed to move, but not move, if you know what I mean."

Kafan smiled. "You mean, teleported. Yes, I can do that. In combat, I can do it very quickly, to anywhere I can see or directly sense. Out of combat, I can go much farther, to anywhere I have been often enough to have ... well, call it a sense of what the place is really like."

"So my eyes weren't playing tricks on me. Still, that's a hell of a power to have."

"And *not* one I recall you having to such an extent in the old days, Kafan."

For an instant, there was a flicker of that dead black look, but it disappeared, leaving Kafan simply looking cautious. "No, I didn't, Father. But I can't talk about *why*, not now anyway."

"No problem. I do have one other general question," I said.

"Only one? Dear me, Jason, then I must have already said far too much!" Verne said, relaxing.

I laughed. "No, seriously. You've often mentioned, offhandedly, things about 'other worlds' and how somehow magic was removed or sealed away. I guess my question is ... where *is* the magic? And will it come back?"

He looked thoughtful. "This is not the first time I have considered that question, Jason. To put it simply, magic exists everywhere to at least some very small extent, but its focal point, if you will, is a single world. Why such a truly cosmic force should be so focused I do not know—I never studied magical theory—and the reasons behind such a phenomenon were probably only really understood by a handful of wizards of Atlantaea.

"However, there was a link—a conduit, one might say—between that world and Earth. Kerlamion and his forces either severed or blocked the conduit. If severed, it might well act as would a similar item in the real world, spraying its cargo of power out into the 'area,' if one could use such a term, of the break. Where that would be, of course, is a question far beyond my ability to answer. If it was sealed, on the other hand, the power has been building up behind the blockage. Perhaps there is some maximum which is already reached, and thus the barrier will remain unless something breaches it; or, perhaps, eventually enough pressure, so to speak, will build up and shatter even the Seal placed by the Lord of Demons."

I thought for a moment. "So, to summarize, 'I haven't a clue' is your answer."

Syl gave an unladylike snort that turned into a fit of coughing; she'd just been taking a sip of tea when I skewered Verne. As I apologized, the others finished laughing. I sat back in my chair, feeling a crinkle of paper that reminded me of something.

"Oh, Verne, I've got something for you." I handed him the check.

He stared at it. "Jason, I appreciate that you wish to repay me, but we're hardly done yet. Besides, after what I know you've spent, I know you cannot possibly afford this."

I grinned. "It sure shows that you've been too busy to keep up with events lately, or you'd have seen the news articles on it. Verne, I'm rich now."

"What?"

I opened up the paper. "Take a look. After the Morgantown Incident, werewolf paranoia showed up everywhere. And since there's only *one* known way to detect the things, people, including the Feds, started making Wood's Werewolf Sensors, or whatever they wanted to call them. Well, a little pushing from the right lawyers—and the president—and the patent office recognized that I'd done the design work and owned the rights to every version of the thing being produced. In exchange for a real generous licensing deal to allow them any number of the sensors for government use, the Feds made sure that the private-sector manufacturers coughed up the bucks real fast and either got out of the business or started licensing from me. I'm probably going to have quite a substantial income for a long time to come."

"Truly it's an ill wind that blows no good, Jason. Even Virigar has brought something good out of his visit. My congratulations."

"Speaking of those things, have they actually proven to be of any use?"

"According to government sources—who naturally don't want to be talked about—a number of, um, 'paranatural security breaches' were detected through its use and related approaches. That's one reason they're very happy to work with me."

"So all's well, then," Verne said. "It is well done with."

"We're not done yet," I said. "There's still the question of Senator MacLain. And of Kay and your daughter."

Kafan nodded, lips tight.

Verne smiled. "True, Jason. Yet I have confidence that we will find a way to deal with these things. The Lady is with me again. I have friends. I have my son.

"Faith, friends, and family, Jason. What more do any of us need?"

Part V

Live and Let Spy

September 2000

CHAPTER 47

Categorization and Catharsis

"Good evening, Jason," Verne said. "Is there a reason you come bearing a laptop?"

"Evening, Verne," I said, sitting down in the large, comfortable chair I usually took when visiting. "Yep. Remember, I asked you if you were free this evening. I want to pick your brain, or at least get a start on it."

"Not spending the evening with Lady Sylvia?"

I shook my head. "No. Syl got an emergency call from a friend of hers, Samantha Prince. A young girl she knows disappeared and so Syl's down to see what she can do. I guess Samantha and this girl, Aurora, were pretty close."

"Dear me. I hope things will turn out all right." He then raised an eyebrow at me, curious. "So you would pick my brain... about what, in particular?"

"Well, when I first met you and ended up with Elias Klein turning into a charcoal briquette, I thought, 'Well, now, that's something to tell my grandkids,' but figured it was a fluke. Then Virigar and his litter of homicidal puppies showed up, and I thought, 'Jeez, twice in a year. But that ought to be that.'"

Verne sat down in his own chair. "I believe I see where this is going."

"So then along comes Ed Sommer, genetically engineered contractor-assassin, following your time-displaced contradictory-backgrounded long-lost son, and I get an infodump on the Secrets Man Was Not Meant To Know," I continued. "At this point, I think I have to accept that as long as I'm involved with you, the Weird Crap of the World is going to keep coming to my door.

This puts aside the fact that along the way, I, personally, have gotten pretty high on the hit parade of several nasties—Ed and the Colonel's former organization, whatever's left of them, the vampire who sent Klein after you at their request, and of course the King of the Werewolves himself.

"So I figure that as long as I'm going to be in the deep end, I might as well know what else might be swimming around under me, nibbling at my toes." I plugged my laptop into the wall and powered up. "I've set up a database for the weird here, and I want you to help me fill it in, as much as possible, so that when I run into something, I'll have a chance to figure out what I'm dealing with."

"I cannot argue with the logic of this enterprise," Verne admitted. "Whether I agree that I, personally, am the focal point—it could, I think, be argued with equal facility that you are yourself the crux—I am a firm believer in destiny. Giving you more information to work with has always served us well. Ask and I shall answer, to the best of my ability."

Kafan appeared in the doorway. "Do you need my help, Mr. Wood?"

I shook my head. "I don't think so, Kafan. Verne probably knows more about the current State of the Weird than you do, given that you spent most of your current life either locked in a lab or hiding in some Viet jungle. If I have to ask about things specific to you, I'll let you know. By the way, I got a message from the senator; I'll be having a meeting with her day after tomorrow, and the three of us will have to decide how I'm going to approach it. But I'll do that tomorrow as a strategy meeting."

Kafan clearly wanted to discuss it now, but he restrained himself admirably. It had taken more than a little effort to hammer it through his head that there simply was not going to be any quick and easy way to get his children back. "I'll see you tomorrow, then," he said finally. "I'm going out for a while, Father. Morgan says that he and Meta will watch Genshi."

"Very well, Kafan. Enjoy yourself." Verne turned back to me as Kafan left. "So where shall we start?"

"Well, why not with you, Verne?" I asked. "Over the last few months, I've gotten piecemeal ideas about what hurts you or helps you and so on, and you told me that your powers derive from your...goddess," I stumbled over the word; it was still difficult for me to casually refer to things as fact which had been myth to me a year previously, "and that Klein's type of vampire was made in mockery of what you are, but I'd like to have a unified idea of what you can and cannot do, and why, and then we can compare this to the Klein type of vampire, and move on from there."

"I have no objection." Verne settled back and steepled his fingers in thought. "As you know, the Lady Eönae blessed me with these powers. She is the essence of the living world; you can think of her as a spirit who reflects the nature of life and the magic of the soul. During the destruction of Atlantaea, I was one of her priests—high in her hierarchy, but not at the top—and at the time the blow fell, I was serving as...how should I put it... a minister or chaplain to the Royal Family. Seeing the demons unleashed, the Eternal Queen told me to go swiftly and protect her son, Prince Mikael, who had only shortly before left for the Great Temple. She did this partly out of kindness, I am sure, for she knew that my own wife and children were of necessity at the Great Temple as well."

Verne's voice took on a trace of that ancient accent, and his eyes became dark and sad as he continued. "It was while I raced down the Diamond Way that I was attacked by a mob of demons. Individually, they were no match for me at all, and as a group, they should not have been able to defeat one of my rank and training. But even as I summoned the power of the Lady to oppose them, I felt it falter. For the first time in living memory, something was threatening the strength of Eönae herself, and because of that we, her chosen, were weakened at the very moment when we so desperately needed her power." He sipped from his crystal goblet, eyes staring into the past. "Yet still had Queen Niadeea placed her command and charge upon me, and I would not fail her. With the shadow of power still mine to command and with my own will and training, I managed to fight my way free of the demons, but they had grievously injured both body and soul. I should have died there, moments after that desperate victory, but I could not—*would* not—yield my life without reaching the Great Temple. I refused Death, forbade it to touch me, and swore upon all the Powers of the Two Worlds that I would still reach the Temple and see Prince Mikael's living face, even were my very heart torn from my body.

"Around me, as in a nightmare, I could hear the destruction of the city—screams of terror and pain, the snarls of demons and monsters, the crumbling of buildings, the flare and thunderclap roar of spells and mystic weapons against the invaders. My breath seemed to give me no strength, yet I forced one foot in front of another, following the wavering path onward towards the building I must reach."

I found myself gripping the laptop tightly, knowing what was coming. There was pain in Verne's voice, a pain that literal ages had not been able to entirely erase. I hadn't intended to ask for his past story, just for something on what he could do, but I realized that this was a story he hadn't told for a long time indeed, and maybe a story that he *had* to tell.

"The steps of the Great Temple were covered in blood. The echo of the Lady's presence was fainter. I staggered up the steps, my shattered ribs grating, blood trickling down my side, vision narrowing until it seemed I walked down a black tunnel, a tiny sliver of light ahead of me revealing bodies, torn tapestries, nothing but death, death and destruction everywhere." For a moment, his voice, the smooth, deep voice which almost never varied its controlled pitch, caught, wavered. "Then I saw them.

"Mithanda lay atop Nami and Suti, futilely trying to protect them to the last. The beast that had slain them turned towards me, grinning, feeding upon my horror and despair. I screamed, I know that, and swung my staff of office, caring nothing of how I died now. But the staff carried the enchantments, as did almost all weapons in those days, and the monster had seen my wounds; it had thought me unable to fight, and its lunge took it straight into the path of my blow. The staff shattered, but the mystic force slew the monster in that same moment.

"I could do nothing for my family now. I had to see if the Prince was safe. Surely, he would have been taken to the Heart, for the Sh'ekatha to defend him. I had nothing left, only the command of the Queen. Somehow, I still moved, leaving them behind. Mourning would be for later." He drew a deep breath.

"But the Prince was not there. The Sh'ekatha was, but he was already near to death. The Lady was one of the demons' greatest enemies, so one of their greatest killers had been sent to make her cult impotent. It had not been easy, not even for one of the Great Demons, but even as I entered, Balgoltha broke the Sh'ekatha's back over the Heartstone. My cry of protest was barely a cough, so weak was I, but still the Demonlord heard it and turned. Wounded though he was, he laughed, and rightfully so. I was no threat to such as he—not even had I been unhurt. The Lady's power was faint, and fading. I had no more hope or help to give, and I had failed the Queen, for surely the Prince was dead or captured now. With no other recourse, I used the last of my strength and staggered into the Mirror of the Sky; at least I would die in a place where no demon might touch my soul."

He swallowed, eyes still focused on things long gone to dust. "But the Lady is wise, and has the craft of the Earth within her. In that very instant, she drew upon the strength of the world entire, and I . . . I became the Sh'ekatha.

"Balgoltha had tried to seal the power, but even he had failed to realize how strong the Lady could be; by the time he reacted, it was too late. Here, in the center of the Great Temple, I rose from the Mirror, healed and touched by the very grace of the Lady, and Balgoltha knew he was no match for me, not in that moment, not as he was. It would have pleased me to fight him, finish off at least one of the enemy, but he was no fool, and fled with a curse.

"Atlantaea was ended, and the demons scoured the Earth. With the Lady's blessing, I could hide from them, but little else could I do for long, long years. Only when they had left, confident that their work was done and only harmless savages remained, did I emerge and, taking those few things I could salvage, begin to rebuild what had been lost."

There was a long silence then. Finally, Verne shook himself and looked apologetically at me. "Dear me, Jason . . . I became rather carried away there. I had no intention of talking so long on a topic, which is, at best, a side issue to the one at hand."

"It's okay. I think you needed to talk that out."

He hesitated, then nodded slowly. "You may be right, my friend.

"And though it's about half a million years too late . . . I'm sorry."

"Your sympathy is appreciated." He sipped from his goblet, and then with visible effort, cast off the feeling of brooding sadness. "Enough of this. It was only after that time that I truly began to understand what I had become, and why. The powers of a Sh'ekatha, and their limitations, are all part of what it means to represent Eönae, the Lady of the World.

"Firstly, I drink blood. Blood is in many ways the essence of life; it carries all that sustains a living being, and thus I depend on it as all living things depend on each other. I am strong, a strength that represents both the unity of life and the solidity of the Earth, and a strength which grows as time does pass, just as a forest can grow from a single seed in time. Only things that are living, or that derive directly from the activity of life, can harm me as weapons. This reflects the fact that the existence of life itself is not truly dependent on the Earth's decisions, for life is a natural consequence of the world; only the turning of life against itself, or an unnatural form of life, can destroy life.

"I cannot enter a dwelling place of intelligent creatures unbidden, because the very nature of intelligence is to control nature; nature only enters a dwelling if the owner permits it, and therefore one who is the living avatar of nature may not enter without permission either. I can change my form, since life is itself mutable, and nature exists in many guises; yet the forms I can assume are constrained, because in nature the rules constrain the ways in which life evolves.

"Sunlight harms me and those of my kind, if any others still exist, because it is the source of energy for all other forms of life, but the Sh'ekatha draws his strength from the Earth itself; he is reminded, by this separation, that he is different from all other things that live because he, alone of all things, is tied to the Spirit of the World directly and can do no harm to her without feeling it rebound upon him, nor can anything long harm the world without harming him. He can no longer turn to the Sun for strength and light, but must find it within himself.

"I can influence the world, especially the elements of air and water, through the action of my will—although this power does not come to a Sh'ekatha immediately, but grows over time just as the physical strength. This power derives from the fact that life itself can affect and transform the world, and is in fact an expression, by its very existence, of the power of spirit over matter. Similarly, as that which lives can affect me, I can affect it to some extent, and thus I have some power over minds.

"As I represent the Earth, itself, and life in all its guises, no mirror or image made by unthinking machines can capture my essence; a picture of myself can only be created by the power of a thinking mind that sees me with its soul as well as by crude light. As I am living, I can also reproduce, though in a way unique to myself; I can place some of my power in another who is willing, and let that power grow; my life-force acts as a seed and symbiote, creating a new and stronger life, but one with some ties to both me and to the original creature." He sat back and finished his glass of blood. "I believe that covers everything. If I recall anything else, I shall inform you."

I typed, asking questions of him occasionally since I had to clarify certain points—he'd reeled that stuff off awfully fast. Finally, I finished. "Okay. How about those vampires like Klein? Is there a specific logic in the parody of your powers?"

Verne's mouth tightened momentarily. "Oh, yes. Their creator was a magician of vast power, one who, in essence, was attempting to become a demon and perhaps something even greater in darkness. I was one of his major adversaries after the Fall of Atlantaea, because I attempted to establish a new civilization based on the old and had the power to do so. He intended to create his own empire, or so I believe, in order to use the strength of the human race to further his personal quest. In any case, I became a perennial thorn in his side; he could not corrupt the world or its spirit so long as I lived. Eventually, he came up with this curse, which was all too effective.

"The victims of the curse, the vampires, are parodies in all ways. Rather than a purification and extension of the true spirit, they are warped powers, turned against themselves to produce an abomination. They drink blood to represent their ties to destruction—spilling blood rather than accepting it freely. Their strength is the strength of self-hate and destruction, life turned upon itself. They shift in shape to forms of nightmare because terror is their object." He gave a wintry smile. "I suspect their inability to enter a dwelling unbidden, besides being necessary in an overall parody, was also there for a purely practical reason; why permit your own mad and vicious creations to enter your own home without permission? For they were all mad, at least for a time; just as becoming the Sh'ekatha cleanses the mind and spirit and gives you clarity and peace, at least in the beginning, so this dark mirrored version first turns the mind against itself and tests your will to live."

Verne went on, detailing the vampiric abilities and weaknesses and their relationship to his own. After that, things got more complicated as we started discussing other "powers" in the world, what they were like, and how they did what they did.

After a while, I glanced at my watch. "Holy sheep! Verne, it's three o'clock in the morning!"

He smiled. "So you want to make an early night of it, eh?"

I grinned back, probably looking a bit dazed. "I probably should have. I had no idea how big a project this was going to be."

"Remember, Jason, many of these things either do not exist anymore, in all probability, or at the least, are vanishingly rare. If you wanted to do a comprehensive catalog of the entirety of the paranormal, you would never finish in an ordinary human lifetime; however, the number of such things that can even function on Earth as it is today is so small that I believe we can probably finish your little database in a few months of once- or twice-a-week discussion."

"Well, that makes me feel some better. I think. But I'll let you know later. Remind Kafan that tomorrow evening we will be going over what I should do in my meeting with the senator. I'm meeting her the day after tomorrow. And remember that we've got that big reception and art show for Sky Hashima next week."

"I would never forget that, Jason; and I shall certainly remind Kafan of our...council of war on the morrow. Get some sleep, Jason."

"Preferably *after* I get home, of course," I said, glancing at my car.

He chuckled and held the door open as I left.

CHAPTER 48

Femme Formidable

I shook the senator's hand. She had a strong grip and looked as dignified in person as in her publicity shots. I was pretty sure that her "stern schoolteacher" image worked in her favor not only at the polls, but on the Senate floor. "Senator, good to meet you."

"A pleasure, Mr. Wood." She was unaccompanied—something which showed considerable trust on her part, or at least faith that her intelligence-gathering people hadn't missed anything dangerous. "Now, I don't have an unlimited amount of time, so let's not spend too much of it on formalities; you call me Paula and I'll call you Jason and we'll just call things as we see them, all right?"

I nodded. "Fine by me, Paula."

"I'll start," she said. "As you know, I have received the test results for paternity, and they clearly demonstrate that your client is the biological parent of my children. If it comes to court, I won't bother arguing with that.

"However," she continued, "investigating your client's background has turned up some...confusing information. Without wasting each other's time going into details, my investigators are of the opinion that some, or all, of his background was falsified, although they do inform me that his credentials, if forged, must have been faked by one of the very best intelligence services. My investigators also find Verne Domingo's background somewhat disquieting. I don't think I need point out that if this is true, I would be extremely unlikely to agree to allow my children to spend any time—even for short periods—with a man whose real name and background I cannot verify."

She had good investigators. I'd expected as much, but they were *damn* good to have ferreted out that stuff. I'd been pretty sure of the general thrust of what they'd find, though, and because of that, I'd made my decisions about how to approach her. Convincing Verne and, especially, Kafan to go along with those had taken hours of sometimes acrimonious debate last night. "You know, I thought you'd be saying something along those lines," I said finally. "I've discussed the situation with my client, and he's given me permission to tell you certain things, but before I do, I'd like to lead up to it in my own way. The situation is much more complex than it seems, and I'd like to give you the big picture."

She responded with a formal nod.

I stood up and went over to a small glass case at one end of the room, opening it with a key code. Reaching in, I picked up one of the objects inside and brought it over. "Do you know what this is? Careful—it's extremely sharp."

The senator examined the long, slender, sparkling object— slightly curved, razor sharp along the inside edge, coming to a needle-fine point at one end, and about half an inch across at the opposite end. At first she looked puzzled, but then she glanced up suddenly. "Why, this must be a..." she stumbled a bit over the next word, "...a werewolf claw?"

"That's correct," I said. "I want you to think about what you're holding: nine inches of diamond blade. The thing it came from had five of those on each hand, five on each foot, and stood taller than this room's roof if it straightened up. It could run as fast as a car given a straight distance to accelerate, was strong enough to tip a car over on its own, and had a mouth full of teeth just like those claws—a mouth that could open up wide enough to cut a man in half...and it could look just like you or me, or anyone else on Earth."

Senator MacLain gave a small shiver. She had a good imagination, I suspected. "I see. I do indeed, Mr. Wood. I assure you, that's one of the things that most impressed me about you—that you survived being chased by something like that."

"More luck than anything else, Senator, believe me."

She gave a refined, Katherine Hepburn–like sniff of doubt. "Jason, to quote a movie that my older son enjoys and with which you are no doubt well-acquainted: 'In my experience, there is no such thing as *luck*.' Rather, I think people who are competent make their own luck through making the right choices in bad moments."

With a small laugh, I ceded her point. "Okay, yes, I'm pretty good at thinking on my feet. But there are a few other points that some investigators have raised and which are relevant here—and yes, I'll be connecting it to your children in a few moments."

She looked thoughtful. "Oh. Quite so. As I recall, one of the unresolved problems, even after the briefing, was exactly who had assisted you. Some of my colleagues were under the impression that it was some special task force of our own—and from reading the transcripts, I think it's *very* clear that this was in fact the impression that the testimony was intended to give. I always felt that there was more being hidden than told, however. Are you saying that my impression is correct?"

Boy, she was sharp. Winthrope and her unknown employers had done a bang-up job on giving out the story without revealing anything they didn't absolutely have to, and the wording they'd used would have fooled almost anyone into thinking they'd been told all they needed to know. Senator Paula MacLain, however, was not just anyone. "Your impression is bang-on, Paula," I said. "I had help, but it wasn't anything official."

She waited.

"The second question that some people have asked—and quite reasonably—is basically 'well, if werewolves exist, does that mean there's other things like them out there?' The answer to that is 'damn straight.'"

She must have seen where I was going with this, but her expression gave nothing away; she continued to wait to see what I was going to put in front of her next.

"Werewolves are just one of at least half a dozen types of beings we call 'mythical' or 'supernatural,' even though those words aren't accurate anymore; after all, it's not mythical if you can actually prove it's there, and if they're part of the way the world works, are they really supernatural?" I shrugged. "Anyway, the wolves are in some ways the nastiest of all of these things, near as I can tell, and they've got their own enemies. In point of fact, the reason they all came to Morgantown was to hunt down one of their old adversaries, who was living here under the name of Verne Domingo."

Now her gaze was riveted on my face. However, other than its intensity, she still wasn't giving any sign of what she was really thinking.

I took a deep breath. "Verne Domingo is one of the other types of beings; the best, really quick way I can think of to describe what he is would be to say he's a vampire, but that's not accurate. It would give you some idea of his characteristics, though. Verne has...connections throughout the paranatural world. In a sense, he's one of its most respected citizens. While he certainly doesn't know everything about all of them, virtually every one of the beings that lives this kind of double life knows about him, even if they don't know precisely where he is.

"Now, where this hooks up with Tai Lee Xiang is that Verne knew Tai Lee's family, years ago." Verne, Kafan, and I had decided that this "take" on history would be close enough to allow us to tell what we had to without bringing up certain contradictions that had led to other facts, which none of us wanted to talk about. "They saw him as an ally and a protector. Verne left for parts unknown and eventually they lost track of him. But the tradition of the protector was passed down through the family line, along with the unique characteristics that separated this protector from the common man.

"So when Tai Lee Xiang found himself in trouble that he didn't dare bring to the authorities since he was, in fact, being hunted by the authorities for killing a man who had held him and his family prisoner for years, he came to me to find this legendary protector. By that time, he'd reached the end of his resources and was willing to try anything to find his family and stop the people who were after him. With the publicity of the wolf incidents, my name seemed the best possible choice; I knew there were Weird Things out there, and if anyone would be both willing to listen to his story and able to find someone from some pretty strange hints, it would be me." I grinned. "As it turned out, he was luckier than he thought. I already knew Verne, of course, so once he gave me the list of odd characteristics, I could just turn around and phone his family protector."

She'd sat quietly throughout the whole story, gazing at me as though I was on trial and she was the judge evaluating my testimony—which, now that I thought about it, was a fair assessment of the situation. Finally, she leaned back. "That is quite an impressive story, Jason. I expect that much of this would be information your friend, Mr. Domingo, prefers to keep secret, since no mention of him has ever been made in connection to prior events in Morgantown. Why was it necessary that you tell me so much?"

"Glad to see you are as quick on the pickup as your reputation makes you, ma'am," I said. "Because Tai wasn't held in an ordinary location at all. He and his children were the subjects of genetic experimentation. By being involved in their lives, you put yourself in danger, because the people who did the experimentation want their 'subjects' back. Your being a senator has no doubt balked them and caused considerable concern in their ranks, but it will most certainly not have stopped them. Eventually, they'll come for the kids.

"So you have to know the truth about them—not just because it's your right to know about anything that might be endangering you and your family, but also because we just don't know what the ultimate results of the genetic tampering that was done to them will be. You might come home tomorrow to find one of them suffering from some disability or condition which simply isn't even recognizable by medical science."

To my surprise, Paula MacLain didn't burst into a flurry of questions, and she didn't attempt to argue about what was going on. She looked more pale, and after an inquiring glance at me, she lit a long cigarette and drew a shaky breath. A few moments later, she dropped her gaze and considered the half-smoked cigarette. "Usually I take my time on these." She looked back up. "Jason, I appreciate your candor."

I'm sure my startlement showed on my face. "Most people would have said something else, and 'candor' wouldn't be even close to the meaning, either."

"Oh, it's a preposterous story, young man," she said. "Yet I'm old enough to know that sometimes life *is* preposterous. However, that isn't why I accept that most, if not all, of your story is true."

Taking another drag from the cigarette, she continued. "I've been on many different committees over the years. I've seen a great deal of material marked 'Top Secret' and heard all the 'in the interests of national security' speeches. So, I'm familiar with the type of reports I get from my own investigators whenever someone has been nosing around my life.

"After I adopted Jackie and Tai, I started getting hints that *someone* was showing interest. The hints were terribly subtle, though, and whenever I hired someone to poke back, so to speak, they found nothing concrete. Just recently—about the time you first contacted me, in fact—these little hints became more frequent, and my best people came to the conclusion that whoever it was had to be top-level intelligence, and that there might be more than one group of them, all sniffing around my family. I tried using my own connections to find out what was going on, but got nothing.

"At one point, Jackie became aware that I thought someone might be spying on us. That night, he tried to leave, taking his little brother with him. When I got them back, he insisted that he had to, but he simply wouldn't tell me why. He's been worried ever since, and I've gotten the extremely strong impression from him that he is more worried about my safety than his own."

I nodded. "That would fit."

"It certainly would. Now, while I happen to believe you are telling me the truth, or as much of it as you think is safe, I'd appreciate a bit more in the way of solid evidence. I've come here without any meddling lawyers or bodyguards so that we could be honest and say what we want, and so I hope we can get this all out of the way."

I glanced at the clock. "How much time do you have, Paula?"

She smiled. "A bit more than I might have implied at the beginning. Start out with the other side under pressure, that's always been my motto. If you can manage to feed me, I daresay I can stay for the rest of the evening if necessary."

Smiling back, I said, "I suppose I could manage that as we get around to dinnertime." I switched on the air filter—while I don't particularly mind smoke, some clients and friends do. "Assuming that what I said is true, what would your position be with respect to Tai Lee Xiang? He's started a quite respectable carpentry and woodcarving business; he's not a shiftless layabout."

"My position isn't markedly changed, Jason," she answered. "I don't care what dangers come with them, they're my children now, and anyone—mad scientists or otherwise—who tries to take them from me will, I assure you, lose their hands. Their true father is another story, naturally. I have noticed genuine sadness in the boys on the few occasions they've mentioned their father, so I know that he inspired affection. This, of course, isn't sufficient to prove that he was, or could currently be, a good father to them, only that he wasn't such a monster or disciplinarian as to lose the love of his children. If I can be confident that he will be good for the children..." her face worked for a moment, "...well, Jason, we will work something out, I promise you. I lost my family once, you know."

I nodded.

"Then understand—I know what that feels like. If I know that Tai Lee Xiang is a good man, then I will not cause him the same kind of pain. He will see his children again. To do anything else would make me the monster, and while the thought of letting the children leave me—perhaps for months at a time—hurts far more than you could imagine, I would rather bear that pain than know I was taking another person's family away." She was back under control, at what cost I really didn't know. "I hope that makes my position clear enough."

"Perfectly clear. And I thank you, Paula. I'm sure we will be able to work something out." I glanced at my watch. "I think I can give you some more solid evidence, but not until later today."

Seeming relieved to have a break from what was obviously a very emotional topic, she accepted a temporary shift away from the business conversation and spent the next little while quizzing me about the Morgantown Incident—getting my version of the story, rather than the trimmed, edited, and perhaps not entirely accurate version that the press releases contained. By the time we finished, it was getting towards evening.

"Well, Senator," I said, "if your reputation can survive the scandal of being seen out in a restaurant with a younger man, I think it's time to get you the dinner I promised."

She laughed. "Mr. Wood, my reputation doesn't need protecting. And having seen pictures of the young lady you're currently dating, I suspect no one would believe any scandal about us anyway."

"I didn't know my love life was so, um, public."

"It isn't, really, but as I said, I had people investigating. With you being one of the principals in this matter, there was a fair amount of digging into your background as well."

I wasn't sure I liked that, but on the other hand it wasn't anything surprising. I shrugged and offered my arm. "In that case, Paula, shall we?"

CHAPTER 49

Mother and Father

"Senator MacLain, welcome," Morgan said, bowing and escorting us inside. "Master Verne is just this way." He took our coats—it was chilly outside now in mid-fall.

Verne and Kafan—rather, I reminded myself, Tai Lee—rose as she entered. "Senator, what a pleasure," Verne said, quite sincerely. "Allow me to present my foster son, Tai Lee Xiang."

The two studied each other. Tai's face was, if anything, more coldly controlled than MacLain's—not surprising, since he knew that if it came to a dragged-out legal fight for custody, this woman was virtually certain to beat him hands-down. "Senator," he said, bowing formally.

"Mr. Xiang." She extended her hand, which Tai took after a moment. "I will say the same to both of you as I said to Mr. Wood: let's not waste time on formalities. Call me Paula, and I'll call you Tai and Verne, and let's see if we can begin to reach some solution to this problem."

"An eminently sensible suggestion," Verne approved. "Very well, Paula. Where would you like to begin? I presume that Jason has already told you a great deal."

She managed a small smile at that. "You might say that, yes. Let us start with you, Verne. Jason tells me you are no longer associated with any of your drug-dealing contacts. Is this indeed true? For you must understand that any—absolutely any— association with drug-dealing is poison to any political career. If the father of my children is found to be living in the same home as someone of that sort..." She trailed off, having made her point clear without needing to belabor it.

Verne sighed. "To be utterly frank, the answer is yes and no. No longer do I, or any of my associates, have any connection with people who deal in illegal substances. However, some of the 'contacts' I used during my days as a supplier of such substances I now use for other. They have shifted their, how shall I put it, inventory and supply lines."

She looked a bit nonplussed. "You mean that the same people who used to ship, or arrange the shipping of, large amounts of cocaine and so on are the ones doing other, non-drug-related work for you now? They simply dropped such a lucrative trade?"

"Quite so."

"You will pardon me if I find that a bit hard to believe," she said. "Most people who were involved in such a business find that the money is quite tempting and continue in it no matter what."

Verne's expression was slightly amused. "In the majority of ordinary cases, I have no doubt you are correct, Paula. However, there is little that is ordinary in my case. My 'contacts' are not ordinary people, in any sense of the term, and have helped with matters of supply and demand, off and on, for an extremely long time. It is, in fact, their business—one in which they take great pride—to drop one line of supply and, within days or weeks, develop another pipeline of supply for an entirely different class of materials that is, in quality and efficiency, quite the equal of the one they dropped."

Paula opened her mouth, closed it, thought for a moment, then spoke. "Hm. When you say 'an extremely long time,' Verne, am I correct in interpreting that to mean something long to a man of your nature, not merely long in terms I am used to thinking in?"

"That would be correct, Paula. For instance, many of the principals involved helped me obtain some of the materials that recently went on display in Cairo. I received these materials shortly after they had been removed from their proper resting place, due to the fact that my suppliers knew of my interest—very long-standing—in preserving materials of historic and cultural value when I could."

I had guessed at something of the sort, but it was still mind-boggling to imagine some group of people who acted essentially as general-purpose suppliers and had endured since at least the middle period of the Egyptian dynasties.

Something similar was probably going through Paula's mind at this point, but her demeanor didn't change. "I must presume, then, that they are experienced at being circumspect about their activities?"

"If you are asking if it is possible that they can be connected to me, especially in a drug-related context, I would say it is extremely unlikely. It happened once, very long ago, and those were special circumstances. In other words, you do not need to worry about these connections of mine becoming an embarrassment to you."

Paula nodded, looked at Tai. "And yours?"

Tai shrugged. "Mr. Wood made the connection between me and the murderer the Viet were hunting because he thought something peculiar was going on, and because he's very good at what he does. Mr. Wood assures me that the IDs that were supplied to me are unimpeachable. So I don't think any evidence will come to light unless I make a nuisance of myself somewhere and make someone really start digging."

Paula laughed suddenly. "I see! If, for instance, there was a loud, public custody battle, I might cause the very kind of uproar I want to avoid."

Tai nodded.

"All right," she said, "I've had my opening shots; either of you gentlemen wish to return fire?"

"I want to know about my children. How are they? Are they safe, really?"

Paula's face softened slightly. "Jackie—Seb, to you—and Tai are perfectly safe. They're wonderful children. Jackie always tries to do whatever he can around the house, even though he doesn't really need to, and he's so good in his studies. Tai, well, he's a bit of a scamp, but he never means any harm. I would think they're as safe in a senator's house as possible."

Until now, Tai had been taut in posture—like a cat with its back up. But as Paula talked about the children, he seemed to relax. There was no single specific change I could point to; he just seemed to settle back. *Something* had reassured him, far beyond anything her words could have done.

"They'd be much safer here," he said, but there was no confrontational edge in his voice.

Paula raised an eyebrow. "You are so sure of that?"

"I would be here," he said. "And so would Father. I know your military and your security. They aren't bad. But they cannot guard a home half as well as we can."

I could sense that Paula wanted to debate that, but she had intuition as good as mine, and knew Tai was telling the truth, at least as he saw it. "Do you concur with this, pardon the expression, extravagant assessment of his abilities, Verne?" she asked.

"Better, I think, that you ask Jason," Verne replied. "He has more extensive knowledge of modern security than I, and has personally witnessed my abilities and those of Tai Lee."

In response to her questioning glance, I grinned. "Beyond doubt. Paula, you must realize how difficult it is to 'get out' of the drug business, especially if there were highly placed people relying on you. Verne was able to provide them with a convincing argument to leave him utterly alone. By himself. Tai can take care of himself and those around him equally well."

"I see."

Morgan came in, carrying two trays of the sinful snacks he always provided to visitors. It was a good thing I didn't spend more time here, or I'd start to become a far bigger man than I'd ever expected. Like Elvis. "No thanks, Morgan—I really have to cut down."

"I'll have some," Tai said, hungry as usual.

Paula took a sampler plate and accepted a glass of wine. "Now, I was hoping for some direct physical evidence of the more unusual claims Jason has made. He said you would provide such evidence?"

Verne couldn't quite restrain a smile. "I think we can arrange that, yes. I believe the same evidence that convinced Jason should suffice, eh, Tai?"

Tai smiled. "Why not." He swallowed another bite, then went to the stairwell. "Genshi? GENSHI! I know you're up there trying to listen in! Come down!"

That familiar clatter-patter of clawed feet immediately sped down the stairs. Genshi, now used to seeing people come and go, wasn't nearly as shy as he had been the night Sylvie and I met him; he toddled up to Paula, who was staring down at him wide-eyed, and smiled, wagging his golden tail.

"This is my youngest son, Genshi," Tai said. "My son Tai, named after me, can change to a very similar form, but was trained to avoid it. Seb's transformation is considerably less extreme, though still very easy to notice."

Genshi suddenly held his arms up, and Paula, clearly a mother to the core despite her often-demanding profession, responded by picking him up. Genshi snuggled into her as though at home. "Nice lady!" he said.

She looked teary-eyed, but held back. "Well, he's certainly a little charmer."

Tai laughed. "He knows how to use the cute look, yep."

"Will you be requiring a demonstration of my abilities as well, Paula?" Verne inquired.

She glanced over at him, still largely focused on the tailed little boy. "Um... not really necessary, I suppose. It would be silly of me to doubt the rest of the story with evidence sitting right here."

"Will you be needing me anymore?" I asked. "Seems we've gotten over the potential shooting war, and I'd like to get home now if possible."

Paula looked at Verne. "If you can provide me with transportation back to my hotel...?"

"But of course. Go on, Jason. I have a feeling that we have started on a resolution to our problems."

I headed out the door, relaxing finally. Judging by the way things were going, a little sympathy might be in order for the late Colonel's pals; Paula MacLain, Kafan, and Verne were going to be a very dangerous team.

CHAPTER 50

Proposal

"How is it?"

I needn't have asked; the blissful expression on Syl's face told me that the food was everything she'd imagined. "God, Jason, the chef must be a wizard!"

The New York restaurant was famous for its Southwestern-grill menu. I'd brought Syl with me because of her fondness for New York, shopping, and grilled TexMex cooking. She needed the break, anyway; her visit with her friend, Samantha, hadn't gone very well. The girl—Aurora Vanderdecken—had apparently disappeared *en route* to her home, no one had seen her since, and the police had no clues; even with Syl's special talents (and those of Samantha, who Syl thought had similar abilities) they hadn't found a trace. Syl had been there for her friend, but the visit hadn't been cheerful.

So I wanted her to have a mini-vacation of her own, and it seemed to be working; the last couple days, she'd been more herself. Today, she'd gotten in plenty of shopping while I took care of business, and she was now temporarily lost to me as she immersed herself in the delights of cilantro, cumin, and cayenne.

This was ideal for my purposes, since it put her Talent at a definite disadvantage.

"Oops," I said, bending over to pick up what I dropped. Then I went to one knee, opening the little box as I did so, and held it so her gaze fell upon it just as she finished swallowing and opened her eyes.

"Sylvia Rowena Stake," I said, sounding far calmer than I felt, "would you marry me?"

For once—maybe the only time I ever would—I had completely surprised her. Not with the question, I'm sure, since both of us knew it would eventually happen, but she hadn't had a clue that today would be the day. Why I was nervous, I didn't know—it wasn't like I could imagine her saying "no" any more than I could imagine asking anyone else to marry me. Maybe it was just that old fear of commitment making its last stand.

Her eyes widened until suddenly tears started rolling down her cheeks; she closed them and flung her arms around my neck. "Oh, *yes*, Jason, of course I will!"

The entire restaurant erupted into clapping, and camera flashes popped across the crowd. We both blushed, but neither of us could stop grinning as I slipped the glittering diamond ring on Sylvie's finger.

The rest of the dinner was taken up by wedding plans. With the sale of the CryWolf devices, money was rolling in for me and I could afford anything, which I told her. Whatever kind of wedding she wanted, from a quick Justice of the Peace civil ceremony to an all-out extravaganza that would empty any six bank accounts, was all fine with me. "Just keep me from having to spend too much of my own time on it," I said, honestly. "I don't do the big fancy stuff well."

She patted my cheek affectionately. "Jason, darling, don't worry. The wedding's still more for the girls than the guys, even in these enlightened times. You just have to show up and look respectable, and I don't need to worry about you on those scores. The problem will be finding an appropriate person to perform the wedding. I'd ask Verne, he's a priest, but somehow my parents would probably balk at the idea. They're still rather Catholic, you know."

"Yeah, I do." I'd met Syl's parents for the first time recently. They couldn't complain about me as a potential son-in-law, and had done their best to make me feel welcome, but it was also pretty clear that they didn't quite know what to make either of my profession, which seemed somewhat arcane and peculiar to people who weren't computer-savvy, or their own daughter, who had departed the normal world quite some time ago. They often wore the bemused expressions of birds who, after sitting on an egg for months, had watched it hatch into a flying turtle. They loved their daughter dearly—that was obvious—but her religion and business were so utterly beyond the pale for them that they simply didn't know how to deal with it. My parents had raised me so innocent of religion that all religions were roughly equal to me, but this made it awkward to deal with a family that joined hands to say grace, quite seriously, at every meal. Never having encountered that ritual before, I was a bit taken aback the first time. Now I saw it as an interesting and possibly heartening custom, but it was a clear departure from what I was used to—either in my own experience, or in Sylvie's breezy approach to life, the universe, and everything.

Sylvie was right that asking Verne, a priest of an unknown (in this age) nature deity, to perform the ceremony would lead to antacid moments for her parents. Much better to find a flexible Catholic priest and write vows that reflected our real commitment. "I'm sure we can find someone who'll fit the bill."

"I'm not worried," she said, taking another bite. "Mmmm. Since I *knew* we were going to be married, we obviously *will* find someone."

I looked at her. "This destiny thing could become very annoying."

She gave a roguish grin. "And it's only just starting, Jasie."

CHAPTER 51

An Evening in Bondage

I yawned, glancing at my watch as I went to my front door. Jeez. Another three a.m. morning after talking to Verne. At least I was getting a load of data, which hopefully I wouldn't ever actually have to use. Oh, damn. I had to check on the tuxedo—I'd forgotten my appointment. Have to reschedule, and soon—I wanted the tux done long, long before the wedding, and the day was approaching like a runaway train.

I kept my head down, trying to keep the combination of sleet and rain from getting in my face. After a moment of fumbling, I unlocked the door and stopped just short of crossing the threshold. Maybe I was catching intuition from Syl, but somehow I just knew my house wasn't empty. The last time this had happened was when Carmichael's thugs had grabbed me. Since then, I'd added a few tricks, however. After making sure there was no one in immediate view, I nudged the wood above the doorway in just the right way, and a small liquid-crystal screen popped into view, cycling views of the rooms in my house from a CryWolf-fitted set of lowlight cameras, with a running status of the systems showing me what was going on, or not, in each room.

Nothing showed up in any view. Were I in an ordinary line of work, that would've been enough to satisfy my paranoia, but vampires don't show on videotape, film, or anything else; while they have to be invited in, it wouldn't be hard to have an accomplice be invited in on legitimate grounds and come back later to invite the vampire in. That's why I studied the status carefully. The motion detectors were a bit different; they didn't actually produce images and thus shouldn't be covered by the magical prohibition against mechanical devices "seeing" a vampire. They just detected air movement within a given volume. None of the detectors showed anything out of the ordinary since I'd closed up shop, so I shrugged. I was getting jumpy.

So I think I could be excused for jumping backwards with a shout of "what the *hell*?" when I entered my living room to find a man sitting in one of the chairs, waiting for me.

"Sit down, Mr. Wood," he said. He was older than me—forty-five to fifty, I guessed, with a tanned, lined complexion. His eyes were hard, cold blue, measuring me up like I was a piece of fabric waiting to be cut to fit. His hair was brown, sprinkled with gray. Standing, he was probably average height. His voice... level, slightly rough, and direct, reminding me of Clint Eastwood; in fact, there was a vaguely Dirty Harry look about him overall.

I didn't like the whole setup, so I started to reach for my gun, and found myself suddenly looking down the barrel of what appeared to be a small cannon. After what seemed an eternity, my brain calmed down enough to recognize it as a .44—probably an AutoMag. Somewhat old-fashioned, but quite capable of blowing a pretty large hole through me. I couldn't believe his speed. This guy hadn't had anything in his hands just the moment before, and I hadn't even seen him move. The only person I'd ever seen move that fast was Tai Lee Xiang.

"Don't think about it," he said. "I'm not here to hurt you. But I don't like people pointing guns at me either."

"Hey, it's cool," I answered, sitting down slowly. "Clearly, I am not going to be much of a threat to you. Now who the heck are you and what are you doing in my house? And how the hell are you sitting here without my security systems showing you?"

"Um, that would be my doing, actually," said another, much younger voice.

Emerging from my bedroom, where he'd evidently gone to hide during my entrance, was a much younger man—in fact, I figured him for a couple years younger than me. He was slender, very tall, and very blond, and he wore a grin from ear to ear that somehow carried a faint air of apology even while it screamed out "I'm *soooo* good at this!"

Something clicked in my head. No picture had ever been printed, but to do what someone had just done to my security system... "The Jammer."

His grin grew even wider and he gave an extravagant bow. "In the flesh!"

I looked across my coffee table at the other man. "Which would make you . . . the guy who strongarmed the Jammer into not blackmailing me."

The weathered face acknowledged that with a hint of a smile. "Mr. Locke was forcibly employed by my organization, and when necessary we rein him in." He made the gun disappear; I didn't see where it had gone. "Mr. Wood, as time goes on it appears that you continue to become more involved in things that impinge upon some of my organization's most sensitive operations. I would try to recruit you, but your operations here actually serve other purposes for us. It has, however, become necessary for us to meet and get to know each other well enough so that we can, when necessary, cooperate and avoid working at cross purposes. The secrecy of my organization at least equals that of our opposition—some of whom you have already encountered."

I knew that Virigar had been a thorn in their side, but I felt that this guy was referring to something larger—at least in terms of his organization, anyway—and that didn't leave me many possibilities. "Whoever sent over Ed Sommer and his pals."

He nodded.

It clicked then. "Winthrope! She's not NSA or any of the regular organizations, she's with you!" I'd always had a nagging doubt about Jeri—which is why I'd avoided tagging her real employers with a particular set of letters; she'd seemed too open and flexible over certain things.

"Told you he already had it down," the Jammer said.

The older man shrugged. "If he wasn't that quick, he would've been dead already. Yes, Mr. Wood, Jeri is employed by us."

"So you know pretty much everything."

"Everything that you've told her or that she's seen," he said, correcting me. "I am quite certain there's information you have never told her."

"Okay." I got up. "C'mon downstairs. I need some coffee; I've been up all day and was going to go to bed."

They followed without comment. The older guy accepted a cup while the Jammer went for a Mountain Dew. I turned to the older man finally. "If we're going to 'get to know each other' well enough, then let's stop tapdancing. Who are you people?"

"My name is James Achernar," he answered after a moment. "My particular task force is codenamed Project Pantheon, and is part of ISIS."

"ISIS?" I repeated. "The name's very, very vaguely familiar..."

"The International Security Investigation Section," the Jammer put in.

Now I remembered. It was an attempt (an abortive one, I had thought) to create a sort of multinational intelligence and espionage network for the United Nations, some years ago. Supposedly, it was going to recruit operatives from different nations to gather information, prevent international disputes, resolve conflicts, and in general be a truth-checking organization with enough teeth to allow the UN to (at least on occasion) be able to tell who was trying to hoodwink them and who wasn't. There'd been some discussion, preliminary appropriations and so on, but I had been certain that ISIS had gone the way of many a good idea whose time will never come. "Now that's interesting. I thought ISIS never really happened."

Achernar gave a small, cold smile. "We prefer it that way. It nearly didn't, in point of fact, but a number of countries—at the time, the US and USSR foremost—recognized that despite various competing agendas, we also needed an independent group that would try its best to defuse problems that could be caused by smaller countries, terrorist organizations, and even large corporations. The result was an intelligence organization operating out of a non-profit front sponsored by the UN, whose full scope of powers and operations wasn't realized by anyone save the people who made it. All participating countries supplied authentic intelligence materials for their contributions—such as genuine IDs and so on—and were given certain controls to prevent their own contributions being used against them.

"Pantheon is a subdivision of ISIS, established shortly thereafter to deal with the most extreme and unusual intelligence situations."

"The X-files," I said.

He gave a wry smile. "Not precisely, although of late it has started to seem that way. We do have other problems."

I studied him. "All right. Now, you said something to the effect that I was making a habit of getting involved in your affairs. Once obviously isn't a pattern, and even twice wouldn't make it certain, but I'm not able to think of more than two possibles in my history. The recent conflict that involved Verne and me against that group from Vietnam is one, and I suppose the episode with Virigar counts as another since, as Gorthaur, he was busily chipping away at everyone in the intelligence agencies, but where's the 'habit' coming from?"

He gazed at me expressionlessly. Finally, he said, "I will not give you details at this time, but I will say that even from your early dealings with Verne Domingo, you began to enter into our business. And now that you've connected Jackie MacLain to his family—"

"I should've known: your people are the ones hanging around Paula MacLain."

"Not just us," the Jammer said. "Them, too. The other side. Once you contacted her and someone performed the paternity test, somehow they were alerted. Up 'til now, the kids had gotten away with it—the baddies had lost track of them. Not anymore."

"So who are they, then?"

Achernar and the Jammer exchanged glances. "At this point, you're better off not knowing," Achernar said, with the Jammer giving a reluctant nod. "I know you will find these answers unsatisfactory, but in the main it's true."

I sighed. "Look, if you're not here to give me info, just what *do* you want from me? And why all the futzing around instead of just setting up a meeting?"

He acknowledged my frustration with another faint smile. "To answer your second question, Pantheon doesn't really exist, so to speak. Currently, as far as any official sources are concerned, I am at a psychological convention attending various seminars, and tomorrow morning I will be presenting a paper of my latest research, no doubt to considerable controversy . . . though to somewhat less mockery, thanks in part to an increase in open-mindedness as a result of the Morgantown Incident."

"Seminars . . . you're Dr. J. T. Achernar!"

His response was the seated equivalent of a bow. "Correct."

"Now I start to understand. Your name was one of the more prominent ones I came across when doing paranormal research."

"I had good reasons for being willing to be open-minded myself," he said. "My research has provided few unambiguous results, of course, but as you may now suspect—"

"—part of that is deliberate." I finished. "If you made the

wrong information public, it could get very dangerous for a lot of people."

He nodded. "As for what I wanted to accomplish by coming here ... by letting you know who is behind Jeri, you will understand if we start sending hints in your direction. We may ask for your help, through her, or request an interview—perhaps with Dr. Achernar—or in some other manner either request your assistance, or offer some subtle assistance of our own. But we have to avoid being visible. This is a shadow war, Mr. Wood. The world at large does not know of these kinds of things—even after the werewolves. Many forces exist, some of which you would not believe, and many of them are quite willing, in their own way, to trigger a holocaust if they feel that their operations are threatened."

I had to hide a smile. I'm sure Achernar meant every word he said, but the truth was that after Verne's revelations, not only would I be able to believe just about anything, but I probably knew stuff that made everything Pantheon knew put together look like small change. "Well, I'm always willing to help. And I'm already kinda in your debt after the little assist you gave me with the IDs for Tai Lee Xiang."

Achernar nodded. "That was our intent, although as I said, that connected to one of our operations. Let me put it this way: I'd have arranged the same thing for him myself, whether you requested it or not. So don't feel it was a tremendous favor; you just gave us a chance to do something for the enemy of an old enemy."

I studied him narrowly. "And you're just going to leave him and his kids alone? Not 'recruit' them at some later time?"

"No government, and no agency—not even ISIS and Pantheon—can be trusted with them," Achernar answered.

"He's telling it straight," the Jammer put in. "Part of my job at Pantheon is to arrange for certain kinds of data to just plain disappear."

"I find it *extremely* hard to believe," I said, "that even the UN, in its best days, would like the idea that its own agents are taking it upon themselves to decide what data should and shouldn't be reported up the chain of command."

"They wouldn't," Achernar said bluntly. "But my immediate superior created Pantheon specifically to be able to make such decisions. No, there isn't anything like that in the written files, but our meetings always touch on how much of what we learn is going to stay hidden and how much will be reported. Yes, we could all be arrested for treason or something similar if the truth somehow came out. Fortunately, our opposition generally wants the truth hidden even more than we do, so for the most part, the only people who might ever be in a position to blow the whistle on us have a vested interest in not doing so."

I shuddered. "Mr. Achernar, no offense, but I can only hope to God that you'll never get a mole in your organization."

"As do we all. We do our best to avoid that possibility. It may happen one day, but at the moment, we have no better alternative; someone must deal with these problems, and thus far, we have proven to be sufficient to the tasks at hand. Of course, your work with the wolves eliminated the one actual threat of such mole infiltration that we've ever had."

I had to admit that I'd missed that point. Virigar's poking through intelligence files actually made more sense now; he had, almost certainly, encountered something that indicated Pantheon's existence and was trying to find out what various governments might know or guess. After his existence had been blown wide open and the CryWolf gadgets put on the market, he and his furry friends had to back out of that business, at least for a while.

"So, in that sense you owe me at least as much as I owe you," I said finally.

"I'd agree with that," Achernar said. "In any case, I'd like you to memorize this number." He handed me a card with a phone number on it. I concentrated and committed it to memory by a few mnemonic tricks, then handed it back. "If it ever becomes necessary for you to contact us directly, rather than through Jeri—she's unavailable, got herself killed, or you're too far away—that will get in touch with me. But do not use it barring a true emergency."

"I won't. Obviously, you already know how to contact me. Are you planning on trying to reach similar arrangements with Verne?"

That got a short laugh. "No, I don't think so. Mr. Domingo has his own game, which he's been playing for a lot longer than any of us. If he needs our services, he'll ask for them, and there isn't anyone on Earth that can demand his help." He looked at me. "Except his friends, of course, and I'm afraid that in my business, you rarely have the time to make friends."

There wasn't much to say to that, so I finished my coffee. "Anything else? No offense, but I'm exhausted."

"Not at the moment. Our apologies for disrupting your schedule. With luck, you'll hear very little from us."

I suddenly remembered a problem that I'd been trying to solve for a couple of weeks. "Hold on. There *is* something I need from you guys—probably mostly the Jammer's field, actually, but it touches on your interests, too. Consider it payment for breaking into my house and scaring the crap out of me."

Achernar waited, eyebrow raised.

"Two things, actually. First, I want the Jammer to help Verne get top-level security for his house."

He didn't hesitate. "Done. And the second?"

"Now that he's a patron of the arts, Verne's getting a lot of invitations to go various places. He has to accept at least a *few* of them, the ones that are important. One of them's coming up now, an art show and reception for Sky—"

"—by Miss Danielle Lumiere, yes. What about it?"

Fine, show off how informed you are. But that makes it easier. "So I need someone to address the obvious problem."

Achernar blinked, then suddenly gave a low laugh. "Ah, indeed. Security people will be *most* distressed by guests who do not show up on a camera." He looked over to the Jammer. "What do you think?"

"Not a problem," the Jammer said after a moment. "If you're going to authorize me to do it, hey, I can get in there, intercept the feeds and substitute appropriate imagery. You'll have to do me a favor and put some RF IMU sensors on him—preferably under his clothing, some on key parts of his clothes, for motion and position capture—but if he'll go along with that, I can make sure that all the security feeds show him. I can probably do the same with any press vid cameras, too." He looked at me seriously. "You're on your own with respect to other people snapping pics, though."

"I *think* Verne can handle that on his own," I said, "barring the presence of any other vampires or werewolves as guests, and they won't want to call attention to Verne that way."

Achernar nodded. "Very well, I'll authorize it." He got up. "Oh, there is one more thing."

I glanced up.

"Congratulations."

I couldn't help but laugh. "My God, is there *anyone* who doesn't know I'm getting married?"

CHAPTER 52

Fangs for the Recommendation

"Jason, Sylvie, please meet Father Jonathan Turner," Verne said.

I shook hands with the cheerful-faced priest. He looked to be a mere twenty-five, hair dark and curly, wearing the traditional uniform of his profession.

"Pleased to meet you, Father."

"It's a genuine pleasure, Mr. Wood." Father Turner's rolling, English voice carried the warm, comforting tones that the very best priests usually have—a kind of voice that makes you willing to believe that God does speak through them sometimes. I'm not religious, but I recognize the dedication a real priest has to have. "And Miss . . . Sylvia," he went on, avoiding the name pitfall that most people—including me—fall into when first meeting her. "Verne has told me a great deal about both of you. I understand you are looking for a priest who will be, shall we say, flexible in the ceremony while remaining acceptable to the more traditional elements of the wedding party?"

Sylvia smiled, obviously taking to him on first glance. "Exactly right. My mom and dad are old-style Catholic and if I don't have a Catholic wedding of *some* kind, they'll worry that I'm heading to Hell one way or another."

Father Turner smiled back and shook his head in a resigned way. "Not, I'm afraid, an uncommon state of affairs these days. Now, my dear, you were baptized Catholic, weren't you?"

Sylvie nodded. "Not practicing for years though."

"No matter. Would you be willing, both of you, to agree to teach any children you have in the Catholic faith?"

"How do you mean that?" I asked. "I'm basically agnostic—I'll believe in the Almighty when I see evidence for him—and you seem to understand what Syl is."

"Let's put it cynically," he said, taking a seat across from us in Verne's living room. "As a representative of a church that's come under hard times, my job is to try to make it look more attractive than previous generations have seen it. Sometimes, you have to deal with people who are using the competitors' product, so to speak. Well, we don't win points with such people by insulting their choices; on the other hand, if I'm going to perform a wedding, it's incumbent upon me to try to get a wedge in the door to increase our membership. Yes, I generally get paid for doing the wedding, and that isn't something to be lightly brushed off, but I take my job seriously. If you'll agree to make sure that any children you have are exposed to the Catholic faith—taught the beliefs and values—I'm gaining something out of it. I'm willing to bet," he said, turning to me, "that you had almost no exposure to organized religion in your childhood. Am I right?"

I nodded. "Some attendance at Sunday school for reasons I can't remember now, and some time at the Unitarian church when I was much older, but no, not much at all."

"And without your making a promise of this sort, your child or children would most likely follow a similar path—or be exposed only to Sylvia's faith or to that of this decadent old bloodsucker," he said with a grin, hooking a thumb at Verne, who chuckled.

Syl and I were both startled by that; clearly Jonathan Turner knew a great deal about Verne!

"So, at the very least, I gain the potential of children who grow up knowing our system and aren't inherently hostile to it."

I glanced at Syl; she nodded, so I said, "I think we can agree to that. If you're not requiring us to teach them *only* in that faith, it's no problem."

"Jolly good; we should be able to get on famously," he said.

"Pardon me for asking," I said, "but just how do you come to know Verne so well?"

He was very serious all of a sudden; he looked at Verne for advice.

"It is entirely up to you, old friend," Verne said. "You know how much I trust them; let your reluctance be only personal. If you wish not to speak of such things, do not, but they are of my family, as though by blood."

"Quite, quite," Father Turner agreed. "It is a long story, and I'm not sure how to tell it without leaving out too much, or sounding as though I might be boasting in some way. Unless you would care to explain the essence of it yourself?"

Verne accepted the invitation, apparently feeling that some explanation was appropriate. "Jonathan is one of the accursed—taken by one of the vampires of Klein's type many years ago. He has, however, managed that which no other in my memory has done: opposed the curse's madness with will and faith, and maintained himself in a state of innocence. He has killed no one, hunts no human prey, and has become stronger because of it."

Father Turner seemed to blush slightly, though that reaction in such a being was hard to credit.

"Is this evidence for the truth of the Faith, Father?" Sylvie asked.

He smiled sadly. "Of course I believe so, Sylvie. Yet I cannot deny that other priests—some at least as devout as myself—have been preyed upon over the years and fallen. God's will has helped preserve me, but there is no reason for Him to have saved me while permitting others to be damned. And without such reason, I am afraid I cannot convince others that it is a genuine Miracle. Verne would have it that it was my own strength; yet I don't see myself as being so much stronger than others."

He shrugged, obviously uncomfortable with the thought, and I realized that there wasn't any false modesty with him; he sincerely doubted he was that strong. "I had friends and others who depended on me, and perhaps that helped. Yet the same could be said for so many others. Still, having found my mind spared and my soul unstained, I realized that I must minister to those who had no others they dared trust. There are still some of the accursed who try, with all their will, to turn from the path the curse lays out for them, and so long as they try, I am there for them—as confidant, helper, and perhaps as an example that it can be done. This is the task Our Father has set before me, and at the least I can accept it knowing that it is a worthy goal, even if I myself am hardly equal to the burden." He took a breath and shook himself. "But enough of this. Let's talk about your wedding. I spend enough time fighting darkness, it is a positive joy to be able to work in the light."

I glanced at him. "Would that be literally true? Because we'd like to have the ceremony during the daytime."

Jonathan nodded. "I can walk in the sunlight; the Lord has seen fit to bless me in certain ways, perhaps to help me in my mission. Our friend Verne, of course, is more than strong enough for such things."

"Goody," said Sylvie. "Then let's get down to planning the whole ceremony."

I looked around for some more snacks. This might take some time.

CHAPTER 53

Reception of Revelation

Verne looked nervous as we waited for Sylvie to join us at the ballroom entrance. It was an unusual expression indeed. "Jason, I know I have asked, but—"

"*Trust* me, Verne. The cameras are taken care of. The Jammer and his bosses were confident they could do it, and they gave me the thumbs-up a couple of hours ago. If you can keep from being directly photographed, you'll be fine."

He sighed. "That I can do, Jason. It is just ... difficult to take this risk. Yet I must, if I wish to be fully a part of society. I am just sorry that I must rely so much on others to do so."

I grinned cynically. "I think they're probably *relieved* to have the chance. Means that you're not undetectable by them, that you have limits and weaknesses, and that you will owe them something if they keep doing this kind of thing for you."

A brief smile in answer. "Yes, I suppose. A wise man, your Mr. Achernar; one who would rather cement alliances than divide."

"I'd say so. Now, I need your help to keep me from committing any *faux pas* this evening, Verne," I said.

"I will do what I can," he answered with a quick smile, "but as this is Sky's night, I think he is the one who should be nervous about it all."

"Well, at least this is *his* shindig," I said. "After all, Ms. Lumiere arranged the reception specifically to showcase his art."

"But," Syl said from behind as she slid her arm into the crook of mine, "it's not like you'll be able to escape attention."

"Hopefully not too much." I looked her in the eyes. "Are you going to be okay?"

"I'll be fine, Jason. I know they still haven't found Aurora... but I have a good feeling about it. She'll turn up, somewhere, somehow."

That relieved me. "Okay." I gave her a hug as I said over her shoulder, "Have you met Danielle Lumiere before, Verne?"

"Honestly, Jason, I have not paid much attention to business or social events until recently, so no. I do not, I confess, even know what she looks like. I did read a quick *precis* of her history, and I will admit to considerable admiration for her ability to not merely survive rude blows of fate but to maintain a head for business at an age when most children are not yet ready to leave school."

"You can say that again," I said, checking my tie one more time before we entered. "This is only the second event she's attended since her friend was lost overboard almost a year ago and the first one she's thrown herself, so let's make sure it's a good one."

The doors opened and we were actually announced to the room, something that I hadn't seen done outside of old movies. "Mr. Jason Wood, Miss Sylvia Stake, and Mr. Verne Domingo," a gentleman next to the door said; a hidden microphone conveyed his quietly spoken words to loudspeakers tuned *exactly* to the level of audibility but below the level of intrusion. *And to manage that, they've got a sound crew being paid a few thousand dollars an hour, I'll bet.*

There were a couple hundred people in the long, shining ballroom aboard Lumiere Industries' floating headquarters, the modified cruise vessel Danielle Lumiere had christened *Valinor*. I'd never seen so many tuxes and extravagant gowns outside of a James Bond marathon. Despite my *extremely* expensive outfit, I felt like an utter impostor.

A tiny, energetic figure popped out of the crowd and walked very quickly towards us. "Mr. Domingo! Mr. Wood! Ms.... Sylvie!" she said, evading Syl's problematic last name. "Dad's really glad you could all make it," said Star Hashima.

"We, also, are very glad we could come," Verne said. "And allow me to say that you make an exquisite hostess this evening, Star."

She grinned and spun around, showing off her brilliant green and sea-blue dress; it contrasted very well with her night-black hair and eyes. "Thanks! But if you think *I* look good, wait 'til you get a load of our real hostess, Miss Lumiere."

"I look forward to it," Verne said.

"Well, you'll get your chance right away. Dad sent me over to make sure you found him easy. C'mon, he's like on the other end of the room."

"Slow down, Star," Syl said with a laugh. "Genteel, remember. Your dad isn't going to disappear in the next five minutes."

Star did a creditable job of reining in her obvious need to run from point to point, but I could see the repressed energy. "Boy, Sky must have his hands full with her," I murmured to Syl.

"No doubt," Syl answered. "But she obviously loves her father to death, so he's doing a good job, I think." Syl looked . . . *dazzling, actually,* I thought to myself. *Incredibly gorgeous.* I hoped we might be able to dump Verne later on, actually, much as I enjoyed his company. *And in a couple of weeks . . .*

We finally emerged from a thick ring of *real* VIPs—I noticed Steven Cameron, the director of some of the biggest hits in Hollywood (including some of my favorites, like the wildly successful *Lensman* adaptations); Angelina Weaver who was the most bankable action-movie star these days; and a bunch of others, including the Vice President of the United States.

Sky Hashima was in the center of this knot, answering questions and pointing to various paintings and sculputures positioned around this part of the room. While he kept a calm, confident smile on his face, I could see by the stiffness of his back that he was *very* nervous.

He relaxed slightly as his daughter came into view with us in tow. "Star! Thank you for getting them so quickly."

I stepped forward and shook his hand. "Congratulations on this event; looks like everyone who is *anyone* is here. But I don't see our hostess."

"She's on her way," Sky said. "I don't know if you heard, but there was a major fire at one of the manufacturing plants that started just before the event, so I actually haven't met her or her right-hand man yet—they've both been in an emergency meeting." He turned and gave Syl a hug. "Been a long time since my first visit to your shop, hasn't it?"

She hugged back. "Not all *that* long."

"Seems like half a lifetime ago to *me*," Sky said, and then bowed to Verne. "And I owe you a *lot* of thanks again, Verne."

Verne waved it off. "I merely began the process to expose

your work to the proper audiences; it is your own work which has produced success from that exposure."

"Maybe, but the genteel form of advertising sure doesn't hurt." Sky glanced to one side. "Oh, I think that's them now," he said.

I saw a very tall man—taller than Verne—with carefully trimmed brown hair and a square, tanned face. He was wearing a suit that must have cost several thousands of dollars and which seemed ready to bust at the seams trying to contain shoulders of heroic proportions. The man was escorting someone so tiny that she was barely visible. Then the crowd parted and let them through.

I suddenly felt a crushing grip on my *left* arm—Verne's side, and glanced over, opening my mouth to protest; my objection vanished as I caught sight of him. Verne had gone paper-white and looked as though he was about to faint dead away; I followed his gaze—straight to our hostess.

Danielle Arwen Lumiere wasn't called "The Golden Girl" for nothing; cascading waves of gold-blonde hair framed her face and fell nearly to the floor. I'd seen pictures of her, but they hadn't conveyed the *beauty* adequately. I wasn't used to finding myself staring at someone like that, but for a moment, concerned though I was about Verne, I couldn't keep from doing so. Scarcely five feet tall, the sixteen-year-old owner and CEO of Lumiere Enterprises Group—from her sunshine-gold hair to her brilliant smile and huge, gray eyes that somehow were both familiar and exotic—outshone everyone around her. Danielle's dress made her look like a delicate fairytale princess, stepping straight from a book into reality—a reality that was a bit too gray and dull to hold her.

I blinked and looked back at Verne. "You okay?"

He made a visible effort, and the touch of color returned to his pale cheeks. "*In'e valahet . . .*" he murmured, then straightened, letting go of my arm, which had gone numb. *Jesus, I'm gonna have bruises there tomorrow.* "My . . . apologies, Jason. Yes, I am . . . okay now."

Good. But you're going to owe me an explanation later, I thought.

The big man stepped slightly forward. I thought I glimpsed a strange look exchanged between the man—Rex Hammersmith, Danielle Lumiere's bodyguard and right-hand man—and Sky

Hashima, but whatever I did see, it was gone almost instantly. "Mr. Hashima," he said, "allow me to present Miss Danielle Arwen Lumiere."

Sky took her hand and bowed over it. "Thank you *very* much, Miss Lumiere, for giving me such an...extravagant event."

She smiled and the temperature of the room seemed to rise by a degree and a half. "Oh, just call me Danielle, if I can call you Sky. Your work's *wonderful*. I had Rex buy two of your pieces just yesterday. And I have to apologize for not having been here to meet you; I had to make sure they got the fire under control..." her brilliant smile faltered momentarily, "...and that the families of the people who got hurt or...worse were being taken care of."

"Well," Verne said, now apparently fully recovered, "it is good to see that you continue the traditions and practices set by your parents. Lumiere has a most...salutary reputation in a field filled with other corporations of...often questionable motives and morality."

"Why, thank you...Mr. Domingo? Yes, of course, you must be Verne Domingo. Thank you for such kind words; my mother and father taught me that a company that cares is one that will survive when others fall. And, of course, I have to thank you for bringing Sky to everyone's attention. I can't *think* how he was missed for so long." She turned that stunning gray gaze on me, and suddenly, I realized where I'd seen eyes like that before.

Danielle Lumiere's eyes were virtually identical to those of Xavier Ross.

I was distracted by this realization, so I don't remember her greeting or my response to it. I did notice Syl studying her with unusual intensity. I had no idea what was going on, but I had the feeling that the answers to many mysteries were flying around *just* out of reach, and I had not a clue what the mysteries *were,* let alone what the solution to them might be.

To my great relief, after asking a few questions about the Morgantown Incident and congratulating us on our forthcoming wedding, our hostess kept to her mission and focused on Sky and his work for the remainder of the evening.

However, this wasn't true of many of the guests, and despite trying to escape it, I found myself being questioned about everything werewolf-related. By the time we finally left, my throat was sore from talking.

"Well, Jase," Syl said as we got into Verne's limo, "Miss Lumiere is *very* interesting, isn't she?"

I shot a glance at her to see if she was trying to yank my chain for staring too much at first, but her face was dead serious. "She's...unique," I said finally.

"I've never *seen* such a perfect example of...oh, *charisma*, I guess. And she doesn't seem conscious of it, really," Syl agreed. "I could *sense* something special about her, and so could most of the people in the room, even if they couldn't say what it was."

I looked at Verne, settling into his seat across from us. "What do *you* think, Verne? And before you answer, you damn near crushed my arm."

Verne bowed his head. "I apologize, Jason. I am...rarely surprised. And this evening, I had such a shock as I have not had in centuries. Many centuries."

"Didn't know blonde high-schoolers were your type," I said wryly.

He neither smiled nor looked irritated, which told me how serious this was. "Imagine, Jason. Imagine being who I am, with the history you know. Imagine that there was a person from your living days, one who was a bright and shining symbol to all your people. A symbol snuffed out on the same day that your world was turned upside-down by monsters and sunk beneath the waves.

"Then imagine, half a million years later, that you came face to face with her, exactly as she had been when you last saw her, the same smile, the same eyes of the King, the same hair that shone from out of the midst of a crowd, and that you *sensed* her in that moment—sensed her, and knew it was the same girl, the same *soul*."

I stared at him wordlessly. Sylvie broke the silence. "Verne... you mean to tell us that Danielle Lumiere is someone from... Atlantaea?"

"Not that she, herself, was transported from Atlantaea, no," Verne clarified. "But she has been somehow...reborn into a body that seems utterly identical to one from five thousand centuries ago. She is even known by a name so very similar, for then she was called 'Dahnelle,' and her name in Atlantaean meant, quite simply, 'the Golden One'; ancient Atlantaea—you should be aware—had virtually no people of fair skin or light hair. It was a rare and remarkable sight indeed for most of us."

"Holy crap." I thought for a moment, as Morgan—the only driver we'd trust on this sort of expedition, so far from Verne's home—put the limousine in gear and started the drive home from New York City. Finally, I said, "I'm guessing that you don't come across... what, reincarnated Atlantaean souls very often?"

"Never," he said, and there was hollow agony in that single word. "Understand, Jason, Sylvia: the Great Sealing ritual performed on the magical link between our world and the other, Zarathan, was *powered* by the souls of the dying. Those who died that day, nearly to the last man or woman, were *consumed* in the ritual that Kerlamion performed. They were neither reborn into the cycle of life, nor taken to any of the realms beyond life; they simply *ended*, and so none of the millions in the great City, none of my friends and family and colleagues, none of them have been reborn or found their true destination beyond. Only those few who fled before the ritual and survived the destruction were complete... and she was—she must have been—one of their primary targets."

He shook his head. "So she *cannot* have escaped. And yet... she is here. Unaware of her past, and I suppose I should leave it so. But I fear that any who remain of our old enemies will wish to complete their work. In that summary of her life, I saw that she has already lost her parents, and—more recently—one of her few true friends of childhood. I wonder already whether this is pure accident, or more."

"It's not your responsibility, Verne," I said. "If she really was the *same* person, maybe, but you yourself say she's more, what, a reincarnation?"

"Yes. Yes, you are right, Jason. Yet... she *would* have been my responsibility, for she was to be wed to the one for whom I was responsible, the Prince himself." He took one of his rare deep breaths. "But... without revealing much that would endanger her in and of itself, there is little I can do. So you are, I am afraid, correct."

"Verne," Syl asked after a moment, "what did you mean when you said she had the 'eyes of the King'?"

He managed a smile. "Ah, of course, that would mean nothing to you. Torline, the Eternal King, had extraordinary eyes, eyes of gray, most often described as of the color of stormclouds reflected on a blade of steel, large and expressive eyes which seemed to look through you. Oh, there are and have been many others with eyes of shades of gray, but *those* eyes, *that* shade of gray ... only the King, and those of his near blood—within three generations—ever showed *those* eyes, and few even of those."

That put a new perspective on a few earlier events. I pulled my laptop out and opened it, as Syl said, "But wait, you said she was supposed to marry the Prince. That would make them cousins or something, wouldn't it?"

Verne chuckled faintly. "Well, yes, it would. But is it not true that many royal families of your own history encouraged inter-marriage?" Syl nodded. "But in this case it is more complicated. Torline and his Queen were married at the dawn of Atlantaea's rising. It is no exaggeration to say that the fact that they *existed* was what led to Atlantaea becoming what it was. Yet in all that time—one hundred thousand years—they had but *one* child between them. That one, at the end of their reign, was Prince Mikael, and his birth was the greatest joy of the age, for we all knew how desperately the Eternal King and Queen had longed for a child that was theirs *together*, and how they had long accepted that it would never be.

"But the two Immortals, with such life before and after them, were not jealous nor wishing to see their lines end; and so it was not unheard of for someone of great accomplishment to catch the eye of either the King or Queen and become one of their favored; from these unions there were other children, and all saw this as strengthening the Empire of Atlantaea, for how could the child of one of the Eternal Rulers be anything but a strength and blessing to our people?"

"I guess that does make sense," Syl said after a moment. *I think I still have the files,* I thought, as I searched a couple of directories. "So there were a lot of semi-distant relatives pretty much *everywhere* in the main city."

"Maybe not just there, either," I said, and spun the laptop to face Verne. "How about *that*?"

Verne leaned forward, staring at the image of Xavier Ross, and once more he looked as pale as a ghost. "Who ... who *is* this?" he said finally, and his voice was shocked.

"That's the kid I think I got killed, Verne. Xavier Ross."

His head snapped up. "*This* is Xavier Ross?"

"Yes."

Slowly, he leaned back.

"Do you recall," he said finally, "how we discussed the changes in the world, and how I felt that you might equally be called the center of these events, as much as I?"

"Yeah, hard to forget it; that was the first time we started really going into details about the world."

"Well, I must amend that. I believe that there is more to these events than I had yet imagined. You stated once that you did not believe in coincidences. I, also, do not believe in coincidences of such great improbability."

He looked out the window into the city-lit night. "I think it is time I begin to seek out the meaning behind these events... before it is too late to see what the outcome may be."

CHAPTER 54

Home Security

"But of course, Jason. Indeed, I would be honored. How long will it be?"

I considered. "I've put a 'price no object' priority on it, and with my various contacts smoothing the way, I figure our new house should be finished in about three months."

"Then think no more of it, my friend. Your possessions may remain here until that time."

That was one small load off my mind; I knew that with the moderate-sized wedding Syl had planned we'd still end up with a sea of presents. It seemed that the public actually cared about what happened in my life—my fifteen minutes apparently hadn't quite come to a close—and so there were likely going to be some attempts at gatecrashing and certainly gifts from all over the place. This ignored people who wouldn't be at the wedding but that one or the other of us knew well enough that we'd be getting something from them. And Christmas wasn't all that far away either, so there might be *more* gifts before it was all done.

"You did say something about increasing my security?" Verne prompted.

"Hm? Oh, yeah. You remember that I had Jeri's people provide you with cover at Miss Lumiere's party?"

"Naturally. I could hardly forget it, when it was the first time I had dared appear at so public an event in many years."

"Well, I arranged with the same guy to provide security for both of us—top-level security systems."

"That would be this 'Jammer' person?"

"Yep. They agreed that it was in our best interests to maintain

293

maximum security, so sometime before the wedding, the Jammer will be by to help out. Put up with him; he's younger than I am, and he has that wiseass geek attitude that I mostly outgrew, but he's the best of the best."

Verne smiled tolerantly. "Jason, I assure you that I can 'put up' with any temperament. Geniuses are often immature or asocial in many ways. For a greater degree of security, I will have no objections. I will of course emphasize, in my own way, that they are to not leave any special privileges for themselves in the systems."

I grinned. "I rather thought you might. And someone like you will probably get through his hide." I saw Kafan going by the doorway. "Hey, Kafan! Is the senator coming to the wedding?"

He smiled. "Paula says that you'd have to lock the doors to keep her away. And she's bringing Seb—I mean, Jackie—and little Tai!"

I smiled back. Legal wranglings could be murderous, and establishing truths in court almost impossible, but Paula and Tai Lee Xiang had found a way to cut through all the potential barriers. Tai Lee knew, by scent that never lied, that Paula was a devoted mother who loved children; and Paula, from long experience in judging people and promoting children's rights, could tell that Tai was a loving parent. She also saw Tai and Genshi together often. Once the two recognized the other as someone who genuinely cared about the well-being of their children, they were no longer adversaries, but rather allies who simply had a complicated problem to work out. The storybook tale of the orphans' father returning was bound to come out soon; in fact, Paula was laying the groundwork for the press releases already. The stories would be of a *fait accompli*, not of a potential legal firestorm. "That's great. I'm looking forward to meeting them myself."

"Master Jason, is this list from Lady Sylvia the most accurate?" Morgan inquired as he entered, carrying a sheet of paper.

"I think so. Yeah, that's the current guest list. All the ones in red have confirmed. The names in black are people we expect to attend but haven't gotten confirmation for." It was Morgan's concern because we were having the wedding and reception here, on Verne's extensive grounds.

"Very good, sir."

Suddenly, there was a shout from down the hall, followed by a voice: "Hey! Let me go!"

Verne smiled and leaned back in his chair as Camillus entered, carrying the Jammer in a move-along hold. "Is this the young man you expected, Jason?"

I raised an eyebrow at the Jammer. I should've expected he'd try something like this. "Caught so soon? Yes, Verne, but he's kinda disappointing me."

The Jammer flushed. "I'd like to know just how you managed to catch me at it, since I know for damn sure not one of your alarms went off."

Verne gestured, and Camillus deposited the Jammer in one of the chairs. "Mr. Locke—"

"How the hell do you—oh, Wood."

"To an extent, yes, but I have my own sources. You are Ingram Remington Locke, former resident of Long Island. I know a great deal about you, Mr. Locke."

That got the Jammer's attention; he knew that Achernar had mentioned his last name, but not his first. "Damn."

"As I was saying, Mr. Locke: you are apparently suffering under the misapprehension that my security is only technological. While you are correct in that none of my electronic security systems notified anyone of your presence, I was able to sense you once you entered my demesnes. I then notified Camillus of your whereabouts and the direction in which you were moving, and he was naturally then able to capture you."

The Jammer rubbed his arm and glanced at the door through which Camillus had left. "Naturally. Well, if you've got that kind of warning, I don't know if you need anything more."

"Oh, assuredly I do," Verne said. "I do have to rest, and during that time, my senses are less sharp. There are also various ways in which my senses can be eluded that would not evade properly designed technological security. Magic is not inherently superior to technology, merely different. I would be very pleased if you were to design a top-of-the-line security system for my home. I will not offer you money, since I am sure that is not a major consideration for you; rather, I offer the challenge of making such a large, old, rambling estate secure enough to meet your own exacting standards."

The Jammer laughed. "Okay, Dracula, you've got me pegged pretty well. My friends sent me out here to do a job, but damned if you didn't go and make it look fun to do, too. I hope you won't take this the wrong way, but I'm going to keep trying to get in here without you knowing."

Verne ignored the vampire witticism and nodded. "I expect no less. In fact, I would demand that you try everything at your disposal to enter this place unbidden, so that any flaws which may exist can be fixed, either with your techniques or my own."

"Then can I get up and start working?"

"By all means." As the Jammer rose, Verne said, "*However...*"

The Jammer froze; Verne's tone had shifted without warning, to something cold as winter ice, and his level gaze impaled Locke. "Let me make one thing clear, Mr. Locke: your work will remain exclusive to me in this instance. You will have no 'backdoor' codes, no special privileges, and no records, after the fact, of the work. This will also be true of Jason's home. I am aware of the way your sort of person thinks, and I warn you that I will not be amused if I discover anything in my or my friend's security systems that appears in the least suspicious. Is that understood?"

The Jammer was a shade paler. "Understood, sir," he answered.

"Very good, then." Verne's voice had returned to spring again. "Carry on."

I watched the Jammer leave. "It's amazing. When I was younger, I didn't believe that crap about people with a 'force of personality' that you could actually sense. The past year or so has made me a believer. You've shaken him up pretty good."

"My sense of the matter is that he has already encountered someone with a similar force of personality." Verne commented. "Someone whom he respects and thus associates with my own exhibition in that arena. But I agree; we will not need to worry about him inserting unwanted material in our security."

"Good. Because, lord knows, I've got enough to worry about right now..."

CHAPTER 55

They Never Knock

I looked around the office one more time. It was a little intimidating to realize that I wouldn't be back here for quite a while and that when I came back, I'd be married. We'd be spending our wedding night at Verne's before setting out on our honeymoon.

Everything looked in order—ordinary, even, and I found that startling in and of itself. When I'd first moved in and started WIS, I would have laughed at the thought of vampires and werewolves. And now I knew things far stranger were real. It seemed somehow strange that my office still looked ordinary.

I turned back towards the door and jumped back with an inarticulate yell, yanking out my pistol at the same time and pointing it dead-center at the towering apparition that stood there.

It looked like a man—but one that topped seven feet in height. He wore some kind of robed outfit, mostly blue and brown and gray, and a peculiar five-sided hat which had symbols on it that I couldn't make out. The hat shadowed his face, so while I could see white hair and a sharp-edged chin, I couldn't see anything else clearly. One hand gripped a staff as tall as he was, an elaborately carved staff with a complex crystal headpiece that chimed when he moved it.

And despite the utterly outlandish appearance of the figure, I was struck first by the eerie feeling that I'd seen him before.

"Who the *hell* are you, what are you doing here, and how the heck did you get *in* here?"

The vaguely visible mouth turned up in a smile. The answer was in a very deep, resonant voice that reminded me of a cross between James Earl Jones and Charlton Heston in his old Moses role. "I am Konstantin Khoros, Jason Wood. I am here...to see you, mainly. See you separate from others, in isolation, for only thus can a man be understood as an entity unto himself."

"Does that also make you incapable of *knocking*?" Despite my anger, I lowered the gun. This guy didn't seem interested in threatening me, and he also didn't seem to give a damn that I had pointed a gun at him in the first place.

He chuckled. "Not incapable, no. But in this case, it served my purpose better to not do so. An old friend of mine contacted me recently, and as I suspected, it was you who set him on the path that would lead him to do so."

There weren't too many candidates, and given this guy's out-landish garb..."Verne?"

Khoros nodded. "He spoke to me of coincidences and miracles, and I could hear that he was much changed since last we had spoken. I had wondered what would become of him, the day it began for you. I am pleased to see the results are all I had hoped."

The day it began...I suddenly remembered that day, and the very first hint of strangeness, an impossible image out of the corner of my eye..."That was *you?* You were watching me then—before I even started—"

He shook his head, and the staff chimed faintly. "Not before you started; for already you had the photographs taken by Klein in your possession. I guessed where such an event would lead."

"More than *I* could have guessed," I admitted.

"I have had somewhat more practice than you at these things," he said, and began to turn. "Tell the Sh'ekatha when next you see him that I have the answer I have sought, and the answer to all his questions that can be so answered is yes; as for his other questions, there are no coincidences, and I have entered the endgame."

"Why the heck don't you tell him yourse..." I began, and trailed off as Khoros disappeared in a chime and a shimmer of golden light. I stared for several minutes. "Dammit."

It took only a couple of moments to dial up Verne's house and get him on the line. "Yes, Jason? What can I do for you in this most hectic of times?"

"I just had an unexpected visitor. Tall guy with a weird hat and a staff."

He was silent for a moment, then I heard him sigh. "Khoros."

"That was the name he used, yeah. Verne, he's been watching me since the day I started working on Klein's photos."

"I... see." Another pause. "I will be there momentarily."

Since he could travel with the speed of a whirlwind, it literally was moments; I'd only just hung up the phone when a breeze swept out from the doorway and Verne materialized from thin air.

"I guess I should get used to that," I remarked. "Khoros disappeared from the same place a few minutes ago."

"Yes," Verne said, eyes distant. "I can sense his magic— unmistakable, when he allows a trace to linger. He wanted me to be able to verify it was him."

"Why wouldn't he talk directly to you? You called him up, didn't you? About Ms. Lumiere?"

"And young Mr. Ross, yes. What exactly did he say?"

"Several things, none of them very informative. He did leave a message specifically for you." I made sure I had the phrasing right. "He said that he had the answer he had sought, that the answers to all your questions which could be so answered was *yes*, and that as to your other questions, there were no coincidences and he had entered the endgame."

Verne's eyes widened and he muttered something in the ancient language that I now knew was Atlantaean. "And he has been watching *you* that long?"

"Yeah. I actually saw him that night, it was just so quick I figured it was a trick of the light somehow. What did he mean by all that, and is he always that much of a... twit?"

Verne gave a snort of laughter. "He was somewhat less of a... twit, as you put it, in the old days. But he has been searching ever since the Fall for answers to a specific set of questions, and that search... *obsession* would not be too strong a word to apply to it. It now seems he has found those answers, and that all that has happened is either part of, or is being bent to, his ultimate goal. A goal, I hasten to add, which is a worthy one. Of his methods... I say less."

"*All* that has happened? What 'all'?"

"Possibly literally everything of note that has happened since you received those photos—Klein's attempt to frame me, Carmichael's ill-advised kidnapping, Virigar's return, Kafan's involvement with the Project, the appearance of your client Mr. Ross, and our encounter with Danielle Lumiere."

"What? He couldn't possibly have set that *all* up himself, and if he did, he's a murdering bastard, but you don't seem to view him that way."

Verne smiled sadly. "I would be inclined to say that he did not in fact set it *all* up, but that he *did* know much of what was going to happen, and in some fashion it serves his purpose. You have undoubtedly heard of some people called 'chessmasters'— people who manipulate events and other people to cause results that might be impossible to achieve by working directly?"

I nodded.

"Understand, then, that Khoros is one of those, only playing in a grander game on a scale that even I do not truly comprehend. He has been doing this since the Fall of Atlantaea." He caught my glance. "Yes, Jason, he is one of those few survivors I mentioned. And no, I do not agree with his tactics in many cases. He is no longer the man I knew then. He is still on the *side* of good, understand; but he is, himself, no longer a good man."

"How does that work?"

"He believes that the end does not *justify* the means, but that the means may be *necessary* for the end. That is, he will do or allow things that in no sense should be considered good, and these are not justifiable or defensible to him. Yet they *must* be done, in his view, to achieve a vastly greater goal."

"A goal that's taken him this long to reach? How the hell can he live with himself if that's the case?"

"I do not believe," Verne said, after a moment, "that he *intends* to live with himself once the task is complete."

"And do you know what that task is?"

Verne nodded. "In essence...to shatter the Great Seal, and bring to justice the ones behind the destruction of Atlantaea."

"By *himself*?" Given that the demons who'd taken down the ancient civilization had literally rewritten continental geology, the thought of one person trying to oppose such forces was mind-boggling.

"I suspect... something more complex, something involving your young friend Xavier, Ms. Lumiere, and others. But in the end, yes, I think he will take a direct hand. Somehow, Jason, you are part of those plans. As am I."

He shook his head. "And I do not know how all this will end."

CHAPTER 56

Vows and Threats

"Ready, Jason?"

I took a deep breath. "All set." I wasn't nearly as nervous as other grooms I'd known; my nervousness was only an echo of the proposal now. I was more excited than anything else.

I walked up the sunlit aisle, lined with flowers—incongruous against the browning grass of winter—that ran between the rows of chairs on Verne's back lawn. Many people had wondered *why* we were having an outdoor wedding in winter. Syl wanted a wedding in the light, and what she wanted, she was going to get. I strongly suspected, however, that the unseasonably warm weather in the last week was not accidental, but due to intervention by a certain priest of Eönae.

Verne, of course, was Best Man. I saw my mom and dad—Mom's hair still clearly blond (maybe dyed, but I'd never dare ask), Dad's a distinguished gray—both smiling broadly. Sylvie's mom sat just across the aisle from them, and was already dabbing at her eyes with a handkerchief. Why do so many people cry at weddings? Jeri Winthrope was also near the front, leaning back in a relaxed pose as she waited for the vows, having already sat through Father Turner's quick little introductory sermon; Morgan was next to her, straight as a ramrod in his proper butler manner. Kafan was with his three children and Paula, looking happier than I'd ever seen him. I saw Camillus and Meta a row back, along with several other members of Verne's household who I'd only glimpsed on occasion.

Then I saw Sylvie, and everything else faded. She'd chosen a traditional shimmering white for her gown, and I no longer saw the laughing gypsy princess... or, rather, I saw the shining angel who'd hidden behind the gypsy façade.

I heard the vows, and responded, but at the same time I hardly heard them at all. Sylvie was the only one who mattered.

"You may kiss the bride," Father Turner said finally.

I lifted the veil and bent down. I don't know how long we stood there.

Then the party began. But as a favorite character of mine once said, that's a deceptively simple statement, like "I dropped the atom bomb and it went off." The reception and dinner went on for hours, and no one seemed inclined to leave early. Hitoshi had outdone himself, and even with my newfound wealth, I shuddered trying to imagine the bill for this one. Imported caviar was a trivial garnish, and I was quite sure that if I'd asked for a truffle, I'd be handed one the same way other people might give you an apple from the fridge. Butterflied lobster, some kind of imported beef that cost twenty times what any other cut might, abalone, the list went on and on. The cake itself was a stunning edifice of the pastrymaker's art. I learned later that Verne had imported, not the cake, but the cake*maker* from Paris just for this one cake.

Finally, with most of the guests cleared out, our inner circle gathered in the living room and Sylvie and I started going through the remaining presents. Most of them were exactly what you'd expect: silly knicknacks, small appliances, we all know the kind of thing. But there were a few...

I studied the long, slender package. "Damn. Feels pretty heavy. What, a crowbar?"

Jeri smiled. "Open it and see."

I stripped the wrappings off and opened the box. "My god!"

It was a sword—katanaesque in its design, with strange upward-spiking crossguards and a hilt that could be grasped with one or both hands. There was something strange about the metal of the blade, maybe a color or a shimmer. I glanced questioningly at her. "Okay, you people seem to have found out that I collect swords, but I'm stumped on this one. What is it, exactly?"

"Sort of a joke," Jeri said, obviously pleased that it wasn't instantly clear to me. "Since you seem to get involved in all kinds of unearthly strange stuff, we thought an unearthly blade would be appropriate."

"Unearthly...?" I stared at it. "Meteoric metal!"

"Bang on," she agreed. "There's a couple outfits that make things like this, so Achernar and the rest of us chipped in to get it."

"Well, thanks!" I hugged Jeri. "Convey my thanks to the rest of the spies."

"Will do. Hey, go help your wife over there."

Sylvie was wrestling with the wrappings on something that stood about six feet high. Finally, the two of us convinced the box to open. Sylvie gasped. "Oh, my..."

It was a vanity table—wood so polished that it seemed to shine from within, a mirror sparkling in the center, drawers so carefully fitted that they slid in and out with only a whisper of sound.

"Oh, Kafan, how beautiful!" Sylvie said, throwing her arms around Verne's foster son. "You shouldn't have!"

"Bah," said Kafan, blushing. "I don't have much money of my own yet, so all I could do is make something. Jason's got matching bookcases and a dresser, but I didn't wrap those up—take up too much room."

I thanked Kafan, and while Syl hugged him again I chose another package. This one had elegant writing on it that could only belong to Verne. Opening the small box, I found two rings, formed of gold and what appeared to be platinum and ruby, intertwined like growing vines. "What..."

"Gold and platinum, imperishable metals, the essence of the Earth," Verne said, "and ruby, the bloodstone, symbol of life ever-flowing." His own ruby flickered, and I thought I saw a faint answering shimmer from the twining ruby threads.

"They're amazing, Verne," Sylvie said. Her eyes became distant momentarily, and then widened. "No, Verne, you can't!"

I understood then. "We can't possibly—Verne, you took these from your true home! We can't accept them!"

Verne shook his head. "My friends...my very dear friends... in my culture, such rings were one way that couples to be married would symbolize their vows. In my own collection, they do nothing save gather ages of dust and memories. What better thing could I do with them, than to see the two people who brought back my very heart and rekindled the flame I thought lost wearing the last rings of the Lady? I insist."

Syl hugged him even more emphatically than she'd hugged Kafan, and I just gripped his hand. There weren't words to express this kind of thing properly, but he understood.

We went back to wading through the mass of gifts.

"Look, Jason, another blender!" Sylvie said, laughing, from the pile. "Oooh, look at this one!"

"This one" was a large box in shimmering silver-and-gold paper.

"It's heavy!" I grunted, setting it on the table. It had no card on the outside, and Morgan vaguely recalled that it was among the large number sent to us via special couriers. Presumably, it would have a card on the inside, as most of them did. Sylvie and I undid the wrappings, revealing a hardwood-sheathed box held by a clasp at the top. It had an interesting symmetry of almost-invisible lines down the side, indicating that it opened in a unique fashion; when I undid the clasp, the sides fell away like the petals of a flower.

Sylvie gave a shriek and leapt back; I sucked in my breath and recoiled. I heard both Verne and Jeri gasp.

In the center of the table, the focus of the radiating sides of its box, stood a crystal sculpture of a wolf in mid-leap, facing us with savage glee. Carved on the water-clear base were the words, "'Til Death Do You Part."

Fear washed away at that taunting, threatening phrase. I glanced around for something heavy, then reached out to heave the glittering reminder through the window.

"NO, Jason!" Verne and Sylvie both shouted.

The desperation in Verne's voice halted me, even more than the fear in Syl's. "Why the hell not?" I demanded. "The son of a bitch—and I mean that literally—wants to send me a message, I'll send him one back!"

He plucked the statue from my hands. "Please, Jason. Sit down."

My heart still pounding from a mixture of terror and fury, I did so, a little shakily. I hadn't realized just how scared I really was of Virigar until I saw the statue. "Okay, I'm sitting. Now why shouldn't I break the thing?"

Verne sighed. "Because, my friend, it would have terrible consequences. I do not argue with you what his purpose was in sending this to you, for that purpose is obvious: Fear, uncertainty, to ruin your future with thoughts of your eventual demise at his hands, and to do so on your very wedding day, yes, this is undoubtedly his purpose. Yet you also must understand that Virigar is not an ordinary adversary. He is not even what you believe him to be. He is an ancient being, evil, yes, perhaps more so than you realize, yet with a majesty and a pride that you cannot begin to comprehend. That statue was carved with his own hands, Jason. I have seen a few works like it in my years, and I cannot mistake that inhumanly perfect hand; you have been gifted with a creation the likes of which few mortals have ever even seen, and even fewer have owned. Throwing it away would be a mortal insult, one which would almost certainly require that he turn his immediate attention to your painful demise. It is, in its way, a salute as much as a turning of the screw. You are an enemy who has actually bested him, in a manner that he found artful, original, and worthy, and further, one whom destiny favored sufficiently to save from your second confrontation. For that, he has chosen to terrorize you in a manner worthy of your stature. See it that way, please, and take heart in your own success. He may threaten, but only you can fear."

Syl nodded, so scared that she couldn't speak, but obviously seeing the truth in Verne's words.

I saw the truth, as well. I'd faced Virigar in person. I sensed that what Verne said was true, and more, that the whole thing— even being beaten—was to the King Wolf nothing more than a game. If I played by his rules, I had a chance. If I didn't, I would be risking the lives of everyone associated with me. "Okay, I'm cool now. But I know what I *am* going to do with it." I turned to Kafan. "Could you do me a favor, just once, and let me borrow your transport skills?"

Kafan nodded, confused. "On your wedding day, of course. Where are we going?"

"One second. Verne, that case over there, the one you emptied the other day—can I use it?"

"Certainly, Jason. Consider it a gift." He measured it by eye. "It will fit the statue admirably, actually."

"My house, Kafan."

He took my hand, and there was a flickering dislocation; I suddenly stood in my kitchen. "Whoa. I always wondered what teleportation felt like."

"It is less disorienting after you get used to it," he said. "Why are we . . . ?"

"Just a second. Then we can go back." I ran to the living room, got what I came for, came back. "Okay, we can pop back now."

It was still disorienting, so I presumed that it took more than a couple of times to accustom oneself to instantaneously crossing distances. After I refocused, I went to the case, in which Verne had just placed the statue, and around it placed six other sparkling objects. "I'm sure he'll find out somehow what I've done with it; let this be my message to him."

Verne smiled broadly, and Sylvie gave an emphatic nod.

The wolf still sprang, triumphantly leaping upon its cornered prey.

But surrounding it were werewolf claws.

Part VI

Mirror Image

March 2001

CHAPTER 57

Honeymoon Hotel

"Jason, you're sure about this?"

I looked over at Sylvie, who was looking through one of the Florida guidebooks. "Sure I'm sure. One of my classmates back in high school used to come here every summer with her family and found at least two."

She sighed and smiled. "Okay, Jasie. We can spend a few days in the area looking."

"Hey," I said, "it's not like we weren't planning on spending weeks at the beach anyway. Venice has a really nice beach—that's where you look for the Megalodon teeth."

Sylvie put on a mock-indignant expression. "So we'll be at the beach and all you're going to look at is fossil shark teeth?"

I reached over and grabbed while keeping my eyes on the road; her sudden giggling shriek told me I'd grabbed the area I'd intended. "Not a chance."

I glanced over at her again, quickly admiring the sight of my brand-new wife in shorts and a tight shirt—a huge change from her habitual "Gypsy Princess" look, which ran to layered skirts, puffy tops, multicolored handkerchiefs, and acres of sparkling crystal necklaces, earrings, and bracelets, all of which concealed the details of her figure from any prying eyes. I'd always thought she was pretty, although it was a lot more than that which had drawn us together and, almost a month ago, led to our marriage. It had been my immense delight to discover, after the wedding, that the gorgeous face was matched by the rest of her. Yes, as a matter of fact, we had *not* slept together before our marriage, not that it's any of your business. We had all of our lives to make up for that lost time, after all. And I certainly intended to spend plenty of that time admiring her whenever she chose to wear something like the glittery bikini she had bought earlier today.

Venice looked much like other Florida towns—built low, no really tall buildings, the newer homes and condominiums tending to follow the same vaguely Hispanic pattern while the older ones often had more individuality. It was, however, smaller than many others we'd visited, and as such was less built up and felt more relaxed.

I chose one of the nearby hotels that had beachfront—with my current finances, I didn't need to worry about how much I spent on our honeymoon—and parked in a lot that was surprisingly empty of cars, with only a green Ford, an orange Saturn, and a couple of dully colored Hondas taking up spaces. Once more expending the effort that put the "lug" into "luggage," Syl and I dragged our stuff into the lobby.

"Reservations?" the big, cheerful-looking man behind the desk asked.

"Actually, no; I was hoping you had some openings."

"As a matter of fact, we do!" he said, grinning. "Y'all are in luck; had a small convention here over the weekend, and when they left, it gave us a small hole to fill. Just the two of you? Newlyweds, I'll bet?"

"Yep," I said, answering both questions with one word. "How'd you guess?"

He chuckled. "Guess? My friend, after fifteen years in the business, there ain't no such thing. Seein' two people walkin' in like that, draggin' a hunnert pounds o' junk without so much as a groan or a gripe, an' tryin' to stay as close together as they know how, you know they just got hitched." He went to his computer and glanced at another monitor near it. I knew from its location, the glance he gave it, and the odd camera unobtrusively pointed right at the check-in desk, that it was a standard CryWolf system ($250 retail, $350 with monitor) as provided by Shadowgard Tech under license from me directly. "How many days you folks plannin' on stayin'?"

"Two or three. Say three."

"That'd be two nights, then." A few taps on the keyboard, then, "Cash or charge?"

"Charge. Here."

I handed him my card. He turned around to his credit valida-
tion scanner, slid the card through, and sent the query through
the lines which would determine whether or not my plastic was
worth anything.

Had I been in a different line of business, or not been looking
straight at his back, I might have missed it. But as the little credit
gadget's screen lit up, I saw him stiffen, like a man opening his
eyes to discover a scorpion sitting on his stomach. It was just a
moment, but I was sure I'd seen it. "Anything wrong?"

He was just a hair slow in answering, and the first few words
lacked the breezy, relaxed tone of our earlier conversation. "No.
Not at all." His voice came back to normal. "Sorry, got distracted
there, remembering something I gotta do—one of the rooms needs
work and I plumb forgot. Not yours, don't worry 'bout that." He
turned around, the credit slip in his hand, and gave me back the
card. I signed, he did the ritual of glancing at the card and my
signature, accepted that the scrawls looked similar enough, and
handed me back the yellow copy. "Okay, Mr. Wood, you're all
set. Here's two keys, I've given y'all one of our oceanside rooms,
that'd be number 240. Just take the elevator there—here, lemme
help you with that." He hefted our bags onto a rolling cart. "There
ya go. It'll be the second door to the right after y'all get off the
elevator. All the rooms got cable, air conditioning, plus the doors
have the new CryWolf peephole gadgets so's you can make sure
any visitor is who they say they are. Pool's open from ten to
ten, and we own the beach out front there. Lifeguard's around
from ten to eight on the beach—after that y'all are on your own.
Thanks for coming, have yourselves a great time, and if y'all
need anything, just call down to the desk here. My name's Vic."

"Thanks, Vic, we will," Syl said.

We wheeled our luggage to the room and got it settled. While
we did so, I mentioned my observation to Sylvie.

Syl frowned. "Hmm. I didn't see it myself, but I know how
good your observation skills are. Still, Jason, I didn't feel any
hostility from him. I don't feel there's any immediate danger."

"Good enough for me. Let's get down to the beach."

CHAPTER 58

Never Off-Duty

"This really is a pretty little town," Syl said as we walked down one of the sand-strewn sidewalks in flipflops, looking very appropriately like tourists. She glanced around at the palm trees whose sunset shadows stretched towards the other side of the street.

"It certainly is that," I agreed. "Though not nearly as pretty as you." I luxuriated in walking on a solid surface after having spent the afternoon either sifting gravelly sand for fossil shark's teeth or chasing after, and sometimes catching, a certain black-haired enchantress in a bikini.

"Are you flirting with me?"

"As usual, of course." We kissed. "Hey, how about I pick *you* out something pretty?" I said, as we were passing a jewelry shop.

Syl grinned. "What girl could refuse? Even if you do have questionable taste in gems."

"I make up for it by my taste in girls."

She gave me a nudge in the ribs as we entered Marie's Jewelry Box. "That had better be *girl,* singular, Mr. Wood."

Aside from the clearly visible CryWolf camera pointing at the door, the store itself was a not-so-subtle reminder of the changes the events in Morgantown had wrought. In the old days—barely a year distant—silver had been the most popular metal for affordable but adequate jewelry. Now there were considerably fewer silver pieces on display, even in large jewelry stores, and those that remained were far more expensive, and some had been designed with an eye towards defense as much as beauty. For a while, silver had eclipsed gold in terms of price per ounce, and even after the immediate hysteria had subsided, silver's price remained far, far higher than it had been before the werewolves had made their debut.

I noted even fewer silver pieces in this store—only two, in the back and not well-displayed. The majority of items were gold and platinum. Syl and I spent quite a while looking around, comparing, arguing gently on occasion, before we finally decided on a platinum-and-gold bracelet encircled with a spectrum of multicolored stones.

"A lovely choice," the owner, Marie, said, smiling—not surprisingly, since it was also one of her most expensive pieces. "Can I wrap that for you?"

I shook my head. "No," I said, slipping it onto Sylvie's wrist and kissing her hand, "I think we've got a perfectly good way to carry it, thanks."

Smiling, Marie took my proffered credit card. Her smile froze momentarily as she glanced at it. She looked back at me, eyes wide. "J-Jason *Wood*? As in . . . *the* Jason Wood?"

I sighed. I might not be at movie-star-celebrity level, but I was already resigned to the fact that I was no longer a completely private individual either. "Yes, I'm Jason Wood."

She smiled. For a moment, I thought it looked a bit forced, but then it relaxed. "Well, then, welcome. Lord, what a change *you* brought down on us, eh?"

"Heh." I acknowledged the (unfortunately all-too-familiar) mildly amusing sally. "Not entirely my doing."

"Of course not," she agreed, and turned to run the card through. "Changed my own business enough, though—that I can guarantee you. Hardly any silver jewelry available anymore, and the silver *dust* business—well, I'm sure you know all about that."

I nodded, noticing that the standard-issue box for silver dust packets was present but tagged "out of stock." She noticed my gaze as she handed me the slip to sign. "Oh, my suppliers ran short on everything silver this month. I'm expecting a resupply in next week, if you were needing any . . . ?"

"No, no," I said, passing her the white copy. "We won't be here more than a couple of days, just driving around."

"Well, thank you very much for your patronage, Mr. Wood—and congratulations. I hope you will both be very happy together."

"Thank you," Syl replied. "So far, so good!" She giggled as we left, jangling her new bracelet against the others she already had on.

But her face grew serious after a few more paces. "Jason?"

"Hmm?" I pulled my mind from the distraction of certain parts of Sylvie's anatomy. "What?"

"She seemed friendly enough and all, but I could have sworn... when she first saw your name, I thought I sensed fear—almost panic."

I blinked. "Why the heck would she be afraid of me?"

Syl shrugged. "I don't know. It was a momentary impression—a flash, you know—and then everything seemed perfectly normal. Just thought I should mention it."

"Great," I grunted. "Guess I'd better check our supplies tonight. Just in case."

"Really, it's probably nothing; I don't have a bad feeling about her or anything. Let's get dinner."

It was fully dark when we finally left the Cactus Steakhouse. (Steak, yes. I love seafood as much as anyone, but this vacation had been awfully seafood-heavy and we both decided on a change.) The stars glittered overhead, at least those which could overcome the town lighting, as we walked back towards our hotel. "Oooh, that was good," I said finally.

"It better have been, seeing as you ate so much," Syl replied indulgently. "Jason, just because we're married now I don't want you settling down and growing a potbelly."

"Hey! I always eat a lot. And we were doing a lot of exercise this afternoon."

She was about to reply when something caught our ears. A... grunt? A cough? A slight gasp or something? I couldn't quite place it, except it sounded somehow terrified. It was coming over the fence of a nearby yard. I glanced at Syl, to feel my stomach knot; her "feeling" face was on, that frighteningly intense gaze that focused on nothing, yet saw beyond anything. "Be careful, Jason!" she hissed, knowing my actions even before I'd decided.

I nodded and gestured for her to stay where she was, near the fence, while I moved forward toward the gate. Cautiously, I pushed; it was open and swung easily. I wished I had my trusty ten-millimeter on hand, and wondered if I was going to be one of the cats that curiosity killed.

The yard was dark; there were no lights were on in the house to which it was attached, and my eyes were still accustomed to the streetlights. But I could make out something on the ground, about thirty or forty feet away...and I thought I saw movement across the yard, another gate opening, and someone going through. It was nothing I could put my finger on...but something about that distant, moving figure sent a sudden shiver down my spine. "Hello?" I said tentatively.

There was no answer, though I heard the faint *clack* of the other gate shutting in the distance. "Sorry to intrude, but I heard something...?"

Still no answer, but no sudden attacks in the darkness either. I took a deep breath and stepped inside, walking slowly towards the object lying on the ground in front of me. Even before I reached it I had a very nasty feeling I knew what it was. I pulled out my keyring and turned on the mini-flashlight, pointing it downward.

Lying on the ground before me was a dead man.

"Oh, for crissakes," I heard myself say. "I'm on *vacation,* dammit!"

CHAPTER 59

Problems and Premonitions

"Well, isn't this just peachy," I said, finally stripping off the clothes that had become steadily more uncomfortable during our police interviews. "Why couldn't I have chosen somewhere else?"

As the people who found the deceased—apparently the *very* recently deceased—Jerry Mansfield, not only had we been extensively questioned by the police but were issued the standard request to remain in the area.

Syl managed a sympathetic smile, though she couldn't have been feeling any more comfortable. "Jase, darling, I think we have to face the fact; it's your karma. You attract these kind of things. If we went somewhere else, that's where we'd find the trouble. Even before you met up with Verne, the cases you got involved with had some odd features."

I admitted that this was something I couldn't argue, loath though I was to admit that there was anything to Sylvie's "karma" theory. "Maybe this one will be resolved quickly..." I started, as I turned on the shower. I caught her narrowed gaze, sighed. "...or maybe not," I said. "That feeling wasn't just death?"

"It was very, *very* bad, Jason. I haven't felt anything like that since...since I saw Renee and knew she was going to kill you."

Renee's name sent a pang through me, despite the year that had gone by. I missed her hardcase-cop façade and quiet friendship. "Did you see his face?"

Syl nodded. "Horror."

"Well, it could have been a rictus of pain, but I agree, Syl. The first thing to come to mind when I looked at him was that he died in terror. Eyes wide open." I frowned. "I looked over the body quickly, and without touching or moving him I couldn't find any traces of injuries, either. No vampire bites, no slashes, and so on."

"A werewolf doesn't have to cut you," Sylvie reminded me.

"True," I said, stepping into the shower to let the hot water blast the sand off my body, "but, according to Verne, they do have to get awfully close to you in order to suck the life out of you without physical contact. You didn't check out the area near the body, did you?"

I could just make out Syl shaking her head through the mist-fogged shower door. "Not really—we didn't want to muddle things up with more tracks."

"There was silver dust scattered over a wide arc in front of him—some of it was even on his clothes. If it had been a wolf, I'd have expected it to either be dead next to him, or at least to have made a rather loud protest about the stuff. They never are very subtle once they are hurt. But if I actually did see the killer leaving, he or she left dead silently, smooth and without great hurry either."

"But," Syl pointed out, and it was a mark of both my worry and tiredness that observing her silhouette undressing only slightly distracted me, "the fact that there was silver at all is a pretty damning clue."

I didn't answer immediately, but lathered my hair and washed. "I dunno, Sylvie. It just doesn't quite click for me. Sure, the wolves can kill without the slashes, if we take Verne's word for it—and I don't doubt him—but still . . . I've never actually heard of them doing it that way. And even less would they do it if the victim started showering the area with silver." I chewed it over in my mind as I ran soap over the rest of me.

"Actually, I think you're right, Jason," Sylvie said. "It didn't really feel like a wolf to me either. But if it wasn't, why the silver?"

I'd come up with a tentative answer. "Well, if you know that wolves can shapeshift, and you know something is trying to kill you without touching you—and the victim sure was scared about something—wouldn't you think 'werewolf!' right away, no matter what the thing looked like?"

"Oh." I heard the faint sounds of Sylvie brushing her teeth. "That makes sense! Confronted by the unknown, you'd try whatever weapons you have available in the hopes that they might work."

"Now the real question is," I said, getting out and toweling off, "why the heck I'm spending my time trying to figure it out. Let the damn cops deal with it."

She kissed me and stepped into the shower herself. "Because you know perfectly well that they're not going to deal with this one. It's ours. Wood'n Stake ride again."

I snorted. "Bah. I'm probably making a mountain out of a molehill. The autopsy will come back saying he died of a heart attack, and the silver dust will be glitter or something from a kid's birthday party."

Syl's outline against the glass shivered. "I hope so, Jason... but I don't think it's going to be that way."

When I pulled out the ten-millimeter and loaded it, she knew I felt the same way.

CHAPTER 60

Touched with Silver

Sheriff Carl Baker was a big, tired-looking man with thinning hair combed over the top of his head and a white-sprinkled mustache that also drooped tiredly. "Sorry to have ta drag you back here, Mr. Wood," he said.

"It's okay," I said. "I know what it's like when you're doing an investigation."

"Guess y' do, at that. Anyways, to be honest we're kinda at a loss. Jerry may not have been the friendliest guy in town, but he sure weren't the nastiest, an' I don't have a clue about who would've killed him."

"Are you sure he was killed?"

Baker's moon-round face twisted in a sour grimace. "Ain't sure of anything, right now. Coroner says that so far as he's concerned, Jerry should've been gettin' up off the damn slab before the autopsy. Not a thing wrong with him—heart in great shape, brain jus' fine, everything jus' fine—'ceptin', of course, that he happens t' be dead." He grunted and handed me a file. "Ain't procedure, but you've got yourself a rep in more than one way—I checked out what the cops up north had ta say 'bout you. Anything in there give you an idea?"

"Well, I'll see..." I opened the file, started reading. Sheriff Baker, relieved of the responsibility of talking to me for the moment, went into the outer office.

Baker wasn't exaggerating; while I'm no doctor, I know how to read ME reports, and this ME was clearly frustrated. Jerry Mansfield, twenty-nine, had apparently been a health nut. He was in perfect shape—not too fat, not too thin, medical records showed excellent cholesterol and blood-pressure measurements, and so on and so forth. The coroner really truly had no idea why this man was dead. There weren't any marks on his body, no foreign substances on his skin aside from a bit of dirt and silver dust. The latter had been found on his clothes, most heavily concentrated on the hands, head and neck, and...

Wait one minute. I thought back to last night. There had been the regular sea breeze, but there was no way a significant amount of wind would have been getting into the high-fenced yard, and even if it had, the direction was wrong. What the hell...

I flipped back to another section of the report, looking for something. It wasn't there.

"Sheriff..." I called.

Baker stuck his head back in. "Found something?"

"Can you have the coroner check for something specific?"

"Sure. What do you need?"

I looked back down at the report. "I want to know if Jerry Mansfield had any silver dust in his lungs. Your ME may be doing an autopsy on a former werewolf."

"That's ridiculous!" Baker burst out. "Jerry couldn't *possibly* have been a werewolf!"

I raised a skeptical eyebrow. "Oh?"

Baker looked nonplussed for a moment. "Well...look, he shopped with everyone else, didn't he? Everyone's got those things you designed—hell, there's one right over my door here. Stands to reason the man couldn't've been anything other than one of us."

I had to admit there was something to that. Unless a wolf had replaced Jerry Mansfield very, very recently, it was hard to imagine how he could maintain the masquerade in a place like this one, which as a tourist area had apparently made it quite a point to have everything covered from the wolf perspective. "Well, have him check it, anyway."

Baker shrugged. "I asked ya to look, I suppose I oughtta go along with it. You got any particular reason for this here idea?"

I pointed at the photos of the body and the description. "There was silver dust all over the area in front of Mansfield, but if you look at the way it's distributed, it wasn't *Mansfield* doing the throwing; someone threw silver dust *at* him. He's got it on his hands where it would be if he tried to shield himself, but mostly on his head and other areas where it would have been if someone tried to throw it at him. Now, I don't know about you, but the only good reason I can think of to throw a hundred bucks' worth of silver dust over someone is if you think they're a werewolf."

Baker looked at the photos and swore mildly. "Goddamn. Now that y' point it out, it's plain as day."

"The clincher, of course," I finished, "is that Mansfield didn't *have* silver dust on him. No pouch or dispenser or anything like it. So it *had* to be the other person or persons who did."

While Baker went to call the ME, I continued studying the report. Footprint and track analysis was very disappointing. While you could, with difficulty, make out my prints and some of Jerry Mansfield's, there were hardly any readable tracks elsewhere. One investigator said it appeared that something had been swept heavily across the area leading from the body to the other gate, which opened up into a well paved side street. If that was the case, it obviously was a murder of some kind—someone had erased the tracks. I studied the pictures for a few moments more, then put them back.

Baker hung up. "Okay, he'll take a look an' get back to me soon. I hope you're wrong, to be honest. I mean, Jerry was a friend. Not real close, but enough that it'd kinda shake me to find out he wasn't what he seemed."

"Not to mention the other can of worms that would open if it turns out he was one."

"Noticed that, did ya?" Baker grimaced again. "Oh, yeah. What do I do if he was a damn wolf? Ain't no laws dealing with this. The man paid his taxes an' didn't cause no trouble, so on that account, I oughtta treat it like any murder. But if he was really one o' these shapeshiftin' killers...no thanks, there's a headache I just don't need."

"Well, Sheriff, I did what I could. Sorry if it causes you more trouble."

He waved it off. "Nah, believe me, I'd rather have the answer than not. I'll let you know what the coroner says."

"Thanks. I'm afraid that aside from that one offbeat suggestion, I don't see anything else. If I think if anything, I'll call." We shook hands.

CHAPTER 61

Close Call

A few minutes later, I was letting myself back into the hotel room. Syl came out of the bathroom, gave me a hug and kiss which took a few moments in itself, and then asked, "How'd it go?"

"The sheriff was actually more interested in getting my professional advice than in raking me over the coals," I answered. "Handed me the ME report, which did tell me one interesting thing: the silver dust wasn't Mansfield's. It belonged to whoever or whatever presumably killed him."

Sylvie stared. "You know that doesn't make any sense."

"Unless Mansfield was a wolf, and as the sheriff pointed out, that'd be hard to pull off in a town that's as wolf-wired as this one is. Or unless..." I trailed off. "Doesn't quite work, dammit."

"What?"

"Well, whoever threw silver dust at Mansfield *thought* he was a wolf. And it struck me that we do know of one supernatural type of creature that kills werewolves whenever it can get away with it."

Syl's face showed enlightenment. "Vampires, of course! Verne told us about that secret war they had."

I nodded. "Problem is that there weren't any puncture marks on this guy. Werewolves can kill without touching people, according to Verne, but he never said vampires could." I turned to the phone. "I'll call Morgan and see if this kind of thing rings a bell for him."

As I reached for the handset, there was a knock at the door. "Who the heck...?"

I went to the door and looked through the peephole. A

well-dressed man about my age, black-haired and brown-eyed, stood there, waiting expectantly. "Yes? Who is it?" I called through the door.

"Sorry to disturb you—but you *are* Jason Wood, correct?" he answered in a tenor voice. "My name's Karl Weimar, sir. I know this is irregular, but I have some information about Jerry Mansfield that you might like to know and I'm not sure I want to go to the cops just now."

I closed my eyes for a moment, sighed. No rest for the suckers. "Oh, all right, hold on." I unbolted the door and slid the chain off, turning toward Syl.

Her eyes were wide, mirroring an inner vision of disaster.

I dove away from the door, drawing the ten-millimeter as I did so. At the same moment, the door slammed open so hard it almost tore from its hinges, and the dapper young man lunged through, shapeshifting into an all-too-familiar towering mass of black-brown fur, glittering claws, diamond teeth, and glowing soulless eyes.

But Syl's unspoken warning had been enough. I had moved and was not where "Karl Weimar" expected me. It skidded to a halt, talons ripping great gouges in the carpet, and turned on me, to find itself staring down the barrel of my gun.

"Believe you me, this thing's loaded with silver. And if it weren't for two things, I'd blow you straight to hell right now."

It snarled. "And those two are . . . ?" it asked in the unearthly deep timbre of its kind.

As I glanced at Sylvie, I amended my comment. "Three things, actually. The first is that I'm curious about what brought you here to kill me. The second is that, based on Virigar told me, not one of you would dare touch me or Sylvie since he'd marked us for his own—and you sure as hell are not him. The third is that my wife thinks I shouldn't shoot you right now, for some reason of her own." I had no idea what the reason was, but Syl had communicated that I was doing the right thing, so I didn't argue.

The expression of savage hunger and fury left the werewolf's face. It looked positively taken aback. "You think that the King's ban would be enough for one who's already hunting His people?"

"What?" I must've looked even more confused. "Hunting you? Sure, I'd expect that you guys would defend yourselves if I was going around shooting, and I'd presume even Virigar himself wouldn't argue about that. But I haven't been hunting any of you. Do I look crazy? Do you furballs think I *like* having clawed monsters chasing me around?"

"You killed Mansfield, thinking he was one of us," it retorted sullenly.

"*I* killed...? Do you wolves smoke some of the same stuff we do, or what? I just found the goddamn body! If he wasn't a wolf, and thus dead from sucking silver, I haven't a goddamn idea what the hell killed him. You think I can kill people—wolf or otherwise—by waving my friggin' hand?"

It stared at me a moment, eyes flickering like evil lamps, then abruptly reverted to its human form. "Well, *scheiss*," said Karl Weimar. "Now I'm just as confused as you are."

"I doubt that," I said.

He reached into his pocket, pulled out several bills and dropped them on the table. In the back of my mind, I noted that in wolf mode he had no clothes, let alone a wallet, which raised an interesting question regarding the authenticity of the cash. "For the damage. My apologies." Weimar turned and walked towards the door.

"Hey, you bastard, you can't just pop in, scare the crap out of people, and pop out without a little explanation!" I shouted after him, ignoring the obvious fact that he was doing just that.

I closed the door, which scraped a bit from nearly being torn off, and collapsed into an armchair. "*Jesus*, that was close."

Syl nodded and came to me; we hugged, trying to get over a serious attack of the shakes.

Suddenly, I stood up, almost dumping Syl on the floor. "Jason, what...?"

"The peephole!" I answered, digging into my larger travel bag for my kit.

"What about...oh, my God."

"Exactly," I said grimly. "If my CryWolf gadgets aren't working, it means they've figured out a way to hide from them...and all the people buying them are no safer than the poor bastards who bought shark repellent and thought it would keep sharks away."

But when I started checking on the door, the results were even more disquieting.

The external shell was a CryWolf sensor, or a good replica of one, complete with the logo...but the interior was nothing but an ordinary peephole lens. There wasn't even a power lead in it.

"That son of a bitch," I heard myself growl.

"Who? That wolf, Karl?"

"No," I said, standing up and wrenching open the door, "Our 'cheerful host,' Vic. He's ripping off everyone in the hotel—putting fake sensors on the doors to make 'em feel comfortable, but not spending the money for the sensors themselves. Well, he's about to get a little talking-to."

Vic was at the desk; the lobby was deserted. He looked up, started to smile a greeting, then stopped at the look on my face. "What's wrong, Mr. Wood?"

"I was attacked in my room just now. By a werewolf."

Vic looked horrified. "But..."

I tossed the dummy sensor on the desk. "And don't even try to tell me it's impossible. Give me one good reason I shouldn't call about a dozen lawyers down on your ass right now."

Vic's gaze barely flickered to the sensor; the fact that I had been attacked seemed to have overwhelmed him. "But they couldn't have gotten in here...?" he said, looking pathetically frightened.

Then I remembered my prior brush with death at Verne's house and how Verne had also nearly died. Vic probably didn't install his own stuff any more than Verne did. "Then you got screwed by your contractors, Vic. If the one in my room's a dummy, I'll bet all of them are."

His expression went from shocked disbelief to fury. "All of them? Jesus H. Christ, sir, I'll be lookin' into this, you can bet on it." He frowned. "What can I do in the meantime? Please, don't mention this to the other guests...?" He made the request a question.

I nodded. "Okay. I don't want to ruin your business, but get it fixed fast. Don't worry about my room—I have my own CryWolf gadgets, of course."

"But you don't have to..." he began, then realized that I had to do this myself, since at this point I couldn't trust *his* sources. "Yes, 'course you do, sir. Well, I'd better get on the phone and start kickin' some."

"I suppose. And get a ruglayer into my room; the wolf tore it up something fierce."

"Yessir."

I didn't feel like going back to the room right now, and by her expression neither did Syl. "Want to take a walk, then maybe go for dinner?"

"As long as you'll be on the lookout. I don't know what that wolf was up to, but he may not be the only one with that idea."

"Damn straight," I said, putting on my special glasses. They were a trial addition to my CryWolf technology. I wanted to use some of the more advanced circuitry currently available to make a detector which would, in theory, be just as good as my original clumsy goggle-mounts, but that looked just like those light-adjusting sunglasses. I glanced back at Vic to offer him a stopgap solution in the form of one of the other gadgets I'd brought, but he was in the office behind the desk, and I could hear his southern voice rising, with the words *lawyer* and *sue* audible.

We spent a couple of hours wandering around on the beach, avoiding people in general. While the town was a pretty place, recent events and our forced residency were unfortunately starting to rob it of its charm. As dusk began to fall, we made our way back towards one of the restaurants. Remembering the layout of the town, we turned into a smaller alleyway that would take us to the next road.

In the growing shadows, I thought I saw someone coming down the alley ahead of us, and slowed to let him go around. Then I realized he or she was just standing there.

"Hello?" I said to warn them that we were approaching.

The figure didn't move or respond. As I got closer, I saw that it was all the same grayish color—a statue of some kind?

Sylvie gave a sudden gasp and stepped back; my reaction was to step forward, staring incredulously.

Gazing back at us, face frozen in an expression of terror, was Karl Weimar.

CHAPTER 62

A Perfect Little Vacation Spot

I poked at the thing several times. It was stone, all right, solid stone of a generally grayish cast—in the current light I couldn't do much to identify it. But the detail I could see was amazing. I glanced at Syl.

"It's not a statue," she said, confirming my gut intuition.

"Right," I said. Realizing I hadn't brought my cell phone with me, I headed up the alley to the nearest open store, which happened to be Marie's, the jewelry store we'd visited...was it only a day ago?

"Hi," I said, walking towards the proprietor, "I was wondering if you..."

I'm not sure how I controlled voice or expression in the next few moments; perhaps a part of me already knew and was prepared. As I neared Marie, her image began to shimmer, glittering with a network of lines and sparks...

Without more than a slight pause, I heard myself say "...would show us that lovely necklace in the third cabinet again?"

Marie smiled and headed for the cabinet in question. Syl stared at me for a split second, obviously wondering what the hell had gotten into me, but she knew I must have a reason, and followed Marie over. As she reached the third cabinet, Marie entered the effective range of the CryWolf camera over the door, and I turned and studied the image on the display behind her counter. I had to crane my neck to do it.

She and Syl both showed as perfectly normal on the monitor.

In that second the oddities I'd noticed all made sense, and I think it is a great accomplishment that I did not, in fact, scream out in horror. Instead, I turned and walked to the counter next to Syl. As Marie turned with the necklace in her hands, I said casually, "So...is the sheriff one of you, too?"

She blinked. "I don't quite..."

I tapped the glasses. "These are CryWolf—experimental model."

Syl, realizing my meaning, stepped back and slid her hand into her purse for her gun.

Marie stood for a moment, face utterly expressionless, then closed her eyes and sighed. "How did you guess? You weren't wearing those last time."

"Since then, one of your people tried to kill me, apparently thinking I was out hunting wolves."

"Who would possibly be insane enough to... oh, I know. Must have been either Kheveriast or Mokildar." She shook her head. "Children are always fools."

The full implications finally made their way to Sylvie's consciousness. "By the Earth, you can't mean...Jason, the whole town can't be wolves!"

"Not every single family, no," I said, "but all the key people and a bunch more residents is my guess. Right?"

Marie nodded.

"And you make sure it looks like everything's covered with CryWolf sensors, so no one ever gets an idea to start checking around otherwise. What I don't quite get is *why*."

Sheriff Baker's tired baritone spoke from behind us. "You don't get why, Mr. Genius Wood? *You* are the reason why."

"How...?" I asked, then looked at Marie. "Ah. You can communicate with each other over some distance."

He glared at me, hands on his hips, and continued as though I hadn't spoken. "Ten thousand years, Wood. For ten thousand years, I have walked the face of this planet, with all my people, and never did we have anything to fear from you mortals. Oh, if one of us was blatant, stupid, clumsy, or unfortunate, a silver weapon could end it for him or her, but all in all, that was just as well; if you have no respect for the potential danger of the cattle, you become fat and lazy, unworthy of being one of the great ones.

"And then *you* come along and invent a little toy." His hand lashed out, snatched the glasses from my face and pulverized them. "A *toy* that gets more of us killed off in three months than in my entire lifetime, save only the time the blood-drinkers made war on us. A toy that gets our race publicized so we actually have to deal with people knowing—not guessing, but *knowing*—what walks among them."

"That," I indicated the crushed glasses, "will cost you about ten grand."

His expression became a snarl and his features rippled slightly.

"Unless you want me to blow the gaff on your cozy little tourist village here, or you assault me against your King's command, that is."

He seemed to be considering it through the bit about his village, but when I spoke of the King, he instantly backed off, clearly frightened by the mere mention of Virigar. "N-no. You aren't intending to tell about us?"

"That depends on how you answer my question." I let my heartbeat slow down. It looked like things might not end in a blaze of claws and gunfire. "Again, why the hell are all of you down here? Or is it just to give the words 'tourist trap' new meaning?"

He chuckled humorlessly. "The temptation is certainly there. But no, we don't kill anyone here. We can feed without killing, if we must, and if we control ourselves; and control is the complete and absolute law here. If we permitted killings, no matter how subtle, your law-enforcement people would eventually notice a change in the statistics and come to look." He gritted his teeth at my inquiring look, and finally forced himself to continue. "We are... we are *hiding* here."

I couldn't restrain a guffaw. The wolves were running scared! "So you're living like cattle now, hoping none of the bulls with silver horns catch up with you?"

He growled, a very inhuman sound coming from an apparently human throat. "For the moment... until we have decided how to properly deal with this new threat. So you didn't kill Jerry Mansfield?" he asked, changing to his human guise's voice.

"Nope. Had no idea there were any wolves around here until one of them tried to kill me earlier today. Now I understand your bit about denying he was a wolf, though; you can't have any suspicion of wolves being present at all."

"Mansfield was human," Baker said. "Someone thought he was a wolf, looks like, but I guarantee you, he was human."

"The plot thickens," I commented. This was an interesting

sidelight on the matter. "And since I didn't kill him, we still have a mystery on our hands. A real wolf would have known he wasn't one. So Mansfield was killed by someone who wasn't wolf and wasn't human either." Suddenly, I remembered why we'd come here in the first place. "Hey, Sheriff, do you know a wolf who goes by the human name Karl Weimar?"

He nodded. "That'd be young Kheveriast. What about him?"

"He tried to kill me earlier, assuming I'd been trying to hunt wolves, but that's not why I ask. If you go down this alley at the side," I pointed, "you'll find a statue of him. Except I think it probably isn't really a statue."

Marie looked puzzled, but Baker's face was a study in dawning horror. "A . . . statue?"

For a moment I actually felt sympathy for Baker—but I remembered that despite his fight to save his race, his speech had indicated no remorse for his people's actions and had confirmed the usual wolvish tendency toward megalomania. "Gray stone, incredibly detailed."

He got a grip. "Mr. Wood, I have some calls to make. We will speak again. This business may concern both your people and mine."

"Maybe," I said. "Why would someone have thought Mansfield was a wolf?"

"He worked for us," Baker answered after a moment.

I blinked. "What?"

"I said, he worked for us. While we have a fairly good grip on this town, new humans who move in can't be easily controlled— and if they start installing their own sensors, none of our people dare get near the house. Jerry was . . . I suppose you'd call him a special agent. He would arrange for any active CryWolf sensors to become inactive. We'd use him to meet with agents who might be carrying their own gadgetry. Another reason we have to keep things low-profile here, obviously; if the Feds come in, they might bring CryWolf-equipped cameras, goggles, and so on, and that would ruin it all."

I was utterly floored by this revelation. "What in the name of God could convince a human being to work for things like you?"

Baker grinned. It wasn't a comforting expression. "Your people are no angels, Wood. We can offer plenty to a wise human, espe-cially when, as is now the case, you humans have something to offer us. And we generally play fair; after all, even your people don't butcher every cow—you keep some as breeding stock, some as working animals, and even a few as pets. If you weren't associated with Domingo, I have no doubt our King would have made you an offer to switch sides."

The very thought of someone—of a human being—working for these monsters, knowing what they were, was so repellent that I simply couldn't reply for a moment. Finally, I got my voice back.

"Okay, Baker. I won't blow your cover...for now. But I am not working with you anymore. I will give you no help, no hints, nothing. So far, whatever it is has targeted you monsters or someone who was working hard to give up his humanity. As far as I'm concerned, that means they're doing the world a friggin' service."

Baker stepped forward again, glaring. "Wood, you'll assist if we say so, or I'll—"

"You'll what? Come on, tell me." I threw my own sarcastic grin back in his face. "You can't do a goddamned thing to me, Baker, and you know it. I'm too well known to just disappear. If I get killed, your cover's blown for sure, and once the country realizes what you're up to, there won't be a safe place for you bastards anywhere on the planet. You'll have to go to ground in wilderness, away from all the comforts you've obviously come to like. Even if you keep the Feds out of it, Verne Domingo will deal with you. And I don't think the King will stop him in that instance." I took Sylvie's arm and started to walk out.

"I still have an investigation ongoing, Wood," Baker said, with a cold intonation. "Leave town and I can have you brought right back here."

"Oh, I won't leave. Yet. But you finish this investigation—pin it on either the real crook, or one of your own people, I don't care which—and let us out of this infested hellhole within the next week. Because I swear by God that if we have to hang around here any longer than that, I'll phone the authorities anyway."

"You wouldn't!"

I whirled around, grabbed his collar and shoved him back against the counter. "The hell I wouldn't! Do you think I'm an idiot? That I can't do a little simple math? It's been less than a year since Morgantown, and here you are, in charge, hundreds of you furry bastards living like so many Addams-family rejects behind a coat of Brady-Bunch paint. You didn't win any elections to get here—you whacked hundreds of people and took their places. The *only* reason I'm not blowing the whistle right now is that when your kind are cornered, you kill, and I don't want to be responsible for another bloodbath. I'll take your word—for the moment—that you're not killing anymore. Maybe it's true. It had better be true from now on, believe you me." I let him go, turned back to Sylvie. "Let's go."

I ignored the crawling sensation between my shoulder blades and didn't look back as we left.

CHAPTER 63

Dealing With a Devil

"Why the hell can't you keep your fifty thousand makeup things off the darn counter?!" I exploded as three bottles fell over.

"Probably for the same reason you can't put your stupid clothes away when you go to bed!" Syl snapped back. "Do you know how disgusting it is to leave your dirty clothes on the floor?"

I opened my mouth to fire back, saw the mingled anger and hurt in her eyes, and closed both eyes and mouth. "Jeez, I'm sorry, Syl. This thing's really getting to me."

She came over and put her arms around me. "Me, too."

"Some honeymoon *this* is turning out to be."

Venice and Nokomis were still lovely places, but just how are you supposed to relax and enjoy your stay when you're aware that any one of the nice people around you—on the beach, in the store, on the street—could be a soul-eating monstrosity just hiding out until such time as they can gain the upper hand on your own species? Baker had come through with the money for destroying my prototype, but without access to my homegrown lab and materials I wouldn't be able to duplicate the things. I was now carrying one of the commercial CryWolf goggles, but I didn't bother wearing it while out and about. I could do without drawing that much attention, and I really didn't want to know just how many wolves were around me at any given time.

"The first part was fine. It's not your fault that we've found ourselves stuck in another strange circumstance."

I took a deep breath and tried to relax into her. There was no point in letting this drive me nuts. "Maybe not, but Verne did say that *I* might be the focal point of everything. The fact

we've run into the weird *here*...well, he might be right." I took
another breath, smelling her hair and letting my eyes close. I'd
given Baker a week, and it had only been two days. If I didn't
get a grip, I'd be saying something I'd never be able to make up
for by the time another five days were past.

There was a knock on the door. Both Syl and I jumped, showing the state of our nerves. "Who is it?" I called back.

"Sheriff Baker sent me over, Mr. Wood. Might I come in?"

I went over to the recently repaired door, put on my goggles,
and opened it, keeping the chain on as I studied the man standing there. He was a tall man, over my six foot one, with thick,
wavy brown hair brushed back from a high forehead, piercing
blue eyes, and sharp, patrician features. He was slender, though
apparently fit, and his clothes were of impeccable cut—clearly
upper-class. I glanced back at Syl to make sure she didn't have
a nasty feeling about the next few seconds, then nodded, taking
off the CryWolf goggles and sliding the chain to the side. "Come
on in. What's this about?" I asked.

"I have a...business proposition to make you, Mr. Wood,"
he said. He bowed to Sylvie. "Lady Sylvia Stake; I have heard of
you. An honor."

As he was paying his respects, Syl was checking him out. His
voice had a faint English accent, but with perhaps a Canadian
influence? "A business proposition, Mr...?"

"Carruthers, sir, Alexi Carruthers," he replied, shaking my
hand firmly. "Yes. I would like to see if I can persuade you to
reconsider your refusal to assist investigating the current string
of unusual murders."

What had been a pair was now a string. "There have been
more?"

Carruthers nodded, taking a seat when I indicated that he
should. "Three, two wolf and one human."

"Was the human another of the wolves' allies?" I asked.

"She was," Carruthers acknowledged. "This may be coincidence,
however. Out of necessity, as many townspeople as possible had
been recruited. It is not improbable for a killer to run into two
collaborators."

I shook my head. "What's in it for me, Mr. Carruthers? So far,
as I told Baker, this whatever-it-is seems perfectly happy killing
wolves and traitors to humanity. Since the wolves perpetrated

mass slaughter to move here, and don't show any sign of regret, I'm not particularly motivated to try and help them. I'm supposed to be on my honeymoon, not working."

Carruthers smiled faintly. "I suppose monetary recompense would be foolish?"

I snorted. "I may not be the richest man in the world, but I've got more money than I know what to do with."

"I told Baker that myself," Carruthers admitted, "but it was the simplest offer I could make. When he called me in, I warned him you would be difficult to deal with; you have many reasons to not wish any of us well."

I studied him. "Did you say 'us,' Mr. Carruthers?"

He smiled again. "Yes, I did."

"You're a wolf?"

"I am."

The terrible, hollow feeling I'd had after Karl Weimar had attacked us returned. The wolves *had* found a way to hide themselves from the detectors. "Damn."

He looked momentarily confused, then laughed. "Ahhh, your clever little CryWolf device! I must compliment you on that—an inspired piece of design. One that couldn't have been done effectively even a few years ago."

"Useless now though," I said, trying to keep the bitterness out of my voice.

"Oh, far from it!" Carruthers assured me earnestly. "Really. Only a very, very select few of us can pass such devices with impunity. Only those of us who are truly Elder Wolves, and of course the King himself."

"Baker isn't an Elder?"

"Baker? Little Hastrikas?" Carruther's laugh filled the room with a rich baritone sound again. "Why, he's no more than eleven millennia—barely more than an infant, really, all things considered. No, no, Mr. Wood, there aren't more than a handful of the Great Elders left alive. I, of course, am one of them." For a moment, his eyes flickered, became soulless glowing yellow orbs. "Virigan, at your service."

Both Syl and I gasped—in a way, that partial, instantaneous transformation was more macabre than the full-scale change. "So," I said, "you're saying that the CryWolf devices are still reliable?"

"In the vast, vast majority of cases, indeed."

He still seemed relaxed and cheerful. "You don't appear particularly disturbed by this...situation. If you don't mind my asking, why aren't you on the warpath along with the rest of your relatives?"

The smile faded; now Carruthers looked serious. "Mr. Wood, most of our people are children by our standards. Even the older ones, like Baker, have had easy times. They need to learn that sometimes prey can turn on you, and they need to know how to survive such times. If they cannot, they do not deserve to live; other worlds are not nearly as forgiving as this one has been. We are the greatest and most powerful of all beings that have ever lived; only those who prove their worthiness again and again should have the right to even approach that potential. So has it ever been. If they wish a different course for our people," he smiled coldly, "all they need do is challenge the King for rulership. And win, of course.

"But enough about us, Mr. Wood; let's talk about you." Carruthers studied me for a moment. "I actually wanted to meet you quite some months ago, after you interfered with something I'd been working on for years." He raised an elegant eyebrow, waiting for me to guess.

I didn't have to think long; there was really only one viable guess. "So you were one of the people behind the Project—the one in Vietnam, with Tai Lee Xiang."

"Very good. I was in fact *the* person behind it all, and have been for several decades now."

I thought about that for a moment. "That would mean you were working on this stuff while the OSR was still active."

"Correct."

"Now, just what would a werewolf want with a human genetic engineering project, Mr. Carruthers?"

He waved a finger in a "no-no" gesture. "Ah-ah, Mr. Wood, we are getting sidetracked again. The answers to such questions should remain mysteries; all the better to intrigue you. We are here to discuss your employment."

I smiled back with an easy laziness I didn't feel; I was in a room with one of the most lethal creatures on Earth, and knew all too well what it would do to me if circumstances changed. "No, *you* are here to discuss my employment. So far, I'm here to listen to whatever interesting facts you let slip and otherwise laugh at the very idea of helping you."

Carruthers gave a heavy sigh. "Yes, I rather thought so. Let me make you a more concrete proposal. Your interference in the Project cost us immensely. There are a number of people—human, my kind, and, well, *other*—who feel that you would make an ideal target as an example. The game of international intelligence, on this level, is not played in the standard way, since, if we are being honest, neither side admits of this level's existence. More grim and direct methods tend to be used in our realm of business. Your termination, despite certain allies who present formidable obstacles, would serve as a clear warning to others who have begun to gain an annoying brashness in their intrusions.

"I am willing to offer you amnesty—we shall write off the cost of the operation with respect to you and your lovely wife. Since the King's decree protects you from my kind, this will essentially place you back at where you were before ever you were involved in such affairs; only mortal concerns to worry you."

I nodded, considering. I hadn't forgotten the possibility that the Project would take my interference amiss, but Carruthers had now made it a concrete threat, one that I couldn't afford to ignore, especially now that I had a wife and, potentially, one day, a family of my own.

"What's your angle, Carruthers?"

He raised an eyebrow. "What do you mean?"

"I mean, you're a bright guy. You have the Project for resources, plus the gods only know what else. Why the hell do you want me in on this? What is it that prevents you and your furry family from solving the murders?"

"A matter of symmetry, you might say," Carruthers responded. "You ruined one project, now you present yourself in a perfect position to rectify another."

"Bullpuckey." I glanced at Syl, who nodded, glaring at our visitor. "Don't *even* try lying to me, Carruthers, or you can go sit on a silver spike and spin. Try again, the truth this time, or you can kiss any chance for a deal good-bye."

Carruthers' eyes narrowed, and for an instant, the wolf looked out, hungry, furious at being balked by this lesser creature; then the urbane mask was back. "As you will, Mr. Wood.

"Certain . . . features of this case are disquieting to my people. There are a few possible reasons for the . . . particular condition of the corpses, but all of them imply a form of death which our people fear above all others. At least one of the possible causes would make us more, rather than less, vulnerable to this attacker than human beings, and in most cases, the attacker will grow stronger with each kill. None of my people want to be involved— not only is the type of death truly hideous, especially to a race that is by all rights immortal, but if the one explanation proves correct, those investigating would be potentially supplying our enemy with ever greater power. A human being will be less vulnerable and, if he fails, will not provide much of a boost to our adversary."

I snorted. "So you need an intelligent but dispensable agent who won't prove to be a battery for this bozo."

"Succinctly put."

"You're being awfully low on the details here. If you expect me to look into anything, you'd have to be a bit more forthcoming on them."

A nod acknowledged my point. "Indeed, but you have not yet agreed to the position, Mr. Wood. The more you learn, the more dangerous you could become to us, true?"

"True enough." I thought for a moment. "I'll make you a counteroffer, Mr. Carruthers. You will arrange the same immunity for *all* those associated with me—specifically, you give up on Tai Lee Xiang and all his relatives. If his wife or daughter are still in your possession, or in that of anyone you have influence over, you'll hand them back. Verne Domingo, Sylvie, myself, and, to be blunt, my whole damn hometown is off-limits to you and your gene-twiddled friends."

"Have you completely taken leave of your senses, Wood?" Carruthers stared at me. I couldn't completely blame him, I had upped the ante a bit, specifically in his own project's area.

"Hey, you're the one who came here. Take it or leave it. I'm not interested in only personal immunity—that's not enough to make it worth playing this game with you. I'll trust in Verne and Tai Lee to whip the crap out of any of your assassins who happen to wander through." I turned my back on him and got myself a ginger beer out of the fridge and congratulated myself that my hands hardly shook at all.

I turned back to face Carruthers' silent glare. I returned it with a raised eyebrow and sat back down.

Silence. None of us moved.

After what seemed an hour but was probably only a minute, Carruthers broke into a smile and spread his hands. "You have my measure, Mr. Wood. It is, indeed, that important to me. I accept your terms, with a single exception: Jeri Winthrope. While she is not, at present, high on our list of targets, she is connected to an organization that is in an adversarial position to us; I will not agree to something which would potentially leave me bound to permit an enemy to strike without my own freedom to strike them as I saw fit."

I didn't like the exception, but I also knew what "organization" he had to be referring to, and whoever they were, they played their own brand of deadly hardball. A warning to the Jammer should suffice to make sure they kept their eyes open.

"Agreed."

"Excellent!" Carruthers stood to go.

"Whoa, there," I said. "I want you to swear to this agreement."

"Certainly," he began, but I held up my hand.

"In the name of the King himself."

His mouth tightened, then relaxed. "Yes, I suppose you would guess that one. So be it. I, Virigan, one of the Eldest Five, swear, by the name of our Father and King, the Final Devourer, Virigar, that from this day forth no forces under my control, or under the control of any I influence, involved with the Project or of our people, shall seek to harm, kill, interfere with, or otherwise inconvenience Jason Wood or any of the people associated with him as follows: V'ierna Dhomienkha, known as Verne Domingo; Tai Lee Xiang and any of his family; Sylvia Stake; and any and all residents of the community of Morgantown, New York, current or future, with the sole exception of Agent Jeri Winthrope and any that she recruits or imports to the area, aside from those already mentioned. In addition, I swear that if any of the family of the previously mentioned Tai Lee Xiang remain in the custody of any I control or influence, they will be returned to Tai Lee Xiang and will enjoy the same status of protection.

"In return, Jason Wood, you swear that you will undertake the investigation of these killings in Venice and environs, and will devote the same ingenuity and effort that you have to prior investigations, ignoring considerations of our races' differences in the pursuit of the perpetrator. Have I your word?"

"You have my word of honor, yes. I'll do the best I can."

Carruthers bowed. "Then it is agreed and sworn to. I would suggest you call the Sh'ekatha; he will be able to tell you many things about what you may be facing. In the meantime, I will be instructing my people to cooperate with you fully—including giving you information on ourselves and our enemies which we would otherwise never reveal. I shall not be available; I must return to my own duties elsewhere." He extended his hand, which I shook reflexively, a shiver going up my spine. "Good-bye, Mr. Wood. I doubt we shall meet again."

The door closed behind him. I looked at Sylvie. "Why do I have a feeling that despite having him over a barrel, I *still* got the short end of the stick on this one?"

CHAPTER 64

Set in Stone

"You may have been tricked, Master Jason."

I closed my eyes for a moment. "Why, thank you, Morgan. Just what I needed to hear."

Sylvie and I had just finished filling Morgan in on the details. After I had called Verne to tell him the situation, he cut me off, not wanting to discuss things by phone, and sent Morgan down by chartered jet. Another peculiarity of Verne's existence that I hadn't known until now was that he could not travel a great distance from home, or stay away for any length of time, without significant preparations. Therefore, he had sent Morgan—his oldest living friend and retainer—as his right-hand man.

"Would you mind explaining?" Sylvie asked. "Exactly how we were tricked, I mean?"

Morgan smiled slightly. "Perhaps 'tricked' is too harsh a word, but slightly misled, certainly. While it is, technically, true that there are several ways to produce the effects that you have described, only one seems to me and Master Verne at all likely—and even that one is so unlikely that only the very existence of these crimes would make us consider the possibility at all."

"I see," I said. "What you mean is that he made it look like the thing they were afraid of wasn't necessarily here, while in fact he was pretty darn sure that it was, right?"

"Essentially true, yes, sir. In our opinion, you are dealing with a *Maelkodan*."

I typed the word into my laptop and frowned. "That word does *not* come up in the little database I made a while ago, Morgan."

"Master Verne realizes this and sends his apologies, sir. The

341

creatures were rare even before the disaster, and usually not found on Earth in any case; it did not occur to him that any such could have survived until now."

I noted the word. "And just what is a . . . Maelkodan?"

"As the werewolf is the origin of several legends—that of the lycanthrope, several demons, and so on—the Maelkodan is the original source from which the legends of Medusa, the basilisk, the catoblepas, and so on have derived. They are monstrous creatures, intelligent and devious, of vast mystical potential.

"As were so many monsters, they were created by sorcerous experimentation. In the case of the Maelkodan, a misguided attempt to create a creature capable of hunting down werewolves produced a monster with the requisite abilities, but with its own agenda. As nearly as Master Verne can determine, this was due either to a genuine mistake by the wizards creating the design, or to deliberate interference by someone—perhaps Virigar, perhaps one of the magicians themselves playing a deeper game. The Maelkodan was created from a combination of werewolf, human, and Teranahm souls and bodies."

"So," I said, "a group of powerful but possibly not very forward-thinking wizards went ahead and made this weird crossbreed. Um, what was that last species? Tera . . ."

"Teranahm," Morgan repeated. "The translation would be 'Great Dragon.'"

"Ooog." It wasn't the brightest-sounding rejoinder, but I wasn't able to think of an appropriate word.

"Indeed, sir. The resulting creature lacked the fluid shapeshifting ability of the wolf, but as both wolf and Teranahm have this as an inherent ability, a Maelkodan nonetheless has three forms. The first is its true form, which from the fragmentary descriptions available would be something akin to a slender lizardlike body with a vaguely humanoid torso rising, centaurlike, in the front. It has wolflike claws and teeth, and the scales are excellent armor. Unlike the werewolf, it is in fact not vulnerable to silver, but on a much brighter side is vulnerable to ordinary weapons, as a general rule, though if they become powerful enough their armor will withstand blows from swords and so on wielded by mortal strength. Master Verne and I are of the opinion that bullets will remain effective."

"Well, praise the Lord and pass the ammunition, will wonders never cease; a horror from beyond time that I really can just shoot dead," I said. "By the fact that the wolves are scared of this thing, though, I guess it must have something to make up for the fact that it can be killed conventionally."

"Indeed, sir. Several." Morgan paused, knowing I liked to work things out myself if possible.

I considered what he'd said so far. "Okay. Given what you say it originated in the way of legends, it has a death gaze. If it looks at you, you die. I'd guess that you would have to also be looking back at it—not only is that what the legends say, but if it could just kill by looking around, the thing would be virtually impossible to defeat, and I'd guess the things did get killed on occasion."

"Scoring pretty well so far, Wood," Baker said from the doorway, carrying a box of papers, presumably the records I needed.

"What I don't get is the different methodologies. Why did Mansfield end up just plain dead and Karl playing statue?"

Baker shook his head. "Not different methods, Wood. Different kinds of beings are affected by the Mirrorkiller differently."

"Um, 'Mirrorkiller'?"

"It's what we call the things. For what it's worth, the damn things fulfilled their design purpose. They like hunting us. They just like hunting everything else, too."

"Quite so," Morgan said. "They were supposed to inherit some human behavioral traits, but instead apparently became mostly wolfish in their outlook."

"Enough," I said, as I realized Baker was taking it personally as a snipe—which it may have been, but with Morgan's English-butler reserve, there was no way to tell. "Three forms, you said. What are the others?"

"One is human," Baker said after a moment. "A secondary shape it can assume while hunting. The third shape is the shape of the last person it killed. So when first hatched, it's only got two forms until it succeeds at killing."

"Why does it cause humans, for instance, to drop dead, and wolves to turn to stone?"

"That has to do with the difference in the essential nature of human versus wolf," Morgan answered. "Correct, Mr. Baker?"

"Yeah," Baker said. "Ya figured out our basic nature when ya made that gadget, right?"

I nodded. I thought I was starting to get the picture. "You're really energy matrices inhabiting a physical form. That's why you can perfectly duplicate a human being without becoming the human being."

"Right. Now, the Mirrorkiller, it eats the soul—the essential energy of any living thing. Being related to us, it's basically the same kind of thing."

"Now I understand. Since it was made using part of your essence, your people can't simply sense it—it can hide from you just as well as you can hide from us."

Baker grimaced. "Uh-huh. Now, when it gets you in its sights, it tries to eat your essence. But a human being, he's tied to that body. The body and the soul, they're just part of the same thing for you people. So it's got to rip the energy out of you, bit by bit, until the meat that's left falls over." Baker gave a shiver, a genuine sign of fear. "With us...it establishes, um, whattyacall-lit, a resonance, two similar patterns, and it damps part of ours out—negates part of the will to move, to fight. The resonance makes it take on the shape of the one it's killing."

"Thus 'Mirrorkiller.'"

"And then it moves to the target body, eating directly, leaving its own behind and taking over the shell."

I blinked. "So it's not really Karl's body out there carved in stone?"

"Not really, no. That's the mass which the Mirrorkiller was using beforehand. The next victim we found, well, that was Karl's body after the Mirrorkiller was done with it."

I had to admit that it was a pretty creepy picture. "But then Mansfield's body..."

"Well, of course that was the real body," Baker said. "The Mirrorkiller doesn't waste energy forcing its body to maintain a biological structure when it's moving to a new one. And it can't move into a human body the same way—it needs a soul connection to do the move, and it has to rip the soul out of a human first, rather than being able to move in via the resonance. It can use the resonance to paralyze the same way for a human, but that's the most it can manage."

"Okay, so it killed Mansfield. Then, as itself or Mansfield, it could—"

"No, not as Mansfield—where'd you get that idea?"

I looked at Baker. "You said its third form is the last person it...oh, I see, the usual wolf attitude: we're not people. It only takes the form of people whose bodies it's taken over."

"Right."

"In the legends," I said, "basilisks could be killed with mirrors. Is this true?"

"As it so happens, yes," Morgan answered, consulting some notes. "The Maelkodan retain some tendencies of physical creatures; they must see their target with physical sight first, before their soulsense can engage. For them, the eyes are indeed the window to the soul. The mystical connection between sight and soul is exceedingly deep for them; therefore, when they are engaged in the hunt, seeing themselves in a mirror—in attack mode only, mind you—triggers an attack upon their own soul."

I nodded slowly. "I see...yes, that makes perfect sense. The energy matrix is of course its own, and by trying to establish a suppressive phase shift, it's going to in essence cancel itself out."

Morgan blinked, as did Baker. "If you say so, sir."

"You emphasized 'in attack mode only,' Morgan. I suppose that means that we can't track down the Maelkodan by looking to see who might have no mirrors in their houses, or by lining the streets with reflective glass?"

Baker chuckled. "Sorry, nope. Only when it's chasing prey is it using the death-stare, focusing its own soul to attack. And they're all pretty well aware of the Perseus dodge, so it ain't easy to catch one off-guard." His tone became more serious. "And a wolf don't have much chance of getting away with it. A human, he can catch a glimpse, get a jolt but maybe stumble on, break eye contact and keep going. One of us, once the lock starts... it's over."

"So there's two things you're more vulnerable to than us," I said, musing.

"Mr. Carruthers mentioned that these creatures gain in power as they kill," Sylvie said. "Can you clarify that, Mr. Baker? Do they have other abilities besides this death-gaze?"

"Ayup," Baker said dismally. "Humans ain't got much, for the most part, on the power scale. Oh, there's a few what have trained in certain disciplines whose souls burn more bright, but for the Mirrorkiller they're strictly potato chips—you gotta eat a whole bag to get much out of 'em. One wolf, even one of the puppies around here, gives 'em a kick like fifty or sixty mortals. As they get more soul energy, they get stronger. More powerful energy matrix, in your terms—they can do a lot more with it. Physically, they get more powerful, no doubt—by now, the bastard we're up against could probably toss a small car with effort. And at some point, they'll be able to access the Draconic heritage those damn-fool wizards mixed in. That means magical effects. What with the pathetic magic ratio on Earth these days, at least we don't need to worry much about 'em casting spells, but inherent magical effects ain't out of the question. Poltergeist stuff, at least."

"Moving things by sheer will? Telekinesis?"

Morgan responded. "Yes, sir. Now, it's tied to the spiritual side, which means that it cannot directly affect people—of any sort—but other objects are fair game."

"What about the cosmic mind-woogie?" Sylvia asked.

"Beg pardon, Lady Sylvia?"

"I mean, both the wolves and the vampires can mess with people's heads. How about these things?"

"Ah. Yes, well, they apparently have some small ability to do this, but it is more along the lines of standard hypnosis—anyone who is aware of what they are facing is really in no danger."

I noted that down, looked at the rather intimidating summary. "That about it?"

"Think so," Baker said.

"Okay. So let me summarize. The thing kills by mutual sight—even a glance is enough to lock down a wolf; a human has a chance to break eye contact if he's lucky, but a few seconds will finish anyone. It has three forms—one a lizardy-centaur kind of thing, one a base human form—that's a preset, right? I mean, it's born able to turn into some specific human appearance?"

"Right."

"One base human form, and one form that changes with each kill of a wolf or similar, um, energy-matrix being. So if it kills Joe Wolf, it can then be either its default form or Joe Wolf until it kills Jack Wolf, at which point it loses the option of looking like Joe, but gains the ability to look like Jack. Can these things kill each other?"

"Probably," Baker said. "They don't seem to hunt each other down much, though. There never were many of them, thank the King."

I nodded. "Okay, then we've got several possible investigative avenues. First, where'd the thing come from? Your people seem to keep fair contact with each other, at least for big important stuff, and I'd guess you'd have known if there were statues turning up before now. Besides that, I've been doing a search through police files across the country and even in other countries I've gotten access to, and there doesn't seem to be any pattern of people being found dead without marks on them. So as a first guess, this thing just recently became active. How and why, and from where?

"Second, we follow the movements, as best we can, of the victims; see if we can come up with anything they had in common that might lead us to the killer's home. It's a damn shame about the statue trick; it doesn't give us much info on time of death, and that means that since the killer can take on the appearance of its last wolf victim, sightings of the victim at any time during the day preceding the statue's discovery could actually have been the Maelkodan using the victim's shape.

"Third, we remember that the creature has to be living here somewhere. Probably in the form of a human. If that's so, it must be using its default form. So, you want to look for people who have arrived here recently but who have been here since the first killing. Aside from myself and Sylvie, of course."

"You, I'll grant," Baker said. "But just out of sheer cussedness, why can't *she* be the one?"

I stared at him, speechless for a moment.

"Y'all gotta admit, the timing fits. And I hear tell she can sense us coming. That's impossible for a human. Nothing can find us except our own kind, and even that depends on how strong the other one is and how bad they want to hide. So just how can she sense us . . . unless she's either one of us, or a Mirrorkiller?" Baker's gun was out now, pointed straight at Sylvie . . . but his head was turned sideways, keeping him from looking at Syl's eyes.

"That would be extremely good evidence," Morgan said quickly, "were your statements entirely accurate. They are, however, not quite correct. It is true, sir, that there are very few things capable of sensing the wolves, but as Master Jason's device demonstrates, it is not entirely impossible. In point of fact, there are a few examples in Master Verne's experience of human beings and others who had the true Sight—they were not seeing through the disguise, so much as sensing an outcome of events, watching the very flow of time in the short term. From my experience with Lady Sylvia, I am convinced that this is, in fact, how she senses your people."

Baker's gun hand wavered slightly. He was listening.

"And also," I said, "Syl's been living in Morgantown for years. No such killings ever took place there, and hell, during Virigar's visit there were so many wolves around that I can't imagine one of these Maelkodan things being able to restrain itself; instead of Verne killing wolves in a warehouse, he would've gotten there to find a wonderful display gallery of statues and a Maelkodan so juiced up it'd be telekinesing city blocks for fun."

Slowly, Baker lowered the gun and raised his head cautiously. Looking at Syl, I saw what he did in her eyes; mild amusement, relief, and a trace of sympathy. "Well, even a Mirrorkiller would've thought two or three times about trying that with the King nearby, but I guess y'all have a point." He sighed. "Damn, but it would've been a simple solution."

"The simple solutions rarely work out," I said, relaxing. "Now that we've got an idea of what we're up against, let's get to work finding the damn thing before it kills anyone else."

CHAPTER 65

They Don't Just Come From Nowhere

"Baker, what do you think about this?"

He looked up from his desk and took the sheet of paper from me. "Hmm. Ayup, I was wondering about that."

"Three disappearances in the same general time period. One of them from your department. Think maybe the Maelkodan might be responsible?"

He frowned. "Problem is... why the hell are these guys disappearing when there are others standing out in plain sight? It ain't like hiding some of its victims is going to put us off the trail, the thing'd have to hide all of 'em. Or at least all the wolf victims, anyways."

I nodded. "It's a puzzler, that. But I'm still putting these guys down as possible victims. Are these people all wolves?"

He glanced at the names again. "Yep. All of 'em."

"I'll make that 'probable' victims, then. You've made it clear that you people work together and talk to each other in this town, so people don't go running off without a word to anyone... and offhand, I can't think of easy, accidental ways to kill you people off."

"S'trewth," he agreed.

"Any progress on movements?"

"Damn little," he growled, obviously frustrated. "Karl Weimar, easy enough—we know he busted in on you, then left, talked with a couple others, then said he was heading back to talk to you again. Timing makes it likely he got nailed right after that. Mansfield, well, he was all over town the last few days, bein' one of our contact men and all. Since he was killed at home, though, that don't tell us much. Same for the other victims—looks to me like the killer's picking vulnerable times and places, not waitin' to ambush a sucker who gets close."

"Which means we'll need to trace movements of people who might be the killer, rather than tracing the victims' movements."

He nodded. "O'course, without some decent suspects, that'll be a mite difficult. Can't run a trace on everyone."

"How about the correlation with recent arrivals?"

"Aside from you and your wife, you mean? Ain't looking very promising neither. If I give it about a month for new arrivals—assuming the thing decided to take a couple weeks to settle in an' decide how it wanted to start the killing—we've got about eight possibles. Problem is that so far it looks like at least half of 'em have ironclad alibis for Mansfield's murder, an' the rest might be a problem for some o' the others."

"Damn." It was starting to look like the creature might be hiding somewhere in its actual guise, not living among regular citizens. While in theory that might make it easier to find because of the limitation of how many isolated, hidden areas there might be, in practice, the thing could just pop out in its unknown "default" guise whenever it needed something, and since that default still wasn't known, no one would think twice about its appearance. Baker and I agreed that we might get somewhere by seeing if a stranger had been seen in the general area—that is, if our monster was at all interested in living the civilized life, it had to be picking up its cokes and chips somewhere, and even if it varied the routine, after a few weeks it had to be repeating locations. If we were lucky, someone would remember that. If it wasn't into the comforts of the twentieth century, we might be in for a long, hard search.

"How about your end?"

I shrugged. "Depends on how the thing got here. So far, we haven't found any probable entry times or points, but hell, we don't know if it slithered here under its own power, walked in as a human being, or got shipped here as a Ronco Peel-O-Matic in a little cardboard box."

"Maybe not, Wood, but you're missing the point."

I was always open to suggestions. "And the point being...?"

"Well, if'n we're right about this thing not bein' active until now, that means someone woke it up—either it hatched, or someone found it trapped somewhere and let it out."

Maybe it was all the paper-pushing, but I didn't quite see what he meant. "So?"

He gave me a "stupid human" look. "So, big shot, there's damn few places there'd be a Mirrorkiller—egg or suspended—hangin' 'round to be found. It'd have to be someplace where the coverup job on the Old Civilization wasn't complete—real heavily defended vaults, places like that. Now, I ain't up on the geography of that time, but you got friends who are. I'd ask them."

I smacked my forehead. "Okay, thanks, I deserved that. Of course. I suppose the Greek legends came from one that was released in a similar fashion?"

Baker shrugged. "Probably. I don't know firsthand, but makes sense; seem to remember something of an alert on one of the things being on the loose 'bout two, three millennia back or so, but I was in Asia most o' that time. Ask your friends, they oughtta know."

I gave a tiny shiver. Just when I was half-forgetting what he was, something would happen to bring it home. Verne always had that otherworldly air about him, courtesy of the movie-vampire image, which he happened to fit, and his own immense dignity. Baker, on the other hand, was as down-to-business a southern cop as you could imagine, and hearing that drawling voice casually mentioning a memory from before the time of Christ was unnerving. "Okay, I'll get on it. Add in those disappearances and see if it gets anything new on the timing end."

"Will do."

CHAPTER 66

Research Expedition

"That few?"

Morgan nodded. "Ten is the largest number of reasonable sites that Master Verne can think of. You have been told the power involved, Master Jason. You must understand, the demonic forces did their very best—at the direction of their ruler—to eradicate every trace of the original civilization, and Atla'a Alandar apparently suffered a similar fate." He unrolled a set of maps and began to lay them out on the floor of our hotel room. "Seven of them are, of course, at the locations of the Seven Towers; these were the bulwarks of Atlantaea's defenses, and even in destruction may have continued to defend at least something in their immediate area from complete eradication."

"Odd," I said. "I'd have thought that such areas would've been the focus of specific clean-up efforts."

"They most likely were, sir. However, according to Master Verne, the Towers' very nature made them difficult to destroy completely; even in destruction, it seems, they may have cloaked some material from detection."

I studied the maps and started marking off the locations on the globe. It was a jolt to notice that instead of exotic, faraway places, one of them appeared to be somewhere in the vicinity of Cape Cod. The rest of the ten locales were scattered around the globe, ranging from somewhere out in the middle of the south Atlantic Ocean to Germany.

"Now that you have this information, sir, do you have any idea what you will do with it?"

"Yep. That much I knew as soon as I asked. Obviously, this

Maelkodan thing wasn't mobile on its own before now, and I'll bet money that, even immobile, it wasn't anywhere with easy access." I was using my laptop to access my home machine and set up the search criteria, tapping in the commands and specs. "So someone just dug it up, or in the case of the ones in the ocean, maybe dredged it up."

I waited for that set of commands to be acknowledged, entered the next. "So what I'm doing is setting up a bunch of search parameters to, first, locate any expeditions or events that might have uncovered something unusual in the ten areas you've given me. In the case of deep-ocean sites, that'd have to be major scientific expeditions—no one goes down fifteen thousand feet in a casual dive. In land or shallow-water situations, there's more potential for casual digs and dives that might happen to turn up something that Man Was Not Meant to Know."

"I see," said Morgan. "And after that?"

"Then I tie this in with law enforcement files."

"Why law enforcement, Jason?" Sylvie asked, looking over my shoulder.

"Think about the scenario. By far, the most likely is this: Jane Doe finds something unusual—maybe it looks like an artifact, a fossil egg, whatever—on a dive or a dig. So the Maelkodan either wakes up right then, or it wakes up after she's brought the thing home, or to the university, or on board the ship. In any case, when it wakes up, what does it do? Barring some ridiculous coincidence involving its default human form looking just like one of the people present, it can't just slip out unnoticed, even assuming no one was looking when it woke up, hatched, whatever. Even if it *does* slip out, the finders are now missing part or all of their interesting find."

"Very clever, sir."

"Yes, I see, Jason. Either you'll have someone who disappeared, someone who got killed, or some item or artifact stolen or disappeared."

"Right. Now, if it was incredibly lucky, there might have been a werewolf available when it woke up, and then it could have assumed a form known to the people around. But even so, that person would have had to leave the area and end up here—or rather, it would likely have said it was going to some particular locale but came here to throw off any possible pursuit. Either way, it's likely that someone would be looking for them by now unless the person in question was in the habit of just dropping out of sight for weeks at a time."

"How long do you think it will take to do this?"

"Now that I've put in the parameters? A few hours, maybe, depending on how much stuff there is that makes a close fit."

Morgan shook his head in amazement. "I still find myself shocked at the speed of such things, Master Jason. However, are you not making a bit of an assumption that what you are looking for is indeed online?"

"To an extent, certainly, but news services generally carry most of the kind of thing I'm looking for. If we come up completely dry, we'll have to try something else, but let me give my machines a chance." I pulled out a deck of cards. "Anyone for a game?"

A couple of hours later, I was glad we were playing for pennies. I'm not a complete putz at cards, but I'd forgotten that Morgan was probably older than the sheriff. He was clearly trouncing both of us. "I should've suggested a game of Magic," I muttered as I shuffled and began to deal. "One-eyed jacks and the suicide king are wild."

"My geeky husband, you forget that you'd be the only one with a deck," Syl said, checking the cards as I dealt them.

"Couldn't lose then, could I?"

"Actually, Lady Sylvia, I happen to have a very nice red-black deck," Morgan said, causing Sylvia to boggle and me to chortle. "Although I confess to not going by tournament rules and hardly being up-to-date on my cards."

"No problem, Morgan, it's not like I'm a fanatic who has time to keep up—" my laptop played a small fanfare. "Oh, goody—I mean, oh, darn, I guess I'll have to sit this one out," I said, dropping my cards on the table.

The others dropped theirs, too, and Morgan collected his winnings. I keyed in my go-ahead and data began to scroll across the screen.

"Anything?" Syl asked.

"Excavation in Chile...nope, nothing there...dredging... possible, but...digging for old Indian relics in New York, nothing promising there...well, well, what have we here?"

I highlighted the article and brought it up. "Doctor J. I. O'Connell of the University of Oxford Archaeology Department led a team of researchers in the past few months on a survey of supposed underwater ruins off the coast of Cuba and other Caribbean islands. Their purpose was to find an accessible site to see if they could uncover anything in these ruins which would verify their age and origin."

"Looks quite promising, Master Jason."

I grinned. "Yep. And the physical nearness is encouraging. I mean, if you're in Mongolia and looking for some wolves for lunch, it'd probably be a lot easier to head for China. But if you're in the Caribbean, you head for the good old USA." I keyed in a request for a search on more information on O'Connell, this recent expedition, where he might be presenting the results, and so on.

A few seconds later, the results popped up. One carried the red flag signifying it was a law-enforcement file. "I'll be damned," I said. "Look at this."

Syl read aloud. "Missing Persons Report: James I. O'Connell."

"I believe we have a winner," I said grimly.

"Even more so, sir," Morgan said, pointing to the bottom of the list.

From the screen, I read: "Underwater archaeology team hopes to present results at conference in Florida."

A double-click brought up the entire article, which was an interview with Dr. O'Connell and a few of his students. In it, O'Connell indicated that he hoped to present at least a preliminary review of the results at the UAR (Underwater Archaeological Researchers) local conference in Florida. I read from the article. "'This is all very tentative,' O'Connell said with a grin, 'since we don't know our exact timetable yet, let alone if we're going to have any decent results to present. Still, I've given them tentative notification so they'll be ready.'" I looked up at the others. "Bingo. A few calls, and we'll know exactly how and when our little friend entered the country."

A Web search found the UAR page (after encountering the acronym in use for things as diverse as a Mac networking program, a UK asset recovery agency, and Russian architects, I had tp specify what UAR was) and a listing of their event schedule. A chill went down my spine as I read:

"Local Archaeology Conference: February 22–25, Venice, Florida."

CHAPTER 67

Showing Up Without Being There

I listened to the ring tone. Again. Again.

"Hello?"

The London-accented voice was that of a young woman.

"Could I speak to Mandy Gennaro, please?" I said, making sure I was reading the right name.

"Speaking. Who is this?"

"Ms. Gennaro, my name is Jason Wood."

"Not *the—*"

"Yes, the," I said. I revised my estimate of how many people knew my name; given how much the Morgantown event had forced the revision of people's security systems, it might be that I was currently a household name throughout the entire civilized world. I wasn't sure what to think about that. "I'd like to ask you a few questions, if you have a few minutes."

"Hold on!" I heard footsteps hurry away, a clatter, then footsteps returning. "Sorry, had something on to cook. Is this about the professor?"

"In part, certainly. I know the police have already gone over everything with you, so I'll try to make it quick."

"How are you involved, Mr. Wood?"

"It's rather complicated to explain. In a nutshell, I've gotten involved in an investigation here in the States which may be connected with Dr. O'Connell's disappearance in some way."

"Right, then. Go ahead."

I ran through a short list of questions, establishing that she knew O'Connell quite well, having had him as her advisor for the past three years, and that she had been his right-hand person on the expedition.

"So you were very familiar with the sites, then?"

She had a nice laugh. "No, no. I was in charge because I'd done underwater investigations before—on an old Greek merchantman in the Mediterranean. So I understood the limitations and requirements more than most of the other students. You don't really grasp the dangers unless you've been down in the muck yourself, you see."

"Was all the equipment yours? The University's, I mean?"

"Oh, lordy no. 'Twas a joint project, you understand—your own National Geographic Society helped sponsor it, and we had a few others to help. Submersibles and so on, they aren't cheap, not even for a big university."

"I understand that Dr. O'Connell vanished at the airport."

She hesitated. "It did seem that way . . ."

It was an obvious opening. ". . . but?"

"Is this confidential?" she asked suddenly.

"Well, I'm not a lawyer or priest—I can't be protected under law against talking—but I won't say anything about this conversation that I don't have to legally to anyone not directly involved in the investigation I'm doing," I answered. "If you want to verify that I am who I say I am, I can give you some numbers to call to verify my bona fides."

"Oh, no, no. It's just that the issue's a bit touchy now, and the police are still being a bit hush-hush about it all," she answered. "Here it is. The night he disappeared, he left in a bit of a hurry. There were some last-minute notes about how he wanted the materials handled and so on, but he said he'd had a sudden personal emergency and had to leave immediately. He got himself plane tickets out, right there at the airport, but he never actually left."

I nodded, then remembered she couldn't see me. "I get you. No one who knew him actually saw him from any point after . . . when?"

"Dinnertime. He went off to the lab to finish some notework on our finds, and since we were already getting ready to pull out, the rest of us were more into relaxing a bit."

"So if someone got to him on board your ship, they could've just left the notes and then used his card to buy the tickets."

"Right."

"Were the notes in his handwriting?"

I could almost hear a shrug in her tone. "Could've been.

I wasn't studying them hard then. Since, well, they don't look quite right, but then if he was in a hurry and upset...anyway, the police will probably be able to say for sure."

"Anything else odd?"

Again, she hesitated. "Not at the time. But...well, we brought our finds to RLAHA when we arrived—"

"RLAHA?"

"Sorry, the Research Laboratory for Archaeology and the History of Art," Mandy clarified. "And just the other day they found something very odd. We'd uncovered this thing—some of us thought it was a sarcophagus, others thought it was a vault box, and others thought it was some kind of storage chest for holy relics—but whatever it was, it was big, had a lid, and seemed hollow. Anyway, RLAHA and our team started going over it so we can date it, open it properly and all, and what do we find? It's apparently already been opened—in the air."

"Dr. O'Connell wouldn't have done that on his own, maybe out of curiosity?"

The tone of her voice indicated she was somewhat offended, somewhat tolerant of my ignorance (partial ignorance, actually—I thought I knew the answer, but it didn't hurt to ask). "Mr. Wood, no archaeologist worth his or her degree would even think of it. We're not playing Indiana Jones up here. Such an object is like a time capsule, but a very, very delicate one. Open it under the wrong conditions, and you can destroy what it can tell you."

"I understand. Was this sarcophagus, or whatever, one of the things you discussed at the UAR conference in Florida?"

There was a long pause. "I'm a bit confused, Mr. Wood. I wasn't at the UAR conference—Dr. O'Connell intended to go himself. He was going to confirm his travel plans with them either the night he disappeared or the next night, in fact. That never happened..." Her voice trailed off, then came back, "...but it is a bit odd...I did get a letter a few days ago from Dr. Rodriguez of the UAR, discussing some of our finds. I thought it a bit odd, but I haven't really read it carefully yet."

"You didn't attend the UAR conference in Venice, Florida?" I repeated.

"No, I did not, Mr. Wood. Why?"

I looked down at the flyer in my hand, printed from the UAR site. "Because, according to the UAR, not only were you there, but you presented a quick but fascinating overview of what you found," I answered. "Ms. Gennaro, would you do me a favor? Fax me a picture of yourself, so I can show it to some of the attendees?"

She was silent for a moment, probably still trying to absorb what I'd just said. Then, "What...? Yes, yes, of course. If someone's running around pretending to be me...well, I don't know what to think. Your number?"

I gave her my fax number—actually an e-fax number, one that would send the fax as an e-mail so I could retrieve it anywhere.

"Will there be anything else?"

"No, not at the moment. You've been immensely helpful, Ms. Gennaro."

"You're welcome. Could I trouble you to at least let me know what you find out?"

I hesitated. I could probably come up with a bowdlerized version that would be close enough for her to hear. "I certainly will."

I hung up the phone and turned to Morgan, Baker, and Sylvie, all of whom were waiting. "We have our smoking gun."

"The damn thing came to the conference?"

"Right here in this hotel," I said, enjoying Baker's expression. "And apparently wowed them with the presentation, too. It must've absconded with some of O'Connell's notes and slides."

"Slides, yeah, but it wouldn't need the notes," Baker said, looking chagrined. "Assume it killed O'Connell, then it knew pretty much what O'Connell knew—about recent events, leastwise. Dunno just how extensive it is, but they sure steal enough to be able to get by. Probably just grabbed some rolls of film an' chose some good shots."

"And then, finding that the conference just happened to be in Wolf City, it decided there was no reason at all for it to move on."

"Ayup," Baker said dismally. "When's that girl going to send her pic, so we can go around and trace her movements?"

I grinned. "Receiving it now, but I'm willing to bet half of what I own that not one person will recognize her."

"What? Oh, damn. It booked it under her name because its default human form is female, but no way it looks like her, right?"

"Maybe close in the written essentials, but not close enough to fool anyone, unless it's so lucky that it oughtta be playing the lottery every day." A photo-quality print came out of my little inkjet. "There you go."

Mandy wasn't bad looking—cute, with a round face, dark hair in a sort of pixieish cut, and a reasonably trim body as you'd expect from someone fit enough to do diving archaeological work. "There you go, Baker."

"Nope, rather it was you. Remember, more contact I have with the outside, more likely I run into some paranoid who finds out what I am."

I sighed. "Fine, fine, look, you do the hotel staff anyway, will you? I'll handle talking to the UAR people."

"No need to bother," Syl's voice broke in.

Baker and I looked at her. "Why?"

"Tsk, tsk, Mr. Information Man. While you were talking, I did a few searches under the members' names, and looky what I found on Dr. Jesus Rodriguez's web page."

On the screen was a photo of a tall, slender, dark-skinned girl of long hair and exotic beauty, pointing at a slide image showing a large stone object. The caption read, "Mandy Gennaro showing some of the spectacular finds from the University of Oxford's Caribbean excavations."

Syl smiled at me smugly. "I think you get to keep everything, Jason."

CHAPTER 68

Hiding in Plain Sight?

I looked at the stony face and sighed. "Another one, I see."

"Fourth, or if we're right about the disappearances, seventh of us." Baker grimaced. "I swear, the thing's probably out there laughing."

I shrugged. "Maybe. We certainly aren't having luck catching it. The question is where the hell did it go after the convention? Plenty of people saw 'Mandy Gennaro' there, but afterwards?"

Baker shook his head. "Nothing. We've been around with photos, checkin' the stores all through the area. Couple of people saw her during the convention, but not afterwards."

I turned away from the statue of the late Deputy Arnaud and headed up the stairs to Baker's office. He shut the door behind us and followed. "So, she went into hiding. But that's not a nondescript appearance; she's going to be noticed if she was looking like that."

"Ayup. But..." Baker's eyes narrowed; for a moment I almost thought I saw a yellow gleam. "Now there's an interesting possibility. Look here; it's hard to tell, but it looks to me, if we take best guesses, that we end up with a new statue around the time we get a new missing persons report. There's been a lot of events in the past couple weeks, so I dunno if we can say it's a real pattern, but...what if she's killin' people, takin' their place for a while, then shifting to someone else? The people who been disappearin', she actually killed 'em days before. Then she hits someone else for a quick fix, uses them that day to scout out a new sucker, an' takes them. An' a few days later, it starts again."

I sucked in a breath. That theory made sense. "I see. Yeah,

quite a bit. If that's so, then she's got to be either hiding the statues near the kill sites, or she's got herself a good storage spot for a bunch of statues..." I smacked my forehead. "Duh! She's not keeping the statues. She's pulverizing them." I gestured out the window, where you could occasionally get a glimpse of blue ocean. "Your *habeas corpii* are probably out there on the beach."

Baker looked like he wanted to kick himself as well. "Right, right, Wood. Shoulda thought of that. Ya must've hit it on the head. Damn."

"Around here, it's easy to get rid of something like that. Getting rid of a body like Mansfield's, that's harder. Unless this thing eats flesh, too, and lots of it."

"Nope. They can eat—an' some do, just like we do—but they ain't like us in that area. Me, I could've polished off Mansfield in three or four bites, bones an' all, but the Mirrorkillers don't do that."

"But then why the hell is it leaving statues?"

Baker pursed his lips, thinking. "Well, I'm thinkin' it's like running a business. Location, location, location. Even at night, if you're out in the middle of town like she was with Weimar, it's gonna draw attention if someone sees ya lugging a statue down to wherever it is ya plan to do the rock-crushing. Sure, by now she can probably do it with her bare hands, but it's still gonna be noisy."

"Right," I said. "So the ones we find are just stopgaps—she takes the form like you said, uses it to find someone she can nail in a more private location and then replace them for a while. You people all work together, and once she killed a couple of you she'd know everything about who she could and couldn't talk to about what was going on—from your point of view, I mean. So I'd guess it wouldn't be hard for her, as one of you, to talk to the right people and get them into a convenient locale."

"Nope," Baker agreed. "We gotta be ready to cooperate with each other here, especially in shifting people around. The humans that work with us sometimes'll have to be in two places at once, so to speak, and it's our job to cooperate with 'em to that extent."

"Oh? Why do they have to do that?"

"People in any business that's got a lot o' contact with outsiders. Either the ones doing the interaction have to be human, or we need humans who can do jobs that we can swap places with. You have no idea how complicated this can get. So any of us can call on the others to help out—moving bodies, switching places, whatever."

I nodded my understanding. "So it would be very easy for her, in the guise of her stopgap body, to get someone else to accompany her, or let her inside their house, or whatever."

"Ayup," he agreed.

"Then we've got her. Just make it so that people can't do it that easily—they have to coordinate it with you, or some other central group. Next time she tries it, *bang*, she's finished."

"Can't be done," he said heavily. "The masquerade can break with just one bad run o' luck, and my people've gotta be able to respond to an emergency right away. Besides, ya don't realize just how hard it is gettin' wolves to work together this way if'n you ain't the King. They hate bein' shoved into coordinated slots, an' it's takin' me just about everything I got to keep this thing workin' as it is."

"Well, we've got a chance now, anyway. Look, she can't be sure of exactly when the statues of her quick kills are going to be found, so she's got to move fairly quickly. So somewhere around the area should be the place where she found her new longer-term host, so to speak."

"And how does that help us?"

"I think there might be a way to test it. The Maelkodan isn't vulnerable to silver. So if we can check all the wolves in the area, you just need to find one that doesn't react. Wear a glove or something with a little silver on it and shake hands; anyone who doesn't get burned or whatever is your monster."

Baker gave me a respectful look. "Y'know, that might just work. I'll get my people on it...right after I give 'em a hand-shake m'self."

CHAPTER 69

Lie Down and Reflect

I put down the phone, sighed, and sank into a chair, toying with the just-finished duplicates of my CryWolf glasses. One advantage of working for the wolves was that I wasn't restricted in movement if I stayed on the case, so I'd ordered the custom parts, then taken a day, flown up, and assembled the things. At least now I could be subtle. I put them on, adjusted the fit.

"Bad news?" Syl asked sympathetically.

"My bright idea was a bust. All we've got now is a bunch of werewolves with itchy palms, and I don't mean that they're looking for tips." I chewed my lower lip idly. "Now, this could mean Baker's idea still works, but she's going farther afield than we thought looking for her replacement."

"Why does she have to switch so often, though?"

"Remember her basic limitation, Syl. Every time she whacks a wolf, she gets a brand-new face. She doesn't keep a record of the old ones in her matrix, so she can't just go back to where she was..."

I saw it then; it was, in its way, sheer genius. It wouldn't work forever, but certainly for longer than it had already. And I could confirm it so easily...

Picking up the phone, I called Baker and asked him a few questions, as though I was clarifying something. Then I hung up. Sylvie watched as I checked my gun once more. "What are you going to do?"

"The rest of my job. But I'll do it my way, not Carruthers' or Baker's way."

She nodded, serious. I started to say something else as she

began to put on her own gun, but I stopped. She knew what I was going to do before I did it, and there was no arguing with her when she decided what part she was going to play.

Besides, I needed her to play that part.

I went down to the lobby, where Vic glanced up. "Hey, Mr. Wood! Need anything?"

"Actually, yes, Vic. But it's kinda private...?"

He nodded his understanding—certain business, after all, not being something to discuss in non-secured public areas. Even though it was late, there was always the possibility of someone dropping by at the wrong moment. He hung a "back in 15 minutes" sign up and we went into a back room. "Okay, how can I help?"

I studied him. "First, let me congratulate you," I said, to his image sparkling in the glasses. "I almost didn't figure out how you were doing it, and without that, we'd never have caught you."

He froze for a moment, just as he had the night we checked in, then sighed. "Goddamn. If you don't mind my asking, how'd you figure it?"

"Partly the timing of the killings, partly luck, and just a few little things that nagged at me," I said, making sure I was not blocked in and had at least two ways to run. "Baker's theory on what you were doing wasn't bad—and it was actually close, in some ways—but when we came up with nothing on that, I started thinking it was a complete bust. But then there had to be some explanation for the pattern. So I was thinking...why? If you're not moving from life to life, what's the point of the pattern of one person disappearing, one person being found?"

He nodded, sitting down on a crate some distance away. Apparently, he really did want to hear the explanation. "Go on."

I was careful to avoid staring directly into his eyes; despite assurances that an alert human could probably break contact fast enough, I wasn't taking any risks. "Then there was the whole Jerry Mansfield episode. It didn't quite fit with the others. Especially the silver dust bit.

"But it did make sense if I assumed someone got a little panicky. The wolves certainly did. Mansfield was a quick and dirty attempt to get rid of me. His death made it look like someone was out hunting wolves the conventional way. Once I'd weathered that threat—when Karl Weimar left me alive—it was clear that the quick impulse had failed. You knew who I was when I registered, and it flustered you. Here you were, still adjusting to the way this world works—and even with your ability to grab people's knowledge, I'll bet that still takes some getting used to, the changes in the world since you were last out and about—and along comes this guy with a reputation for dealing with Weird Crap. No warning. You knew you'd killed a fairly important guy already, the cops were looking for him, and if they'd gotten a whiff of the weird, well, who would they call? Jason Wood, of course.

"Naturally, you knew who and what everyone in the town was, and Mansfield made a perfect target—vital to the town's functioning, but wouldn't die in that all-too-telltale stony way. By the time the wolves stopped panicking at my presence and the silver evidence, I'd be dead. Maybe. You didn't have that much to lose, since you planned on settling down here to eat anyway."

He hung his head. "I'm sorry about that. Really. But you're right, I just...what's your idiom? *Freaked*, that's it. After uncounted thousands of years, I was finally, finally *free*, and suddenly there you were."

"The first 'disappearance' was about due to be reported, anyway; Karl Weimar gave you the perfect chance to start confusing the trail," I continued. "Your first victim was expected to be away for some time, so you had latitude. And you'd already figured it out. Everyone knew you couldn't go back to a form you had already had. And you couldn't take the form of human beings, only wolves. So Victor Spangler, long-time resident, and well-known human collaborator, was a doubly safe identity.

"I didn't get all the clues to this puzzle until recently, or I might have caught on sooner. If I'd just been going by your movements en route here, Vic would have been high on the suspect list; this is a fairly central location, you have contact with everyone, and so on.

"The key, of course, is the masquerade. The wolves have to cooperate in order to keep the secret from being blown, and they *especially* have to do so with their human collaborators—the ones who sometimes have to be moved around quickly so as to be the interfaces with human outsiders who might possibly be carting around CryWolf gadgets. These collaborators are of prime importance in all areas that have high contact with outsiders: convenience stores, gas stations, restaurants...and hotels."

He chuckled and nodded. "Right, right."

"I found out that the day the conference ended—the day before I arrived—Vic had to go work at one of the other hotels. Someone had to take his place here—a wolf who had changed himself to look just like Vic! You noticed the substitution and that was when the idea hit you. You killed that wolf and took his place, and assumed the guise of Vic the Human. Once you were 'in,' you could use that cooperative requirement to get other wolves to take on Vic's form—on the excuse that you were needed elsewhere. You had to destroy the other bodies to hide the fact that, otherwise, there'd be quite a collection of Vic Spangler statues around. All I had to do was find out if you were a collaborator—I asked Baker as though I assumed you were a wolf, he corrected me—and check a couple of timing issues with your assumed ID."

He spread his hands. "You got me, all right. Had to kill the real Vic, too. So now what?"

I frowned. "Aye, 'there's the rub,' as Hamlet put it. On paper, you're a murderer, or a dangerous animal, depending on who you ask. And I can't say I'm comfortable with the whole idea of what you are, or of letting you go after you killed a harmless archaeologist. On the other hand, I also really hate being strung over a barrel by the wolves. Their King's put me on reserve as a personal chew-toy for later, but they've bargained with me to solve this mystery in exchange for my friends' safety. I want to see if we can find a resolution that doesn't include my using this," I pushed my jacket aside and eased the gun out, "to turn you into a colander. And I'm also a bit of a conservationist, I suppose; killing off the entirety of a species doesn't sit well with me."

Vic sparkled; the shimmer intensified. It was like watching clouds of sunshine-touched mist dissolve and then reform. The Maelkodan appeared in its natural, default-human form. I admired its tactical sense; if it wanted to play any sympathy cards, it knew perfectly well that a beautiful woman would have a better chance with me than even a nice, cheerful hotel proprietor. "As I see it, the problem is that I need to eat."

"Not nearly as much as you have been," I pointed out. "They already told me just how much power you gain; by now you're getting quite a ways up there."

"And you believe everything they say?" she challenged.

It was my turn to chuckle. "Not at all. Unfortunately for you, Morgan was the source of confirmation on that information."

Her lips moved in a pout or a tightening; I couldn't be quite sure which without looking her in the eyes. "Ah, the one who feels like something from home. But really, Mr. Wood, does it matter? Aside from Dr. O'Connell, who just happened to be the one present when I finally broke free and acted on my instincts, the only ones I've killed have been wolves or their friends. Do you really care what I do to them?"

I acknowledged the point. "In truth, not really. I think the world's better off without them. But there's the issue of my own word versus theirs. I did promise to investigate this fully and track down the killer. Now, I could weasel *some* technicalities around, but I do have to solve the problem for which I'm hired, and saying 'Well, I did find the killer, but too bad, I'm not doing anything about it' really violates the spirit of the contract. The very *last* thing I want to do is encourage them to start playing technicality games with me."

She nodded. "I could just move on."

"Will you really be able to stop killing? Be honest, because if you lie about it and it comes out later, I will, beyond any shadow of a doubt, come after your ass."

She paused for a long, long moment.

Finally, "No. No, I could not. It is what I was created to do. I am a hunter. I hunt anything, mostly wolves, but even your people. The hunt is part of my life. They made me that way. You would eventually hear of more deaths. And they would continue, so long as I live."

My heart pounded painfully against my chest. "Then let's settle it here."

"You have not called the wolves?"

"No. I wanted to find out if there was a chance first. And if not, I want to deprive them of the pleasure."

She stood up, slowly, and shimmered again, her hands in a "wait a moment" gesture. Rainbow-shimmering clouds formed, dissolved, coalesced, solidified.

Before me stood the Maelkodan.

The centauroid torso and head were just about my height; the body itself, perhaps three to four feet at the hip. It was twelve feet long, covered with iridescent scales in beautiful geometric patterns of green, black, red, silver, and gold. The legs, three-taloned like a Jurassic Park raptor's, moved smoothly, shifting back and forth nervously. The arms were edged, with wicked spikes at the elbows, and I could see the glitter of diamondlike teeth in the mouth. I couldn't focus on the head without risking eye contact, but it seemed to be crested and fluted and spiked, as though wearing an elaborate helm.

It bowed low from the waist. "You risk your life and honor me. I shall cherish your soul."

"I don't intend to die."

"No more than did any of the others." The eyes glowed suddenly, an iridescent flame that I glanced towards reflexively, eyes drawn by the sudden moving change.

It was like simultaneously being hit on the side of the head with a mallet, combined with the fascination of every forbidden pleasure ever imagined. I knew—with absolute truth—that if I didn't look away, I would die, yet for a frozen instant of time I couldn't do it; I yearned to do nothing more than stare more deeply into those windows of horrid revelation.

But memory, duty, and Sylvie's face warred against that lure, forcing my eyes shut against the terrible siren call. Still, being blind is a bad combat situation, and I heard it starting forward.

Right on cue, Syl kicked open the door from the hotel. I went out the back way, as I'd intended all along. Sylvia's gunshots, unexpected as they were, convinced the Maelkodan to head out into the street with me, even though public locations were hardly where it wanted to be caught.

I sprinted down the alleyway. Behind me, I heard the swift scuttling of taloned feet; I whirled, keeping my eyes low, and snapped off two shots; the Maelkodan writhed sideways, behind a dumpster, giving me back the lead and allowing me to round the corner.

More gunshots from Syl's Smith & Wesson sounded out. I kept running, knowing I'd hear the creature on my tail in moments. It wouldn't try to charge Syl who was in the cover of the doorway and who was, I felt sure, firing with accuracy while her eyes were squeezed shut. Her Talent had many uses.

Skittering rhythm of claws on pavement behind me—and then a screeching of tires. I spun around, just in time to see one of the police cars slide to a halt right next to the Maelkodan. It flowed up and to the other side of the car, and I heard a suddenly-cut-off shriek. There was a metallic ripping sound, and

I saw the passenger-side door fly out onto the street, shattering the statue which had been the Maelkodan's body a moment ago.

Then the whole car was hefted into the air.

I almost made eye contact again, goggling at the scene. The creature had its legs splayed wide and dug into the street, tail counterbalancing, performing a comic-book feat of strength with a wide grin on its fanged mouth. With an effort that sent it skidding backwards, tearing grooves through the blacktop, it hurled the cop car straight towards me.

I ran and dove aside at the last second; the impact was so close that it sounded like the crack of doom. *Jesus Christ, the thing was strong! Maybe as strong as Verne!*

As I rolled to my feet, I emptied my gun in its direction to slow it down and ran through another alleyway, slamming in another magazine. I'd heard one squealing roar of pain—must have at least nicked the thing. I realized I'd been subconsciously underestimating the creature; our estimates of its capabilities had been based on it having killed three wolves; by current estimate, that was off by at least a factor of two, maybe more if it had gotten lucky and caught a few others we hadn't noticed yet. I exited the alley and turned down the street. I was, naturally, cursing myself for having these ideas of fair play and justice when dealing with monstrosities from beyond time, and promising myself I'd change my ways if I could just live through this.

A shadow within the darkness was my only warning as the Maelkodan dropped to the street fifty feet ahead of me, having apparently run and jumped along the tops of buildings to do so. However, in landing it paused slightly, perhaps enjoying the effect and its power, and I took full advantage to center my ten-millimeter on the torso and fire three times.

The creature's eyes flared just as I fired, and I saw three sparks of light in line with my aim. In the glow from the streetlights, I could just make out three tiny objects floating in the air scant feet from the thing. Telekinesis.

"I should have known, I should have known, you can *never* kill a monster with bullets, never, it's in the friggin' Monster Union Rules!" I heard myself half-wail as I turned and dashed inside a nearby supermarket, which was mostly empty. The gunshots had drawn the attention of the proprietor, who had unlimbered an impressive-looking shotgun. He never had a chance to use it, however. With a roar like a jet engine going into overload, the Maelkodan demonstrated its newfound power by blowing the entire glass storefront inwards, blasting us off our feet and sending racks of candy, magazines, sunglasses, and other sundries tumbling end-over-end. I took advantage of the impetus to skid and roll down one of the aisles. Its shape and size would give me a slight edge in narrower spaces. I hoped.

"Let us prolong this no longer, Mr. Wood!" the Maelkodan called, its voice oddly human; perhaps it, like the wolves, could shift parts of itself while in motion. "I will try to kill no innocent humans during our hunt, but the more you resist, the greater the chance that one will get in the way!" It sounded sincere, and oddly enough, I believed it. The creature was, perhaps, as soulless a killer as the wolves, but even some wolves seemed to take pleasure—perhaps honest pleasure, perhaps the pleasure of a properly played game, but pleasure nonetheless—in following through on a commitment. I had shown the Maelkodan more consideration than it might have expected; it was trying to live up to the standard I'd set.

"It's not in my nature to stand still and die," I shouted back, moving down another aisle. "Honestly, I doubt we'll get out of this store with both of us still moving."

"True enough," it said, and I felt a wave of force ripple past me . . . and then the shelves—the entire aisle's worth of shelves and products—were moving, toppling inward towards me.

But I was close enough to my goal, slamming my way through the door and finding it was just large enough for my purpose.

There was a pause, one in which I recalled all too well a similar moment, waiting behind a door to see if the King of Wolves would take the bait or not.

I heard a genuine laugh from the Maelkodan, something like a steamkettle rattling. "The men's room? How clever." The door burst open. "But did you forget—"

"That you could turn off the killing mode and enter mirrored rooms safely?" I said from my position on the other side of the door. As it turned its startled, momentarily harmless gaze on me, I pressed the button. "I *counted* on it!"

There are commercial versions of that gadget, but I like making my own. The Dazzler detonated like a magnesium flare in that enclosed space, leaving a spotty afterimage on my eyes even through closed lids. I was diving back through the door even as I triggered it.

The Maelkodan shrieked. My ears felt like spikes were being driven through them. The creature's tail gave a convulsive movement that whipped me fifteen feet across fallen cans and shelves. No telekinetic shield could have protected it from that blazing luminescence scarcely a foot and a half from its eyes. And as Morgan and Baker had both said, it had to be able to *see* its prey to use those eyes. It cursed and shouted in a language so ancient that only Verne and Kafan might have understood it.

For the next few minutes, it was much less dangerous. But that trick had been meant as a last-ditch effort; I'd expected to kill it long before this. Once it recovered, I'd be meat. Even if it kept playing fairly, it was clearly going to wear me out, and then it would all be over. I picked myself up groggily, staring across at the scattered wreckage, candies, displays...

"...smarter...than I thought...Mr. Wood," it gasped, backing out of the bathroom clumsily. "Much smarter. I've been far too long without a decent opponent, and it shows, does it not?" It rubbed fiercely at its eyes. "Alas, my eyesight shall recover momentarily, and I am hardly harmless!"

Canned goods began floating into the air. I muttered a curse of my own; it was going to play Darth Vader, and I was no Luke Skywalker. I threw myself down on the floor, ignoring the increase in bruises, and slid towards the front of the store as a hurricane of metal cylinders started streaking randomly around the enclosed space, ricocheting off the still-standing shelves, walls, support columns, an occasional one bouncing off the floor or me. I restrained the grunts and groans of pain—I didn't need to give it any help in targeting. Somehow I'd lost the CryWolf glasses. I was going to put in a hell of an expense account to Baker...

Lost my...

I somersaulted forward and moved into another aisle, hunkering down. My gaze roved frantically, searching.

"Ah...there...starting to come back..." I heard it mutter. The cans stopped moving, and I could picture it standing there, listening. I knew I couldn't be noiseless, not in all this destruction. Despite my attempts, there were rustlings, cracklings, clanks of cans rolling. In the distance, I heard sirens, but they wouldn't be here in time...assuming any wolf was brave enough to enter the Maelkodan's range.

Clawed feet rattled through the supermarket stock, making a beeline for my aisle.

Where, dammit, where—Ah-HA! I grabbed, then dove for the end of the aisle away from the creature—but my foot slipped on a can.

As I came down hard, jarring my chin so much that I bit my tongue and tasted blood, I thought to myself that at the least I'd managed to be convincing in that slippage. Next time, perhaps, I might consider learning how to do it without hurting myself. Behind me, the Maelkodan scuttled at lightning speed. Taloned hands grasped me, and rolled me over, the sculpted head bending to deliver an unavoidable stare...

It had time for a single horrified "NO!!"

In a blaze of rainbow-clouded energy, the creature neutralized its own matrix, leaving a bending statue. With difficulty, I wiggled free of its now stony grip, and slowly hobbled away. I lowered my right hand, which had been pressed tight against my temple, and extended it towards the shaking, wide-eyed clerk who had just risen from the wrecked counter.

"I'll take these," I said, placing the mirrored sunglasses in front of him. "And most of your stock of Band-Aids."

CHAPTER 70

Souvenir

Baker stood staring at the statue. "I can't believe it," he repeated for the fourth time. "You beat the thing."

"What you hired me for, isn't it?" I said, rather gratified by the reaction; it was nice to know that the wolves were honest-to-God terrified of something and that it hadn't just been a matter of trying to make the human do their dirty work. "One Mirrorkiller, packaged for transport."

Baker finally got ahold of himself, and turned to face me. "So we're square up, then?"

"You make sure Carruthers understands that I carried through on the spirit as well as the letter of our agreement," I said. "No trouble from any of his people or yours, you won't have trouble from me. And two other things—one I just want to reinforce, since I warned you before, and one new one."

He looked at me suspiciously. "And those would be ...?"

"First, no more killings. I've got a good idea how many you had to do to take over here, and it's sickening, but we've gone into that. You just make damn sure no more people—either natives or visitors—get killed by your people, or under their orders."

Baker glowered at me. "We have to protect—"

"That isn't my problem." I cut him off with a cold glance. "You work your masquerade without killing, at least until you're ready to take all of us on, or you *will* be taking all of us on. If you think someone's getting too close to your secret, figure out a way to mislead them, or get ready to pull up stakes and move on. It's your call, but if you push me into blowing the whistle, you can bet that not one out of ten of you will get out of Florida alive."

Baker spat on the ground, looking like he yearned to do something else to me, but we both knew I was off-limits. "Fine, fine. I got your message. What's the other thing?"

I pointed. "The statue. I want it carefully packed up and shipped to me."

Baker looked startled. "Oookay, if ya say so. I cain't say anyone in this here town's likely to want it for a decoration. I'll spring for that." We shook hands on the bargain, my skin only slightly crawling. "So, you know y'all are welcome to stay here for free—I know you were on your honeymoon, an' the beaches here are—"

I couldn't restrain a laugh. "Baker, it's a lovely town, but there's no way in hell we're staying here any longer. Right, Syl?" I said, as Sylvie finally crossed over the hastily erected yellow tape barrier and grabbed me in a hug that nearly cracked my sore ribs. "Ouch, watch it!"

"Sorry—I'm just sooo glad you're alive, Jason. I thought you would be, but you can never be sure." She glanced at Baker. "And he's right. We're out of here as soon as we can get packed." She looked up at me. "So, Romeo, wherefore art thou taking thy wife for the rest of thy honeymoon?"

I winced at her mangled semi-Shakespeare, but smiled back. "Home to Morgantown, Syl. I think we've had enough adventure for now. Maybe we can go on another trip later."

She snuggled into me. "Sounds perfect to me."

CHAPTER 71

Saved For Later

"Oh, I had a king-sized attack of the shakes after it was all over," I admitted, leaning back in the comfortable, oversized recliner near Verne's fireplace and hugging Syl to me. "More than one. Cursing myself for giving it any chance at all, and so on."

"No, no, Jason. All in all, I think you did precisely the right thing," Verne said. "Perhaps it is merely that I am a relic myself, but I feel that there is such a thing as respecting one's opponent, and part of that respect is, in fact, giving him or her...or it... the chance to not be your enemy. It is evident that the Maelkodan shared that respect for you. It could have attempted to kill you much earlier, and even later in the combat, there were tactics it might have used to kill you more efficiently. But just as you hadn't arranged for a multiple crossfire or something of similarly lethal nature, it did not attempt to use—how would you put it?—ah, *cheesy tricks* to finish the chase."

I chuckled, then sobered. "On that note, what do you think of Carruthers' offer? Is he going to play fair on the deal, since I delivered the goods?"

"I would say without any shadow of a doubt, my friend—and I thank both your good fortune and good business sense for that bargain. Yes, he will abide by those terms; while some of the young wolves may sneer at such commitments, a true Elder knows better than to contemplate breaking a bargain sworn to in the King's name. And if Carruthers' name is truly Virigan... well, then he is more than merely Elder; he is one of the only surviving Firstborn." He frowned, swirling his usual drink in its crystal glass. "I must admit, Jason, that I am as mystified—and concerned—with his outré interest in human genetic engineer-ing as you. Such a thing would not, as far as I can tell, enhance the spiritual power or aspect of humanity—which is what they consume, as you know. Thus it cannot, at least directly, be concerned with improving their food supply. Indeed, tampering that interferes too much with certain aspects of humanity could actually damage humanity's usefulness to them, so Virigan must be interested in...something else."

I shrugged. "No hurry, I think. We'll keep looking—or rather, Jeri's outfit will, right?"

Jeri, still looking somewhat uptight at being in a meeting that so casually discussed burn-before-reading secret material, nodded. "You can bet on it. Since we're not excluded from their hit list, unlike the rest of you, we also have no reason to hold back. I might note that when I gave my interim report on this incident, my boss did something I've never seen him do in all the years I've known him: give vent to an utterly spontaneous curse."

"Why?"

"It seems," Jeri answered, "that Mr. Carruthers was, in a way, sending us a message by appearing to you in that guise. Obvi-ously, as a wolf, he could have chosen any shape he wanted. As far as we knew, Alexi Carruthers was killed off a number of years ago in a manner that remains classified. By showing us what he really is, he is telling Pantheon, and through Pantheon all of ISIS, that we're dealing with something much nastier than we'd suspected...and be assured, we already suspected some seriously nasty things."

"Well, Miss Winthrope," Morgan said courteously, "I am sure I speak for us all when I say that you can count on our assistance if we could ever be of service."

I glanced at Syl with a raised eyebrow. She gave a secretive smile. Morgan did seem to like Jeri, which was strange; I would never have thought she was his type. Whether Jeri had any interests outside of her job was something none of us would ever know unless she decided to tell us. "I have to give Ms. Gennaro a callback; it's been several days already. I'm just trying to decide what to tell her."

Kafan growled something, then sighed. "Twisty problem. Can't just tell her to stop poking around in those things—it's her job."

"Besides that, trying to shove her out might cause talk by

itself, and certainly wouldn't keep someone else from going to the sites," I pointed out.

Verne nodded. "I am afraid, Jason, that you will simply have to use your own judgement. You and I are safe—at least until that day when the King decides to try us again—but if she or her people learn too much, there will be more disappearances, regardless of whether they discover another monster or not. I would, in fact, judge it unlikely they will find anything of that magnitude again, but the discovery of even a few more artifacts whose age they can accurately measure would be greatly troubling to certain people. The demons cannot rework the face of a planet, not with the changes wrought on Earth since those long-ago days, but the few of their agents who remain are more than strong enough to obliterate prying scientists."

"If it will help, I can always throw an international security umbrella over the work," Jeri offered.

"No!" Kafan snapped, jumping to his feet.

Jeri looked uncertainly at him, aware of his capabilities. "Why the panic?"

"Control yourself, Raiakafan," Verne said.

He closed his eyes, opened them again. "Because any such move would make it look like the governments are directly interested. The very last thing any of them want is for humanity, or its governments, to take a deep look into these things. That's why you and your agency numbers are all going to be dead sometime soon." He said the last line the same way I might have said "I'll be ordering pizza for dinner tomorrow"—a casual statement of fact, impersonal but inarguable. "Your people ride the edge, and Carruthers' signal just means that he's marked you as needing his attention, or that of some of the other surviving forces. If you start doing things officially, they might decide that the whole world's getting too close to the truth, and then they'd have to start a war or something."

"A nuclear war would definitely be interfering with my life," I pointed out, half-joking. I really didn't like considering this entire shadow war thing right now.

To my surprise, Kafan and Verne seemed to take the idea seriously. "Jesting aside, you may have something of a point," Verne said. "Carruthers' own projects would be unlikely to survive an extreme sanction against the world order, and so he would have a vested interest in promoting maximum tolerance. Still, I agree with Kafan that unless there is no other choice, overt involvement of any intelligence agencies in such matters would be playing with fire."

"Hey, just offering," said Jeri. "And unless these demon thingies *do* still have the power to reshape the world, don't be counting us out, Mr. Raiakafan Tai Lee Ularion Xiang. If someone does come gunning for us, you can bet they'll know they've been in a fight."

Kafan nodded to her, a mark of respect if not agreement.

I got up, leaving Syl on the recliner, and picked up the phone. I needed to contact Ms. Gennaro at the University. She was readily available, preparing a paper on some of the finds.

"Mr. Wood!"

"Yes. Nice to speak to you again, Ms. Gennaro. Your information was invaluable."

"Please call me Mandy. So what exactly happened?" Her voice seemed slightly tense, as if she was trying to be relaxed but not quite succeeding.

"You can call me Jason, then. There was a series of murders in Florida..." I gave an expurgated version of events, leaving out things like werewolves, my bargain, and so on. "...And so, I was finally able to kill it off. Some of this you might see on the news soon, even though there was a heavy lid clamped on it at first."

She was silent for a few moments. "So...you're saying that this 'Maelkodan' was inside that casket we brought aboard?"

"Yes," I answered. "And you were right, of course; Dr. O'Connell never left your ship. The Maelkodan killed him when it emerged. It, like the wolves, gains knowledge of its victims, so it was able to figure out a way to—at least temporarily—leave a false trail."

"How horrid." I could almost hear a shiver in her voice. "If it weren't for the events in Morgantown, I'd think this was insanity. But...when we opened the casket, there were some odd traces that we didn't know what to make of. Any dating we do on the casket at this point will be questionable, since it was not in controlled conditions when it was opened. We have a few other items from the same dig, however, so we are hopeful that we may be able to date them."

I took a deep breath. "Mandy, I also have to give you a warning."

"A . . . warning, Mr. . . . Jason?"

"I can't—nor would I—try to tell you not to continue your line of research. However, I do have to caution you; you've heard the old expression 'Things Man Was Not Meant To Know,' of course?"

She gave an uncertain chuckle. "Um, yes . . . ?"

"I never gave much credence to that idea myself, but as it turns out, there are some things that . . . well, not to go into detail, but Things That Put Man Or Woman In Real Danger If They Know. Your research has just uncorked one nasty genie from a bottle; there are worse genies—some of them forces that just don't want certain things known. Think paranoid. Then think worse. I'm already in the soup, so to speak—there's no way for me to reduce my danger."

"And is there for me? Aside from abandoning these sites, which I really cannot imagine doing?"

"I'm not sure. Legitimate archaeological work can't be stopped, after all, and even if you did stop on my vague say-so, someone else would surely try their hand."

She was quiet for a moment. "Does the danger in question include things like this Maelkodan, or are you referring more to the fact of our knowing and publishing certain things?"

"The latter more than the former, although as we have both discovered, the former isn't to be discounted."

She thought for another few moments. "Mr. Wood, could you, personally, recognize these dangerous elements if you saw them?"

"I think so," I answered cautiously. In point of fact, I could probably recognize most dangerous subjects, and with Verne and Raiakafan to back me up . . . "Yes, I could."

"Then perhaps this would at least minimize the risk; in view of this bizarre discovery, I could recommend to the board that you be hired—if willing—as a consultant, who will examine finds for potential risks that lie outside of our normal expertise. In this way we would be able to pass material found at the sites in question to you for advice on how best to handle it, and you would be able to determine what time bombs—informational or actual—we may have unearthed."

I felt my tension ease a bit. Mandy Gennaro was clearly one smart cookie, and willing to listen. "That sounds excellent, Mandy. You can count on me. Obviously, I'd try to reject as little as possible—and the final call would still be yours. I'll work on getting together a risk assessment methodology, so that you can make informed risk decisions."

"Right, then. I'll contact the board immediately, in view of what happened to Dr. O'Connell. You have told the police about this?"

"I will be informing them shortly after I hang up with you. I felt you deserved to get the news first and directly from me."

"I truly appreciate that, Jason. Now let me get the ball rolling here; I'd like to be able to run all discoveries past you pronto so that we can get publishing soon."

"By all means. Thank you, Mandy. Take care."

"Ta." She hung up.

"Smarter than many," Kafan said. "I guess she decided if she was going to trust you, she had to figure you knew what you were talking about."

"It is rude to eavesdrop, Kafan," Verne said mildly.

"You heard it, too," Kafan retorted.

"Well, yes, but a gentleman doesn't admit to overhearing things not meant for his own ears. I agree with your assessment; a woman of uncommon good sense. She recognized Jason as trustworthy, and thus no matter how outrageous the subject area, he was worth paying heed to."

"So you think this will work?" I asked.

Verne gave a seesawing motion of his hand. "It is far better than nothing. She will still be running grave risks, but this approach may keep her and her people alive, or at least give them sufficient warning to know when they are, in fact, at risk of death or worse. And it is a far, far better thing that we have direct contact with those who may be uncovering traces of the past than that someone we know nothing of be doing the digging."

"Well then," Jeri said, getting up, "since that's taken care of, I'll be off to file a report and recommend that it be marked closed in our files."

"I shall show you out, Lady Jeri," Morgan said, and the two left.

"So, will you continue your honeymoon?" Verne asked.

We laughed. "Eventually, sure," I said. "Not that being home means it has to stop." I grinned lecherously at Syl, who poked me in one of my still-very-sore ribs. "Ow! In any case, there's lots for me to do here."

"And we can do it with less to fear, now," Syl said.

"Indeed. Again, Jason, I thank you. By good fortune and wise choices, you have lifted what was in truth a burden of worry and fear from us all."

I grinned and blushed. "Aw shucks, weren't nothin'."

"Do not sell yourself short, my friend."

I nodded, still smiling. "Okay, okay. You're welcome. I guess we're safe now. Well, except for the demons."

"Perhaps even from them, at least for now," Verne said, lifting his glass. "As you deduced in that adventure which nearly killed me in my own home, the Project certainly must have connections to the remnants of those who caused the fall of Atlantaea originally. Given that, they will know that we are endeavoring to keep the number who know certain facts low, and, more importantly, that you, Lady Sylvia, and myself are explicitly reserved for Virigar's attention."

"Oh?" I said, skeptically. "Even if they do, so what? I mean, Virigar's the Big Bad Wolf, no doubt about it, but these guys obliterated cities, rewrote the surface of a planet to fit their own schemes, and didn't destroy it only because of some mystical connection that they didn't want to risk. What's to stop them from laughing in Virigar's face?"

Verne stared at me, then gave a faint, hollow laugh. "My friend, there is nothing I have seen in all my hundreds of thousands of years that I fear more than the Werewolf King. And I tell you, in all earnestness, that there is no being I have ever known—man, dragon, vampire, demon, ghost, living god—that would dare to laugh at him, if they knew what they faced. No, my friend, while the Great Demons might, under the right circumstances, disregard the Werewolf King's claims on someone, even they shall never do so lightly. I believe that if we continue to limit the sharing of our knowledge, keep any struggles against them a secret, and move not against them, they should be willing to leave us alone. They do not want to borrow trouble they could easily avoid."

I stared at him, realizing that he meant every word. I shrugged. "I don't know if I should consider this comforting or not. Okay, the big demons will leave me alone, but any day now I could be a wolf appetizer."

"Unlikely in the extreme, sir," Morgan said, returning. "Uncertainty and fear are part of the King's stock in trade. It will suit him far better to wait several years—and with the disruption to his people you have caused, he will have many better things to do with his time for a while. Both Master Verne and I are of the opinion that the Werewolf King will trouble us no more for quite some time to come."

I did relax at that. Something about Morgan's calm, English voice was infinitely reassuring. "In that case, I say we should celebrate."

Morgan nodded and turned towards the kitchen. "An excellent suggestion, sir!"

CHAPTER 72

Blasts From The Past

I heard the door open and winced inwardly. *No, please, no more haunted houses, no more sightings of Bigfoot that you think is really a space alien, no more—*

"So, Mr. Wood, you've given up on customer service and don't even look up?"

That voice was a relief to hear. "Agent...I mean, of course, *Officer* Winthrope," I said, getting up and shaking Jeri Winthrope's hand. "If you'd had to deal with the customers I've had in the last few months, you might start questioning the value of customer service, too."

"I don't doubt it. You'd better figure out something better than a one-man storefront operation, then."

"I'm thinking about it, believe me. Though I don't want to desert what I used to be, either."

Jeri nodded. "Yeah, it's tough to change the whole way you operate."

"So, what brings you here, Jeri?"

She put her case on my desk, unsnapped it, reached in, and handed me a disc. "Unfinished business from a while ago that I happened to run across and figured I'd finish—in view of certain questions you'd asked about an old case."

"Old case?"

"Yeah. The Ross case."

Oh. "How do you see it as unfinished?"

"Came across Lieutenant Reisman's last notes. She was planning to talk to you about it again."

That's interesting, I thought with a pang at the reminder that

384

Renee was dead, and had been now for well over a year. "Any idea why?" I asked. "Even the family had accepted that I didn't know any more."

She shrugged. "Some, but you'll get that out of the file. You'll *also* get the additional stuff I managed to dig up, with the assistance of my...associates."

New information? That would interest Verne, and that was of course the reason I'd asked Jeri about the case at all. The discovery that apparently Xavier Ross had been a close descendant of the Eternal King had made the whole subject a lot more important than I'd originally estimated. And if Jeri's "associates"—Project Pantheon—had done digging... "Thanks. I'll look it over right away. Thank Achernar and company for me."

"Will do. Oh—I know you don't need this warning, but just to stick with proper form—you're technically not allowed to see any of that, so don't let anyone else know about it. I'll deny ever giving it to you if you do."

I grinned. "Yeah, I know. As long as the disc won't self-destruct in five seconds."

"It'll last about a day and a half," she said seriously. "So copy anything you want before that happens."

I really should learn that making jokes like that just gets me in deeper stuff than I want.

After she left, I checked my watch. Four thirty-two. I decided to close up a little early.

It didn't take long to peruse the disc and realize I had some very interesting—even disturbing—material to talk with Verne about.

First, I stopped off for dinner; after all, Verne wouldn't be up until about seven-thirty at this time of year. And even later as time went on. *Must be a pain to be a vampire during high summer. I guess it gets balanced out in winter.*

The door's Jammer-improved security recognized me and let me in without having to bother Morgan. That's how I was able to walk into Verne's huge living room without him knowing I was there.

I stopped in utter shock.

Verne sat, face in his hands, shoulders heaving and the unmistakable sound of sobs racking his tall, usually elegantly poised frame. Morgan stood next to him, hand on Verne's shoulder.

"Holy—Verne, what's *wrong?*"

Startled, he lifted his head—and I saw my impression had been completely wrong, because his face...*shone*, that was the only word I had for it. Despite the tears streaking his cheeks, Verne was *smiling*, a smile so wide and joyful that he looked almost like a child, someone given a gift so lovely and perfect that they cannot even *speak* because there are, literally, no words to express what they feel.

I stared at him. "What...happened?"

Wordlessly, he gestured at the huge television screen that dominated the other side of the living room. Frozen on the screen was an image of three people, something clearly taken from a news video.

I had no trouble identifying two of the people; I could hardly forget Danielle Lumiere and her right-hand man, Rex Hammersmith. But next to Danielle was a young man I didn't recognize. He had dark Middle-Eastern skin and expressive eyes of what looked to be red-brown under dark brows. Above those brows, a profusion of curly brown hair tinted with red and gold grew in an almost uncontrolled mass that tumbled down over his shoulders. The face, though young—no older, I thought, than Danielle—had lines of determination graven on it, and though he seemed barely, if any, taller than the Golden Girl herself, his body was a compact mass of muscle that looked rock-solid.

I heard another small sound from the other side of the room, and looked past Verne and Morgan to see Raiakafan—Tai Lee—staring at the screen with his mouth completely open in astonishment. The expression vanished, but I was sure what I'd seen. *That's...interesting.*

"I see she's got someone else with her, Verne, but what...?"

Verne took a deep, shaky breath—one reserved for deeply emotional moments—and closed his eyes, smiling, wiping the tears away, finally, with a white handkerchief. "Of course, you would not recognize...Even Morgan could only do so from pictures I had shown him long, long ago." He pointed. "Miss Lumiere rescued that boy, found him drowning in the Caribbean, just a week or so ago. Until now, there were no pictures..." He smiled again, brilliantly. "But that, my friend...that is Mikael Valanhavhi."

I blinked. "Mikael...you mean, the son of the Eternal King?"

"The boy whose life was in my care. Whose soul I thought

I had lost, who had disappeared on that very day that the Great Seal was formed and so I, and his father, had accepted that he was gone forevermore. And now..." his eyes shimmered with new tears, "now...I find that I did *not* fail. The failure that I have regretted for all these millennia, that was partially the cause of my own fall...it did not happen. I did not fail, *Eönae* did not fail, the King. His son is, somehow, returned to us."

I hated to be a wet blanket, but... "Verne, that's just a picture. You were talking before about people from...back then planning to kill her. They might—"

He looked up sharply. Then the smile returned, though muted. "You are entirely correct, my friend. I do not believe this is such a trap, however, for a number of reasons. Yet I shall certainly avail myself of the opportunity to sense him directly."

"He could be a wolf."

"If Rex Hammersmith has failed to thoroughly douse such an unknown in silver dust," Morgan said, "then I would be very disappointed in him. I am quite certain that such tests would be applied in an extreme fashion before Mr. Hammersmith would allow anyone to remain in close proximity to Miss Lumiere, and as we know, even Virigar is not immune to silver."

That did make sense. "Okay, then. I hope you're right about who he is. I'm sure it won't be hard to get a chance to drop by *Valinor*, given how happy she is with Sky's work." I studied Riakafan for a moment. *There's another mystery, though...*

"I will certainly arrange it," Morgan said. "But now, Master Jason, what is it that brought you here?"

"Something maybe associated with that deep past again. Not nearly so exciting, probably."

Nothing would be likely to dent Verne's good spirits, but he turned to me more gravely. "Then by all means, tell me."

"Xavier Ross. I just received some more info on his case from Jeri, and some of it's...pretty interesting."

"Go on."

"Well, before she died, Renee had pushed for further investigation on his disappearance; the whole thing had bothered the hell out of her, coupled with the fact that the *reason* the kid went out in the first place was that no one out on the Coast was willing to reopen the case of his brother's murder. So she'd called in a few favors and from what I read here, she even put some of her own money into a couple of PIs to poke around and ask questions. Wish she'd mentioned it to *me*; I'd have kicked in a few dollars."

I shrugged. "Anyway, knowing where they thought he got hit, they were able to interview people who might have been in the area, and they did find a couple of people who thought they noticed someone fitting Xavier's description. One in particular is very interesting—a guy who works in an office facing the right area of the street." I put down a couple of printouts, pointed to a paragraph midway down the first page.

Verne read aloud, "Interviewee David Ringo said that he recognized Xavier Ross from the photograph. 'I especially remember because he was talking to this really tall guy, kinda a weirdo in a funny outfit and a strange hat.'" Verne's head came up slowly. "Khoros."

"Seems likely; but that's only *part* of the fun in this one. Take a look at *this* later report. Apparently, Mr. Ringo called back to the station some months later and gave *this* tidbit. 'Hey, I think I saw that kid you were looking for, Ross! He was right near where he was last time—I think he'd just come out of the alley. And that same guy with the five-sided hat was there.'"

Verne's mouth tightened. "So Khoros is not merely peripherally involved. Did Mr. Ringo say where they went?"

"According to him, he ran out the door and tried to follow them, but they'd vanished around a corner, even though," I continued, with a meaningful glance at Verne, "there seemed to be nowhere they could have gone." I checked the dates once more. "And if the dates are right, it looks like this sighting happened one year *to the day* from the time Xavier Ross vanished."

Verne muttered something in Atlantaean which I was pretty sure did not constitute a compliment to Khoros. "Then it *is* all related, my friend. Anything else?"

"Well, they did manage to find members of a gang that had apparently assaulted Xavier, but according to their testimony they never got to finish it because someone interrupted."

"Khoros, of course," Verne said, nodding.

"No, actually." I *did* enjoy surprising Verne on occasion, and his eyebrows rose at my response. "The two punks interviewed both agreed on a bunch of things, once they stopped trying to pretend that nothing had happened. First, they *had* attacked this kid cutting through the alley. Second, someone had knifed the kid pretty bad—in the gut, probably. Third, just before they had a chance to finish him off, this old guy showed up out of nowhere, and beat the living *hell* out of the entire gang by himself."

Verne blinked. "An 'old guy,' you say?"

"Yep. White hair, long mustache, they guessed he must be seventy at least. But according to the one guy they picked up..." I looked until I found the part I wanted. "Yeah, here. 'That old man told Colt to stop it, standing there just like...like nothing could touch him. And when Colt went to shoot him, he just... was *there*, twenty, thirty feet from where he'd been and taking Colt's gun away without even a *pause*, you know? We all went after him...and it was, you know, like we didn't even *matter* to him."

I looked up. "He goes on to say that he thought the old man killed three or four of them and knocked out the rest, except a couple like the witness who ran like hell when they realized just how badly they were outclassed. No one ever found any bodies... but Jeri checked, and the ones that the witness thought were killed were never seen after that day." I shook my head. "Twenty-two people—gang members—against *one* old man? What the hell was this guy, and how's he mixed up in this?"

Verne picked up the paper and studied it; a faint smile appeared on his face. "Perhaps..." he said slowly, with that smile brightening, showing the same hope I had seen in his eyes before, "just perhaps...the father came for his son."

Part VII

Shadow of Fear

May 2001

CHAPTER 73

Rude Awakening

The scream was so piercing that I was up, cradling Syl in my arms even before I was fully awake. "What? What is it, Syl?"

She was shaking, and for a moment she couldn't speak, just clung to me tightly, staring into the darkness of our bedroom as though something monstrous lurked there. As there was enough moonlight coming through the windows, I could tell that in fact there *wasn't* anything lurking anywhere in the room.

Finally she relaxed her grip. "Something...something *happened*, Jason."

"Not to be sarcastic, Syl, but...that's not very clear on the 'something.'"

"I..." She swallowed, reached out to the side table and grabbed the glass she usually kept there, and drained all the water left. "Better. Jason...I don't know what it was. It was...a shock, a ripple, like the whole *Earth* was struck by something huge."

"What? You're saying...what, a meteor or—" I had the terrible image of a dinosaur-killer having hit somewhere on Earth and us being just minutes away from annihilation by fire or water.

"No, not...not struck Earth *physically*. It was almost like being hit myself, inside, where my Talent is."

I blinked sleep out of my eyes, gave her another hug, and sighed. "Okay. Wish I knew what that meant, though."

I waited until her shakes died down, then got out of bed and turned on the light, glancing at the clock. 3:25 a.m. "Hope we can get back to sleep in a bit, but I know neither of us is ready just yet." I turned on my computer and switched on the TV; Syl often watches TV until she falls asleep, and I figured I could do some quick searches to see if there was anything I could connect to her "shock."

As the TV came on, however, I realized I probably didn't have to search, because the normal late-night programming wasn't on; instead there was the serious face of a main cable news anchor, staring out at us, saying: "...no response as of yet, but current reports indicate a nuclear explosion."

He cut to images—clearly taken with cheap, easily available cameras—showing a huge mushroom cloud rising over some forest or jungle. "These are the first images coming in from Gabon. They appear to confirm that a very large explosion has occurred somewhere within the country."

I frowned. *Hard to think of this as coincidence, but I doubt that nuclear bombs would have some kind of psychic shockwave or whatever. And what the hell would someone be doing, bombing Gabon?* I checked some online maps. Making some guesses based on what the newscaster said as to the location of the images, it looked like the blast would have happened...basically in the middle of nowhere, rainforest without a single valid military or industrial target within at least a couple hundred miles.

The phone suddenly rang. I glanced at Syl, who was still riveted to the newscast, shrugged and picked it up. "Jason Wood."

"Mr. Wood." The rough-toned voice was instantly recognizable. "It seems you are already awake. Would I be correct in assuming your wife woke you up?"

"You would."

"My sympathies to you both. I'd like to invite you to join the investigation."

I nodded to myself. *Of course.* "You don't think it was a nuke."

"I'd bet everything on that, yes. And since you're the world's current authority on the strange, getting you in on it early will look properly proactive."

"Not to mention," I said, heading over towards my dresser as I talked, "if I'm working for you, you can tell me whenever you want me to look the other way. Harder to do that if I work for anyone else."

The short chuckle indicated I'd hit the mark. "I'll take that as a yes?"

"As long as Syl comes along. Face it, she's more likely to be useful than I am."

"If she wishes to accompany you, I won't object."

"Of course I'll come," Sylvie called from the other side of the room, where she was sorting out clothes and starting to pack. "Mr. Achernar has some of the Talent but I have *much* more experience in this kind of Sensing."

"Excellent," said Achernar. "By the time you reach the Albany Airport, I will have a fast transport waiting."

I followed Syl's instincts in packing—which suggested that we'd be there for a while. *I've never been* anywhere *in Africa. Shame this isn't a vacation trip.* I made sure to pack stuff ideal for hot-weather bush-hiking; Gabon had actual rainforest and sat right in the middle of the tropics. It was a good thing that I always kept a travel pack of essential toiletries and such ready; saved me a lot of time.

It was well over an hour before we were in the car and on our way to the airport. "Wonder what Mr. Achernar will have arranged?" Syl mused.

"My guess? Something we won't expect," I answered, pulling into the parking lot. "He plays on a different level than the rest of—"

My new cell phone beeped. "Jason Wood here."

"See you've arrived, Jason," came the Jammer's voice. "I'll let Mr. Achernar know."

"How the heck did you—"

"Traced the phone, cell tower triangulation, called once you stopped moving."

Showoff. "All right. You coming on this trip too?"

"No, I'm staying at HQ, actually. Not that I mind field trips, but the amenities out there in the bush aren't going to fit my usual preferences."

"Where am I—"

"Just go in the main entrance, you'll figure it out."

I rolled my eyes. *Super-spies employing wiseguy hackers really should stay in bad suspense novels.* "Okay."

Syl was already pulling her luggage out of the trunk; I followed and the two of us eventually made it to the entrance—where I saw James Achernar waiting.

"You're playing taxi *yourself?*"

"For something like this? Yes. I'll brief you on what we know along the way."

Waiting on the tarmac, far away from the usual commercial jets, was a plane of a type I'd never seen before—though with its shadow-black color and sleek, almost bladelike design, I could tell that the SR-71 Blackbird had to figure heavily in its ancestry, though there was something oddly out of place about parts of its engine mountings. "What is *that*?"

"HSC-2 *Hermes*, high-speed courier aircraft. Only three like it on Earth," Achernar answered. "Fastest operating aircraft in the world. She'll get us there in under three hours."

"That's almost six thousand miles in less than three hours?" I said, trying to grasp what I was hearing.

"Correct."

We entered *Hermes* and found that it was set up more as a small private jet than a military vehicle...though all the seats could be locked down and equipped for full military acceleration, and—I was able to see as I studied them carefully—also had full ejection setups; they looked like Martin-Baker manufacture with mods.

"Strap in," Achernar said, and to my surprise he went to the pilot's seat. "I want us in the air as soon as possible."

"You know how to *fly* too, Mr. Bond?" I asked as I followed his instructions. Syl didn't seem as gobsmacked as I was, probably because she didn't spend a lot of her time thinking about technology and its limits.

He laughed briefly. "I have an...eclectic skillset, yes. Not, unfortunately, the equal of that particular gentleman, but I have advanced degrees in aerospace engineering as well as psychology, and training as a pilot and driver of multiple vehicles. And a few other less commonly useful skills involving things like handguns."

The jet engines began their rumbling whistle—surprisingly faint. *Must have very good soundproofing here.* "And a master of the martial arts, I'd bet."

Hermes began to move slowly down the tarmac. "Tower, this is Courier Seven, requesting clearance for takeoff," Achernar said into his headset, then in answer to my question, "Actually, no. I'm not completely incompetent in hand-to-hand, but in all honesty, our mutual friend, the Jammer, could probably beat me in that area."

That was a bit of a surprise; I'd started imagining Achernar as the classic superspy, and his wide range of talents had seemed to fit with that. "Really?"

"Really. There are unfortunately a lot of things I don't do well—which is why I need a team, after all."

"Courier Seven, you are cleared for takeoff on Runway Two," the tower said.

"Roger. Courier Seven cleared for takeoff on Runway Two," Achernar acknowledged.

A few minutes later, *Hermes* roared thunder from both main jets and pushed us back in the seats with more force than I'd felt in any normal takeoff. Syl was wide-eyed at the power the plane demonstrated. Swiftly, the nose lifted and the plane streaked into the sky, the lights of the city dwindling away below us as we arrowed away towards the gray light of approaching dawn.

A screen deployed from the ceiling, and the lights dimmed. An image appeared of a green jungle with a huge, bare, perfectly circular crater in the center, surrounded by countless thousands of trees blown flat like matchsticks in a gale, radiating outward from the crater; a significant number were on fire, or had been, and smoke fogged the image. "Holy *crap*."

Achernar unstrapped, having set the plane on autopilot, and came back. "Okay, we'll start the briefing. First, the summary of what we know so far.

"At 7:02 GMT, sensing stations at various locations registered a shallow seismic pulse located in Mwagne National Park, near the border between Gabon and the Congo. Fortunately, one of our low-level satellites was in position to get a picture within ten minutes of detonation; this is the image you see here.

"The diameter of the primary crater is one thousand, seven hundred forty meters. From this, surrounding blowdown effects, and initial seismic pulse, we estimated a detonation on the order of eighty to one hundred megatons." He looked at me and Syl. "What's wrong with this picture?"

I thought a moment, then pointed to the trees. "Only some of them are on fire. The thermal pulse from a nuke—or from a meteorite, for that matter—should have cooked *everything* closer than a certain distance, and I'm thinking that distance should be quite a ways out."

He nodded. "*Very* good, Mr. Wood."

"And mundane explosions don't send out mystical pulses, either," Syl said firmly.

"Agreed," Achernar said with a wry smile, "but I can't put

that into a *For General Release* report. In fact, I probably don't want to put it in more restricted reports, either. The fact that you and I—and probably a number of other people—sensed something cataclysmic at the same time is very important to us, but not something we want known outside of a *very* limited circle."

I was studying the picture carefully. It had the usual distortions and limited resolution of satellite images; contrary to popular myth, you can't just whistle up a satellite and read the newspaper over someone's shoulder. But there was still a fair amount of detail...

I got up and walked to the screen. "What's *that*?" I asked, pointing.

In the very center of the crater, almost obscured by drifting haze, was a darker object, maybe greenish.

"Good eyes, Mr. Wood. That is very much what we want to know, and why we are trying to get there as fast as humanly possible—before anyone else can, hopefully."

"You mentioned a team; you have people other than us, I hope. I'm no forensics expert, and this would be out of even a normal forensics guy's league."

"Oh, I've got *several* more people coming." He looked back at the crater and grimaced. "I wish I had even more, but there's a limit to how many I can trust...and how many I can get there. One more thing...what do you think it was that we *didn't* find so far?"

Given that they didn't have boots on the ground yet, that left remote monitoring of various sorts. So... "Radiation. You haven't picked up any increase of radiation."

"Not one extra click on the geiger counters, no," he acknowledged. "Mystery enough for you?"

"Mystery enough, yes. Hopefully we'll learn something useful."

"Oh, we will, Jason," Sylvie said, and her voice had *that* tone in it. "We will."

CHAPTER 74

Smoking Gun

"Well," I said finally, as staring failed to make sense of what I saw, "it's . . . *definitely* not what I expected."

Achernar's expression probably matched mine—the dumbfounded expression of a man who'd opened the hood of his car to find that the engine consisted of three hamsters running a giant wheel at three thousand RPM.

Syl didn't look quite as surprised, but she was obviously overwhelmed by the sheer scale of destruction . . . and, I guessed, the lingering traces of the power that had echoed to her halfway around the world.

A crater over a mile across was impressive enough from the air, but on the ground the sheer scale was terrifying, especially as we'd had to pick our way through flattened forest giants that had been smashed like dry grass in a tornado.

But what held *my* attention was the answer to our mystery— an answer, however, that gave us more mysteries. In the precise center of the crater was a small patch of untouched greenery, no more than three feet across, on a pillar of earth and stone that rose from the bottom of the mile-wide bowl. That little bit of green was at the exact level of the remaining jungle floor surrounding it.

I looked at Achernar. "You have any idea what the heck happened here?"

"It *looks*," he said, slowly, "as though the blast was centered right above that untouched column, and somehow didn't touch *anything* in a narrow, narrow cone—maybe a degree or so—from that region, and blew completely outward from there."

"I don't think you could pull that off with explosives."

Achernar shook his head. "I know something about demolitions, and I don't think you could even come close to that. The nearby concussion would shatter the stone at the base and the whole thing would have collapsed before we got here. I'd *really* like to get a good look at the top of that, but I'm afraid it'll fall down if anyone tries to climb it." He pulled a small satellite phone from his pack. "Sif, this is Thor."

A pause. Then a contralto voice answered, "Sif here. Go ahead, Thor."

"Did you pack Hugin and Munin?"

"We did. You want them deployed upon landing?"

"Yes. What's your ETA?"

"Seven minutes to land, ten to unload, ten to your current position."

"Acknowledged. Thor out."

"What was all that about?" I asked, as he put away the phone.

"My other teammates will be arriving in about half an hour. With a couple of UAVs—Unmanned Air Vehicles—which will give us a chance to get a good look up on top of that column. Until then, let's just look around—carefully."

I was sweating, but the open area allowed a reasonable breeze, so walking the perimeter of the crater wasn't that bad. I honestly didn't expect to find anything; if a bomb or something like it had gone off, I couldn't imagine that any pieces would be left; aside from bomb fragments, I had no idea what I could be looking for.

"Syl?"

She gave a start. "Oh! Sorry, Jason." She was following me, but her gaze was clearly not exactly *here*.

"Getting anything?"

"It was...magical. That's all I can say, so far anyway. The traces of magic are so intense I can't make out anything else; even my...talent feels fuzzed. It doesn't feel like anything I've ever felt before."

"No sign of anything...well, anything that *did* this?"

"I haven't got any sense of..." she paused, frowning. She closed her eyes for a moment and seemed to...*extend* herself somehow, without actually moving in a way I could describe. When she opened her eyes, she looked confused.

"What?"

Syl glanced around quickly, eyes scanning the area, focusing on one particular location about two hundred yards away. "*Something* was watching. I think. But it's *gone* now."

I drew my pistol and moved forward carefully. It took several minutes to work our way to that area.

At first, it didn't look any different than the other parts of the crater rim: fallen trees, flattened brush and blasted dirt. Then I looked closer.

In the thin layer of dirt I saw footprints. Shoeprints, actually. I knelt down and stuck the little yellow marker flags Achernar had given us into the dirt just off to the side of each print, then studied the actual pattern.

"Looks like...whoever it was...came up out of the crater," I said finally, not without some reluctance. There seemed to be some scuffmarks right at the edge, and maybe even some smears and smudges on the glassy surface of the crater itself. "Then he or she sat down on this tree trunk." The footprints bent towards the trunk, which showed slight smudges in the coating of dust that covered it. New footprints faced out from the tree and seemed to overlap those that had approached the tree. I knelt again, looking carefully at the prints. "Looks like sneakers or maybe running shoes. Size...six or seven in men's, maybe."

"So someone a little small if they were a man, but normal-sized for a woman."

"Right." I looked back across the crater. "Damn. Camera's over there. Honestly, I didn't think I'd find anything. C'mon, let's go get it and tell Achernar what we found."

She glanced at me. "You have that 'I know something they don't' look on your face, Jasie. What is it?"

I grinned faintly, but the situation was too serious for me to find it amusing. "Strange mystical events intruding on our world makes me think of a certain incident..."

"Oh. *Oh*. And...?"

"Near as I can tell from Verne's sketchy guesses, we're standing right on top of one of the sites of the Seven Towers."

"But why in the *world* would one of them...explode or whatever *now*?" Syl muttered as we made our way back around the crater.

"Not a clue. Maybe Verne will have one, when we get back. But we'd better not say anything more; don't want to drag them into *that* mess."

Syl nodded. Project Pantheon might *think* they knew what was hiding behind the façade of normality in our world, but we knew that there was another, much more dangerous layer, and the last thing we needed was government agents poking into the history of Atlantaea.

Getting back was a little quicker. Finally, I caught sight of Achernar about fifty yards away, a pretty woman of about his own height talking to him while two men—one a tall black man, the other large, solid, with short bright-red hair and the pale complexion to go with it—unpacked a couple of crates nearby.

All four of them instantly stopped and glanced in our direction, seemingly aware of everything going on around them. *Definitely from the Super-Spy Academy of Paranoia*, I thought.

"You found something," Achernar said as we got closer.

"How'd you guess?"

"Aside from your expression? You're back much faster than I expected."

I supposed that made sense. "Found footprints. Coming *out* of the crater."

His eyebrows climbed skyward. "Really. You marked them?"

"Flag for each print and for a couple points of interest. Came back for the camera."

"Very good. We'll go check it out. Let me just introduce you to the rest of the team." He turned first to the black-haired woman, who I could now see was, at least partially, Japanese and maybe Chinese, too. Something about the way Achernar looked at her gave me the feeling that he thought of her as more than just a colleague. "Bambi Inochi, Jason Wood."

I tried not to grin at the name, but she caught it. "Blame my parents' love of Disney," she said as she shook my hand. I recognized her voice as the one that had answered to the codename "Sif" earlier. "Pleased to meet you, Mr. Wood."

"Thanks, Ms. Inochi. This is my wife, Sylvia Stake."

Achernar then quickly introduced us to Derek Fairchild (the tall black man) and Donovan Grant (the red-haired man). "You finish getting the UAVs set up," he said, grabbing the camera case. "I'll want a flyover of that...column as soon as possible. I'm going to accompany Mr. Wood to—"

His and Sylvie's heads snapped around, and I turned just in

time to see a flash of light. When it died down, dust was drifting in a thick cloud near the edge of the crater.

Just about where we'd found the tracks.

Achernar's gun was already out, but Ms. Inochi was *moving*— cutting across part of the glassy crater at a high sprint, somehow not slipping on the steep, slick slope. The other two stayed back with the equipment.

I thought I was in pretty good shape overall, and I've certainly learned how to run fast when the occasion demanded, but Achernar was outdistancing both me and Syl, and by the time he was halfway around the edge, Bambi Inochi was already standing at the point where the flash had occurred. But I was already close enough to be sure.

The entire area had been wiped clean as a blackboard with an eraser. There wasn't a trace of the footprints . . . or of the flags. Achernar looked at me. "You're sure this was the place? *Exactly* the place?"

"I'm afraid so. The prints came from down there," I pointed, noting that even the surface was now pristine, "to up about here. They walked to here, and whoever it was sat down on this log, which now is missing its bark for about three feet on either side of where the person sat, and then continued on."

Achernar frowned. "And both Sylvia and I sensed . . . something, just as this happened. Someone's here, or was here just minutes ago."

"Syl said she felt someone watching before."

"Whoever it was must have realized you found clues there, and when you went back for the camera, did . . . whatever that was . . . to erase the evidence." He looked to his companion. "Bambi? You got anything?"

The black-haired spy walked lightly across the ground, jumped onto one of the fallen trees and followed that for a while, surveying everything around her. Finally, she came back. "Sorry, James. Not a thing. The evidence says someone had to have been here . . . but I'm not seeing a trace. Whoever it is . . . they're *good*."

"And might still be watching us. Dammit."

I looked around a little warily. To instantly strip something like eight feet of bark from a big tree and wipe everything else clean over forty feet in one shot . . . that would take a hell of a lot of power and control. Verne could probably do it; he'd shown some impressive telekinetic abilities. But this was someone and something else, and the thought they might be waiting there, watching...

But there was another side to this. "You know, he or she *could* have done a lot worse."

Achernar glanced at me, then his eyebrows came down slightly. "I suppose they could have, yes. Whatever did this would probably be easily capable of injuring or killing us. They made sure that no one was nearby before doing...whatever this was." He looked around slowly. "Not inherently hostile, then. Sylvia, what was it you sensed?"

She gave an apologetic smile. "Sorry, Mr. Achernar. Most of my senses are overwhelmed by the power still lingering. I just suddenly sensed something was *going* to happen. What about you?"

"Just for a split second...it was a feeling of concentration, of something pent up and released in the same moment." He gazed off into the distance. "Nothing else, really. I've taught myself the best I can, but I just don't have much of the Talent. Maybe that's why I don't feel blinded here; I'm *almost* blind to begin with."

Derek Fairchild waved from the other side. "Hey, James, *Hugin*'s ready. What's the plan?"

"Send her up and criss-cross that little standing garden in the middle of the crater," Achernar said, giving a shrug and heading back in that direction. "How close can you get?"

Fairchild and Grant both studied the pedestallike column through binoculars for a few minutes as we made our way over. "No lower than about ten feet," Derek said finally. "That one bush must be close on seven feet high, and I don't want to cut it close; one snag and *Hugin* will go straight down to the crater floor, and that's all she wrote."

"Okay. Try to make it as slow as possible."

Donovan Grant nodded. "Just at stall speed when we go over."

I had to admit it was neat to watch. Remote-piloted aircraft weren't new, but a semi-autonomous and instrumented drone like these UAVs was a refinement I hadn't seen. Assembled, *Hugin* had an eight-foot wingspan and a four-foot body; I could see a camera projecting downward below the nose with some other mounts that looked like sensors out on the wings. Derek checked the unit, activated it, and simply threw it out into the crater like a giant paper airplane.

Hugin's engine purred to life and the little drone came up and steadied. Donovan was guiding it, and after a few moments it climbed back up and glided low over the mysterious green spot.

Images flowed by on the screen, but when we froze the image stream they were slightly blurred—something that obscured crucial details. After several overflights, Achernar cursed mildly. "Bring *Hugin* in. We're not getting anything this way. It's just too small a target and we can't move slow enough."

Bambi had been staring at the column all this time. "I think I could get on top of it and take a look."

Achernar looked at her narrowly. "There is no way in hell even *you* are getting up that thing without falling or, more likely, hitting it somewhere so it *does* come down on top of you."

"I'm not talking about getting there from *below*."

I suddenly understood what she was getting at. "You landed your courier jet on VTOL mode, like a Harrier," I said. "So if you flew it that way—"

"With you hanging underneath, in the *jetwash*? To keep from messing up any evidence, I'd have to be at least a hundred feet up, probably twice that. That's *hellish* maneuvering to get someone safely on a three-foot-wide target!"

"And if *anyone* can do it, James Achernar, it's you."

I could see that Achernar was torn. He *really* wanted to get a good look at that little piece of untouched land, and probably wanted to do it well before anyone else got here. But he also didn't want to risk her life. Finally, he turned to Syl. "What do you think?"

I was surprised for a moment, and so was she; but both of us realized why he was asking her, after a moment. "Well," Syl said slowly, "I . . . don't get a *bad* feeling about you trying it. But—no offense—you're not very close to me and usually that sense of mine triggers when it's something to do with me or very close friends."

"I suppose so," Achernar sighed. "All right, Bambi. But you be *careful*."

"That's *your* job, James," she said with a smile. "*I* just have to get a good look at it."

"Is it really *worth* the risk?" I asked, nervous about interrupting. "What do you think could possibly be *up* there that makes it worth the chance of screwing up?"

The four members of Project Pantheon looked at each other. "Maybe nothing," Achernar said. "But maybe something, and we need anything we can find. Look at this again." He gestured, taking in the immense smoking crater. "*Something* blasted this area with more concentrated power than the biggest nuke ever detonated, and yet—somehow—that little column was protected from it. Maybe this is a freak magical accident. Maybe it's some kind of... natural but mystical phenomenon. Or maybe it's something *deliberate*—a test of a technique. I can't afford to *not* get that information. Understand?"

I nodded. "I felt it had to be asked, though."

"It did, I think," he agreed. "Thanks."

About twenty-five minutes later, I heard the rumbling howl of *Hermes'* engines, and it wasn't five more minutes before the craft drifted slowly into view. Below the sleek black jet with its now down-turned engines, dangled a figure in black. "Jesus," I muttered. Bambi Inochi looked like a tiny spider at the end of a thread, but if she fell off she wouldn't just land and scuttle away; it was over a two-hundred-foot fall to the bottom.

Hermes floated towards the column, slowing ever more until it finally came to a halt over the strange column. Bambi twisted her body slowly, damping out swinging motions and compensating for the unavoidable slight rocking of *Hermes* as Achernar kept her poised, immobile over that impossible dot of green.

Gradually, Bambi lowered herself until it seemed she was just about touching the bush on one edge. I couldn't be sure, but I *thought* she was taking pictures.

Then Syl jumped, *Hermes* twitched, and there was a flash from below, right at the base of the column.

The column shuddered, then began to tilt with a low groaning, cracking sound. *Hermes'* engines instantly roared louder, lifting upwards, as the two-hundred-foot anomaly sank and shattered in a new cloud of dust and debris.

Hermes swung around, slowed over our location and let Bambi drop off before going to land. "Well, *that* was exciting," Bambi said.

"Get anything before it fell?"

"Pictures only," she said. "And I have *no* idea if there's anything to see here, but at least shutter speed should've prevented the blur."

I sighed. "So we won't know until the film's developed."

She grinned brightly. "*This* is a digital camera."

"Really?" I'd seen the recent releases of digital cameras, but they were too expensive and the resolution wasn't nearly on par with real film. "I don't recognize the brand."

"You wouldn't," Achernar said. "Custom design. You'll probably see something like this on the market in . . . oh, seven years. Maybe."

Bambi had gotten a cable out and was connecting it to the same portable computer that had been running the UAV. After a few minutes, she brought up a graphics program, showing a top-down view of green and brown—some bare earth in the center, short leafy plants hiding a few sticks, a tall bush and a shorter one. I was startled by the sharpness of the images; yes, real film would have gotten better detail, but the *immediacy* of this was amazing. *Once this technology gets out there,* I mused, *I suspect film cameras are going to die a fast and final death.*

"Darn," she said after a bit. "Nothing."

"No, there's *something*," I said. "Flick through the last three again." The images clicked by, changing perspective slightly to parallel the change in Bambi's position as she had swung above the enigmatic patch of land. "There." I pointed to a faint blackish line.

Achernar and Bambi squinted, zooming in on the area—to end up with a more-pixelated image. "Well, okay, you're the expert in interpreting data," Achernar said after a moment. "There's *something* there, but damned if I know what it is, and it's gone now."

"Probably. But maybe not. If we look for it *right now.*"

Bambi raised an eyebrow; Derek and Donovan had similarly skeptical expressions. I noted, with some satisfaction, that there wasn't a trace of skepticism on Syl's face. "I can't *look* for something, Mr. Wood," Bambi said slowly, "if I don't know what it *is.*"

"It's a thread. About seven inches long. Not quite sure about the material, but I'd lay a *lot* of money on it being a thread; it's dead black in color, too."

"You can get *that* out of this blur? Without analysis?" Derek looked unwillingly impressed.

I grinned. "The human brain's darn good at analysis. And this is, as Mr. Achernar said, one of my specialties. Down there," I pointed, "is roughly where the top part of that thing came down. If we go look right now, we *might* find it before the wind comes along and blows it away."

James Achernar shrugged after a moment and gave a small Clint Eastwood-like grin. "What the hell. Not like it'll hurt to try."

The six of us fanned out across the region of the crater—being *very* careful not to slip on that impossibly glassy surface until we got to the safer, dirt-strewn area—and began searching.

It was about twenty-five minutes later—I was getting pretty tired of studying one dusty clod of dirt after another, and developing a healthy respect for the four agents' patience—when Syl suddenly turned, took two steps to her right and bent down, tweezers in hand. "Ha!" she said with satisfaction.

Achernar and his team seemed to materialize around us, staring at Syl's find.

It was a long black thread, frayed, with signs of having been torn from something else.

Achernar extended a sample bag and Syl dropped it in. "Very good, Sylvie. And Jason—I'm impressed. It may not be much... but you just helped recover evidence we probably would have missed. Oh, the Jammer would have figured out what was in the pictures, but that would have been too late to actually get the thread."

"Thanks. Glad to be of assistance. Though... is that really going to be of much use?"

Donovan Grant's grin was predatory. "Mr. Wood, believe me; you'd be amazed what we can get out of a thread."

Achernar suddenly cocked his head; a moment later, I could hear why he did: faint, distant fluttering, humming sounds. "Okay. Looks like we've done what we can for now. Company's coming. Bambi, you guys hold things down here. I've got to get our consultants out of sight and home."

"Thought you were planning to use my presence as evidence of your proactive nature," I said as we followed him towards *Hermes*.

The smile was a quick flash of light. "The *official* interviews will be sometime tomorrow or the day after. But I don't want them knowing you were on site *now*, or seeing *Hermes* up close, for that matter. Too many things I don't want anyone knowing."

"And I'm guessing that when we get home, they're things we don't know, either," I continued, starting up the ramp.

"Hell," Achernar said, following us up, "when I'm off-duty, they'll be things *I* don't know."

CHAPTER 75

Client Referral

I opened up the fridge and poked around. "I think I'm out of AB, but this bottle of A is new."

The vampire to whom I addressed the comment leaned back comfortably in one of my new office chairs. "That's just fine, Jason. Verne's the connoisseur; I try actually *not* to cultivate a discriminating taste."

"Given that you're theoretically still cursed, I suppose it's probably a good idea. Here you go." I placed the bottle in front of Father Jonathan, probably the most atypical vampire alive, given that he was a fully ordained Catholic priest and had chosen to visit me during a lovely sunny late spring afternoon.

The priest studied me as I sat down, maybe a little heavier than I wanted to. "You look absolutely exhausted, Jason. I hope married life isn't a problem...?"

I responded with a small chuckle. "Oh, Syl and I are doing just fine. I'd be a lot more tired if I didn't have her around; she generally screens my public calls and filters out like ninety-five percent of them as total crackpots, and most of the rest I can dump off on other people who can do the looking as well as I can. But even the remaining one percent seems to be getting bigger all the time. Then when something really big and flashy happens, guess who gets called? I just got back from Africa last night." *For the second time*, I noted to myself. No one was going to know about the first.

Father Jonathan gave a startled laugh. "Oh, how silly of me. Of course you would have been called in on that."

"Yeah." I acknowledged. "Since the Morgantown Incident

that just about everyone's heard of, plus a few other things that Certain People know about, I'm called in for everything weird these days. Thank God the Cold War's over; a multimegaton blast back in, oh, 1960-something would probably have caused missile launches without anyone asking questions first."

"I fear you're correct." He sipped at the blood, straight from the bottle. "And did you find anything of interest?"

I shook my head, frowning. "More a 'dog in the night-time' case, actually. What we *didn't* find was pretty revealing. No sign of radiation. No sign of chemical explosives—not that a hundred million tons of high explosives could be smuggled into the middle of a jungle without causing talk—heck, I don't think there's that many conventional explosives OUT there. Not a trace of meteoric dust or iron, either.

"Of course, certain sources that we know," I glanced at him and he nodded, knowing I meant Syl, Verne, and a few others, "all felt 'something' when it went off, but that's not the kind of evidence I could bring to the table down there. Though it created the kind of crater you'd expect, it hadn't burned everything for miles around. No one still alive nearby had seen or heard anything unusual before or just after the blast." That wasn't *quite* true, but what they *had* seen just raised more questions than answers, and I was too tired to go into the details, and not sure how much I could tell Father Jonathan, even if he was in the more unusual category himself. "Anyway, what brings you to the office?"

He looked mildly concerned. "I hadn't realized how busy—or tired—you are, or I wouldn't have come to you for what seems a relatively trivial matter."

I waved that off. "If anyone *isn't* going to be coming to me with a crackpot problem, it's a guy who's a vampire himself. What's the problem?"

"Monsters in the closet," he answered, looking embarrassed.

Well, that's a new one. "I'm presuming it's not *your* closet. My guess is you could take care of your own problems."

He laughed. "No, you're correct there. One of my parishioners, Dave Plunkett."

"Plunkett...that name rings a bell. Is he with Plunkett Security Incorporated?"

He nodded, pleased. "He *is* PSI, yes."

"Okay. Not the sort of guy who's likely to come to you with a BS story, then."

"Not at all. I've known Dave for, oh, ever since I came to this area. Years. He's one of the most cheerful and down-to-earth people I know."

"So what's the story?"

"Dave has a summer camp, on forty-eight acres up in East Galway, if you know it?" At my nod, Father Jonathan went on, "So you know the area has no amenities—no water, electric, or sewer—but Dave's grandfather built a large house there many years ago, and his family—Dave, his wife, and their two children—have spent several weeks there every year.

"Up until the last couple of years," Father Jonathan continued, "they've had no real problems; oh, the usual kid's complaints about isolation, a few nightmares, people calling the house 'creepy,' you know the sort of thing, but the worst you could really say was that it was...an 'atmospheric' place. Their kids actually liked the slightly scary atmosphere, and it was popular with some of their friends too. Then..."

"...it stopped being just atmospheric." I finished, not entirely surprised. It really did seem that something was changing, something that started when the wolves appeared, or maybe when Raiakafan first showed up. Verne had hinted about that more than once. One of these days, I was going to have to sit down with him and go into these things in-depth.

Father Jonathan agreed that was a good, if all-too-brief, description of what had happened, and after I asked a few more questions, it was clear to me that I needed to talk with Mr. Plunkett personally.

"He lives in the area," Father Jonathan said. "I know this is important to him, so if you don't mind I'll have him come over tomorrow."

I checked my calendar. "That should work. I don't have anything specific scheduled. Just have him give me a heads-up about half an hour before he's coming over and that'll be fine."

"I shall." Father Jonathan rose and shook my hand. "Thank you for listening, Mr. Wood."

"No problem. Like I said, if *you* are the one bringing me weird-sounding problems, I'm gonna assume they're legit. I just hope I can help Mr. Plunkett."

"So do I," he said, looking pensive. "Because as I said, I know Dave. He doesn't scare easily. He's been in security and law enforcement for twenty years. It's *hard* to scare a man like that.

"But when he came to me, I could tell by the way his voice shook...he was *terrified*."

CHAPTER 76

Camp Fear

Dave Plunkett was of about average height, with red hair and beard—both showing a bit of gray—and a face of the sort that normally looked open and cheerful. Now, though, he looked more worried than anything. "Sit down, Mr. Plunkett. Father Jonathan gave me a really quick summary of your problem, but I'd really appreciate hearing it from you, straight."

He shifted uncomfortably in his chair. "It's . . . kinda hard to talk about it. I mean, in the daytime, here, it doesn't seem real. Well, no, that's not it. I know it's real, Jesus Christ, yeah, but . . ."

". . . you feel stupid talking about it because you wouldn't believe it yourself." I finished for him. "Mr. Plunkett—"

"Dave."

"Dave, I understand completely. I still find it really hard to say the word 'werewolf' without wincing. And I've seen the damn things up close more times than you can count, or would want to. If Father Jonathan thinks you have a problem, he's probably right. Just tell me about it. Start with what happened last year; I know about the camp."

Mr. Plunkett scratched his head nervously, then started talking. "Right . . . well, last year, we—that's me, my wife Jenny, and my kids Elizabeth and Mitchell— went up for our usual trip."

"How old are Elizabeth and Mitchell?"

"Oh, Lizzie's fourteen now, and Mitch is eleven."

"Okay. Just needed to visualize the group of you. So they were thirteen and ten when this started?" He nodded. "Got it. Go on."

"Okay . . . we got there in the afternoon, dragged in all our stuff, I grilled us some dinner, and then we all went to bed—well, we usually do some reading first, then we go to bed early the first day.

"About a half-hour later, Mitch screamed—loud enough to wake me right off, and I'm a heavy sleeper. Mitch said he'd seen something, something huge like a monster peering in the window, a black shadowy thing with faintly glowing eyes.

"Since this was just a little while after Morgantown, you can imagine what I was thinking; I had a shotgun with silver loads along, just in case. So I checked all around the house very carefully."

Still listening to his narration, I mused that Mr. Plunkett would never have *thought* about doing a careful search if he'd ever actually *seen* a wolf. Or, if he did, the "checking" would have consisted of firing blasts of silver shot in all directions as he went around the house.

"I didn't find anything; I even checked for prints outside of Mitch's window. Mitch was positive he'd seen *something*, but he admitted that it was kind of blurry and that maybe the moonlight through the trees had made the pattern. So we pulled the curtains tight shut in his room and went back to bed." He took a deep breath, then continued. "It wasn't twenty minutes later that another scream jolted us awake, but this one was from Lizzie.

"We all rushed into her room to find her backed up against the wall with her bush knife in her hand, shaking so bad that she couldn't even hold the thing straight. When she finally calmed down, she told us she'd glanced at her closet—well, really more a cabinet bolted to the wall, but a tall one a couple of feet deep—and noticed the door was open. That was just barely visible in the moonlight coming through her window. She was already falling back to sleep and trying to decide if it was worthwhile to go over the cold wood floor to close it, when she saw the door opening wider... and wider... and she could see *something* inside, something dark and huge with faintly glowing eyes and a wavering, fanged smile.

"Of course, we didn't find anything. Her closet door was open, yeah, but she had it so crammed full of clothes you couldn't have fit a kitten in there, let alone some seven-foot monster. Still, the kids were both scared as hell and Jenny was getting kinda creeped out by the situation—and, I gotta admit, so was I. Lizzie and Mitch hadn't had those kind of nightmares in years, and nothing ever that bad, and it just didn't make *sense* that they'd both suddenly go all scared overnight. Still, we were already there, it was late, driving back was out of the question at that hour. So we moved sleeping bags into the main bedroom and left a small oil lamp on until the kids fell asleep. Once me and Jenny were sure that both of them were sleeping, we turned out the light to go to sleep themselves."

"And?"

Dave swallowed hard, then continued. "About ten minutes later, just as I was drifting off to sleep, I heard a faint creaking noise, and saw the bedroom door opening very slowly. You can bet I came awake right away then. But I didn't say anything, didn't even move, except to slide my hand over to where I had the shotgun. Just kept my eyes slitted almost shut, open enough so I could see the door. Mr. Wood, I've been in security for twenty years, been in my share of fights, even had guys trying to honest-to-God kill me, but I'd take all that over again rather than lie there like that, watching a door open that couldn't possibly be opening, because I knew I'd shut it myself.

"It was *black* outside that door, black as pitch, and it kept opening, and then I saw a faint light; I thought I was finally seeing the window across the living room, and then I saw it was an eye. A glowing eye, and I swear to God I felt my heart stop dead right then. The door just kept swingin' open, and I saw more and more of this black *thing* standin' there, blocking out the faint moonlight from the windows, and grinning like some walkin' jack-o-lantern. Then it moved, like it was getting' ready to come in.

"Lemme tell you, *that* got my heart and the rest of me moving. All I could think of was that Jenny was right there next to me, and the kids off to the side, and there wasn't any way I was letting this thing get them. I sat up and let that thing have it, three rounds as fast as I could pump it. There was a lot of screaming and jumping and moving, and I couldn't see right away because of the muzzle flash, so I couldn't see or hear where it went, but when the smoke cleared there wasn't anything there.

"That was the last straw, though. We cleared out right away and drove home. The next day, we were still creeped out, but it sounded pretty silly, so we didn't say anything about it, we just said that one of the kids got sick and we didn't want to stay up there then." He leaned back, looking slightly defiant.

"Somehow," I said, "I don't think you're the kind of guy to leave it at that."

He grinned, a tired grin, but real. "You've got that right.

Sure, the next weekend I went up there by myself. Jenny didn't like that, but someone had to go check it out. I brought portable lights, security cams and stuff like that, wired the place up, and watched all night. Had a couple of moments where I felt something was watching me, but nothing happened, and I felt pretty silly—not to mention tired—by the time morning came. So I caught me some sleep that afternoon and decided to go to stealth surveillance mode. I cut the lights and went to near-IR."

I nodded my understanding. Many electronic cameras were sensitive in the near-infrared spectrum, and it didn't take much power to send out enough NIR "light"—actually, heat—to illuminate a wide area while leaving it pitch-black to the naked eye.

"So again I was watching the little screens, but . . . well, I hadn't really gotten a full night's sleep and I'm not as young as I used to be, so pulling all-nighters really takes it out of me. I fell asleep. And I had nightmares, of all the doors around me opening, and monsters like the one I saw coming at me. But I couldn't wake up for like the longest time, and those nightmares just went on and on, until finally I felt like I had to *rip* myself out of sleep—you know that feeling when you're awake, but you feel like someone dragged you out of sleep with a tow chain? Anyway, I was totally—I mean, totally—soaked with sweat, breathing like I'd done a marathon, and I look up and there the damn thing is, standing over me, reaching towards me. Now, I ain't proud of what happened next, but I don't know if anyone else wouldn't have done the same. I screamed like a girl and I ran. Lucky I was in the dining room and not far from the door, because the way I was thinking, or not thinking, I'd've dove straight through the nearest window. I practically flew to my truck, had the remote starter start her up and turn her on as I was running, and I dove into the cab. I could feel that thing right on my heels, and as I slammed the door, I swear it was not three feet off. I left the cab lights on, gunned the engine, and got the hell out of there. Went back the next morning to get my equipment, and even then I was jumpy."

"And did your cameras show anything?"

He slammed his fist on the desk. "Not one damn thing! They blacked out! Didn't show crap!"

"Hey, take it easy. If they were independent units, that's actually a pretty interesting fact. They shouldn't have failed all at once. Was there anything wrong with them?"

"No, sir. I checked them all out before, and I checked 'em out again afterward. They all worked." He gave me an apologetic look. "Sorry about bangin' on your desk."

"No problem, you've been through a lot. So what about in the time since?"

He recounted a few other incidents, which boiled down to the simple fact that no one—not him, not his family, and none of the few friends he'd dared tell about the problem—had been able to spend a night in that cabin since. Some of them wouldn't even walk in the door; they got a feeling of dark foreboding that something terrible was waiting just inside. "So the damn place is going to fall to pieces. Ain't no one been inside to clean it since that first time we ran out—I didn't do any of that on my surveillance trip—and no one has stayed long since."

I nodded. "Sounds like it happens mostly at night. Is that right? Has anyone run into this thing in daylight?"

"Well...no, not really. The cabin feels a lot creepier and less friendly than it used to, but no one's ever seen or heard anything in the daytime."

"If all it does is scare people, maybe you could use that."

He gave a short, explosive laugh. "Yeah, a tourist attraction. Thought of that, actually. But a real tourist attraction, you still have to know what you're dealing with and be able to control it. I don't know that this thing is just trying to scare us. It can move doors, at least, so I have to ask myself: what else can it do? It sure don't seem friendly."

"No, you're right there. If I look at it as thinking even vaguely like a human being, well, a person who liked doing that is the kind of guy who tends to escalate—they start out small, then get worse. You're doing the right thing. If you still have the surveillance data, I'd like to look at it."

"Sure, no problem. I didn't find anything on it, but if you can, more power to you." He looked apprehensive. "Um, how much is this going to cost?"

I shook my head. "I don't necessarily charge if it's important enough, or interesting enough. There are advantages in being The Guy Everyone Calls, and my contract for CryWolf gadgets means I don't actually *have* to work. Let me talk to a few consultants first, then I'll get back to you with an estimate."

CHAPTER 77

Awakening Power

The cave ceiling glowed faintly like a starry sky overhanging the small trees and grassy sweep of lawn below it. I leaned against the altar at the center of the Heart, admiring the view. "I swear, it looks brighter in here."

"Your perceptions are most accurate, Jason. It is indeed brighter, a fact of considerable concern." Verne's dark-skinned, aristocratic features, with their underlying vampiric pallor, mirrored the concern of which he spoke. He stood at the edge of the Mirror, the mystic pool which was the true center of this underground temple to the Earth goddess Eönae.

"What's the problem? Light is pretty good for plants; seeing them growing underground like this is still quite freaky."

The wry smile showed the sharper canines more than the other teeth. "The light, by itself, is not the problem. It is that such brightening is the first objective indication I have had of something we were before only speculating about. The strength of the Powers is indeed increasing, in a very disturbing manner."

He frowned. "The . . . Gabon Blast is another worrisome indication. I am afraid that even after some investigation, I cannot say why such a detonation should have occurred at the site of one of the Towers. It has been, as you observed, half a million years since the Fall; any energy in the sites should long since have been released or dissipated." He gazed into the Mirror for a few moments. "But if . . . for some reason . . . the power is returning, somehow leaking past the Great Seal . . . well, many things may happen."

"Do you think Mr. Plunkett's problem is related to this?"

"I would, in fact, be quite astonished if it was not—and if similar problems are not occurring elsewhere."

"We really need to sit down and talk about this sometime. Soon. And if this kind of thing is going to keep happening, I may have to start hiring. Syl can't keep being the filter on my answering machine; she has her own business to run and since she started studying with you, that business has gotten a lot more serious, for those of us who get to see behind the fluffy exterior."

"I am very much afraid, Jason, that you cannot escape your destiny to be at the very center of such events. Yes, we must discuss the overall implications, and soon. But first, to the very interesting problem of Mr. Plunkett and his no-longer-friendly vacation home."

I nodded, moving away from the altar stone. "I've brought all the stuff with me. Coming up?"

"In a moment. If you would, please stay while I speak with the Lady."

I remained, staying respectfully silent. "Speaking with the Lady" was Verne's phrase for prayer, but unlike in prayer sessions in other places of worship, I had gotten more and more the feeling of Someone being present when Verne closed his eyes and spoke in the ancient tongue that had not been heard in half a million years. I'd asked him if he thought other religions were false. His answer was vehemently negative:

"No! Never should one judge the truth or falsity of religion based on such nebulous things—or even, truth be told, on far more objective events. If the Powers be present, there are those deities who will show themselves openly; there are others who do not. There is a myriad of reasons why they may, or may not, manifest to their worshippers in physical ways. It is my belief that most religions are true in one way or another; they simply focus on different aspects of the Creator and Its Children."

This time, that feeling of Presence was even stronger; I thought I saw a luminous glitter from the Mirror as Verne bent over it and touched its surface gently with spread hands. Then he rose. "I am now at your disposal, Jason," he said, his archaic turn of phrase complementing his theatrical style of dress, which echoed all the best cinema vampires—or, perhaps it would be better to say, his style seemed to be emulated well by all the best actors of vampires.

We sat in the large yet cozy den into which Verne had had me dragged when we first met, almost two years ago. The usual tray of snacks was already waiting for me; Morgan always anticipated my need for additional fuel when researching the weird. Verne, of course, had his usual glass of blood.

"You mentioned that the security images were not entirely without value. You obtained some images of interest, then?"

"Yep. Here, take a look."

The critical frames were taken from the moment that the cameras had faded out. To someone viewing them casually, it just looked like the camera failed; the screen went black. But the human eye doesn't discriminate shades of dark nearly as well as a camera can register them, and playing with the original data showed something very different. The darkness didn't hit the camera in a uniform fashion, but started on one side of the field of view and spread—very quickly, within one or two frames—to cover the entire camera. And in a couple of those frames...

Verne nodded thoughtfully. "That looks like part of a hand, does it not?"

"Yep. Blurry as hell, and black as pitch, but there's *structure* to that darkness that covers the cameras. The blur might be from movement, or the thing itself might be blurry. So, any ideas, Verne? This a ghost, a demon, what?"

Verne considered for a while. I knew enough not to bug him, but instead ate a few of the spiced roast beef crackers that Hitoshi had made this evening. Finally, Verne sighed. "The problem, Jason, is that I have entirely too many ideas on this subject. The described events and behavior could be caused by a large number of supernatural creatures and forces, and it will require some effort, investigation, and deduction to determine which one."

I made a face. "I knew this would happen one of these days—that I'd get a case where the answer didn't just drop obviously out of the events. Even the Maelkodan pretty much narrowed the field down quickly once she left a statue out for us to see." I still felt a slight twinge of regret over the Maelkodan's end. I really wished I could have found some way around the creature's death, but even the Maelkodan itself admitted that there was no real chance it could stop killing—especially humans and werewolves.

"If there were no signs of the Awakening, the answer might well be narrower," Verne said. "But as the overall level of power increases, things that were too weak to manifest previously become much more likely to be seen. I would say that the three most likely candidates are a *ryunihav*, a *zarbalath*, or one of the *thansaelasavi*."

I knew the first two; "ryunihav" was the Atlantaean for ghost, though I needed details on what they meant by "ghost." "Zarbalath" was one of a number of words which basically meant "demon."

"What's that last?" I asked, activating my Lumiere SmartCall phone so I could record this for later transcription.

"*Thansaelasavi*," Verne repeated.

"Okay, got that...um, if I remember right, that'd be 'magic... something.'"

"Very good, Jason. An exact translation would be difficult, mainly because it is a shortened form of a far more descriptive phrase. The best description is 'creatures born of and sustained by the magic of life.' Some believed such creatures were the creations of wizards or deities; others that they were natural products of a world steeped in magic, that evolution would act upon magical traits exactly as it would upon ordinary genetic ones. In my view, likely all of these are true for some particular group of *thansaelasavi*.

"For our purposes, unfortunately, it is a very broad category. All of these creatures derive much of their essence from the energies of other living beings, somewhat as the Great Wolves do. However, they do so mostly through interaction with living beings and their...auras, as Sylvia likes to call them. They are also quite diverse, as they may derive from natural creatures, or are a living essence of some mystical element or another—fire, earth, and so on. Some of these creatures are symbiotes—the typical 'familiar' attributed to some schools of magical practice, for instance, would be a *thansaelasavi* of cooperative nature, exchanging the affection and power derived from its linked partner for the services such a familiar could provide. Others are much more sinister, parasites which influence the minds and emotions of intelligent creatures to generate more energy for themselves and to weaken the creatures in question until they die. Such *thansaelasavi* cannot directly kill the soul, as could the Maelkodan or Great Wolves, but if someone dies when they are nearby, they can consume the released essence."

"Well, that last description sounds pretty much like our friend in the cabin, doesn't it?"

"If only it were so simple. A number of demons could, and would, operate in the same fashion. Similarly, so could a *ryunihav*. Each, unfortunately, implies differing means of dealing with it, and far different threats for the investigator."

"This thing comes out at night, or so it seems. Why don't you come out with me? There isn't much on Earth that could mess with you."

Verne considered. "What you say is true, certainly. But by the same token, such things will tend to conceal themselves if I am present. In this case, even if what you are dealing with is a demon of considerable comparative power, I am sufficiently formidable that you would find yourself in the position of a hunter trying to catch a rabbit while a tiger is prowling nearby."

That did make sense. "You can't hide yourself from them?"

He shrugged skeptically, finishing his glass as he mulled the question. "In truth, I do not know. If I knew for a fact what was there, yes, probably. But without clear knowledge, I would have to be something more like a wolf to be able to conceal my nature from all such presences. I am afraid, Jason, that you and, possibly, Sylvia will have to visit this place without my direct participation."

I sighed. "It's never simple. I guess we'd better go over all the details. If I'm going to figure out what ancient horror from beyond time is awakening in the Adirondacks, I'd better have a good Field Guide to Horrors available."

CHAPTER 78

And Then There Was One

The cabin loomed before us like a sleeping volcano. Despite the bright sunlight streaming down through gaps in the overhead foliage, the area around the cabin seemed darker. The sounds we'd heard surrounding us in the woods during the walk up the hill to the cabin—scuttling chipmunks in the brush, birds, the *tap-scuff-tap-tap* of deer moving cautiously through the woods just out of sight, the drone and buzz of insects—were almost totally absent, only coming to us faintly from some considerable distance.

Syl swallowed hard. "I don't think you need my intuition." Her voice sounded unnaturally loud in the silence.

I shook my head. "There's *something* in there, that's for damn sure. Finding out *what*, now, that might take a while."

"No simple tests for this case," Syl agreed, staring at the cabin and showing not the slightest indication of wanting to move closer. "Can we deal with something like that?"

I shrugged and started forward. "Verne seemed to think so. He said that even though the world seems to be 'Awakening,' as he put it, it's a long way from reaching high power levels for quite a while yet. He also said something about the 'mark' on me that he thought might have some effect." I turned back. "You have it?"

She blinked, then shook her head. "Sorry, Jasie. I have to focus a bit. Here. Remade with everything I could put into it."

I took the crystal hammer charm, a carved model of one version of Mjölnir—Thor's hammer—which Syl had given to me shortly before a vampire almost ripped out my throat. Even then Syl had been "for real"; the charm had made Elias Klein back off just long enough.

Now, after studying under Verne, she was beginning to understand, not just the fragments of true magic which had managed
to survive or be rediscovered in the time since it had been mostly
sealed away, but the real basis of enchantment and the powers
of the mind. She had taken the charm back and put everything
she could into it. *I don't have much sensitivity to those kinds
of things*—Verne had said, with an apologetic smile, that I was
as pure a mundane in that sense as he'd ever seen—but even I
could feel a difference as I put the charm back on, as though
the clearing had become just a little lighter. "Thanks, Syl. You
coming in?"

She nodded. "I just don't understand why I'm having so much
trouble. We haven't even *seen* anything yet."

"Dunno. Maybe after soaking in all the mystic woo-woo from
studying you've gotten too sensitive. Or maybe it's just that right
now we haven't any idea what we're looking at; all the other
times, we did, and something we don't know is usually scarier."

The cabin door creaked atmospherically as we entered. Inside,
the light was dimmer, and it felt as though the ceiling was low
enough to bump my head on, even though a glance upward
assured me it was at least two feet over my head. "Mr. Plunkett's
grandad built 'em big." I sniffed; a faint, sharp smell reached my
nostrils, the echo of something far stronger. "Gunpowder. Long
time ago, but I guess the smell lingers in a closed room." I stepped
forward, felt something move, looked down. Little metal balls,
mostly black in color. I picked one up, rubbed it hard against
my jeans; it sparkled like a mirror. "Silver shot. He really meant
it when he said no one had cleaned up."

I glanced around, remembering the diagram Dave had given
me. "Okay, that's the master bedroom there. Don't move, Syl. I
want to check some things."

I studied the floor carefully. A lot of evidence had been
disturbed—several people had been here since the night the
whole family was chased out—but I didn't need any more tracks
marking things up. Lots of pellets once you got outside of the
main traffic path. I went into the main bedroom, studied the
doorway. The sides were chewed up pretty badly in a pattern that
confirmed Dave's story: he had unloaded three blasts from his
shotgun right at the doorway. Some of it had hit the doorframe,
of course; shotgun blasts spread, and if he was firing from the

bed...yeah, it could easily spread that much, depending on how it was choked. Still, most of the shot would go through the door and end up on the wall opposite.

Better get some pictures. I got out the digital camera—twin to the one Bambi Inochi had been using, which had been my fee for services rendered. Standing near the bed, I sighted through the door. "Syl," I said, "go stand against the wall there. No, a little over...over...stop."

That put Syl just about in the path of Dave's fire pattern. "Okay, you can move out," I said, and then took several carefully focused digital shots of the wall and surrounding area. I wasn't sure, but I thought I was seeing something. "You getting anything?"

Syl's normally cheerful blue eyes were haunted; her black hair seemed duller. "Too much. There's fear...loss...loneliness...fury, hatred..." she closed her eyes. "Feels like a revenant, a ghost."

"What Verne calls a *ryunihav*."

"Possibly. Verne says true ghosts, in the sense of a living being's spirit refusing to either dissipate or "go on" to some other place, are vanishingly rare—though not impossible. What's much more common are mystical echoes of the presence of a powerful person or soul, accumulations of their essence that take on a circumscribed life of their own. That's a *ryunihav*. With the increase in magic, such "echoes" would start to replay again."

"So it's like a CD on repeat, and someone just turned the power back on?"

"Except that these things can take actions, sometimes dangerous ones. But they're usually not capable of reason. You have to banish or neutralize them."

"Well, that's good. Can we try that and see if it works?"

Syl shook her head. "I have a bad feeling about that idea. I have to do the ritual while it's present; if it's stronger than I think, the ritual could backfire on me, and if it's *not* a *ryunihav*, the focus I have on the ritual could leave me open to attack from whatever it really is."

I don't argue with Syl's "bad feelings." Even before I knew there were such things as real monsters and magic, she'd convinced me that she had *something*, and she'd only gotten better at it. "I don't suppose you can 'feeling' your way to telling me which way to go on this?"

She shook her head again, looking apologetic. "According to Verne, a lot of what I'm doing is precognition. Sensing the future. With the werewolves, I wasn't sensing *them*, because that's almost impossible; I sense what's going to *happen* in a few seconds, and I know it's bad. But future sensing is *hard*. Even as old as he is, Verne's known of very few people who could do it *reliably*—maybe ten or twenty in his whole life—and none of them really *saw* the future. Raiakafan's the only other living person he knows with that power.

"So I might get a good feeling or bad feeling about some approach to something, but that's about it. And from what's happened before, I think it really doesn't work all-out unless someone I care about is in danger."

I nodded. That fit with the way things had worked before. "Okay. Then let's finish checking out the cabin before the sun starts getting low. I want to get back to the hotel and figure out my approach *before* I get caught in this cabin after dark."

She nodded and we got to work. Time passed, and the light was slanting a lot lower by the time we headed back to the hotel.

"Now *that* is interesting," I said a while later.

Syl came and looked over my shoulder. "What?"

I pointed at the twenty-three-inch flat panel I was using for a display in our hotel room. "That's the pattern of shot that hit the wall when Dave Plunkett tried to blow away the thing in his doorway."

She nodded. "Shot hit the wall. So there wasn't anything there?"

"No, that's what's interesting. Dave is a good shot. I was able to use the pattern of shot that grazed the doorframe to reconstruct his shots pretty clearly. He made a darn close grouping, centered here, here, and here." I poked my finger at three points in the main image. "After picking up some of the shot, I know what kind of load he had in there, and the spread tells me the choke, or lack thereof. He had a cylinder barrel, which means that at fifteen feet the grouping was about seven and a half inches, and about twenty inches on the far side of the common room, where the wall is. Big house. And I personally wouldn't be using number four shot for werewolves, but hey, that's his choice. Does give me a nice number of pellets—around a hundred forty per ounce."

"So you reconstructed the shooting."

"Exactly. Now, look; I'm assuming ideal patterns, which don't exist, but I can come fairly close. When I run it through someone firing three shots at these angles, I get a pattern very close to the one I found at the edge of the doorframe; standing at the bed, he was a little off to the side of the door, so he clipped it a bit. But take a look at the pattern on the far wall." I ran it through several cycles. "Compare that to the real pattern—I've reduced it to the same wall with dots that I get from the sim."

Syl studied it for a minute. "It looks...denser than the real thing. More dots."

"Quite a few more. And I've run it many times. I never got *anything* that low, or even close. But the doorframe proves he really did fire three times, with the same kind of shot. My best guess is that about half of the first load never reached the wall."

"So...some of it did?"

"Yeah. It's not missing a whole load's worth, which is really weird. It means that whatever was standing there wasn't solid enough to stop *all* the shot cold, but *was* solid enough to stop *some* of it. And it *wasn't* there for the second or third shots." I looked at the screen, feeling grim. "That means that this thing can be solid enough to stop bullets. So much for it not being able to be dangerous."

Suddenly, Syl's cell phone began playing a song by U2, causing us both to jump. "Hello? Yes...*what?* Oh, my God! Yes, of course..." she looked at me in shock. "Hold on...Jason, it's Samantha Prince. She says Aurora's back."

I understood the shell-shocked look. Samantha Prince ("Sam" to her friends) had been one of Syl's closest friends in college. Her open personality made her a magnet for everyone with a problem...including a certain girl named Aurora Vanderdecken, who apparently had a *lot* of problems. Samantha had been a friend and confidant to the girl for months...and then Aurora had vanished, no warning, no letters, no trace.

This had happened at the same time Raiakafan had shown up, about a year or so ago. After that much time, even Aurora's family had started to accept that she was gone forever. "Is Sam sure it's her?"

"Very sure. But she's not in great shape, and with her background...Jason, I don't want to leave you alone with this, but..."

I hugged her and took the phone. "Samantha? Jason. I'm glad she's back. Look, Syl thinks you could use some help."

Samantha's voice sounded relieved. "I know this must be an inconvenient time for you...my goodness, with what you're involved in I suppose there *are* no convenient times...still, Syl has always been such a help whenever I've needed her. Aurora isn't making a lot of sense, but she's clear that she doesn't want me to contact too many people. She's insisting that we not even tell the police yet. It's very confusing."

"It's no problem. I'll send Syl down right away." I handed the phone back to Syl.

A few minutes later, having hung up with Sam, she came over to me. "Are you sure you want to handle this without me?"

"Want to? Not exactly, sweetheart, but look, I know how close you and Sam were, and I like her myself."

"Yes, I noticed," she said, trying to sound like her usual lighthearted self.

"Can't blame a guy for looking," I said, grinning. "Anyway, you go help her out. Charter a flight if you need to on this short notice. And if you need anything, well, give Verne or me a call."

"Thank you, Jason...I love you." She hugged me fiercely and we kissed. "Oh no, I didn't drive up here separately! I can't take the Hummer; you need the equipment!"

"Then get a taxi. It's only money. Or better yet..." I pulled out my cell, hit my speed dial.

"Domingo residence, Morgan speaking."

"Morgan! Hey, look, a personal emergency has come up for Syl; she has to go visit some old friends, and we're stuck up here on that investigation. Can you—"

"But of course, sir. I will send a car up immediately."

"I could call a taxi—"

"That would never do, sir. Master Verne would insist."

"Thanks so much, Morgan." I hung up. Syl was packing away her things. "Gonna miss you."

"You just be careful while I'm gone, Mr. Information Man," she said, using one of her old nicknames for me. "I want a home and a husband to come back to." She looked up at me. "It's going to take at least an hour for the car to get here."

I raised an eyebrow. "Something you'd like to do in that time?"

Normally, she'd have countered by playfully withdrawing her implied invitation. Instead, she just said, very softly, "Yes," and came to me.

After she left, I stared out into the darkness that had swallowed up the limousine. That almost overenthusiastic "good-bye" session had told me how much she was worried. She knew that I never left an investigation unfinished. And she couldn't see where this one would end.

"Great," I sighed. "Now *I'm* worried."

CHAPTER 79

Now I Lay Me Down to Sleep . . .

I checked all the connections again. I'd spent the entire day wiring the cabin with a multiplicity of sensors, lights, and other gadgetry, all hooked to a dual redundant set of generators and controlled both from the laptop computer in the master bedroom and from my Lumiere smartphone. I was taking no chances that my preparations would fizzle at the wrong moment, especially now, as the afternoon sunshine was starting to fade. I made sure I had fresh batteries in everything I was carrying, and tucked the Mjölnir charm inside my shirt.

Syl had called around noon, to let me know what I'd already guessed: whatever was going on with Aurora was going to take some time to figure out and I had to deal with this one on my own. Apparently Aurora's problem wasn't exactly "normal" and she needed the aid of Syl's particularly deft touch. Verne and Meta had given me some advice on useful approaches that didn't require the talents of a wizard to pull off. I'd put as much of that advice to good use as I could in designing the pattern of lights and other devices around Dave Plunkett's cabin.

I glanced at the west windows, where the remaining shafts of sunlight were definitely reddening, and went outside to grill a steak. No point in facing some Unknown Horror from Beyond on an empty stomach. I used a combination of spices, including cilantro, red pepper, and paprika, and sesame oil, cider vinegar, and honey, taking my time in the preparation and trying to keep my other senses alert. I wanted to evaluate the process of how this presence, whatever it was, acted. Any little quirk in its behavior might help determine what it was and how I might beat it. Oh, I thought I'd already come up with a weapon or three, but at least some of the possible explanations for the thing made it possible that killing it wouldn't be necessary.

By the time the rub had worked its way in and I was ready to grill, the sun had gone down. I switched on one of the outdoor lights I'd rigged and started grilling. I could already feel a ... *pressure*, was the best way to put it, an oppressive, nondirectional weight that dragged at my spirit. Concentrating on the pleasant, hot smell of the grilling steak made it feel more like a contest—the "weight" tried to force me to ignore pleasant and happy feelings, while my own focus on my pleasures gave a stronger and more palpable sense of direction (if direction was the right word for something that was purely emotional) to this external influence.

As I sat in the brightly lit kitchen, eating my dinner, I figured out what this leaden depressing sensation reminded me of: it was similar to being in a very bad mood and having to go somewhere that you would normally enjoy. If you didn't know this was external, it would feel like depression, or perhaps the lurking tension of a phobia waiting to strike—as though you were afraid of spiders and didn't *see* any, but were sure that there were a few hiding somewhere nearby, ready to stalk delicately out into screaming sight.

So I enjoyed the steak, but not nearly as much as I might have. Even in the lighted room—and the lighting helped, that much I could tell from having to cross back and forth between the kitchen and the darker deck area where the grill was—the damn thing's influence was insidious. I noticed momentary flickers of fear and sadness in my thoughts: worry about Syl and her flight home, feeling I was simply unable to handle this problem, a creeping sensation between my shoulderblades ... Then it faded back, as though either it had given up on trying to overcome my focus, or else it was planning a more opportune moment for its attack.

The "opportune moment" was pretty clearly whenever I went to sleep. The thing's history made that clear. I could stay up all night if I wanted, but truthfully, that wouldn't help me much at all. I needed to confront whatever it was directly and get some grasp of what I was facing.

So, after taking a walk far away from the cabin to let my dinner settle, I went to bed. That bed, however, had a whole range of controls near it. Even though the mysterious force had backed off, it took me a while to fall asleep. When you know there is a malevolent *something* waiting for you to nod off, it's not exactly easy to close your eyes, let alone go to sleep. Given that this thing affects the mind, I was pretty sure it could tell whether I was asleep. It had probably known the very moment that the Plunketts had awakened, but it had always waited for its targets to fall asleep. Unfortunately, I also couldn't use any artificial sleeping assistance; when I woke, I couldn't afford to be sluggish.

I went to bed around nine o'clock. I think I finally managed to drift off to sleep around midnight.

CHAPTER 80

Nightmares on Demand

It was a terrible sleep, filled with indescribable oozing fear, and a slithering feeling of something creeping ever-so-slowly up on me...with the echoing sensation of complete loss and loneliness, not a friend or companion for a thousand miles. I forced my eyes open.

A monstrous black shadow, barely visible against the gloom of the night-shrouded bedroom, loomed above the bed. Blank eyes glowed the gray leaden color of winter, and a shadowy, taloned hand stretched towards my throat. My heart hammered completely out of control, each beat jabbing pain through my chest. I tried to speak, to even scream, but my throat was drier than dust and only a faint, incoherent croak escaped. The thing smiled, that frozen witchlight limning a mouth filled with shark-like teeth, and one talon traced a sharp, ice-cold line down my cheek, screaming images of dismemberment and abandonment through my head. *I can't move!* I thought, my horror rising.

But that was what it *wanted*. It wanted, *needed* the strength of my fear and horror. I was handing it the weapons it needed. I pushed against it, focusing will against fear, forcing my hand to grasp the little cylinder I'd strapped into it. Unfortunately, my arms were caught in the covers; I probably shouldn't have used any covers at all, but mountain cabins without heat aren't amenable to that sort of thing. I concentrated, trying to ignore my fear and the icy claws near my jugular, pulling my hand out one millimeter at a time. The thing's expression flickered, as though it was nonplussed by my ability to act at all, and a tidal wave of terror thundered down on me.

433

That might have been a mistake on its part. I let that terror galvanize my arm into motion rather than immobility, and my hand came fully out from the bedclothes. Pointing my shaking hand as best I could, I squeezed my thumb down on the button.

A blazing line of blue-green fire seared its way across the room as the overpowered laser pointer sent enough concentrated photons streaking outward to set paper across the room on fire. Seeming bright as the sun in the pitch-black room, the laser carved a razor-thin line across the black shadow. The dead eyes doubled in size and I heard an ear-piercing shriek of agony and shock as it literally stumbled back, unable to just vanish as it had when confronted previously. I tried to rise and give pursuit, but my adrenaline-soaked muscles shook and I fell with an undignified *thud* and *clatter* to the floorboards, the equipment hung over me banging the wood and jabbing into me, feeling weak and shaky as a crippled old man. The thing was clearly worse off, though, and it fled out the doorway, fading; the feelings of horror, fear and loss now focused *outside* of me rather than inside. I knew I must be feeling what *it* was feeling now, and I dragged myself to my feet and staggered after it.

I was shaking, sick to my stomach, and trying to push myself as hard as I could. It didn't occur to me until I was going through the doorway that thing could probably sense what I was doing, or at least where I was and what my intent was. So I wasn't at all ready when black claws slashed across my hand.

The impact was...weak. The thing might be able to assume solid form, but it was still more a thing of spirit than flesh. But it wasn't trying to hurt *me*, I realized too late, as the strap holding the pointer in my hand came apart and the second pillow-soft but swift blow knocked the pointer from my hand. I staggered away, trying to find the miniature laser, but the casing was black and totally invisible in the darkness.

Without a weapon to hand, I faced the monster, towering above me in pain-filled rage. I grasped for the smartphone; enough subtlety, it was time to turn on the lights.

There was nothing in the holster. With renewed horror, I realized one of the clattering noises when I fell out of bed had been the phone falling to the floor. And my laptop was...on the other side of this thing.

It gave a soundless roar, a silent bellow filled with screaming terror and hate and doom, sending my pulse skyrocketing. It snarled and smiled again, keeping between me and my equipment, sending another wave of horror and isolation and loss that almost made me faint. My heart staggered, and I realized that the monster meant to kill me with fear alone. *I have to fight this!*

But... it had cut the strap. It had touched me, but it hadn't actually *hurt* me. I had hurt *it*. And there was something... else, something nagging me...

At those thoughts it moved another step towards me, almost immersing me in twisting living darkness, screaming despair and death into me.

Into me.

Now, I could feel it. It was... it was not quite real. Or the *fear* was real, but the *source* was not. It was the difference between burning with fire, and burning from having soaked in ice water, or swallowing habanero puree. The pain is real, but only one of them is really going to *hurt* you.

And I could prove it, by remembering *real* fear. I remembered fighting Elias Klein, a friend turned monster, and how the terror welled *up* from within in cold flaming waves as I tried to outrun him. I remembered the inhuman colonel as he prepared to sacrifice me in the Heart of Eönae, and the pure *knowledge*—not mere sensation, but bone-deep knowledge—that I had failed, that Syl, Verne, and all my friends were dead because of that. I remembered running down a Florida street, duelling a creature that could kill me with a glance.

The external pressure of fear wavered, hesitated for a moment, and I focused once more, this time on the greatest fear of all. I let myself for once feel it fully, as I had for one moment in the hospital almost two years ago. I brought out that memory and made it *real*, the moment when the urbane and ordinary man before me had transformed into a hulking, shaggy nightmare of diamond teeth and claws, with a shrieking roar that shattered glass and left nothing but total terror in its wake, the moment I had first faced the Werewolf King, Virigar.

And in the moment that memory became the truth of terror, the thing in front of me stumbled backward, shredding and coming apart like mist in a wind, screaming its own fear, fleeing that image of horror in my head, leaving behind a trailing sense of loss, abandonment, sadness, and defeat.

I sank, shaking and soaked with sweat, to the cabin floor. Something had happened here. Something that might just tell me what I needed to know.

I didn't feel a sense of triumph, or even of relief. I felt a tragic loss. And that—more than anything—told me I was on the right track.

CHAPTER 81

Secrets of Ancient Days

"You need what?" Verne looked confused. I had driven back to his house the next day, and slept there while waiting for him to wake up in the evening. I had not gotten much sleep in the cabin, even though the thing had made no attempts on me the rest of that night.

"I need to know about Atlantaea. At least a few details."

He nodded, still clearly not understanding what I was looking for. "I will tell you what I can. But you must understand that I have spent countless centuries *not* thinking about it."

"You've forgotten a lot?"

He sighed. "There are...limits on what a mortal mind can keep within itself, Jason, and though I do not die as do normal men, still my mind is very much that of a mortal man. I never forgot certain events, aspects of the world that were important to me, but as half a million years passed, I had to make choices of what I would keep. The *soul* never forgets, true, but accessing that memory once it is lost from the immediacy of the mind requires, at the least, that the right set of ideas or reminders trigger the recall.

"So, I will try to answer your questions, but understand that I may have no answers."

"Okay." I thought a moment, getting my questions in order. "Your descriptions of Atlantaea were always pretty vague—mainly I guess because you were talking about events that happened, not giving me a virtual travelogue. I've gotten the impression of some kind of, well, shining city of fantasy crossed with super-tech, skyscrapers and aircars and all that, with these Seven Towers surrounding it like a wall. But other things you've said make me wonder—I mean, it couldn't have been just one city."

He laughed. "Ahhh, no, certainly not, my friend. And I apologize for giving you such a, well, clichéd and inaccurate picture. And yet...it is not entirely inaccurate, in its way. The...the impression, the spirit—that is accurate. It *was* a 'shining city,' Jason, the City of the Seven Towers, and indeed that was how many would have represented it, as a city with Seven Towers defending it. But that representation would be no more accurate than picturing, oh, the United States as being the city of Washington flanked by a giant Eagle and the Statue of Liberty."

"So Atlantaea was like Earth today—lots and lots of cities all over the planet—and the city you are talking about was more like the capital?"

He considered that. "Not...exactly. The city that many called simply Atlantaea was the founding location of the government from which the rest of the civilization grew. It was more than the capital, it was the very heart of our culture. There were other cities, other outposts; for example, one around each of the Seven Towers, which were themselves spaced around the Earth in a mystically, but not geometrically, symmetrical pattern. But because Eönae was our patron from the beginning, and because we did not grow from multiple opposed, advanced civilizations, as you have and still are today, we did not spread so randomly and completely over the globe. Many areas were still very wild, even at the height of Atlantaea's power."

"So...you never reached the population we have now." So far, this was actually fitting together better than I thought.

"On the contrary, the civilization of Atlantaea had more citizens than you could grasp, Jason. Because we did not limit ourselves to this world." He gave a soft laugh at my expression. "In a hundred thousand years, Jason, can you imagine that human beings would not have spread out? If they were not to overrun this world, then naturally there was only one way to go. Outward, to the stars."

"Whoa." I had to assimilate this. I realized I was guilty of making the wrong kind of assumptions again. I associated magic, gods, and so on with faux-medieval material; Verne was talking about something far beyond that. "How big *was* Atlantaea, then?"

He gestured upward. "Step outside, and gaze upward, Jason,

and realize that all of the stars you see were once part of the Atlantaean...Empire, I suppose. All of them. At the end, Atlantaea held sway over essentially the entirety of the Galaxy, and was poised to sweep outward to others of those island universes."

"Urk. Okay, I'd better leave *that* for later. So, your *Earthly* population never reached our level, then."

"Oh, certainly not. I believe Earth stabilized at something short of a billion people, of which over one hundred million lived in the capital city."

Biiig city. "What about this area? What was here back then?"

He raised an eyebrow. "I see where you are going, I think. Unfortunately...I cannot be certain. The geography has changed considerably, both due to unnatural and natural forces, since that time. Off to the east, on or near Cape Cod, was one of the Towers, so it was not an entirely deserted area, but this far out...I suppose it would have been something like an isolated suburb. The Towers, due to their nature, attracted many wizards, priests, alchemists, and so on to their general neighborhood, and many such would live relatively nearby; with flight or teleportation capability usually available, 'nearby' could have a very broad interpretation. If you are asking if someone of that civilization might have lived at the site of your friend's cabin, I would say it is entirely possible—even probable, since you have come here asking the question."

"Good. Then, assuming that what I think is right..." I sketched out a plan of attack. "I'm not a magician, but would this work as I've planned it, or do I need someone like Syl to activate it?"

"Normally...yes, but in this case, I think your knowledge and technology can carry the day. And the creature is, after all, aware you are far from ordinary. This will lend a certain mystical force to your actions against it."

"Come again? I thought you said I was a mundane?"

He smiled. "And you are, Jason, but there is no human being—no living intelligent being, in fact—who is so mundane as to have absolutely no connection to the mystical. Life and thought and souls are mystical in the very essence of what they are, and because of that there is some real magic in us all. Magic depends on belief, symbolism, and knowledge. The symbolism inherent in you—in what you have achieved previously, in your dedication to your work, in your courage in facing and defeating this creature already—these will give a not inconsiderable reinforcement to your actions as you have outlined them. Not a spell, as such, but... call it sympathetic magic. If the target believes in magic, and is affected by it—and all such beings as this must be fall into that category—it will, by believing, invest some of its own power into your countermeasures."

"So, I'm basically hitting it with psychological warfare that it's going to make real?"

"Well put." He grew serious again. "But it is not without risk, this plan of yours. Even if you are right, the creature may not be able to control itself long enough. If you are wrong, the creature will attempt to use the weaknesses of your approach against you—and it will do so now with full knowledge of what you can do, and why."

"Not the first time I've been betting on a throw of the dice. But I'd appreciate it if you can hang out close by—as close as you think you can get without blowing your cover."

The black-haired, immaculate head gave an assenting nod. "But of course, Jason. Tomorrow night?"

I nodded myself. "No point in giving it any more time to prep. Tomorrow night we finish this, one way or another."

"Very good." Verne gave a sharp-toothed smile. "But you need do no preparations tonight. Let us relax. I can tell you are not entirely recovered from your ordeal."

"I can go for that," I said with a grin. At least *this* threat wasn't going to be ambushing me. I was going to ambush *it*.

CHAPTER 82

Truth and Dare

Nighttime again. This time, I was sleeping in a sleeping bag on the (no longer pellet-covered) living room floor. Well, more accurately, I was *trying* to sleep. I knew the thing would have to try again; whether my main guess was right or not, it could not afford to lose now that it had started. A ghost would have no choice at all, at least not the automated-recording type. A demon . . . from everything Verne had told us about them, they were ruled by pride more than anything else, and my being able to chase it away and then come back would be more than it could bear. And a *thansaelasavi* . . .

The pieces were all there, even if there was hardly a single shred of evidence I could hold in my hand. But in this particular game, emotions were really the key. I now knew the thing did *not* live on fear alone. It had fled when I offered up a dish of the real thing that wasn't focused on it directly. It had been *scared* by what it saw. Instead of grabbing that image to use it, the creature had been terrified by the Werewolf King.

Fear was what the creature *projected*—maybe because that was a strong emotion easily roused in people who didn't know what was going on—but the emotions I really kept feeling from it, that were an undertone in everything it sent, were very different. Negative emotions, yes, but ones with a common theme indeed.

Of course, that could be a demonic trap . . . or the undertone of a repeating *ryunihav*. But I didn't think so.

Not most of the time anyway. Right now, in the silent twilight of the cabin's main room, I was strongly tempted to beat feet down the mountain and drag Verne back with me.

441

The thought seemed to trigger the event. My cell phone rang, causing me to jump in the semidarkness. I pulled the little gadget out. "Hello?"

"Jason. I must warn you; after our conversation last night, I have done some considerable thinking, trying to reawaken memories that would be relevant, and one just surfaced—one that I find extremely worrisome."

Great, just what I need, more worry. "What is it, Verne?"

"I have mentioned that the Seven Towers protected Atlantaea. It may have occurred to you to wonder, then, how it was that the demons could invade at all." His voice was sad rather than grim. "There was no simple way through the wards the Towers made, and no power that even Kerlamion wielded could have broken those wards swiftly enough to have prevented a truly massive mobilization of our forces—more than enough to have prevented the near-total victory that he instead achieved.

"As those few of us who survived learned later, they had managed—through what maneuverings we could not determine—to recruit one of our own to their aid; at this point the details are not important. For your purposes tonight you need only know this: first, that he was the one who created the vampires of Elias Klein's type, and is therefore likely one of the ones behind his appearance and possibly one of those assisting Mr. Carruthers' group. And secondly, that one of his principal research locations in the old days—his summer home, one might say—was some-where in this region."

Now *that* was a very unpleasant thought. "He's still alive?"

"*Alive* may be an inaccurate term. He is still functioning and active, yes."

"Damn. I thought you and, I guess, Raiakafan were the only survivors."

He gave a slight chortle. "Close. Besides myself and my son's family—who are themselves a puzzle, as you know—there are to my knowledge only three other survivors of Atlantaea itself, with perhaps one other who is not and has not been on Earth since the cataclysm. We will discuss this later. I simply wished to warn you that it is possible that we are dealing with something the *thansaelasavi* summoned, created, or bound. And that would be something very bad indeed."

I thought about it. How sure was I of what I had been sensing?

"I'm guessing that demons or things like them could make me feel things that weren't true, right? Well, okay, the fear I'm feeling when the thing attacks isn't true either, but what I mean is could they be letting me sense other feelings that it wasn't really feeling, to fake me out?"

Verne hesitated a moment; I suppose I hadn't asked the question as clearly as I would have liked. But after he untangled it, he replied, "Yes...yes, they could do so."

"Then I guess it comes down to whether or not I can trust my instincts. My gut says it's worth a try. My head's not so sure."

Verne sighed. "Only you can make that judgment, my friend. Your instincts have served you well, yet anyone can be misled under the wrong circumstances."

I stood silently for a few minutes, thinking. The dark sensation of a lurking threat did nothing to encourage me to stay, and there were plenty of reasons I should just bag this one. But...

"Okay. I might be stupid, but I've never walked out on a job yet. More importantly, I'm pretty good at picking out patterns, and the thing I'm up against *wouldn't* know this. So I don't think what I was sensing was fake. I'm staying."

"I truly expected no other decision, Jason," Verne said quietly. "I shall be waiting with all my senses out and ready to respond."

"That does make me feel better. Hopefully, you won't need to do anything. Bye for now."

"Good-bye, Jason."

I put the phone away, took a deep breath, let it out, and lay down again. I tried counting sheep, working out math problems in my head, concentrating on how tired I was. Still that grim, menacing sensation would NOT let me sleep.

Maybe I could force the confrontation. It was worth a shot. The thing must have picked up the language, or at least be able to get the basic sense of what people were saying, if it had such intimate contact with the minds. I stood up.

"All right, I know you're there. And I know for damn sure you know I'm here." I made myself relax, leaned casually against one wall. "You lost last night's matchup. So what are you doing now? Trying to make me *not* go to sleep, because you don't want to try it again?"

The atmosphere of the room suddenly thickened; it was fear-laden, but with an undertone of fury and desperation. The fear pressed in on me, but it wasn't nearly as bad as last night; for one thing, I was fully awake and it hadn't had the chance to worm its way into my dreams tonight.

"Oh, yeah, like *that* is going to work," I said with a sneer. "Whatever you are, you *know* you don't have what it takes to scare me for real, not if you don't catch me when I'm sleeping. And I don't have to sleep. I can stay up all night and sleep during the day." I pushed away from the wall. "Or... if you want to have another go at me... you can stop being so stupidly obvious and go away for a while. I'm not going to sleep while you're trying to creep me out, but if you take off for the next hour or so, I'll bet I could manage a nap. Then you go for it. What do you say?"

For the briefest moment, I sensed a new emotion; confusion, followed by a flash of angry agreement mixed with challenge. And then the room seemed to brighten, although there wasn't a light on anywhere in the cabin. I opened the window a crack and breathed in the calmness of the night air. I even heard crickets starting to chirp near the cabin.

It had taken the dare. Okay, that meant it *probably* wasn't a *ryunihav*; according to Verne, most of them weren't that flexible. Definitely didn't rule out demon—in fact, that last flicker of arrogant confidence pointed more in the demonic direction than anything.

Still, we'd established a form of communication and reached an accord, even if it was only the equivalent of a temporary cease-fire. Good enough, though. I would be able to sleep now and if I lived through the hour or so after that, Dave Plunkett just might get his cabin back.

If I didn't, well, there were worse places to be buried. I slid into the sleeping bag, closed my eyes, and slowly started drifting off to sleep. I wondered if it would wait for me to go under, or jump the gun...

CHAPTER 83

Rage and Loss

Black acid fire raining down on me as I fled through streets filled with werewolves and monsters. I gave a croaking scream and lunged upward, feeling tentacles coiling tighter, dragging me down ...

No, wait, that was the sleeping bag. I rolled onto my back, started to wiggle out, and suddenly the darkness coalesced into that monstrous bipedal void, grabbing the bag, *lifting* it off the ground. I felt a spurt of genuine, not-generated-from-outside, fear at that; I had never thought it could manage that level of strength.

Possibly it couldn't yet, not for long, because in that same moment I was dropped to the floor with a heavy thud. I shoved my way out of the bag as it slashed at me. This time it actually drew blood, the rake of almost-invisible talons cutting like thorns of ice, injecting terror with the cuts.

Despite the muzziness of sleep and its hold on my dreams, I found I could act. My body was shaky and uncertain, and I sure as hell wouldn't want to try moving around an obstacle course, but I wasn't nearly frozen like last night. I glanced around in the gloom, then pulled the goggles around my neck over my eyes.

Ah, there, light without light. Image intensification with a little NIR illumination made the room bright as day for me. Possibly, depending on how the thing itself "saw," it might be seeing a little light of some kind coming from me, but very little. Damn, damn, damn. Its unexpected maneuver had moved me significantly and it was circling. I had to get it to the right spot before I could act. And if it could sense that, I might never get it there. I had to concentrate on keeping it distracted, off-balance and angry.

"Still . . . can't quite . . . ring the bell, Mr. Shadow," I said, trying to keep the quiver from my voice. "I've gotten worse cuts from rosebushes. I thought for a minute you might actually have something, but all you managed was to cut up my sleeping bag. That the best you have?"

It gave a soundless snarl and took a step towards me. I pulled out my laser pointer. It began to shrink back, then halted as I tossed the little cylinder away. "I don't think I need that," I said. "In fact, you've already beaten yourself, don't you know? Whatever you thought you'd get from people visiting here, it's pretty much over. Once I leave, no one's coming. Ever."

It dissolved, became a black shrieking whirlwind around me with a thousand tiny mouths and eyes, gnashing and mouthing and trying to tear at me but succeeding only in making a few more scratches. I felt desperation echoing from it. "You screwed up. You can't get what you want from animals, can you? They don't have enough . . . life force, will, whatever, for you to work on. They run away, they have no real tie to the land. And you're stuck here. You can't leave, or you won't. So you've driven away the people who used to come here, and pretty soon no one will come here anymore." I checked, took two steps back. The whirlwind parted as I was about to touch it, rematerialized as the claw-handed horror. It was bombarding me with fear now, and part of me—the instinctive part—responded, screaming at me to hide or run. But my mind was still in control. My voice might be ready to dry up or crack, but I was still thinking. "You've lost it all. You can't even scare me anymore. It's *over.*"

The scream in my head was louder, but this time, it was mixed with a wail of despair, confusion and bone-deep sorrow. To my surprise it broke suddenly. I had expected it to continue its assault in desperate denial, hopefully into the trap I'd set. Instead it fled, running from words and thoughts that were too much for it. I gave chase, for this time it hadn't evaporated into empty gloom, but was fleeing as some sort of almost-defined blackness, flying through the rooms as though searching for something. It screamed as it flew, a keening wail of horror and loneliness and abandonment that kept the gooseflesh crawling on my skin even as I pelted after it in the fastest sprint I could manage.

It burst out into the night, circling the cabin, flitting from the edge of the little stream to the well to the cabin and . . . no, not screaming, *crying.* Crying like an abandoned child for a mother that never came, a child in the middle of a dusty, empty house where no voice ever answered back, where no hands came to pick it up and comfort it, no warmth would return to chase away the fear and let it know everything was all right. Nothing would ever be all right, for there was nothing left in the world that cared, nothing that *could* care, because it had been calling, calling, calling, through ages of mankind, and never had anyone or anything answered.

I felt tears start from my eyes and I stopped chasing, panting and feeling a stitch in my side. "I'm answering. Stop it."

With the sudden volatility of that crying child, it whipped around, lunged at me with a shriek of hatred and denial. A concussion of force threw me backward. I could sense, somehow, the pain inside the creature, the injury it was doing to itself, but it no longer cared. It would kill itself in its effort to silence me, and maybe then the pain would end. Sharp-edged rocks and sticks swirled around me in a bladed hurricane, cutting my hands and jabbing into my body, as I covered my face to keep from losing my eyes. Another silent cry of forceful rage lifted me from the ground, hurled me into the stream, and tried to push my face into the water. I clawed at the insubstantial hands on my neck, but there was nothing to touch, just disembodied force shoving me underwater.

But for all its ability to produce momentary force, it wasn't *that* strong. I got my hands under me and *shoved.* It hurt my neck, but I was up on all fours, face out of the water, breathing in fast, frightened gasps. It let go, and I staggered to my feet. I sensed more tearing agony, another terrible self-wounding effort, and heard bone-cracking splintery sounds. With real horror, I saw it had broken thick old pine-branches to jagged-ended spears.

This was officially going too far. Time to call Verne. I reached down and found that my cell phone was dripping water and the screen looked cracked. I tried the phone anyway, dodging the first spear, which embedded itself in the cabin wall. The phone didn't even power up. I wrenched the cabin door open and lunged inside, the second wooden missile ripping along my side, leaving a ragged, bleeding wound. Well, at least I knew it was mad enough to come after me...

Come after it did, like a screaming typhoon packed into a

three-foot sphere of destruction. It was using everything it had to come after me in a truly awe-inspiring tantrum, shredding itself apart like a hurricane coming onto land; it would not survive the experience, but that was no comfort to the poor bastards in its path. It blew the door off its hinges in a shower of splinters, echoing agony from within that was like my own torn side, like ripping out your own heart, but it didn't seem to care. Maybe, down inside, it had finally come to some dim understanding of what had really happened all those ages ago, and death seemed far the better option.

I staggered across the living room, diving for the laptop on the far table. Like my phone, it had all the contingencies loaded; I'd just never expected to have to *use* it this way. The thing flowed across the room, slower now because it was dragging a shard of wood six feet long, but edged like a sword, raising it up to hurl at me with unstoppable strength and undodgeable accuracy in the limited space.

Now!

It sensed my shift in mood just one split second too late, as the trap activated. Blazing like the sun in that pitch-black room, an array of emerald lines of pure light leapt into existence, a seven-pointed star that surrounded the creature in an impassable wall of brilliance. The wooden missile dropped harmlessly to the floor. I felt the thing's influence fade instantly. Potent stuff, that psychological sympathetic magic, especially when the subject was magical.

It screamed silently in loss and fury, spinning like a trapped whirlwind inside the five-foot space at the center of the seven-sided mystical prison, and then hurled itself at the edges, cutting into itself deeply before retreating. I realized that it would kill itself trying to get to me. I took a deep breath and bellowed, *"Hoch'ita!"*

It froze in shock and confusion. Roughly, according to Verne, that word meant "Stop that IMMEDIATELY!" but it carried with it a sense of ancient authority which was never used casually; a King would use it, a general, a powerful wizard, and always it would be an order to be obeyed without question or hesitation. He'd made me practice it for fifteen minutes before he'd been satisfied I'd say it right the first time, and he'd tested me for the next few hours at impromptu moments.

I'd hoped—at least for the moment, correctly—that the combination of the phrase itself, and the fact that it was certainly the first Atlantaean the thing had heard/sensed in the last half-million years, would make it stop.

"I'm sorry," I said quietly.

It tried to gather itself to scream fear and hate at me again, but then collapsed into itself, aware of its own injuries and, with my honest expression of sympathy and regret, unable to continue its berserk frenzy. It was no longer a towering mass of shadows and terror the height of the ceiling. It was shorter than I was now, coiling and writhing in shuddering pain and sorrow.

"Maybe I shouldn't have been as hard on you as I was. But I couldn't be sure—until now—what you were really like. You didn't really *want* to hurt anyone, did you?"

For a moment, it tried to puff itself back up, like a little boy being scolded and trying to pretend that he didn't care. Then it sagged down, even smaller than before, and I felt a tiny thread of sorrow and repentance.

"Fear's just a lot easier to bring out... when that's what's inside you, isn't it?"

It swirled more tightly into a ball, no more than three feet across.

"It wasn't your fault."

Now it raged at me, hammering against the insubstantial walls of light and screaming its self-hatred in crying, hysterical waves of horror and blame that made my eyes sting again with more tears. My *God,* what this poor thing had gone through. It was a wonder it was even capable of this much communication.

"No, it *wasn't.* The demons sealed off magic, you poor bastard! It cut off your master's power, turned you into a faint echo of yourself. There wasn't a damn thing you could have done to help him—or her—and there wasn't anything they could have done to help you. Your master and partner died... and you've been stuck here ever since, no magic to release you, because that death happened *after* magic faded. There was no release, just a binding. You've been here, waiting, for half a million years, as the glaciers came down and ran back, as we rose back from barbarism and spread back over the land, waiting and crying for someone to come that could never come back." I felt the tears that it couldn't actually cry beginning to break forth from it, into me, heard the edge of a sob in my own voice.

"But you aren't alone anymore. You don't have to die. You don't have to scare people just to live. There are still things that endure, things that haven't gone."

It moaned, a cry of abandonment and tragedy, unable to believe that anything had lived from its past, when its...master? Partner? had gone to nothing. I touched one of the controls, then another. The glowing cage faded out. It glanced around in startlement. I spoke to the air around us. "Come in."

Verne Domingo coalesced from the night. The creature shrank back for a moment, but then Verne, who seemed to have instantly understood the situation, simply knelt and held out his arms, saying something low and soft in that ancient language. I heard the words "Eönae" and "*thansaelasavi*," and others, in the tone of a father to a frightened child.

It moved forward, tentatively, radiating disbelief, fear and hope. The undefined monstrous aspect wavered, began to melt away. There was still a shadowy shape, but it neither towered nor threatened. It was exhausted, wounded almost to death by its own efforts, taking hesitant, halting steps forward towards the ancient priest. With a sudden rush, it scuttled into Verne's arms, curling into a tight little ball and now sobbing audibly with a sound like a crying steamkettle, a solid tiny dragon of polished darkness, wounded in a dozen places and bleeding wisps of shadow. "It's all right now," Verne said very quietly. "It will be all right."

I sagged back with a sigh of relief, only then realizing that my entire left side was totally soaked in blood and hurt like hell. "I think...I'm going to need a little loving care myself," I said. Then the darkness closed in on me, pushing me down, down...

CHAPTER 84

Consequences of Hope

I woke up, staring at pastel walls and hearing all-too-familiar beeping sounds. Glancing over, I saw a very familiar head of night-black hair bent over, sleeping in a nearby chair. "Hey, sweetheart," I said, feeling only minimal roughness in my throat.

Syl jolted awake and stood, smiling but with traces of tears in the redness around her eyes. "Hey yourself, Jasie." She hugged me gingerly; even that stung my side, where I suspected I'd have a hell of a scar. "I thought I told you to be careful!"

"You said you wanted a husband and a home to come back to. We're still here."

She smiled faintly. "Well, yes, but I was hoping to have them both at the same time."

I shrugged, which also hurt. "I'll admit that I could do without the regular visits to the hospital, but it beats the alternative." Looking around more carefully, I noticed the room didn't look quite standard. In fact . . . "Um, where exactly *am* I?"

"You are in one room in my home, Jason," Verne's deep voice replied. Dressed in his usual immaculate outfit, he had materialized in the doorway. "We have reason—more than ever, in these days—to keep considerable medical equipment on hand, and your wounds, while certainly significant, were easily treatable by someone with general medical knowledge. So I brought you here."

"And what about . . ."

"You were correct, of course, Jason. It was indeed a *thansaelasavi*, specifically a familiar of a wizard who lived mostly at night and whose magics dealt with light, shadow, darkness, and so on, as well as emotion. I suspect I may have met her—for it

451

was a woman, that much I was able to draw out—once, perhaps at some party or event at the castle. Such wizards were much in demand for such events. Entertainment specialists, you might say."

"Where is it?"

"He, Jason. His name is Arischadel, or Aris for short."

"Okay, where is Arischadel?"

Verne frowned slightly. "Aris is bound where he is. I do not know if I could release him, even if he wanted to be released, but he has spent a near-eternity protecting that spot, as you guessed, like a faithful dog at the grave of his master, perhaps waiting for master to awaken. That has, in turn, bound him ever more tightly to the location. Magic has a way of reinforcing what is being done, of extending and strengthening what already is. He is now more than a familiar spirit, in a way; he is a part of the land in that small area."

"Hmm. Is he going to be okay? I mean, I know he put me here, but I was feeling a lot of what the poor thing was feeling. He was scared and angry and not thinking at all. I got the impression of a kid, even if he is as old as you are."

"Many *thansaelasavi* are mentally children. They are not unintelligent, but are relatively simple, not complex beings." Verne smiled. "Yes, he will be all right. It took much time for me to truly reach him and make him understand, but the strength of Eönae healed and strengthened him. She has accepted his guardianship of that little part of the world, given him a sort of purpose."

"But he's stuck there?" I thought for a moment. "And he's really lonely. And has been for a really, really long time. I wonder..." I had an idea. I asked a few more questions and nodded. First I had to get out of here and talk to Arischadel, but if he was the way I thought...

CHAPTER 85

Happy Endings

"You said you'd solved the problem, so why are you coming up here with us?" Dave Plunkett said curiously.

"Because I said I'd solved the problem, not gotten rid of the cause. I'm going to leave it up to you as to whether you want to deal with what's left. If not, I'm willing to buy the camp off of you."

Dave and the rest of his family glanced apprehensively at me as we continued hiking up the trail towards the cabin. "You mean ... *it* is still there?" Lizzie asked nervously.

"Yes and no," I answered. "You were right, there was something there, and it scared you, but it wasn't what it appeared to be."

I'd thought for a while about how to approach this. I couldn't— for a number of reasons—tell them the whole truth, but I also couldn't just gloss the whole thing over and ignore it. Telling them the truth in general terms would probably be safe, especially if I took certain precautions.

"Basically, you already knew there are stranger things in the world than we used to believe," I said. "Werewolves and such. And then you had your own experience. Well, I'm sure you realize that the strange stuff didn't just come into existence last year. There's been this kind of thing hidden behind the metaphorical curtains for time out of mind.

"We don't know why, but it's become pretty clear that the weird stuff has become a lot more active lately. Anyway, it turns out that your cabin sits on the same area that someone—call it a wizard—used to live. And when that wizard died, her pet spirit, a 'familiar,' you might say, refused to leave. Maybe he didn't really understand death, or just wasn't going to leave his master. Anyway, he's been waiting, and alone, for a really long time, and forgot about working and living with people."

"You're saying it's been there all along?"

"Since long before you guys bought the land. Don't know how long, really. In any case, the thing is that this creature is really mostly spirit. It gets strength from other people living around it, especially from strong emotions directed at it. And in its state, it was easiest to raise the emotion of fear."

Dave frowned. "So . . . it was scaring us so that it could eat?"

"In a way, yeah." The cabin rose up before us in the sunshine. Chipmunks scattered at our approach, as did a couple of birds. The forest was full of the sound of the native animals getting ready for the fall of night. "And probably, like any kid or animal, acting out of its own fear and territorial protection. The more aware it got, the less it understood of what was going on, and that scared it."

Jenny shook her head. "I don't want to go back in there if it's going to be playing those games again. Even if it won't hurt us directly, that's just too much."

"I wouldn't expect you to," I said.

"Hey, the door's trashed!"

"Sorry. Like I said earlier, it wasn't an easy job. Worthwhile, but not easy." I stopped near the entrance. "I said it can get stronger from emotions directed at it. Those emotions don't have to be—and really *shouldn't* be—fear. You don't think a wizard wants to be afraid of their familiar, do you?

"Your resident spirit has a name. He's called Arischadel. I don't know if it would work for you . . . but what he really needs is people who will enjoy having him around. In return, he can do little things for you."

Lizzie looked up suddenly. "Like . . . like the house elves in some stories I read when I was a kid? You'd leave them cookies or something and they'd clean up the house?"

I laughed. "Something like that, but probably not as immediately useful. I think you kids—and adults—will still have to do the dishes, so to speak. But he'd like to play, I bet."

Lizzie shivered suddenly, remembering. "I dunno if I could play with that."

"I wouldn't blame you," I said, remembering my own unpleasant nights in that cabin. "But what you remember isn't what he is."

"*What's that?*" Mitch asked suddenly, pointing.

I glanced up. "That," I said, "is Arischadel."

Around the corner of the chimney, a little narrow black head was looking, with smoky-crystal eyes. It peered nervously out at the group of us, visible in the darkening twilight because of the faint light in the eyes and a slight luminous edging to the shadowed body. When no one made a move—the Plunketts were all staring—Aris edged hesitantly out from behind the chimney. He was a perfect little dragon, about two feet from nose to tip of tail, glittering crystalline scales making him look like a sculpture in dark quartz, huge eyes blinking uncertainly in what was, to him, the brilliant light, batlike wings twitching with caution.

It was Lizzie who spoke first. "Oh my God, he's so *cute!*" she said.

Aris gave a questioning burble, a sort of trilling whistle.

"Are you really the same thing that scared me in my bedroom? You can't be!" Lizzie started forward.

Dave stretched out a hand. "Hold on..."

I shook my head. "It's okay. I guarantee it. She's doing exactly right. She likes dragons, I take it?"

Jenny gave a strained laugh. "Her room is almost completely wallpapered with them. When she was a baby, she had a stuffed dragon that went with her everywhere."

Mitch was following Lizzie, staring raptly at Aris.

Aris scuttled in half-eager, half-fearful steps to the edge of the roof, looking down at Lizzie. I could just sense the emotions he was radiating, hope but fear at the same time, fear that this would end the same way, that there would be a moment of caring and then total loss.

Lizzie seemed to feel it too. "No, no, it's okay. Really. I'm not mad at you now."

Dave and Jenny tensed as the tiny dragon of shadow plucked up courage and dropped down towards their daughter. I couldn't blame them; small it might be on a relative scale, but it still had sharp-looking teeth and claws.

But it curled up into the girl's arms like a satisfied kitten and radiated such incredulous contentment when those arms hugged back that even Dave broke into a broad smile. "So that's it?"

"In a way. You guys have to promise to come here regularly. Aris needs people. But the right *kind* of people, which you are, but not everyone is. You might have to come here more often than you used to. He's stuck here, so he can't come back with you. Maybe one day he will be able to move around, but there's no telling if that will ever happen."

Dave and Jenny looked around at the settling evening. The threat was gone from the darkness; it was a calm and untroubled evening in the Adirondack woods. "Can you guarantee it won't... go back to what it was?"

I nodded firmly. "You're talking about a being so loyal, it hasn't left in over... well, lots and lots of years. If you choose to be his friends and, I suppose, new masters and companions, he'll stay by your side—as much as he can—forever. I know it's weird and scary in some ways, but you guys also seem to be the kind of people who can handle things pretty well. Hell, you came back and faced him a second time, which is more than most people would be able to manage."

Dave nodded slowly. "How... where'd you learn all this, about him?"

"Like they say on TV, there's things you don't want to know. It's up to you what you do. I'll buy the camp if you don't feel it's something you can handle."

Mitch had cautiously extended his hand, which Aris had nuzzled.

"Well..." Dave rubbed his beard, staring at the little creature. "I guess it's better than a dog. Nothing to clean up."

Jenny knelt next to her daughter and looked at Aris. The little draconic spirit looked back and I felt it radiate a tremendous feeling of apology and sorrow mixed with hope and pleading.

That worked. The truth of those emotions couldn't be denied, not by anyone who was reasonably honest with themselves, and the Plunketts were definitely that. Jenny gave a little smile and reached out to gently pat the smooth scaled head. "It's okay. I accept your apology."

When I left a little while later, I could see Lizzie and Mitch laughing in amazement as Aris put on a shadow-show. The little *thansaelasavi* saw me walking away, came flying through the night air and hovered there, radiating thankfulness and apology for the hell it had put me through.

"That's all right. I'm going to be fine." The walk up the hill had hurt like hell, but it was all going to work out. "You just watch over them. You know that there's other forces out there waking up. Keep an eye on them. They're not wizards. And they don't know the truth, and shouldn't."

It radiated iron determination. I smiled and nodded. "Good enough."

I watched as the spirit-dragon flew back to the family that had adopted it, after all that time of fear and darkness, and grinned.

"Finally, a real happy ending."

I turned and headed downhill, toward my own happily-ever-after.

CHAPTER 86

Answers of Mystery

"Well, it all worked out well enough," Syl said as we sat down to dinner.

"Just glad you're really back. Sorry we haven't had time to talk the last couple of days."

She smiled. "Don't worry about it, Jason! Good *lord*, you were half-killed and then trying to get everything fixed up between Arischadel and the Plunketts."

"Still, I didn't even ask you about what happened with Samantha and her friend," I said, cutting her a slice of pork roast and putting it on her plate. "How *did* it go?"

She served herself some mashed potatoes, while screwing up her face in an "I'm trying to figure out what to say" way. "It went...kinda funny."

"How do you mean?" I reached out, found I hadn't filled my own glass, got up and went to the kitchen. "Go on, I'm listening."

"Well...you're going to be getting some big bills coming in."

"Big bills?" I honestly hadn't expected this to be an expensive handholding. "Why?"

"I found out when I got down there that Aurora's first problem was getting *home*. Samantha was trying to arrange it, but while she's not hurting for money, honestly, I didn't want her blowing a couple grand."

"Where *was* she? I thought she disappeared from New Jersey?"

"That's where she disappeared...but she called Samantha from Cairo."

"Cairo...you mean *Cairo*. As in, Egypt?" That *was*...funny,
458

in the strange-funny sense. A girl disappears in America and ends up in Cairo. "What the heck was she doing *there*?"

Syl smiled wryly. "She wishes she knew."

"*Amnesia*?" This was starting to sound like a bad thriller plot. "Aurora disappeared about a year ago. Does she remember *anything*?"

"Almost nothing," Syl said. "And she's not faking it, I could tell. She'd had a big fight with her parents, then saw Sam at the library; Sam almost calmed her down but then Aurora lost her temper again and ran off. She says that the last thing she remembers is realizing that she'd somehow gotten lost, and walking down a road without any houses in sight, just lots of trees, mostly pines." Syl took a sip of her wine, then another bite of pork.

I knew the general area Aurora must live in, given she was walking to the library Samantha worked at. "Wait a minute. There's just no way there's *anything* around there that looks like that."

"We know that, Jason," Syl agreed. "And in one of her other last memories she says there was a *castle* at the end of that road. So we're not even sure if those are connected memories. Aurora *thinks* they followed right after she left the library, but if you ask me, I think she's remembering a couple of things from whatever happened to her after she disappeared."

I gazed off into the distance, thinking. "What do you think happened? Fugue state?"

Syl shrugged. "Honestly, Jason? I think something very strange happened to her. I don't think she just blanked out and ran off, if that's what you mean. Physically, she shows no signs of hardship; no diseases, no injuries, no signs of accidents, abuse, or anything else. She even showed up in Cairo wearing the *exact same outfit* she was wearing when she disappeared. And she wasn't carrying anything she *didn't* have on her before, either."

"Her parents must have been ecstatic at her return, anyway."

"Actually, that's one of the weirdest parts of this whole thing," Syl said. "Her parents hadn't panicked much when she disappeared, and they'd apparently said to the police and to Samantha that they *expected* her to disappear one day, and that they were sure she'd be back."

"*What*?"

"That was *my* reaction too, Jason. Her parents are a little..."

odd. From what I could gather, they drifted around the country quite a bit even after Aurora was born—Deadheads, I think. They still have that...aging hippie vibe, if you know what I mean."

"You mean, the kinda spaced-out look that *you* sometimes use to make people underestimate you?"

She laughed. "Exactly. But in their case, it's mostly not an act. That was one of Aurora's problems; she hated bouncing from one state to another, and her parents apparently told her some stories about her past and such that...weren't exactly sensible, so when she finally went to regular school, she got laughed at a lot. Samantha didn't give me a lot of details and Aurora didn't want to talk much about that."

She leaned back, looking pensive. "But...whatever happened, it *did* change her, according to Samantha. She went back to her parents and didn't have a single word of complaint about them— and Samantha says that she *always* complained about them."

I shook my head. "Well, that's a heck of a mystery. But at least you're done with it."

We finished dinner and started cleaning up; then the phone rang.

"Wonder who *that* could be?" I muttered as I grabbed the receiver. "Hello?"

"Mr. Wood," came a familiar, slightly rough voice. "Glad I could catch you at home."

"Given your resources, I'd be surprised if you didn't *know* I was home before you called, Mr. Achernar."

"Spying on you would be rude. I try to avoid that when I might ask the people in question to do work for me. I called because I thought you might like a quick informal update of what we've learned."

"Hold on, I'll put you on speaker."

Achernar's voice came from the speakers set in the corners of the room. "Ready?"

"We're ready," Syl said. "Hello, Mr. Achernar."

"Hello, Sylvie."

"So what did you find?"

"Completely ruled out any natural cause," he began, "unless I start including magical effects as 'natural,' which isn't going to fly in most departments. There was no known natural phenomenon, or for that matter deliberately designed human phenomenon, which could make such a crater yet leave that one column intact as it was. I had the Jammer and half a dozen other modeling experts try every possible combination and we got exactly nothing.

"Blast effects and stress directions also showed that the detonation emanated directly above that preserved column, in a sphere just slightly wider than the column, while the material directly below was somehow completely untouched."

I whistled. "I knew that's what it *looked* like, but really, that's pretty unbelievable."

"The whole *thing* is unbelievable. We subjected the area to the most intense analysis possible, and there isn't a trace of any chemical or radiological contaminant. People like myself and Sylvia, of course, sensed a huge amount of lingering mystical power. So internally, the explanation is that there was an almost pure magical explosion of physical force that lacked most of the thermal and luminance effects we associate with explosions and which prevented concussive transmission at the center." I could *hear* the ironic smile in his voice as he continued, "Of course, *officially* we haven't even got a clue as to what really happened, since there's nothing on file that can cause this."

"What about the thread?" Syl asked.

"Ahh, the *thread*. Now that turned out to be *very* interesting. Since we discovered it during the initial investigation, it's also not on the official files, at least not yet."

Achernar's voice dropped to a confidential tone. "We analyzed that thread every possible way we could, and we know, or deduce, a lot of things about it. First, it's part of a larger garment, probably a pair of loose pants, and it was pulled out by a thorn that almost certainly was snagging a thread that had been damaged earlier.

"We guess the latter because the thread itself is extraordinarily strong. It's a kind of silk and extremely tough ... but no type of silk we have ever seen before."

"You're kidding."

"Not a bit. This thing is a goldmine of questions, but not so good with answers. It's dyed black ... but we can't identify the precise dye used. There were traces of some kind of pollen on it that don't correspond to any pollen we know."

"Any clue on the person wearing these clothes?" I kinda doubted it, but it was worth asking.

"Only that it was probably a man, based on traces of sweat and its composition, but that's still only a guess."

"Anything from the pictures?"

"The Jammer managed to extract a little bit more," Achernar answered. "There were signs that the brush and other plant life on that untouched piece had been pressed down in a pattern that fits a human figure of moderate size. There was also a mark that looked like part of a footprint, right on the edge of the column."

Interesting. "So there was a *person* there, on the protected portion...and they just somehow up and walked away."

"Wearing clothes made of an unknown fabric, dyed by unknown materials, yes."

"Almost certainly this would be the same person who wiped out the evidence I saw—"

"—and knocked the column down to try to wipe out *that* evidence too, yes," Achernar agreed.

Syl pursed her lips. "Do you *know* that part?"

"You mean that the column was deliberately knocked down? Yes, we do. Besides the flash of light we all saw, we found the precise portion of the column that was hit, and it had suffered an impact something on the level of a wrecking ball...when there wasn't anything to be seen, and no trace of chemical explosives either."

"So now what?"

Achernar hesitated a moment; when he resumed, there was an edge of ironic humor. "Haven't a clue. But I would like you to ask...your own sources...if they have any ideas. I've got some people of my own, but unless I miss my guess your one friend has some connections I'll never match."

That made sense. With something that magical, he'd want advice from anyone he could get. "I will talk to him tomorrow."

"Excellent. I'll let you people get back to your own lives, then."

"No problem; glad you updated us."

"My pleasure. Good night!"

I hung up and glanced at Syl. "Curiouser and curiouser, said Alice."

She nodded, eyes distant and seeing things beyond the room. "And it's not over yet."

Part VIII

Trial Run

July 2001

CHAPTER 87

Back from the Dead

"Yeah, I finally have to admit it," I said reluctantly. "I can't do this alone."

Achernar's voice held just a touch of amusement, but there was respect in it as well. "Frankly, I'm amazed you've hung on this long. Personally, I'd have given it up, oh, a year ago; at most I'd have waited until the Gabon Blast made it obvious that the strange was in our world to stay. Instead, you've tried to do it all yourself for *another* three months. So how can we help?"

"Well, I'm going to have to remodel Wood's Information Service—the building—so I can actually *have* departments. Now that I'm living with Syl away from WIS, I can dedicate the rooms that I used to live in for work purposes. The *hard* part's going to be personnel."

The rough chuckle indicated that Achernar understood perfectly. "No doubt. We have the same problem."

"Exactly. You've got experience in finding employees who are both trustworthy and open-minded. Whoever I hire as my right-hand person needs to know a *lot* about what's going on, including—if I'm going to give them a chance at doing even *part* of my job—some awareness of what's already happened."

Achernar was silent for a moment. "You mean about things like actual vampires and such?"

"If you don't know what's *really* out there, just how can I expect you to sort out the bullcrap from the real stuff that *sounds* crazy?"

"Point." A pause. "How many people are you looking for?"

"I'd say...three. I mean, *anyone* would be a help right now"—I looked at the three other lines blinking red; the message count on

465

my phone now showed twenty-three new, unread messages since an hour ago—"but I think I need someone to run the business side and a couple more at least, to help sort out the crap from the diamonds, and maybe do initial investigations."

"And you'd like Pantheon to see what we can do to find appropriate candidates. Not afraid we'll put a ringer in your organization?"

I grinned, though he couldn't see it. "If you tried really hard, you could probably convince me to *join* you, so it's hardly worth the effort to try to trick me that way. So no, I'm not."

"True enough. Tell you what we can do: you forward all the resumés you get to us, and we'll have them vetted. We'll dig deeper on anyone who passes a preliminary sniff test. You'll interview the ones that pass *that* investigation. We'll be looking for traits that are useful for you, not necessarily to us, in case you're wondering."

"Great!" That took a *huge* load off my shoulders. I heard a chime from the outer door. While Morgantown was pretty far off the beaten track, people were often still willing to make the trip in person and thus get past the answering machine. "Whoops, got to go."

"We'll talk later then. Bye."

I got ready to buzz the newcomer in from the entryway, glancing at the CryWolf image, which focused on his hands; it was unseasonably cold today and the person was wearing a hoodie, so his hands were the only exposed flesh easily visible.

No shimmers or other strange phenomena appeared, so I pushed the button to let him in. "Can I help you?" I asked as the newcomer stepped in and closed the door behind him.

He pushed the hoodie back, and I saw a cascade of long black hair and steel-gray eyes that momentarily struck me absolutely dumb. "Hi, Mr. Wood."

"Xavier? *Xavier Ross?* What the—how...?"

"I'm sorry, sir. I'm *very* sorry that I caused you all that trouble," he said, and I could tell he was being earnest and honest. "I came here straightaway to apologize so you'd get it from me instead of hearing it on the news or something."

I finally recovered enough to think. Xavier looked nearly identical to the way he had when I first met him; the only difference I could see was a very thin, white scar on one cheek. "I sure hope you went to your *mother* first."

His gaze dropped to the floor. "Yeah, I went home first." His voice wavered. "She . . . Mom and Michelle . . . they were really happy I came back. Not *too* mad. And they understood that I had to come here fast, before the news got out."

"What *happened* to you?"

He laughed shortly. "You . . . and that cop, Lieutenant Reisman . . . well, basically I got in the trouble you warned me about. I was almost killed by a gang." His hand went to his stomach, which was where reports said he'd been stabbed.

"That much I knew. Where'd you go? Did the old man who beat up the gang take you to a hospital?"

He looked up, startled. "You know about him?"

"Not much, but there were eyewitness reports from some of the gang members. Said he trashed all of them at once."

Xavier grinned. "And it was *awesome*," he said emphatically. "Wish I could've seen it clearly but I was kinda dying at the time."

He hesitated, then shrugged and went on. "Hospital . . . yes and no. He took me somewhere safe and took care of me until I healed. Then . . . he made me look at myself and what I'd been doing." Now his gaze was more distant, looking at things that weren't in the room. "I'm . . . kind of obsessive. And after what that . . . girl did," for a moment his tone returned to the furious, cold, brittle sound it had held during his earlier visits, ". . . I don't think anyone could really blame me. But he made me see how much I was hurting Mom and 'Chelle by what I was doing. And at the same time, that I probably would destroy myself if I just went home and tried to ignore it."

"And so . . . ?"

"You wouldn't believe me if I told you."

I laughed. "You can always choose *not* to tell me, Xavier, but I guarantee that I've seen things *you* wouldn't believe."

He laughed, a little nervously. "I guess. Man, I'm gone for a couple of years and the world goes crazy. I mean . . . *werewolves*?" He looked serious. "He taught me how to fight. *Really* how to fight. So I could take care of myself when I went on to find . . . her."

I frowned. "So did you? Find her?"

He shook his head. "Not yet. I finished my training with him and came home."

I remembered the reports that Jeri had brought me. "Where does the guy with the five-sided hat come into this?"

His eyes snapped back to mine. "Him? *He* was the one who *sent* me into the alley and almost got me killed!"

"You ran into him again, about a year later."

He blinked. "I don't remember seeing him again—and he's kinda hard to forget. I just came straight home from Chicago. Hitching and walking, of course."

Now that *is interesting. He did* run *into Khoros again, a year ago. What's up with that?*

It was obvious, though, that he either really didn't remember, or didn't intend to say any more on *that* subject, so I just nodded. "All right. I'm glad you're okay, Xavier; I was kinda blaming myself for you getting killed, you know."

He winced. "Sorry. *Really*, really sorry. I... wasn't thinking. At all."

"Okay. Apology accepted."

He straightened up, looking relieved. "I guess I'd better go find Lieutenant Reisman and—"

Crap. "Renee Reisman's dead, Xavier. Sorry. She's been dead about two years."

He looked horrified. "Oh, man. I'm sorry. You... knew her, right?"

"She was a good friend of mine," I said; it still hurt to use the past tense. "And a damn good cop, too. All I can say is she'd have been glad to know you aren't dead. And both of us would hope you've learned your lesson."

He bit his lip, then nodded. "Yeah, I have. I have to think about the people who are *alive* first, instead of the dead."

And that's a pretty good summary. "Good. Then you get on back home; I bet they'll want you to stick close for a while."

He grinned sheepishly. "Yeah, I'll probably be grounded for, like, ever. Or at least a month. And I deserve it, but I don't care; I'm *home*." He turned back to the door. "Thanks, Mr. Wood."

"Thank *you* for stopping in, Xavier. Good luck."

"Bye!"

I shook my head after he left. *There's more to this than I'm seeing. Maybe it's connected with some other things... but I'm not sure I want to poke into it.*

The problem was, of course, that there were elements of this *too* close to that of Aurora Vanderdecken. If I got the timing right, Aurora vanished very nearly the same time that Xavier

Ross had been seen for the second time by David Ringo. And now he'd returned, within a few months of Aurora's reappearance, and neither he nor Aurora apparently remembered much of that period of time, if I was right about his reaction to my saying he'd met Khoros a second time.

After a few minutes, during which all of my phone lines were ringing or blinking, I came to a decision. *I'll leave it for now; neither Xavier or his family need any more crap in their lives, especially since there's bound to be news stories and police interviews.*

But eventually—and not too long, either—I'll have to ask Verne what the hell *is going on.*

CHAPTER 88

Bad Day, Bad Client

There are days when everything goes right. The shower's the perfect temperature, breakfast's cooked perfect, you hit all the green lights when you drive to the city, every client's problem has a blindingly obvious solution that makes you look like a genius, and then when you get home your wife's decided to arrange a romantic dinner that's *just* what you were in the mood for.

This was not one of those days.

I won't even go into the fiasco that was my morning, except to say that the expression "got up on the wrong side of the bed" would apply if you assume that I had a stone wall on the wrong side of the bed and kept trying to get up on that side anyway. But that might have been the high point of the day. Unlike my bachelor days, I now had to drive to work, since Wood's Information Service was in Morgantown and our home was several miles out. The flat tire happened in the most inconvenient location: a stretch of road with no shoulder. During the heaviest rain of the day. At that point I discovered my cell phone battery was dead, then I cut my hand getting the so-called jack out of the back of the car.

As one might imagine, I was not in a chipper mood when I finally arrived at WIS about an hour and a half late. I spent the next several hours dealing with what seemed an endless parade of lunatics and flakes; my association with the Morgantown Incident had made me a focal point for anyone thinking they had a paranormal problem. Unfortunately, even with the increase in real "weird stuff," ninety-nine percent of my callers and visitors were still lunatic-fringe whackos. By lunchtime I was approaching homicidal; I ushered the last person out of the office, locked the door, and switched on my "closed" sign. "Jeeeesus." I sighed. "I *have* to get myself some helpers...and ones with good BS filters."

Syl helped when she could, of course, but she hadn't given up on running the Silver Stake when she married me—and, truth be told, with her being one of the few with real magic potential and being taught the real deal by Verne Domingo, it'd probably be a bad idea for her to stop dealing in the occult directly. More than once she'd found something useful and interesting through her connections, and I suspected that would be more common, not less, if things continued as they were.

I was looking for help that could be trusted. That was of course even harder than it sounds, since anyone who worked with me was going to at least touch on the fringes, and possibly get sucked right into the middle, of Things Man May Be Killed If He Knows. James Achernar of Pantheon was helping me look for candidates, and if we found likely ones they'd have to get past me, Syl, and eventually Verne. This seriously limited my potential pool of applicants. So far, we hadn't found a good one that met all the requirements.

I pulled out my pack...to find that my lunch was not in it. Of course now I remembered putting it on the counter just before I left because I had to put something else into my pack first. And I didn't have much in the office fridge.

"Fine," I growled. "I'll order out."

I went back to my desk. As I was looking up the number of the local Chinese takeout, the phone rang. I found myself reflexively picking it up—years of customer service training taking over. I cursed at myself even as I said in my best Professional Courtesy voice, "Wood's Information Service, Jason Wood speaking."

"Mr. Wood! Thank goodness I got through!" The voice was soft and light, giving me the impression of a woman Syl's size and younger, maybe barely out of high school. "Um, my name's Angela McIntyre."

I took a deep breath. If you're going to answer the phone, suck it up and do the job right. "Thanks for calling, Angela. What can I do for you? I have to warn you, I'm extremely busy, as you might guess. Technically, this is my lunch break." I heard faint sounds of other phones and talking in the background. She was calling from some kind of public area...airport? Conference?

"Oh, dear, I'm sorry. But I really need your help and there's absolutely no one else I can trust, not with something like this." The voice quivered slightly. She sounded serious.

Unfortunately, most of the nuts sounded serious too, and without Syl I didn't have a built-in bullcrap detector. Still, I caught a faint fragment of dialogue in the background that sounded like it mentioned "...the lieutenant...." A police station?

"Go on, please."

"Well, I've been arrested, you see..."

I blinked. "I'm sorry to hear that, miss, but I hope you aren't wasting your one phone call on *me*. I'm an information specialist, not a lawyer, no matter how odd your case is."

"This *is* my one phone call, Mr. Wood, and I know you're not a lawyer, but you're a better choice for me."

This was, at least, a different approach. "What have you been arrested for?"

"Murder. But he was going to *rape* me! It was self-defense!"

I winced. "That sounds terrible, Angela, but I'm sorry, I don't understand why *me*."

"Oh, damn, I'm going about this all wrong. It's because of *how* I killed him that no one else would possibly be able to understand."

Now it began to make some sense, although I *really* didn't like where this was going. She'd probably used magic or psionics on the guy. "And how was that?"

"Chopped him in half, basically," she said.

"Chopped—with *what?*"

"Why, with my *claws*, of course. I'm a werewolf."

CHAPTER 89

Inhuman Rights

Staring at a phone does no one any good, but that's what I did for some number of minutes, trying to grasp the entirety of the situation. Finally, her repeated "Mr. Wood? Mr. Wood? Are you there?" got through.

"Yes...yes, I'm here. A *werewolf?*" I asked incredulously. "Are you serious?"

"I am and these policemen are. They're holding guns loaded with silver bullets on me as we speak, and I think they're discussing silver handcuffs."

I thought for a moment. The situation was so bizarre that it really took some effort to force my brain into its normal analytical channels. First, I'd better confirm that she was telling the truth. "Angela, no offense, but how do I know that you, well, really are a Great Wolf?"

She gave a light, pleasant chuckle. "Hard to prove it by phone, yes. But...Hastrikas told me about having to work with you."

That sealed it. Hastrikas was the real name, the Wolf name, of Sheriff Baker back in Venice, Florida. The number of non-wolves who knew that name could probably be counted on one hand. "Okay, Angela." The irony of her chosen name was, no doubt, intentional. "Then I'll give you the same answer I gave a certain Mr. Carruthers when that deal was made. Why the hell should I care? I know what your people are like, I've killed a whole bunch of you, and I know you'd all kill me in a flash if your King hadn't marked me down as his particular bag of munchies."

"Because, Mr. Wood, you're interested in justice and the truth,

473

and because if you think about the implications, you'll know it's a good idea."

I wondered how old she was, because it was that little speech that set the hook. The thought of a Great Wolf needing to be defended in the name of truth and justice...and that *I* was the one to be their defender..."I won't promise anything yet. I think I need to see this for myself. Where are you?"

"Los Angeles."

It was *definitely* going to be a long day. "Tell one of the officers I need to talk to them."

"Lieutenant Ferrin here. Is this Jason Wood?"

"It is. This is one of the strangest calls I've gotten, and I've had a lot of strange calls, let me tell you."

"You damn near didn't get any call. If she'd stayed in wolf form, she'd have been gunned down, but we barely saw a flicker of the monster, and as soon as we pulled in—"

"Wait, wait, Lieutenant. I do need to hear everything from everyone's point of view—if I'm going to get involved in this case—but this is probably not the best way to do it. What I *do* need to do is see the site, get the information from your ME and CSI teams, all that kind of thing. And I can't do that remotely."

"You're seriously considering helping this...thing?"

I felt my skin trying to crawl. "I'm thinking about it. I don't like it any more than you do. But I may have to." A part of me was already starting to understand what she meant by it being a good idea. "I'll need all the information on precinct or whatever you call it down there—where exactly you're holding her, and so on." I gave him my contact information, while swapping in a new, fully charged battery to my cell. No point in risking it failing again, I'd just keep the old one in case. "I'll be getting airline tickets as fast as I can. Now put, um, Angela back on."

"Mr. Wood?"

"I'm going to be on my way soon. I'm still not promising anything, but if you want me to do this, you have to cooperate with the police until I get there and make my decision. That means you're going to sit in jail for a while."

"I understand. If I want humans to help me, I have to play by your rules," she said calmly. "I will cooperate fully, as long as they do not try to hurt me."

"Good enough for now."

I hung up and started to look for tickets online. At least money wasn't a problem; if I had to, I'd charter a flight. However, a much more difficult problem lay immediately ahead.

I was going to have to explain to Syl why I wasn't going to be home for dinner.

CHAPTER 90

Attorney-to-Wolves

"Are you *sure* about this?" Lieutenant Ferrin asked. "I've seen the videos from that wolf they caught in Vancouver last year. If she decides to take you out, there isn't anything on Earth we can do to save you if there's no one with you."

"Lieutenant, believe me, there isn't anyone on Earth who *knows* that better than me. But I'm sure. She won't try anything on me even if I take a gun out and try to shoot her." I went on through the doorway, which locked behind me.

Angela McIntyre, in her human form, was a dangerously cute young woman no more than five feet tall with straight bobbed blonde hair and bright blue eyes, a Nordic pixie designed by a fantasy artist. She stood up as I entered, a warm smile flashing out as she recognized me. "Mr. Wood! Oh, thank you so *very* much for coming!"

I shook her hand without much of a qualm. Somewhat to my astonishment I was starting to get used to this business. I made a mental note not to let that go too far. I had to remember that no matter how friendly this girl acted, from everything we actually *knew* about the Great Wolves she was nothing but a highly intelligent predator with humans like myself being the preferred prey.

"You're welcome, at least tentatively. I've retained the services of Rosenfeld, Opal, and O'Brien to help me with the actual legal maneuverings, since I am not a lawyer myself."

"A very good defense partnership. I know the firm. I will of course pay all your expenses and a reasonable fee."

I shook my head. "No, this is *pro bono*. You blindsided me

with the original call, but by the time I finished my connection in Chicago, I'd figured out why you'd implied I'd better take the case."

"Of course you did, Mr. Wood. Were you too stupid to figure that one out you'd hardly be alive now."

"Thanks, I think. I'll note that I'm treating this as though I were a lawyer, and Rosenfeld et al have found enough precedent to allow me the same privileges—that is, what we say here stays between us. The only recording of this conversation, or others we may have in the future, is being done by me. That took some arguing, let me tell you." I looked her over. "Now, just to be on the record, the reason I'm taking the case is that I know other, shall we say, nonhuman residents of this world who are not inimical to our existence, and it would be inadvisable for me to permit a precedent to be established that allows human beings to deny these residents rights similar to their own, which allowing you to be railroaded and shot like a dog would indeed establish."

"Exactly right, Jason!"

"Don't get too excited yet. There's a flipside to this, and you're not going to like it. But it's . . . my fee, so to speak." I looked squarely into her deceptively human eyes. "You want legal rights established because your people will then have some leverage to slow down and stop the current all-out war of extermination that's going on. Fine. But TANSTAAFL—there ain't no such thing as a free lunch, my friend. I'll do my best to defend you, but you will accept the decision of the court . . . even if it means you lose."

Her friendliness, alas, evaporated like dry ice on a hot griddle. There might even have been a flicker of inhuman light in the depths of the sky-blue eyes. "*WHAT?*"

"Oh yes, indeed." My grin had all the savagery I'd saved up from the prior Day of Hell. "If they convict you for murder, you'll meekly and obediently let them lock you up for fifty years, if necessary. And you'll be a model prisoner. And if they establish premeditation and go for the death penalty, you'll take that last walk quietly."

The perfect white teeth sharpened and glittered for a moment, and I saw an accompanying snarl on her face. "And just why would I do that instead of trying my best to escape?"

"I told you. You don't get something for nothing. That means that if you want legal leverage, you'd damn well better be ready to accept the decisions of the law. There's no guarantee I can get you cleared. As of yet, I have only your word that it was self-defense, and even if it was, proving that to what's guaranteed to be a pretty hostile jury isn't going to be a picnic. I'm going to be subject to a lot of public outcry for defending you at all; are you willing to take the risk for the gain?"

She glared at me for a few moments, then took a deep breath, closed her eyes, and when she opened them again she was back to being the blonde pixie. "All right, Mr. Wood. I promise that I'll go along with the court's decision."

I laughed. "Nice try. I don't trust you people as far as I can throw one of you in your *real* form. I want you to swear—on the name and honor of Virigar—that from this moment forth, you will comply with all human law and custom as regards criminal prosecution, exoneration, conviction, prison time or other penalties assessed against convicted criminals, up to and including execution for premeditated murder."

The name of the Wolf King had made her wince. I knew from experience that it was the only thing that meant a damn to the wolves; they feared Virigar more than silver. "I will not!"

I turned for the door. "Then we have nothing to discuss."

"You human *worm!*" The last word dropped two octaves and I whirled to see her half-changed and already starting for me.

"*Virigar.*" I reminded her.

She froze, monstrously half-human face working with rage and fear, glowing eyes now on a level with mine. Finally, she snarled something in a language no human had ever used and collapsed back into her human form. "You win."

"Then promise, and don't try any fancy word tricks on me. I promise—on my own honor, which you people know damn well is good—that I'll do my best to get you off on this charge, just as if I were a real defense lawyer, but only if you play this dead straight with me."

Finally, she nodded slowly. "Very well. I begin to see the silver beneath your humanity, Mr. Wood. It is somewhat...disconcerting to encounter it in person, even though I knew how formidable you are from prior events." She took another deep breath. "I swear, in the name and on the word and law of our King, Virigar, and in my own name of Tanmorrai, that I shall comply with human laws as you have specified, even ... even unto accepting penalties in the case of conviction, up to and including ... including my own execution."

"Satisfactory," I said, sitting back down at the table. "Then let's get to it, shall we?"

CHAPTER 91

Innocent Monster

The facts of the case didn't take too long to establish. Angela McIntyre had worked for the deceased, Frederic Delacroix, for the past year and a half. Delacroix ran an extremely high-priced escort service—one of those whose "escorts" *might* actually be top-end call girls, but which was circumspect enough and had customers with leverage enough to avoid investigation or prosecution.

"So was it?" I asked. "Not that this has to come out in the trial, but I'd better know."

"Oh, certainly," Angela said easily. "Not official, you understand, and we were given the latitude to decide if some particular, um, client didn't meet our standards, but sexual interaction was definitely part of our job description."

I looked at her. I could certainly see that she could play such a role, but... "And what the hell do you get out of it? Or did you kill the real Angela and take her place?"

"Oh, no, this isn't anyone else's form, Mr. Wood," she said. "We can choose our own forms if we like. Most of us have at least one human shape that's ours and ours alone. I live in this one most of the time. It's comfortable."

"Still... I can't imagine that you find us attractive, except for dinner purposes. So why this job? For that matter, why a job at all?"

She sighed. "Let's get into that later, shall we? First let me finish the story."

I nodded.

While that kind of contact was part of the work, Angela insisted on keeping relations between her and Frederic strictly business. This had annoyed him, but Angela was a very, very large draw with his clientele and he wasn't about to shoot himself in the foot by firing his most lucrative asset. "I'm guessing your nature gave you an advantage in pleasing the clients."

"How perceptive of you, Jason." She gave another devastating smile. "While of course I couldn't do the trick of becoming the Girl of Your Dreams without giving things away, at close range any wolf can read a lot from your soul. I could always tell the proper approach to take, the right moves to make, that would leave them utterly infatuated. Or not, if I didn't want them around me long."

I nodded. That fit with what Verne had told me about the wolves way back when Virigar had first shown up. They couldn't influence minds the way Verne could, at least not as blatantly, but they had some talents in that direction. "Go on. There's going to be a lot of questions, but let's finish the basic story."

Angela had thought the matter settled; Frederic was annoyed but had a vested interest in swallowing his pride and leaving Angela alone. Which had seemed to be the way it was, until that night. Business was good, and there had been a party at Delacroix's headquarters for some of his top clients. Frederic had socialized and probably drank a lot more than was good for him. When he came across Angela in one of the hallways, he tried to corner her.

A large man in the prime of health, Frederic wasn't someone easily brushed off, but Angela of course had some inherent advantages. She was able to get away with minimal mussing, but she realized now that Frederic wasn't going to give up. If it was just purely sexual attraction, she might have been able to figure out some way to "turn him off," but it was clearly a matter of pride and possession, too. If these clients could have her, so could he. He owned her, after all.

"That went beyond anything I wanted to put up with," she said, "so I left. I figured I could get another job or even start up my own service; my clients would be glad to work with me on that. But it was when I was leaving that I made my mistake. Most of us girls stick together reasonably well, but there's always some of them with knives out for your back. I think Trisha must have seen me leave and let Frederic know; the others would probably have just mentioned they saw me leave with one of the clients, and that would've been okay."

Delacroix had caught up with her at the parking garage. He'd threatened her, then chased her when she tried to get away. "Unfortunately," she said with a wry grin, "*this* body's legs just aren't very good for outrunning former football players." Delacroix ran her down, hit her, and was clearly preparing to rape her.

Angela, while not viewing rape with the same traumatic horror that most human women would, wasn't going to allow that to happen. "I allow humans to touch me when it's part of my job, but for him to force himself on me was never to be borne." I got the impression, despite the arrogant phrasing, that there had been some fear behind her actions, though *why* she might have been afraid I couldn't figure out yet.

So she'd shifted, struck, and shifted back just as the police arrived. "Ironic, of course. He might not have managed to finish his business before the cops arrived, but I didn't know that. Besides, he'd already struck me, which was enough."

I looked at her askance. "You might want to try a different tone when you're on the witness stand. No matter what the law says, whether you get convicted or not will depend—in part—on the impression the jury has of you, and you'll be fighting an uphill battle as it is."

"Oh, I'm quite aware of that, Jason. I'm just being totally honest with you here because you would need to know the truth in order to know how we should 'spin' it. Right?"

I nodded. "One thing that occurs to me is that we need some way of establishing that you really are this Angela. I mean, you *say* you didn't kill and replace her, but how do we know that? And how can we trace you back to certain locations? You can change your shape and just about everything else. I don't even know if you remain constant in your structure. I *do* know that Virigar, as a wolf, could change his anatomy while he was moving."

She smiled. *Damn,* but she was pretty. This girl would be dangerous even if she *wasn't* a wolf. "Scientifically, you can link me by using DNA tests on the relevant locations—my apartment, the crime scene, so on. Certainly, we can duplicate other people on a genetic level—it's necessary for what we do—but in this case, it's *my* DNA footprint. Only another wolf could fake it."

"Or a Maelkodan, I suppose."

She shuddered. "Y . . . yes, they could. But I can prove I'm not a Maelkodan."

I raised an eyebrow. "How?"

"Maelkodan aren't vulnerable to silver."

I nodded in understanding. Pulling a silver knife from its sheath on my leg, I laid it on the flat of her hand. She stoically held still; I withdrew the blade to see a red welt and blister on her hand, as though the knife had been as hot as a stove. "Okay, you're a wolf all right," I agreed. "Still, what about proving that Angela is in fact you, and you haven't just substituted for her?"

"There's some decent evidence available. I suppose I can't *totally* prove it—although I swear in the name of Virigar that I have told you the truth. If you'll have your best professionals examine Angela's background, they will eventually find that it ends as thoroughly as any faked identity does. I obviously didn't spend years growing up from childhood. I started being Angela about eight years ago. The investigation will also show that I had a nondescript but rather decent job as a programmer-analyst up until I changed careers, a change that would be hard to explain for most people, but which makes perfect sense for a wolf."

The timing fit closely with my throwdown with Virigar. I began to understand. "You were doing a completely different job for your own people, using Delacroix's service as cover."

"Oh, excellent!" She clapped her hands enthusiastically. "You really do have the talent for this kind of thing. Yes, and it was all your fault."

"I drove your people into hiding. With the CryWolf units being installed in more and more places, there were fewer and fewer safe locations for you—especially since you couldn't count on any given place *not* having a CryWolf installed. That's why one group of you had to take over Venice, Florida; only if you controlled the major events through the entire community could you have a chance of making sure that any CryWolf units installed would be useless." I frowned. "But you can't do the same in Los Angeles, New York, or any large city. There simply aren't enough of you."

"Well, you know that many of the CryWolf installations were made as supplements or additions to already-existing monitoring units, don't you?"

I nodded. "I designed the retrofit kits for most of those approaches myself. Why?"

"Many of our clients are married." She watched me for a reaction.

Of course. It made complete, if terrifying, sense. Wealthy, powerful *married* men were not going to want a record of them receiving female visitors outside of normal business proceedings. So they could arrange for the cameras to be shut off for a few seconds, especially if a hint was given.

And with the camera off, the CryWolf device was useless.

"But... obviously, you didn't kill off these guys. That would've cut way into Frederic's profit margins, and caused a lot of talk, at the least. So what did that get you?"

"Tsk, tsk, Mr. Wood. The ability to get past the defenses of the building *once* allows me the opportunity to ensure that they will never operate again. It takes some considerable skill to perform the modifications such that self-checking will appear to work, and so on, but I have that skill."

Now I understood. "You basically were working on infiltrating as many business and residential areas as possible and subtly disabling the CryWolf units, allowing your people to return to the major cities."

"*Exactly*, Jason. There are a number of other tactics that I had to use since not everyone would turn off their cameras. I would have to engineer failures from a sufficient distance, but the point was that someone in my position simply wasn't suspected. The advantages of a still-sexist society, you know; it's easy to play dumb when you're a cute little blonde."

I had to agree with that, and the whole situation was giving me the creeps again. At least Virigar had appeared to have some credible threat potential. Angela—or to use her wolf name, Tanmorrai—looked less threatening than Syl. And she was calmly admitting that the purpose behind playing a high-priced call girl was to help render useless the major defense we had against the wolves.

"We probably won't want to bring this up at the trial, " she continued. "It would probably be better for me to just say that as long as we are stuck trying to live in your society, a girl has to do something to eat, and *we* don't have your people's hangups on sexual interaction. Not that we find your people attractive, but as a job, it's no worse than many others. I'd rather do that than be a sewer maintenance worker, for instance."

"Speaking of eating," I said, "how many people have you eaten in your last couple of years—aside from the not-too-lamented Frederic, that is?"

She froze for a moment, then smiled again. "You know I don't *have* to kill to survive, Jason. We might prefer it, but your shaking up of the power structure has made it inadvisable for us to do any more killing. Especially after you made your point so clearly in Venice, where poor little Hastrikas now has to make sure everyone keeps themselves on the straight and narrow, eating what we can get *without* killing the subject or giving them the suspicion that something isn't right."

"That's right, you can do that drain-the-energy trick from a distance," I said. Now that I thought of it, that was probably what she meant by "engineering failure" of the cameras; if you drained the energy from the camera fast enough, it would shut down, then start back up again when you stopped the drain. According to Verne, they could eat essentially any form of energy, but the energy of life—the souls—was so vastly superior that they didn't use that power on other energy sources unless they absolutely had to.

"Exactly. So we might choose some tourist who'd been running themselves ragged, drain them from the adjoining hotel room, and leave them feeling like they overdid it and got some kind of the flu. In a day or so, they're recovering and none the wiser." She grinned, then reached out and touched my hand. "For other purposes, of course, you can reverse the process."

I felt a momentary flood of energy and almost ecstatic well-being, and knew it was due to this gorgeous girl smiling fondly at me. I shook my head, focusing on what I knew was true. The energy and alertness stayed, but I managed to force the attraction out. Well, mostly out. I'm not superhuman, and the cute pixieish types have always appealed to me—I married one, after all—and she was very, very cute. "Do *not* do that again."

"Of course, if that's the way you feel. Consider the energy a gift; you're jet-lagged, but now that shouldn't be a problem." She smiled again, but this time with a nasty edge. "Freddie's soul had to be good for *something*."

I stared at her in revulsion. "That was..."

"Well, yes, I had to get the extra energy from somewhere. Don't worry, it really didn't have much of him left in it."

I picked up the digital recorder and my laptop. "I think we're done for today."

She was laughing quietly as they took her back to her cell.

CHAPTER 92

All So Different, They're Exactly the Same

"So she's cooperating, Jason?"

Just hearing Syl's voice was settling me down. "Overall, yeah. Not without playing games, though. She's a nasty one."

"You like her, don't you?"

I spluttered incoherently for a moment before I found my words again. "I like the way she *looks*, Syl. But she's a *monster*, and she's happy with that. She put a piece of a dead man's essence into me as a demonstration of what she could do for me, what she'd already done to someone else, and I think just to entertain herself with my reactions."

"But you do like her."

It's impossible to lie to your wife when she's a psychic. "In some ways, yeah. She's ... well, she's kinda like Virigar: straightforward, no attempt to pretend she's anything other than what she is, honest in her intent, and I think she has some honest respect for me. But she's also a monster in every sense of the word, and I *hate* the idea that I'm going to be trying to get her out of jail." I paused. "You're not *jealous*, are you?"

She laughed, the sound bringing back memories of the time she'd confronted me with my own jealousy over her and Verne. "Jasie, I know you too well. I'm just making sure *you* know yourself."

"I'm not stupid. It's obvious what she was doing." I chewed my lower lip. "But that approach—without knowledge of its intent—boy, that would really work. She probably used that on some of her clients. They'd attribute their, um, increased energy and stamina to her, but not in the way it was really happening.

486

That'd definitely keep her popular." Something was nagging me about that, but it was the sort of thing that I'd have to wait on; it'd come clear, sooner or later.

"So what now?"

"The cops—CSIs, other agencies—are going to go over the evidence, trace her back, try to show that she's been working there as she claims, dig up proof of her faked background, so that we know there isn't a real Angela who's gone missing, and so on. Mr. Achernar agreed to do extra digging to confirm it's not a double trick, where they made a real person disappear and then eradicated proof that she existed. I have to cover all the bases." There was a knock at the door. "What the . . . Syl, I gotta go. Call you later. Love you."

"I love you, Jason. Be careful."

"Always am. Bye."

I glanced through the peephole, then stepped back, unlatching the door. "Come in, slowly."

Once the man in the doorway was fully in view and my CryWolf glasses showed nothing but human, I relaxed and put my gun back into its holster. "Sorry, but I think you understand that in *this* case, I'd better be double-paranoid. What can I do for you, Lieutenant?"

Lieutenant Kevin Ferrin was one of the most . . . coppy-looking cops I'd ever seen. He could have stepped out of any movie featuring the boys in blue—regular features, trim but tall, short brown hair and sharp brown eyes, a uniform that looked just pressed, and an awareness of his surroundings without seeming to search them. He shook my hand and took the indicated seat as I closed the door. "Sorry for bothering you, I know you're busy."

"Busy, but not off-duty. You don't have anything new for me in the case right now, do you?" Ferrin had already sent over the actual arrest reports and preliminary CSI workup of the area.

"No, nothing like that." He looked slightly embarrassed. "It's actually a different subject. I mean, it's another investigation, but it's kind of strange and I thought, well, since you were already in the area . . ."

"No problem. The strange has become my profession, and if you've got something you've been butting your head against without results, I can take a look at it. I don't make any guarantees, but it can't hurt."

He relaxed a bit. "Okay. Here goes."

The problem didn't take long to lay out. In a city the size of Los Angeles, murder is hardly unusual from the point of view of any policeman, unless it's a murder that remains unsolved. This is not unheard of, of course, and most policemen have at least one or two that they've never gotten a satisfactory answer on, but still it's unusual.

What Lieutenant Ferrin had was something very different. Twenty deaths in eleven separate incidents over the past year or so, and three of them completely unsolved.

"But you're putting them in the same category as the solved ones?" I said. He nodded. "That can't be the official position."

"It's not," he said bluntly. "If this was an official investigation, I'd have asked you to come down to the station and look at the stuff first. Technically, only the three unsolved ones are still being worked on. But..."

"There's a similarity? The others were done in a similar way?"

He shook his head. "Everything from kitchen-knife stabbings to apparent heart attacks or poison." He looked uncomfortable as he said it.

"Common factors, then?"

He wobbled a hand like a seesaw. "The only clear-cut one I could say would be age. None of the victims are under the age of eighteen or over the age of about twenty-five."

I studied him. "Look, instead of making me poke at you, why not just *tell* me what's bothering you about these cases?"

He hesitated, then gave an explosive, frustrated curse. "That's the problem. *I just don't know.* Except...in our line of work, you just get a general sense of things, you know? You see crime day in, day out, and most of the time, things make sense. Even when they're confusing at the start, once you get the answers you say 'oh, right, that's how it was,' and everything's clear.

"Well, not with these. Take this one: Jessie and James Roquette." He pointed to a picture of two bodies—one a very pretty girl lying in a pool of blood the color of her very long hair, the other a slender young man whose good looks were marred by the black hole in his forehead just below his hairline. "Newlyweds, known each other for years before that, no serious trouble—couple speeding tickets, liked partying, maybe into the swinging lifestyle, but still devoted to each other. No one knew anything about a problem between them.

Friends called them an inseparable team—nothing even rumored. They throw a big party, next day, they're found in the kitchen by a neighbor, Jessie with a knife in her gut and James with a bullet in his head. Prints all over the place, but forensics doesn't come up with any alternative answers. Jessie's even got some of James' skin under her fingernails, and it matches pretty close with scratches on his' hands and arms. The gun was theirs, and it was kept right next to where Jessie ended up, so it seemed clear. He attacked her, they fought, she got knifed, went down, but got the gun and blew him away before she died. But..."

"But?"

"Just...it doesn't quite work for me. James was a little farther away; a little off from where I'd have expected him to be in that scenario. And you don't do much moving after a thirty-eight slug ricochets around your brainpan. Times of death seemed a little off, almost as though Jessie had kicked off a little bit before James, which would make it kind of hard for her to have done any shooting. The TOD estimates are always wide plus-or-minus, of course, so there was overlap." He shook his head.

"So then we look at this guy, Joe Buckley; twenty-two years old, perfect health, dating a few girls—who all knew each other and didn't seem to be particularly worried about it—on the rise in one of the movie studios' development groups, goes to a big bash, comes home, found dead the next day without a mark on him." The accompanying photo showed a brown-haired young man lying peacefully on his back, just a slight unnatural paleness indicating that there was anything wrong. "There was evidence that he might have had some company that night, but nothing conclusive. The tox screen came back with a big fat zip—along with the rest of the ME's workup. He said, 'The only problem with this guy is that he ought to be walking around alive and he's dead.' So it was listed as death due to natural causes, some kind of heart condition."

"Okay, so you've got those and some others which are considered solved, but your gut says otherwise." I didn't sneer at gut feelings; they have saved my ass more than once, and for a cop they were critical. "Why do you associate them all as a group?"

"To start with, they're all in the same general geographic area." He pulled out a map of a high-rent area of the city. "I don't have proof there aren't any outside this area. I mean, there's only so much of the city my cases are going to cover—even the werewolf's case is around there. But it's just...of all these cases, only one of them really convinced me that there was a motive for murder, and I don't like the way it ended up. I don't believe it. So I've got at least ten different cases, three unsolved, and all of them without a single believable motive except something like 'crime of passion.' And none of them—not one—with any witnesses at all. The most we got is someone hearing the gunshot in one case. But no one hearing arguments, plans for violence...and the forensics are always...well, they support the verdict, where there is one, but there's always something funny about them to me, even if no one else really sees it. Oh, and never any *living* perp. If we've got a clear case of murder involved, both the victim and the killer are dead, mutual assured destruction."

I got the picture now. "That's not common, is it?"

"Not common at all. One out of ten? Twenty? More? Maybe the killer gets hurt, but he or she walks away. Most people don't expect murder, so when the time comes, they're not ready to defend themselves. And the murderer's got the advantage, unless he's going to talk and threaten like some TV villain. So...most murderers don't end up as corpses, at least not before they're convicted." Kevin Ferrin looked relieved; I suspected that this was the first time he'd been able to articulate some of his concerns with these cases, and he was glad to find that I was taking him seriously.

"Well, Lieutenant, I don't know if there's anything I can do, but give me what you can and I'll take a look. It's an interesting problem, anyway."

The lieutenant gave me a quick, grateful smile. "Thanks, Mr. Wood. I'd really appreciate it. Even if all that you can do is tell me that I'm worrying about nothing, I'd feel better knowing someone else has looked it over. I'll get the files out and you can look 'em over at the station."

"My pleasure." I let him out and reflected on the fact that it was, in fact, a pleasure. The problem with Angela wasn't going to have a very good outcome. Either I'd succeed and a wolf would go free, or I'd fail, which would be depressing and possibly set a dangerous precedent. Lieutenant Ferrin's problem might offer a chance of ending in a way I could feel good about.

I ordered dinner, and then picked up the phone to call Syl back. There was going to be more to talk about than I'd thought.

CHAPTER 93

Proving Her Identity

"You sure this is a secure line, Wood?"

"Absolutely."

Sheriff Baker sighed. "All right, what is it?"

"I'm sure you know what I'm doing right now."

He laughed. "Yeah, I guess I do. Defendin' Miz Tanmorrai in court. That's gotta stick in your craw."

"I've got my reasons for doing it. I need some information from you, though."

"If it's to help the lady, sure. What do you need?"

"I know that there used to be a real Sheriff Baker, and you took his place, just like a lot of wolves did with other humans in Venice. But the Maelkodan had her own human shape, besides the ones she could steal from you." I was deliberately not mentioning what Angela/Tanmorrai had told me. "What about you wolves? Do you have your own unique shapes or not?"

"Well, now, of course we all do. The big furry one. But you mean a human shape. Yeah, we do. When we're young, we practice shape-shifting into human form and everyone chooses one that's theirs."

"Is this a surface shift or a full shift?"

"Oh, it's a complete shift when you've mastered it. No way you humans can tell us from yourselves, except with your little toys."

"And do you trade off these forms? I mean, could Angela use yours, or you hers at some point?"

"Never," he said immediately. "It'd be like shifting to imitate the actual wolf. We get to choose our appearance, and so the selected one belongs to us and it's...very rude to take someone else's shape without permission."

491

"Sort of like copyright or trademark, then?"

He chuckled. "Yeah, you might put it that way, but the penalties are a lot steeper. Like it's generally an insult worthy of at least two cuts, and if you do it in a way that might affect something they're doing at the time, it's a killing offense, maybe even referable to the King."

"So any traces we find to prove her background really do have to be hers."

"Hell, yeah. *Especially* her. No one would mess with *her.*"

"I did notice she called you 'little Hastrikas' like, um, Virigan did. Is she an Elder like him?"

His voice was deadly serious. "Not like *him*, no. Ain't any like *him*, well, maybe two left, but nobody knows for sure. But still, she's old enough, she goes back almost as far as your friend Verne, I think. No one knows for sure, 'cept of course the King and the . . ." he stopped abruptly. "Anyway, you got what you need?"

I really wished he'd finished what he'd been about to say, but I didn't want to push it. "I think so. We have to prove she's the person she says she is."

"You already got most of this from her, didn't you?"

Point to the sheriff. "Some of it. But I had to get confirmation. From another wolf. And you played it straight before."

His voice was not friendly. "Because you have us in a silver trap, Wood. And because the King has required us to maintain a cold, rather than hot, war. For now. But when he decides it's time to kill you, I will be very happy to watch."

"I don't doubt it. But don't hold your breath. Thanks anyway."

He hung up without saying I was welcome, which was rather rude, but I'd gotten what I needed from that call, assuming he was telling the truth. I thought he probably was; not only was it consistent with what Angela had told me, but the additional details made sense. I was, slowly, starting to get an idea of how the wolves' society worked. It was ugly, cold, and vicious, but that really wasn't much of a surprise. And at least the information would be useful.

Project Pantheon, through one of Achernar's associates, had come through beautifully. Angela's background was indeed faked, up to eight years ago. She was clearly a fictional person whose existence was created specifically for the little wolf currently residing in the local lockup. This made winning the case at least possible.

It was, however, still going to be a bitch and a half. I looked down at the dossiers on the table. This was the summary of the important people at the trial—namely the judge and the selected jury. Had this been a lesser crime, it would probably have been weeks or months before we got to this stage, but the high-profile, bizarre nature of the case had ensured that everything was going to move quickly. There were already protesters demonstrating on both sides of the issue. We were going to need an insane amount of high-level security. I had already received death threats for daring to defend a wolf, and heartfelt compliments for my open-mindedness. It was a circus, no doubt about it, but one with a deadly theme.

Convincing the jury was going to be difficult. The prosecution would no doubt paint this as a deliberate premeditated murder, manipulated by Angela for her own macabre gain. Trying to fight that was going to require walking a serious tightrope because there was truth in the suggestion that she was manipulating the situation for the wolves' gain. The last thing I needed was to have *that* come out in testimony. Rosenfeld, Opal, and O'Brien had handled the jury selection, something completely out of my depth, and we thought they'd managed to eliminate the worst possible choices. Realistically, though, there *weren't* any good juror choices for us, aside from a couple of "furries," which had been weeded out by the prosecution.

We had assembled a list of Angela's more important clients. She'd balked at first, but came around once I pointed out that these men were most likely to try and affect the outcome of the trial. I had to get a handle on who they were and *how* they might try to influence it. On the one hand, they wouldn't want word of their involvement to get out, and so they'd have a reason to want Angela out of the way. On the other hand, if they couldn't be sure she'd be executed—and quickly—she had the potential of striking back against them by giving names, dates, and times, and who knew what else she might have learned? So, in that sense, they had every reason to see her set free (and maybe arrange an accident for her *afterward*). The result of that list was that a lot of our challenges in jury selection were based on knowing they were somehow connected to one of Angela's clients.

I looked down the list and sighed. There wasn't much point in looking it over again. About all we'd managed to achieve was to make sure that the jury was as reasonably well-educated as possible; this trial would be better served, for my purposes, by those who were more subject to intellectual rather than emotional argument.

I sat up suddenly. "But I'd better not neglect that emotional side!"

I had a few calls to make.

CHAPTER 94

Opening Statements

"Ladies and gentlemen of the jury," Prosecutor David Hume began, "we are all aware of the unique nature of this trial. In my time as an attorney, I have prosecuted and, on occasion, defended people who might be described as monsters. In this case, we are dealing with a monster in literal fact. The defendant, Angela McIntyre, is not human, despite the innocent appearance she displays for the court. She is a werewolf, a creature capable of taking on any shape for her own purposes, a monster that feeds upon human flesh and perhaps more. Werewolves are known to have killed many hundreds of people, perhaps many times that many, and even with all the technology at our command, it is difficult to either capture or kill these beings. Many people believe that we should be exterminating them, wiping them out as we would destroy some disease. The honorable court, however, has determined that, given the werewolves' status as thinking beings, there is sufficient precedent to justify a trial. We recognize the reasons for this decision, and the State is confident that it will make no difference in the ultimate outcome.

"In this trial, we will demonstrate that the killing of Frederic Delacroix was the result of a cold-blooded hunt, and possibly part of something even more sinister. Angela McIntyre never intended to allow Frederic Delacroix to live once he had served his purpose; his actions, provoked deliberately by the defendant, were meant to allow her to kill him with impunity. She was never in actual danger from Delacroix, and therefore, any contention of self-defense is ludicrous. It is dangerous for us to make any other conclusion; permitting a trial and defense for such a creature is directly counter to the proper welfare and defense of the state and its people—its *human* people—by providing, for creatures who have an admitted view of humans as prey, a means to escape the consequences of their actions." Hume gazed at the jury, trying to make eye contact with each of them to show his clear and forthright nature. "This is undoubtedly one of the most important trials any of us has ever seen, or will ever see. Remember that during your deliberations." He paused a moment longer, turned and nodded to me.

I stood up slowly, then walked to the front of the packed courtroom. Flashes popped; despite some argument against it on both sides, there really hadn't been any chance to make this a closed courtroom. Whatever happened here would be recorded for posterity. So I'd better look good.

"You all know who I am," I said quietly. "I'm Jason Wood. These monsters, as the prosecutor calls them, are the reason you know me. I lost one of my best friends to their King. He nearly killed me in a hospital, where my wife was in critical condition as the result of an encounter with one of his people. I am not their friend. I think it's important you understand that."

The faces of the jurors were intent. I'd memorized all of them: Lucy Aluquerre, Jim Sherry, Darrin Brown, Maria Mendoza, Tony Sestin, Frank Kovalsky, Alfred Flint, Petra Hamilton, Alle Schumacher, Gladia Baley, Steven Jackson, and Verna Stout. I also met each of their gazes squarely. "I didn't take this job to side with monsters. I took it because there's something more important at stake here. This is a matter of justice. Whatever she is, Angela McIntyre was not planning to kill Frederic Delacroix that day, or any other. She was simply living her life, doing her job. Frederic Delacroix decided that this wasn't enough, and tried to force himself on her. She defended herself—as the law allows her to do—with whatever weapons she had to hand. The fact that those weapons were more effective than Mr. Delacroix would have expected simply means that she was able to escape with minimal injury."

I glanced at Judge Freeman, then turned towards the courtroom, still speaking to the jury, continuing to turn so that I once more faced them. "The prosecutor has emphasized that Angela is not human, and implied that this means she is not entitled to proper justice. That sentiment has been uttered before, in settings that many of us are all too familiar with." I saw a flicker of understanding in the dark eyes of Kovalsky, a slight sad smile on the seamed, kindly face of old Alle. "We, the defense, will show that Angela McIntyre did not plan Delacroix's death, that she killed in self-defense to prevent a violent and repulsive assault, and that whatever her true nature, she is here, in this courtroom, a defendant like any other, entitled to fair judgement and justice, not only for herself but for many others."

Angela looked at them out of wide eyes. She had chosen her look carefully today; there was nothing sexy about her outfit. Instead, she'd chosen a blouse and skirt of subdued and modest design, making her look even younger, a frightened, innocent schoolgirl caught in something far beyond her depth. I had to admire the effect, though it made me wince inwardly at the cognitive dissonance. I kept on. "Angela and I are trusting in you to make the right decision. She has chosen to trust *me*—a sworn enemy of her people, a man responsible for the deaths of hundreds of her people—because she believes I understand why she must be defended. And she will accept your finding; she knows that if you convict her, she will be imprisoned, perhaps even executed, and for the sake of the justice she seeks, she cannot use her abilities to fight or escape. Here, today, she is as vulnerable as any of you would be in her place. Her life—and perhaps much more—are in your hands. I am putting my trust in all of you."

I bowed to the jury—it seemed the right thing to do, at least for me—and returned to my seat. It was time for the trial to begin.

"A good speech, Mr. Wood," Angela whispered. "I hope we have enough material to back it up."

"So do I. Your account of your fight—if we can call it that— with Frederic—should give us a good chance, if the evidence bears you out. But even with the best work and evidence, you know this is anything but a sure thing."

She nodded, her eyes momentarily mirroring a real awareness of the danger she was in. "Yes, Mr. Wood. I know."

CHAPTER 95

Testimony and Tactics

The prosecution's case was good. Not that I doubted it would be, and to be honest, not that it *needed* to be, at least at this point. The rest of the day had been devoted to the prosecution, starting with a description of the bare facts of the case and then calling Lieutenant Ferrin to the stand. After establishing Ferrin's name, rank, and relation to the case, the prosecutor asked him to describe the events of the night in question, and then began his examination. "Now, Lieutenant, how did you know for sure that you were facing a werewolf?"

"Well, me and Jack had seen it," Ferrin replied.

"By your own words, 'only for a split second, almost like,' what was it . . . 'a flash of shadow.' That was why you arrested the monster rather than—"

I was on my feet. "Objection, Your Honor!"

"What is it, Mr. Wood?"

"I didn't object during the opening statements, because they're not considered evidence, but the prosecutor cannot refer to my client as 'the monster' or 'a monster.' The term, and similar terms, are prejudicial and shouldn't be used in this context."

One thing I had going for me here was that Judge Freeman was black; I was hoping he would be sensitive due to his likely experience with similarly insulting and prejudicial terms. "Objection sustained. Mr. Hume, unless the term is being used in an evidentiary context, you will refrain from using such terms for the defendant. You will use her name or the term 'the defendant.'"

"Yes, sir." Hume's quick glance at me was something of a minor salute; I'd noticed the tactic and countered it, which as a lawyer he respected. He clearly wasn't worried though. "As I was saying, Lieutenant, by your own report, it was the fact that you had not clearly seen the werewolf—that she had resumed human form—that kept you from gunning down the defendant, and instead arresting her?"

The lieutenant nodded. "CryWolf devices don't work at long range, and shooting down a five-foot-tall woman instead of an eight-foot monster ... well, sir, the department doesn't encourage that level of judgment."

"Understandable, Lieutenant. Still, if you weren't certain enough to shoot, how were you certain enough to take the precautions you did?"

"The condition of the body, sir."

Hume turned to the judge. "Exhibits four-A through four-G show various angles of the body of Frederic Delacroix as the officers found it." A display visible to the jury—but not easily viewable by the audience—appeared on the exhibit screen. Some of the jurors paled; one, Alfred Flint, looked away, clearly nauseated. I knew they were seeing what looked like a man who'd gone through a paper shredder; sliced by four straight bloody lines that had cut through him like a wire through cheese, leaving five *almost*-aligned pieces. "Did you verify that she was a werewolf, Lieutenant?"

"Not at that time, sir. But later at the station we did; she didn't deny it at any time."

"Did she appear upset in any way, Lieutenant?"

"Not really, sir. Calm and clear-headed was my impression, even with the scratches and blood."

"Not exactly like a woman who'd almost been raped and killed her attacker, then?"

"No, sir, definitely not as I'd expect someone in that situation to be."

It continued like that for some time. Hume established how they'd arrested Angela, her call to me, and subsequent police work. He then called the medical examiner for testimony regarding the wounds and cause of death. No surprises there: Frederic had been killed by a werewolf, from in front, in a single strike. I had no direct questions for the ME; what I needed I had found in his report after an examination was performed of certain items found on the deceased. I wanted to bring those points up during the defense. Once I'd explained my reasoning, Mr. Opal (of Rosenfeld, Opal, and O'Brien) had agreed. He was the legal representative of the firm who was sitting with me to provide on-the-spot legal advice. He would also, hopefully, help me catch any tactical lapses or openings on the part of our opposition.

I spent some time during the ME interview examining the crowd. While they weren't participants in the trial, it was not impossible that any large-scale reaction could influence the jury. And, more importantly, anyone with an axe to grind—or an intention to murder my client—might be in that group.

A lined, tanned face with rough-hewn angles and a narrow, sharp gaze stood out. James Achernar gave me an almost imperceptible nod as our eyes met. Agent and, I sometimes suspected, leader of the secret UN intelligence taskforce Project Pantheon, Achernar had not only been assisting in the verification of Angela's background but had applied some level of pressure to ensure that a trial actually happened. I was hoping to find out *why* he was interested in doing this, but for now it was a good thing he was on our side.

Many news reporters were scattered through the audience. I also recognized several other faces—politicians, pillars of the local business community, and others—from the list of clients Angela had given us. Those, and their associates, were worth studying. They had good reason to be afraid of this trial, in more ways than one.

One other face rang a faint bell. I couldn't place it, though. A pretty woman, maybe about thirty, with very long red hair, serving as an assistant to one of the clients. I made a mental note to find out who she was. I didn't see anyone else of significance, so I returned my attention to the stand where the ME was just standing down.

Hume then called other witnesses who, through various chains of evidence, established what type of business Frederic was involved in (while avoiding the details of how far the "escorts" went in their escort duties). The first real surprise was the next witness: Patricia Shire, or Trisha, another escort and the one Angela suspected of pointing Frederic in her direction that night. "Miss Shire, you worked for the deceased?"

Trisha wasn't *quite* as cute as Angela, at least from my point of view, but she did make a good impression on the stand. She was about three inches taller than Angela and more buxom, with long brown hair and eyes which, Angela informed me, were a very attractive green. She wore a subdued business suit and looked forlorn. "Yes, sir."

"Did the defendant also work for the deceased?"

"Yes." She shot a look of horrified venom at Angela, who barely restrained a taunting smile; I saw the corner of her mouth curl.

"So you knew both the defendant and the deceased well?"

"Well...I knew *Freddie* well. I *thought* I knew Angela, but obviously I didn't. I mean, I knew she was hunting him, I just didn't..."

I saw where *this* was going. And it went there quickly. Trisha testified that Frederic had become increasingly focused on Angela since she began working for him, and that Angela continuously teased him. Trisha said that Angela kept stringing Frederic along until he pursued her to a location where there were no witnesses, leaving her free to kill him. By this theory, it was the fact that the police just happened on the scene that screwed up her plans; after all, in just another few seconds, she'd have been gone. Or possibly, Hume pointed out, as it was known that the wolves could rather efficiently dispose of a body if they were so inclined, she'd have returned...*as* Frederic Delacroix. Either way, the fortunate arrival of the police forced her to try this desperate stunt to keep from being gunned down where she stood.

I wondered why they weren't taking it to the next level. While I hadn't thought of the use the wolves were making of Angela's position, it did surprise me that the prosecution hadn't either. There must be some reason they weren't bringing it up. Unless... I had another question to ask Angela.

Hume brought up a few other witnesses from Frederic's agency, confirming his increasing focus on Angela, and then describing her behavior during the night in question. She'd embarrassed him, got him angry while drunk, and then led him out of the building. Angela indicated which one I should cross-examine. "That's Kitty," she said as Hume swore in Kimberley Carronada. Angela and Kitty had been friends, they had confided in each other and traded favors from time to time. Kitty was not part of Trisha's clique.

I got up and walked over to the witness stand. "Kimberley, until that night, you considered Angela a friend, didn't you?"

She nodded, looking uncertain. "Yes."

"Did you see Angela leave the party?"

"Yes. She told me she was leaving."

"Did she say why?"

Kimberley was silent.

"Kimberley, I know the situation is difficult, but remember back to that night. Is it true that she told you that Frederic had tried to take advantage of her?"

I thought for a minute she might simply refuse to answer, given that she now knew Angela was a monster, but it really is hard to believe a friend has changed that much. I remembered trying to argue Elias Klein out of killing me, even when I *knew* he wasn't human and was transforming right in front of me. I counted on that gut-level disbelief.

"Yes," she said finally. "She did."

"Did you believe her?"

"Oh, yes. Freddie was like that when he got drunk, especially when he was mad at one of us for ... well, for not ..."

I passed over the implication. The expressions on the jurors's faces showed that I probably didn't need to; they'd already figured out the score. "Did you see the deceased, Frederic Delacroix, after Angela left?"

"Yes. Just after she left."

"And what was he doing at that time?"

Kimberley hesitated. "He ... he looked really mad. His hair was mussed, and so was his suit, and he was asking for Angela."

"Did he ask you where Angela was?"

"Yes."

"Did you tell him?"

A pause. "No."

"Why didn't you tell him where she was?" I asked. When there was no answer, I sighed. "Kimberley, your close friends call you 'Kitty,' don't they?"

She nodded.

"Did Angela call you 'Kitty'?"

Keeping her eyes averted from Angela, she answered, "Y-yes."

"Then, Kimberley, isn't it the truth that you told Frederic that Angela had gone off with someone else, one of the other guests at the party, because you were afraid of what would happen if he caught her?"

Very quietly, she said, "Yes."

"You heard some of your other friends try to do the same thing, didn't you?"

"Yes."

"Did you hear Trisha tell Frederic that she'd actually just left, alone?"

A momentary flicker of anger. "Yes."

"And Frederic then left quickly?"

"He ran out the door after Angela, yes."

I looked her in the eyes. "And at that time, when Frederic ran out in pursuit of your friend, Angela, did you think Angela was in danger?"

"Y-yes. Yes, I did. I thought Freddie was going to . . . well, hurt her bad."

"Did you have reason to believe this? Had you ever seen Frederic Delacroix hurt someone, or heard convincing evidence that he had done so?"

Her eyes wide, she just nodded her head. A moment later she said, "Yes."

"Your Honor," Hume said, "the dead man is not on trial here."

"True, Your Honor," I agreed, "but establishing the character of the dead man is an important element of the defense. I have no more questions at this time, but I may need to call this witness or some of the others from the prosecution to the stand for the defense."

Judge Freeman nodded. "You're done with this witness for now?" He glanced at Hume. "Any redirect? No? You may stand down, Ms. Carronada."

I saw Angela flash a grateful, relieved smile at Kimberley, who hesitantly returned it. *Damn,* Angela was good. Very, very good. We could—if we were really lucky—actually win this one.

How I wished I could feel good about *that.*

CHAPTER 96

Connect the Dots

I sat down in my fuzzy bathrobe and pulled my laptop to me. I'd rather be pulling Syl to me, I thought, but she couldn't also afford to be spending weeks here in California rather than working on her business (and filtering the nutcases from mine). Syl's psychic friend, Samantha Prince, was visiting, so at least she wasn't alone. I had a computer for company; the best thing I could say about that was that the machine was pretty undemanding.

I'd managed to get one nagging worry cleared up—although the clearing up simply caused me more heartburn. After that day's trial proceedings, I'd had another private conversation with Angela. "The prosecuting attorney in this isn't stupid," I pointed out. "I find it hard to believe that he, or at least some of his investigative staff, don't have any suspicion that you might have had an ulterior motive in working for Freddie. If they figure that out, it won't take very long to discover that someone had screwed with all of the CryWolf units owned by your clients."

Angela laughed. "Oh, certainly, that wouldn't have been good, would it? But don't worry. The first thing my . . . pack, I suppose you could say . . . was to do if any of us were compromised in such a way was to go back and restore the functionality of the systems, immediately. This is obviously a *terrible* setback for us, a year's worth of work totally gone, and we'll have to be even *more* careful for the next few years to make sure no one catches on. But you don't need to worry about them bringing *that* up at trial." She smiled sweetly. "See? All taken care of."

I winced at the memory. Ugh. And as I took my confidentiality seriously, I couldn't tell anyone about the situation. The best my conscience would allow me to do—some time *well* after the trial—would be to hint about the possible approach used by the wolves to circumvent security. Sometimes, having a professional conscience is a pain in the ass.

Right now, I wanted to do some work that didn't threaten me with Pyrrhic victories. I opened my notes on Kevin Ferrin's problem cases, which posed a challenge I could feel better about than the ambivalent hell I had just gone through.

I had—in a way—managed to find a common thread among all the victims, but I didn't know if it was a *significant* common thread. In his original narration of the problem, Kevin had mentioned that both the Roquettes and Buckley had recently attended a party. A quick investigation turned up the fact that *all* of the victims had attended a big bash within a few days of their deaths. Of course, given the higher-society nature of the neighborhood, parties were probably common. And after reviewing the guest lists, we hadn't found any guests in common with the majority of the victims. There were plenty of names that showed up on three or four guest lists, but none that showed up on all of them or even a majority. This again was not a big surprise; people in the same neighborhood with similar interests, or employed by the same or related organizations, could be invited to more than one or a couple of parties, but not all of them.

I studied the evidence gathered in each case. Ferrin hadn't exaggerated about the variety of killing methods. Knives, poison, strangulation; one victim just dropped dead somehow, and one death involved homemade explosives. That one hadn't left much to examine in the way of intact body parts. I found the pictures in that case to be even worse than those of the not-too-lamented Frederic. Still, there was almost *too* much evidence. I agreed with the lieutenant; individually any of these cases was . . . okay, but all of them had something just slightly not quite right in the evidence. The bomb guy, for instance; there wasn't any good evidence he'd had any skill in that direction, just a couple mentions by people that he'd recently mentioned something about how easy it was to make them, and some evidence that he'd hit some webpages on the subject. The bomb used was awfully, awfully good for someone who hadn't been doing this stuff long. Then again, maybe he was just a natural at bomb-making and really, really bad at bomb safety.

I concentrated on the pieces of collected evidence that appeared to have no bearing on the case—that is, the kind of stuff you pick up in the investigation that turns out to not be relevant, like fingerprints from the once-a-week cleaning lady, or undeveloped film which has just pictures of the kids at the beach, or that giant dust-bunny under the bed which simply gives evidence that the deceased didn't do much vacuuming. It was as I went back over the first two folders the lieutenant had given me that it finally hit me.

That woman at the trial—the one with the spectacularly long, red hair—had strongly reminded me of the murdered Jesse Roquette. I grabbed the file and looked up Jesse's maiden name: Grandis. Armed with this new piece of evidence, my search skills, and the name of the politician who the redhead had apparently been working with, it took me only a few minutes to confirm that Virginia "Ginny" Grandis was indeed working with California State Senator Henry Reed, and was undoubtedly the slightly older sister of Jesse Roquette, neé Grandis.

Now the whole thing was clear. Everything made sense. I picked up the phone. I could at least confirm or deny the crucial question. Then it would just be a very tricky matter of proof and timing. Which might get me killed if I screwed it up, but hell, that was no surprise.

"Verne," I said, when he got on the line, "tell me something. You know that little stunt that Angela pulled on me while she was yanking my strings—hitting me with a supercharge from the energy she'd taken from Delacroix?"

"Yes. I understand how such things could work, certainly. What do you want to know?"

"I guess . . . well, you fought these things and even ended up having to do unto one of them as they would've done unto you."

"Yes." His voice was unusually . . . cold? Restrained? Nervous? I knew that particular event embarrassed and upset him, but I thought he'd have been over it by now.

"Anyway, from what I got out of her I guess she used maneuvers like that fairly frequently with her clients. What I want to know is, how much energy would that be in their terms? I mean, if you were a wolf and killed one guy, could you jazz up one client, ten, a hundred times that with the energy?"

"That," he said, more animation coming back into his voice,

"is a very interesting question. Let me think on what I have sensed and what impressions remain from those and similar contacts." He was silent for several minutes. "Not many, Jason. The transfer in that direction would not be tremendously efficient. Humans are not designed for input, so to speak, and wolves are not generally for output, though they are certainly capable of it. More than one, less than ten I would guess."

"Thanks, Verne." I took a deep breath. "Exactly what I needed to know." I hung up after a quick good-bye.

Now the real dangerous game would begin.

CHAPTER 97

Reasonable Fear

I stood before the Court now, the prosecution having just rested its case. I turned to face the jury. "You have heard the prosecution's case, and you have been instructed as to what the requirements of the law are in this case.

"I think it is important, however, to establish that the broad general principle—that non-human, intelligent creatures deserve the same justice as those who are human—is one in need of establishment. If the wolves are what we believe them to be, it would be difficult to argue that there is any justification—for the protection of our own species—for according them such rights." I took a deep breath.

"With the approval of the Court, I am going to present some evidence previously shown only to a very limited number of people, prior to this trial, on which basis the trial was permitted to proceed. In short, I want to introduce you to someone it *would* be worthwhile to protect—by giving them the right to trial."

"Objection, Your Honor," David Hume said. We'd already hashed this out in chambers, but we both knew he needed to get his objection on the official records, and I didn't mind as it meant my rebuttal would be there, too. "Defense is attempting to sway the jury through introducing irrelevant facts designed for emotional appeal."

"In a sense true, Your Honor," I responded, "but if we are honest about this trial and its setting, it would be essentially impossible to get a truly impartial jury. For the past year and a half and more, entire *governments* have changed their courses of action because of the revelation of the existence of the wolves—and not always for the better. I simply want to prove to the jury—and to the world—that allowing such justice is not merely and solely going to be an avenue to permit monsters to go free."

Judge Freeman nodded. "Objection overruled. Proceed, Mr. Wood."

This time the screens were visible to the courtroom. While specific identification had been eliminated from the video, any sufficiently determined and intelligent researcher would probably be able to trace the source, and that was why it had taken a great deal of soul-searching and courage by the principals to allow me to show this video. I felt renewed gratitude towards the whole family as Lizzie Plunkett, face blurred digitally, appeared. "Hi. You can call me...Victoria. I want you to meet my best friend in the whole entire world." Her voice was also subtly altered, but still clearly that of a young girl. "This is Arischadel."

A tiny dragon, seemingly sculpted of smoky black quartz, flew into view. A murmur sprang up around the courtroom. "He can't speak English very well because his throat isn't made for it, but he's just as smart as you or me. So, he's going to write for you."

Arischadel took a little notebook from Lizzie's outstretched hand and, gripping a small pencil in his claw, began to write in a clear, if somewhat shaky, script. The camera zoomed in to show him actually writing each word, and Lizzie read out each line as he completed it. "Hello, ar...arbiters?" she glanced suspiciously at Arischadel. "Is that a real word?" He bobbed his head again. "Okay. Hello, arbiters of justice. I am Arischadel. I am one of many kinds of creatures you would call supernatural or magical. I live with"—here Aris wrote an "L" but managed to convert it to a "V"—"Vicky and her family and watch over them the best I can. I cannot journey to your courtroom, as I am bound to this place." The little dragon looked directly into the camera, large dark eyes giving an appeal which was reinforced by the slightly childlike proportions of the creature's head and body. "I do not ask you to set the one called Angela free for my sake. All that I ask is that you judge her fairly for myself and all other creatures that are not of your blood, but are still of your world."

Lizzie looked up as he finished. "And that's all we ask. We're afraid of wolves, too. But people like Aris need to be protected by the law. That's the point of this trial. Thanks for listening and...good luck."

I nodded to the jury, some of whom were looking startled, a few of whom were looking suspicious. "That video was taken by me personally. It has been verified—and the facts in it examined directly—by personnel from the prosecutor's office as well. You saw no special effects, except the blurring of the girl's face and certain background details to protect her anonymity. Arischadel is a real, living, thinking being, and he is far from the only non-wolf, non-human out there.

"This will be an emotional trial, and decisions are and have always been affected by emotions. But this is also a question, in many ways, of what defines a person, of whether we have the right to pass summary judgment on someone because they are different from us. The wolves are, to us, truly horrifying. Perhaps Angela is just as much a monster as the prosecution wishes you to believe. But her people think, and feel, and hate, and I believe they can choose to love, to care, and to protect. Anything that thinks and lives can do those things. Arischadel certainly can, and certainly has. Remember this, when the time comes to render your verdict."

I turned. "The defense calls Angela McIntyre to the stand."

A ripple of murmurs circled around the courtroom as the petite form of the shapeshifted werewolf entered the witness box. She was sworn in, with a line added specifically for her: "I swear to tell the truth by the name of our King, Virigar himself." Angela had very, very much *not* wanted to accept that change, but in the end, she'd realized that I wasn't budging on that.

I advanced to the witness stand. "Angela, the oath that you've sworn does actually bind you, doesn't it?"

She glared at me, although the glare at this point was mostly for show. "Yes. As you well know."

"What would happen if you were to directly lie on the stand, having given that oath?"

She looked bleak for a moment. "Worse than the death your people threaten me with. I will not elaborate."

I nodded. "Good enough. So we can count on the truthfulness of your testimony at least as much as we could with any other witness."

"More, I would think, Mr. Wood."

I led her through a series of questions establishing her identity and history. "Exhibits ten-A through ten-F verify that the identity of 'Angela McIntyre' is one used solely by the wolf before us, over the last several years. This is not an identity stolen from a human being but a unique identity of her own."

From that point, I quickly rehashed her career with Frederic Delacroix, again avoiding the rather intimate nature of the "escort" duties. "Now, Angela, is it true that Frederic Delacroix pressured you, as one of his employees in a rather...intimate sort of industry, to be more than merely professionally involved with him?"

"Yes. Freddie didn't choose his employees just for the target clientele. He had his own interests."

"Would it be fair to say that he applied this pressure to most of his escorts?"

Angela nodded. "Yes."

"But you refused."

"I did. He wasn't my type, you might say."

"How did he accept your refusal?"

"Poorly." Angela gave a half-smile. "He wasn't bad-looking for a human and he could behave decently, so given that plus money, connections, and his position as employer, I do not think he was accustomed to being refused."

"Did you at any time lead him on, give him the impression that you might be accessible?"

She shook her head emphatically. "I was professionally friendly but no more. I had no interest in him and I tried to make that clear."

"Tell us about the night in question."

The story followed what had already been established, until we reached her flight from the party. "So you left the party?"

"It was pretty clear to me that Freddie just wasn't giving up, he was actually becoming almost obsessive, and I didn't want to put up with it anymore."

"Did you think he would follow you?"

"Most of us girls stick together, so no. I thought he wouldn't realize I was gone until it was too late and he'd calmed down a bit." For a moment, she *did* look venomously angry, glaring at Trisha, who was just visible in the audience. The girl shrank back. "But *someone* told him that I'd gone."

"Were you afraid of Frederic?"

"Not at that time, no."

"What happened?"

"I was about half a block from Freddie's when I heard a shout behind me, and I saw him coming after me. So I ran." She sighed. "But, as you can see, I'm not built to outrun people like Freddie. He was a running back in college, you know."

"If you weren't afraid of him at that point, why run?"

"Because I thought fighting him might be too revealing. I was *trying* to get out of his sight long enough to shift to another shape—one that he wouldn't recognize, so he'd think he lost track of me. But he kept way too close. If he were to *see* me change, well, that would have been bad. I didn't want to kill him and have to leave the area; I had everything nicely set up."

"So Mr. Delacroix caught up with you. What happened then?"

She grimaced, the pretty face looking both repelled and slightly frightened. "He grabbed my arm, said something like 'where the hell do you think you're going, bitch?' and then backhanded me across the face."

"Were you afraid of him then?"

She hesitated, looking almost embarrassed, then nodded. "Yes. Yes, I was, after he hit me."

"Why would you be afraid of him then?"

"Because he *hurt* me." She took a tissue and swabbed makeup from the side of her face. A shadowy bruise, along with some still-visible scarring, came into view.

I turned to the judge and jury. "Exhibit twelve is a photograph of Angela's face shortly after she was taken into custody. You will note the cuts and heavy bruising on her face, in the same place as these scars. Referring to Exhibit four-E, it can be seen that Mr. Delacroix wore a set of rings on his right hand. Trace material found caught on points and angles of the rings has been analyzed and shown to have DNA content identical to the DNA of Angela McIntyre." I glanced over at Prosecutor Hume as I continued. "These rings are described in the accounting of the deceased's possessions, in the ME report, page seven. The most important point of the descriptions is that the two rings which caused the cuts contain a high proportion of silver."

That got a reaction. "Exactly. Until that point, Angela was not afraid of Frederic. But when he struck her, it was with a weapon known to be very deadly to her species, a weapon that could easily kill her if she did not defend herself." I returned to Angela. "Was that when you changed and fought back?"

She shook her head. "Not quite. He knocked me down, and I tried to get away, but he was too fast and pushed me back down. He pulled out his knife and I realized what he intended to do, and *then* I fought back. And then the police came around the corner, *just* at the wrong time. I was not able to get away."

"Thank you, Angela." I nodded to Hume. "Your witness."

Hume was conferring with a couple of people at his table. "Your Honor, as it is getting late, we would like to begin our cross-examination tomorrow."

Judge Freeman nodded. "I have no objection to adjourning until tomorrow. Does the defense object?"

"No, sir."

"Then court adjourned until tomorrow. When we reconvene, the prosecution may begin its cross-examination of the witness."

CHAPTER 98

Lest You Become Monsters Yourselves

"Mr. Wood, do you think you have a chance to win this case?"

"Mr. Wood, don't you feel you're betraying your own people by doing this?"

There were a dozen other questions, all being shouted at once, as I exited the courtroom with Angela. Other questions were bellowed at Angela, but she completely ignored them, looking scared and small. Her Oscar-winning performance continued all the way to the car that would take her back to the lockup. I stopped before I reached my car. "Okay, people, I'll give you some footage. Do I feel I have a chance to win? Yes, I do, as long as the jury is fair. The evidence we just presented shows—contrary to the prosecution's original contention—that Angela did in fact have reason to fear for her life.

"No, I'm not betraying anyone. I don't like the wolves any more than most people, and—in fact—there isn't anyone alive that has more reason to be afraid of them than me. But if we let our justice system be run by anything other than fairness, or at least the willingness to *try* to be fair, we've already lost what makes this country worth living in."

Brian Clement of CNN knew an opening when he saw one. "What do you mean by that, Mr. Wood?"

"I mentioned in court today that entire governments changed after the existence of the wolves became known. The fact is that a lot of the panic over the werewolves has been used by opportunists to get away with things that would *never* fly in ordinary times. The WAS Act—Werewolf Alertness and Security—made a lot of things legal that simply shouldn't have been, all in the guise of allowing the federal government to detect and deal with wolves. Monitoring cameras sprouting up everywhere, background traces to detect discontinuities, my own CryWolf systems doing double-duty as security monitors in thousands of places that never were watched before; there's a serious danger here, worse than anything those monsters could do. They *live* on fear, you know, and if they make our whole *society* based on fear, I'm not at all sure they wouldn't be willing to risk the increased so-called security measures."

"But if that's the only way to be safe—" someone began.

"—then we had better accept that there's no such thing as real safety." I cut him off. "Ben Franklin said it best: 'Those who would give up essential liberty, to purchase a little temporary safety, deserve neither liberty nor safety.' Yes, by not allowing the government to monitor whatever it desires, it's possible for werewolves, or murderers, or terrorists, or whatever, to sometimes get away with something. *That's the price you pay for living in a free society.* Sometimes a monster—human or otherwise—will abuse that freedom to do something to you or yours." I shrugged. "I would rather take that risk than allow a slowly creeping fear to erode our freedom until there's nothing left." I opened my car door. "That's all."

"You're really playing with fire, Wood." Clement whispered.

Thinking of how the endgame of this whole mess might play out, I agreed. Timing was going to be absolutely *everything*... and I had to make sure that all three sides involved—mine, the prosecutor's, and the police—knew the right info, at the right time, to act on it, or else the whole thing would blow up in my face—and I'd be the first casualty. I had the proof in hand, though, courtesy of poor, dead Joe Buckley and a very thorough scene investigator who'd bagged a single hair that was out of place. Now if I could just get through these next few days...

CHAPTER 99

Perry Jason

"Mr. Clarke, what is your profession?"

The prosecution had cross-examined Angela efficiently. Bound by her oath, she had admitted that even with his silver rings, she thought Frederic could not have beaten her to death and that she probably would have had many chances to escape. She also admitted that she could probably have incapacitated him without killing him. She had taken the Fifth Amendment on other potentially incriminating questions, such as whether she had ever killed anyone else. I knew some damage had been done by the time she stood down... but I'd expected that. Thus Mr. Caston Clarke.

"Yes, sir. I am a private investigator. CC Investigations."

"I hired you to perform an investigation, correct?"

"You did, sir."

"What were my instructions to you, exactly?"

"I was to go to the crime scene relevant to this case, at the parking garage, and search outside of the scene in a specific direction for any object or objects which seemed out of place. If I found such an object, I was to call you and follow further instructions."

I nodded. "Tell me about your investigation."

Clarke leaned back. He was a medium-sized man who, at first glance, looked portly, but who was actually mostly muscle, and surprisingly strong and quick. He'd been strongly recommended to me by Lieutenant Ferrin. "Well, sir, I returned to the crime scene and began searching outward from the perimeter in the direction indicated—a fan-shaped area centered roughly northward."

"And did you find any object of significance?"

"Yes, sir. About seventy-five feet from the perimeter, I found an object I considered quite significant in a storm drain where it appeared to have fallen recently."

"You took pictures of the object as it lay and then called me, correct?"

"Yes, sir. You then instructed me to wait until you arrived."

"And after I arrived?"

"I removed the object, using gloves and other means to prevent contamination, while you took a video of the process. We then took the object to an independent laboratory—VeriAnalysis Incorporated—where it was examined."

"What was the object that you discovered, Mr. Clarke?"

"A large combat folding knife, blade found locked in the extended position. Research showed that it was number one hundred twenty-seven in a limited series of three hundred such knives sold by the DiamondEdge Corporation under the brand name Excalibur. Inquiries at DiamondEdge further showed that this particular weapon was sold to Mr. Frederic Delacroix."

After a few more questions from me and the prosecution (which didn't bring out anything of consequence), I let Clarke stand down and called Dr. Herman Dell to the stand. "Dr. Dell, you work for VeriAnalysis Incorporated, correct?"

"Indeed, Mr. Wood."

"What is your job there?"

"I am an independent forensic researcher, specializing in the examination of physical evidence in accordance with proper police procedure. I am qualified through fifteen prior years of work with the New York State Forensics Laboratory."

"Were you the researcher assigned to examine the knife brought to VeriAnalysis by Mr. Clarke at my request?"

"I was."

"Can you describe any significant findings?"

"Certainly. The weapon in question was last held by Mr. Frederic Delacroix. He was holding it in a manner indicating that he had the blade out for use. Blurring of some of the prints and a sharp indentation on the blade indicate that the knife was knocked violently from his grasp. A comparison of the indentation with a number of possibilities shows that the most likely cause of this damage to the blade was an impact by a werewolf claw." He managed to say the last part of his sentence without hesitating, something I still found difficult. "There was a significant amount of blood on the knife, which analysis showed was that of the decedent, Frederic Delacroix. The blade, however, also featured epithelial cells of another individual, which, when analyzed, proved to be those of Miss Angela McIntyre."

"So this is consistent, then, with her statement that she struck Mr. Delacroix when he had her held down with a knife to her throat?"

"Very much so, if we take into account the sequence of events. The photographs of the scene show the orientation of the body. As the shape-changing would have taken place beneath Mr. Delacroix, he would have been elevated and struck by the claws on the arm moving laterally from right to left, from the point of view of the attacker. Given the orientation of the body, the attack lifted Mr. Delacroix up and the claws passed through his body along that line, striking the knife toward the end of their passage as the knife would have been held on the opposite side of the body from the striking claws, and then flinging the knife outward by that impact."

"Thank you, Doctor." I looked to the jury. "There is one extremely significant additional fact of which you should be aware. DiamondEdge's *Excalibur* line of combat blades are a relatively new addition to the market. Their distinguishing feature is that they all include a significant proportion of silver in the blade.

"Such a blade, held to the throat, goes far beyond the threat of beating offered by the silver rings Frederic wore. The deceased was threatening Angela's life. He was attempting to rape her. The silver blade at her throat was a clear, immediate, and credible threat of death, even to a werewolf. And so—just as any of us would have—she struck out in self defense."

"The defense rests."

CHAPTER 100

Free to be Tried

The testimony and cross-examinations were over. We'd each given our closing arguments. Based on the evidence, I felt that we'd done pretty well; the prosecution hadn't been able to seriously damage the evidence of the knife. Whether the jury would consider the evidence more than the monster in the courtroom, however, was still in question. Now all that was left to do was wait for the verdict.

"How long?" Angela whispered tensely for the tenth time.

"You think the jury is going to come back fast on *this* verdict?" I snapped. The tension was worse for me than she realized. "Even if they're all agreed, they'll probably want to make it look good. But, just judging by the looks on some of their faces, I don't think they were all agreed. That is good from my point of view. If they'd all been firmly decided on the way out, I'd be pretty damn sure that they were all firmly decided on you taking a last long walk."

"Which you wouldn't mind."

"Personally, not at all, as you well know, but professionally and tactically, it would suck."

I glanced over at Ferrin, who nodded very slightly. Angela caught it. "What was that?"

"Just exchanging greetings."

She looked at me narrowly. "I think you're up to something."

"I keep my word. You know that. You wouldn't have brought me into this without being damn sure of that. Even your King trusts me on that level, if not on any other."

She nodded slowly.

Time dragged by on leaden feet. I finally got up and went out for a quick snack from the vending machine. I was just watching my selection rattle its sluggish way to the tray when a bailiff came charging into sight. "Mr. Wood, the jury—"

"Of *course* it would be now." I sprinted back to the courtroom.

I sat down next to Angela just as the last of the jurors was seated. "Well, this is it."

For once, she was speechless, staring at the jury, none of whom was looking at her.

"Ladies and gentlemen of the jury," Judge Freeman said, "have you come to a unanimous verdict?"

Alle Schumacher, the sharp-eyed old woman, was the jury foreman. She rose and stated in a clear, carrying voice, "We have, your honor."

"The defendant will please rise."

Angela did so, with a shakiness that I didn't think was feigned.

"Ladies and gentlemen of the jury, what is your verdict?"

Alle looked at the judge, then at Angela and me, and back to the judge. "Sir, we find the defendant, Angela McIntyre, not guilty."

Not guilty.

The words brought me to my feet with a combination of triumph and concern. Angela's face lit up with relief, so innocently beautiful that it was almost impossible to remember what lay underneath. This was going to be the most dangerous time; if anyone in the public felt she shouldn't go free, now was the time they'd try something. But Mrs. Schumacher was speaking again.

"We also have a statement to read, Your Honor, if it please the Court."

Judge Freeman considered a moment. "Very well. Proceed."

Alle nodded to Jim Sherry, who stood and began reading. "We, the jury in the case of State Versus McIntyre (werewolf), recognize the unusual nature of the case we have been presented. Many of us have grave reservations about any finding which could result in the defendant being released, as it is obviously true that she could be a clear and present danger to any other people she encounters.

"Still, we also recognize the points of procedure and law as emphasized by the defense and the much greater responsibility which may result from any ruling we make here. We agreed at the beginning, therefore, that we must come to a final and clear unanimous verdict, so that whatever message this trial might send would not be confused.

"In the end, the judgment came to the evidence and to the question of whether Angela McIntyre, a werewolf, should be judged on that evidence. The evidence is clear and unambiguous to us; were Angela human, there would be no doubt of her acquittal. And therefore, by the letter and spirit of the law, despite our grave reservations as to her personal future conduct, we the jury have rendered the same verdict to her as we would to any human being. Perhaps she does not deserve that justice. But there are those out there who do, and for them and our own self-respect, we give it to her."

The judge's gavel came down. "The verdict has been reached. The accused is found innocent and is therefore free from this moment on."

I turned to the jury. "Thank you. For your statement, not merely the verdict."

Angela had taken my arm. "Thank you, *thank you*, Jason! As soon as I get my wallet, I'll pay the law firm. *You* may be working *pro bono* but I'm sure they aren't."

We continued out through the crowd towards the street, policemen clearing a perimeter around us. I saw Achernar scanning the crowd like radar, alert for anything. We stepped out the front doors into the California sunshine, and the murmur of the crowd turned into a roar, overlaid with a thousand questions being shouted at us by eager news crews.

At that moment, Lieutenant Ferrin came up behind us and in a single swift move, locked a pair of handcuffs on Angela. As she swung around in shock, he stepped back a pace, calmly saying, "Angela McIntyre, I arrest you on multiple charges of murder in the first degree, including the murders of Jessie and James Roquette, Joseph Buckley, and others named in the arresting warrant. You have the right—"

The little blonde gave a snarl three octaves too deep for her shape and ballooned into a towering mass of teeth and fur, crouched low to the ground as if ready to spring. Screams resounded around the plaza and I could see people trying to get a bead on her . . . but there were a lot of people in the way. She whirled on me.

"Treacherous little—"

"Go ahead," I said, looking her in the eye. "Give my regards to Virigar."

She was so furious that her claws started forward of their own accord. "How? *How* did you..."

"It wasn't easy," I said. "You were careful. You never actually said you hadn't killed anyone recently, but you did leave me with that impression at first. None of the murders had any overt ties. None of them had the same MO or same apparent motive. Hardly any real evidence turned up, and no one would have had any reason to tie it to you.

"But there was the fact that all the victims had gone to some large party in the recent past...but that didn't mean much. Not in this neighborhood." I grinned as I saw her collapse back into human form, the broken handcuffs dropping to the ground. "But when I noticed a relative of one of the victims with a certain person, I made the connection.

"Of course, just the fact that all the victims had been at a party where one of your clients had been didn't mean that much. As an escort, you might not be on the guest list—except as "Mr. Client and Guest"—and, in fact, you might have been able to go as a different face. Not hard for you to arrange. But we needed to prove you were the connecting factor. And just as importantly, I needed motive.

"You actually gave me that info."

She snarled something unintelligible, which I generously interpreted as a request to go on. "Two things. First, the fact that you had a shape that was your own, and that no one else would ever use, and second...your little energy stunt. I had to do some digging, but I was able to find out that you couldn't be doing that very often without some heavy-duty recharging—a lot more than you could get from passively feeding off people. A kill gives you a *lot* more power. And you were using a lot, given that you probably used that stunt at least once on most of your clients. You *had* to be killing people. And once I knew that for sure, and suspected your connection, there *was* a little appropriate evidence. Courtesy of Joe Buckley. I suppose he died pretty happy, but you left a little of Angela McIntyre behind. Once they had someone to try a match with, it was open-and-shut."

I saw her glancing around, measuring the crowd and the

police ringing her. "Oh, and in case you forgot, I didn't put any time limit on how long you had to obey human law. And you swore according to *my* wording, remember?"

Her jaw dropped. "You..."

"Good luck on this next trial, Angela," I said. "I think you'll be needing it."

She stared at me for a long moment, icy blue eyes boring into mine. Then, startlingly, she grinned. "So you win the entire game, Mr. Wood. Congratulations." With surprising quickness, she stepped forward and kissed me.

The detonation of ecstasy was like a sledgehammer, such pure pleasure that I couldn't even for a moment remember who I was or where I was, only that this vision of perfection in front of me was the source of paradise. I staggered back, caught by Ferrin while other police pulled her back. As my brain came back online, a sense of foreboding loss began to settle on me. The predator's triumphant grin had returned to her face. "You have won that game, Mr. Wood. But now you will never...quite...be satisfied with anything else on Earth. Will you?"

I couldn't manage an appropriate comeback as they dragged Angela away.

CHAPTER 101

Horror and Home

I sagged back into the cushions of the small private jet. One of the compensations of being rich was *not* having to wait in an airport line and riding among a mob of people; I definitely didn't want to ride in a public conveyance after *this* fiasco. Not until the fuss died down. No, just me, lone passenger, with two attendants to serve me on the flight back to New York and home.

Angela had gotten in a good last stroke, but I'm not an addictive personality, fortunately. She didn't understand the way humans think, I suspect. Yes, for pure enjoyment, luxury of the senses, that one perfect moment would be there forever, but there were pleasures much more subtle, complex, and broad. And going home to Syl was one of those. I smiled and leaned the chair back, closing my eyes.

"An excellent piece of work, Mr. Wood. I particularly enjoyed the endgame," said a cheerful, urbane voice beside me.

Icicles speared my heart as my eyes snapped open.

Standing over me, wearing a cheerful smile without the faintest hint of malice, was a blond man with more than a passing resemblance to Robert Redford. A man I recognized all too well.

"*V-Virigar,*" I managed.

"Indeed." He dropped into the seat next to me. "As I said, beautifully done." He glanced sideways at me. "Oh, please, Mr. Wood, relax. You realize I could certainly kill you now and none of the crew would notice anything. However, there are two excellent reasons why I will not."

"Oh? What are those?" I asked in a surprisingly normal tone.

"Firstly, unless I simply caused you to die of . . . no apparent

524

causes, rather than slashing you to ribbons, the false comfort of your CryWolf devices would be damaged. I find it personally useful, even if my children find them annoying. Secondly, and far more important, is that it would be very unamusing for me to do so. I do not find the kill of a worthy adversary to be satisfying if there's no significant struggle, no chance whatsoever for the victim to win."

This did make grim sense and fit with what Verne had told me about him. "What about Angela? She's likely to be executed. Aren't you a bit peeved at me over that?"

He laughed, a big happy sound at total variance with what I knew of him. "Oh, far from it, Jason. Tanmorrai was old enough, and thought herself clever enough, to actually be contemplating a . . . change in leadership, one might say. I'd been observing her preparations for years. Now, she'll be humiliated as well as killed off."

"And she'll stay there? Not escape? What could you possibly threaten her with?"

He smiled, and *now* I saw the glitter of diamond teeth, the cold joy of hatred. "Why, Jason, I'm surprised you cannot guess. But then, you *are* new to this sort of thing." He looked around the plane, as though examining it for aspects he had not yet seen. "The most amusing thing about your little court case was that you were saying things you didn't entirely believe, yet they are, in fact, all completely true. Any being—even my children—which thinks and feels is as capable as you are of love and affection and tolerance. We all—including myself, you must understand—choose our paths. I chose mine quite consciously. And I want my children to carry on my good work."

The matter-of-fact way in which he said that gave me the creeps. "And what does this . . ."

". . . have to do with the punishment? Oh, everything. You see, there was—once—one of my children with whom I had, shall we say, some philosophical disagreements. He decided he didn't want to follow our path and rebelled against me—protecting, in fact, some of your people. I actually welcomed this little rebellion. You see, it provided me with an ideal—how should I put it?—ah, yes, an ideal object lesson for any others who might ever think they had any freedom to choose."

"What did you do?" I asked finally.

The smile was broader and as cold as a night of glaciers. "I ate him, of course. But in a *very* special way. I consumed his *energy*, but left him *just* enough to be conscious. So he could watch—from within me—as I destroyed all that he had protected. And he still does, to this day. And will, for as long as I live."

I shuddered. I knew that was a victory for him, but I couldn't help it. Now I truly understood why the other wolves would rather face simple death. "You..."

"You haven't words for that, I know. We'll meet again, Jason, and one day—when you least expect it, but when I have the time to devote to it—I will begin to destroy everything you know and love.

"And then, after I've deprived you of your friends, your lovely Sylvia, and even my esteemed opponent, Verne Domingo, I will give you the highest honor of all." I knew what he was going to say even before he finished. "I will place you within me, alongside the Traitor." His pleasant, boyish smile was back, all the more horrid for looking normal and friendly. "Think of it as a favor. Eternal life."

I turned away, trying to think of something to say that had a vague chance of sounding defiant without being futile. When I looked back, he was gone.

I glanced around, probably looking a bit wild. The attendants were both at the front of the cabin. There was no one else in sight.

"Fine," I said at last. "Your point. But I did beat you once. And when that time comes, I'll beat you again." I looked down at my ring finger and thought of my wife. A smile came back to my lips. "And there are some things you can't kill.

"I'm going home."